"You came back," she said.

His response was a kiss. It was the sort of kiss most women only dreamed about—one of those embraces that rendered the knees into a useless set of joints and made a girl feel as if she could be swept off her feet in the manner of romantic movies everywhere. Although she might have harbored doubts about his sincerity a few seconds ago, every bit of hesitation fled as his lips moved over hers again and again.

Monty didn't ask to embrace her, didn't tentatively express his regard. He took, and his mouth said what words could not. Yes, she was wanted. Yes, she was desired. Yes, he would make this happen for her if he had to devour her from the inside out to do it.

"Of course I came back," he said.

**Also available from Tamara Morgan
and Carina Press**

The Montgomery Manor Series

If I Stay
When I Fall
Because I Can

The Getting Physical Series

The Rebound Girl
The Derby Girl
The Party Girl

Because I Can

TAMARA MORGAN

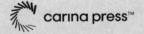

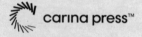

carina press™

ISBN-13: 978-0-373-00471-3

Because I Can

Copyright © 2014 by Tamara Morgan

Recycling programs for this product may not exist in your area.

Dear Reader,

This book started as a dare.

For a writing exercise one day, I was asked to create a list of both my favorite romance tropes and those romance tropes I could do without. While the first list was easy (Marriage of convenience! Friends to lovers! Opposites attract!), I struggled with the second one. There's very little I don't love about romance novels in general, and in the right hands, any trope can be pulled off with flair.

Of course, when pressured, I finally admitted that there was one trope I vowed never to touch myself... the makeover story. Not because I don't enjoy them (Pygmalion retellings are some of my favorite books out there), but because I didn't trust myself to do the story justice.

As is the case with any good writing exercise, the next step was, of course, to tackle that very fear. The result is *Because I Can*, one of my favorite books to date. Georgia and Monty soon became so much more than a simple trope and a simple dare. They became two flawed, beautiful people I enjoyed getting to know both inside and out.

I sincerely hope that you enjoy this chance to get to know them, too.

Tamara Morgan

For Edie Harris, who makes the best doodles.

Because I Can

ONE

"Who, Monty? He's a solid ten, no questions asked."

Monty skidded to a halt as he prepared to round the corner. It wasn't a customary habit of his to lurk along the hallways where the Montgomery Manor staff was hard at work, but he'd been feeling a desperate need for caffeine today. He'd also been feeling a desperate need to unchain himself from his desk for a few minutes, so heading down to the basement-level kitchen to refill his cup had seemed as good an excuse as any.

The eavesdropping was an unexpected perk.

"A ten? Are you sure we're talking about the same man? Monotonous Montgomery? Drudgery John?"

"Absolutely. I'd let him bend me over a table or two."

"You're crazy. Jake is the more attractive brother by far."

"Yeah, but you also admitted you like men with those curly mustaches. I think your taste is flawed."

Even though Monty knew it behooved him to clear his throat or stomp his feet or otherwise put an end to the conversation currently underway behind the swinging metal doors, he leaned forward, straining to place the voices. If he wasn't mistaken, the woman with a flair for the hirsute was Holly, the family cook. He had yet to determine who it was that considered him a ten.

And he *really* wanted to know. As his all-too-familiar nicknames indicated, women weren't in the habit of looking at him and visualizing a sex object. He was too old, too boring and much too tightly wound for that—a vintage toy soldier with moving parts. And not the *good* moving parts either.

"Jake has that whole naughty-playboy thing going for him," Holly said. "Or he used to, before he got married."

"I know, but Monty is bigger. I like a man with some meat on him."

"That's because you're only sexually attracted to guys who can beat you at arm wrestling, which is like twelve people overall."

A robust laugh escaped the kitchen as the pieces fell into place. That sound could only belong to Georgia Lennox—and so could the conversation, now that he thought about it. The owner and operator of the Handywoman Express had never struck him as the type of woman to speak in maidenly euphemisms, and, truth be told, she probably *was* able to beat most men at arm wrestling.

His dad had been utilizing Georgia's services for almost two decades, even though she couldn't be more than thirty years old. He remembered her as a gangly, toothy kid a few years younger than himself, riding over on her bike with a tool belt strapped across her chest like a bandolier, asking if there was anything she could do around the place to pick up some extra cash. Despite her tender years, she'd gratefully accepted his dad's request to build a bridge to continue the footpath that stopped at the West Creek.

And it was a good bridge too—solid oak, a few feet across, still standing to this day. It probably intended to keep standing forever, out of fear she might come at it with a hammer if it didn't.

Georgia was scary. In fact, he wasn't at all convinced

he *could* win against her in an arm-wrestling match. Or that bending her over a table would result in anything but immeasurable bodily harm.

"I don't think a few muscles is too much to ask for in a man," Georgia said, her voice still overloud in its low, deep-throated tone. "It's impossible to look at someone naked and feel all hot and bothered if he has spindly arms. The T-Rex look isn't attractive on anyone."

"Fine. You can give him his ten. I wish you both very happy."

"Oh, no. He's a solid ten in the looks department, but you have to knock off at least half his points for personality. As soon as I was done, ah, admiring his arms, we'd have to exchange a few words."

Monty almost dropped his coffee cup. This was the price of hulking in doorways, listening in where he wasn't wanted, but all the same he couldn't prevent the sense of indignation that rose to the surface. He wasn't that bad. Certainly not a *five*.

"Ha! You're right. He'd probably stare at you for ten minutes before finally offering a few tips for improved performance next time." Holly lowered her voice in what he assumed was an emulation of his own. "Less tongue, I think, could enhance the experience for both of us."

"Is there a reason you kept your eyes open the whole time? I found it quite unnerving."

"How would you rate it when I flipped you over and came in from behind? Three stars? Four? Would you consider it a *bold* move on my part?"

Bursts of feminine laughter had him sneaking slowly away from the door, fearful lest his footsteps sound in the tiled hallway. He only got about five feet when his back hit something soft and warm, and he spun to find himself face-to-face with Amy—yet another staff member, this one the nanny to his three-year-old half brother and half sister. At least he didn't have to fear any sexual judgment from the tall, sunny blonde. Cousinship rendered her safe and neutral territory.

"Oh, hey, Monty." She lifted her empty coffee cup in a show of solidarity. "Mondays, am I right?"

He blinked. "Are you right about what?"

"The daily grind? The need for liquid sustenance? No?" She examined him with pursed lips. "How about this one? I heard they're making this new caffeinated soap so you can skip the coffee and wash the energy boost right into your skin."

It took him a moment to register that she was making small talk, offering those bland bits of conversation that normal people—people who weren't nicknamed Drudgery John—needed to make it through the day. He studied his cup, where a residual pool of ice-cold coffee sloshed, and decided he could go without a refill. Too much caffeine always made him feel jittery and out of control of himself anyway.

It would be a *bold* move on his part to have another one when it wasn't even eight o'clock yet.

"I doubt skin absorbs chemical compounds the same way your digestive system does," he said when it became clear some sort of response was required.

Amy, a woman he knew to be blithely unconcerned for the social comforts and discomforts of others, somehow interpreted this to mean he wanted more coffee. She grabbed the handle of his cup and brushed past him. "Come on. We'll go sweet-talk Holly into giving up some of her wakey-wakey juice."

Monty did a quick mental calculation and decided it

would be less disastrous to follow Amy into the cavernous, glistening metal hull that was the kitchen. At least this way, the other two women would assume he'd come down with his cousin and allow him to save face. There was no reason anyone had to know he'd been shamelessly eavesdropping.

A ten, dropped to a five for my terrible personality.

He had no idea how to handle that kind of insult, but his earlier sense of indignation wasn't abating any now that it had time to settle in. He was a man who paid his taxes on time. He didn't use foul language in the presence of children. He didn't even miss appointments unless there was an emergency, since he hated throwing other people's schedules off.

Apparently, none of that mattered as much as the ability to parry with words. A man could be a charming serial killer and be more likable than Monty. That was where he ranked on the social hierarchy. Right below people who stored dismembered limbs in their freezers.

Amy made enough noise as she walked into the kitchen that the conversation came to a halt long before they became visible. From the scene that unfolded before them, it was clear the two women in the kitchen had been enjoying a comfortable chat. Holly always looked as if she belonged in a five-star restaurant—she was the consummate chef from the tips of her plastic clogs to the top of her dark brown hair, pulled back into its customary braid—but for the moment, she was lounging against the counter sipping her own cup of coffee. And Georgia defied explanation most days, so she could have been hanging from the ceiling by a pair of Spider-Man web-slingers, and it wouldn't have taken him more than a second to adjust. The fact that she was kneeling on top of the stove with her head inside the vent hood, the clank of metal on metal signifying some kind of work taking place, wouldn't stop her from venturing opinions on the state of his manhood.

He'd almost never seen Georgia in a state of inaction, since she was always in the middle of some kind of project around the house. He'd also never seen her in anything but the navy blue coveralls and heavy work boots that comprised her self-imposed uniform. A red bandanna knotted above one knee added a touch of adornment, but he knew from experience it would be the only decoration she'd bother with.

"Hey, Holly. Hey, Georgia. I need some coffee, stat." Amy strode forward and shook the two empty cups until Holly took them. "So does Monty. He was skulking in the hallway right outside the door. I think he was afraid to face you on his own."

Holly turned an alarmed look his way, but it was the echoing laugh of Georgia in the stove hood that arrested him.

"Skulking?" She poked her head out. As he expected, she wore no trace of makeup or jewelry, her tangled brown curtain of hair pulled back in its invariable ponytail. *All* of her was invariable. Although she'd grown out of the gangly, toothy stage from her youth, she hadn't moved an unrecognizable distance from it. Her lips were still thin, her features still prominent, and her complexion bore a windswept ruggedness that would have better served a sea captain or lumberjack.

She wasn't beautiful. She wasn't even pretty. But as the hammer in her back pocket attested, she was more than capable of making do without.

She grinned, bringing life to her features and making

Monty long for the kitchen tiles to devour him whole. "Then it's good we weren't talking about anything inappropriate. I can't imagine how uncomfortable that would make things."

Any chance Monty might have had of playing cool disappeared. One would think that thirty-five years of life on this planet would give a man a certain amount of panache in awkward situations, but one would be wrong. Like a prisoner trapped in solitary confinement, Monty found that the more time he spent on his own, the less panache he was capable of. The less *everything* he was capable of. Even the Count of Monte Cristo eventually discovered a kindred spirit on the other side of the stone wall to save him from the monotony of his own company.

Monty's stone walls kept going forever.

"I wasn't skulking." He couldn't think of anything that might serve as a reasonable excuse, so he left it there.

Holly handed his coffee cup back to him, offering it handle-side-out to prevent their fingers from touching. "You didn't have to come all this way for a refill," she said uneasily. "I could have sent someone up."

"You forget that Monty and I are slaves to our duty," Amy said. "If we didn't break away every now and then, we'd become nothing more than drones of productivity."

Then, as if realizing a drone of productivity was basically all Monty was, she also fell into an uncomfortable silence.

That was his cue to leave. He might not always land on the right thing to say, but he did know how to make a timely exit. In fact, one of the best moves he'd made recently as the head of the Montgomery Foundation was handing over the social obligations to his brother Jake. The division of labor worked so well that Monty had been able to sever most of his ties to the real world and hide away in the Manor with only his spreadsheets for company. He'd never been more popular now that no one had to actually interact with him. He even got fan mail sometimes.

"Thank you for the coffee." He raised his cup in a gesture of appreciation. "I'll let you three get back to work."

It should have been an easy escape, an only mildly distressing break to his routine, but in this, as in all things, he missed his mark. His comment sounded less like a polite parting and more like a boss jumping on his employees' backs for standing around talking when they should have been working.

Technically, they weren't even *his* employees. He didn't own this house, and they weren't hired to cater to his whims. He lived here and he labored here, but he drew a paycheck with the Montgomery name on it just like everyone else. At least the three other women had the option of leaving to go work somewhere else if they wanted. The thing about having your name on the wrought-iron gate leading in was that it worked an awful lot like a cattle brand. He'd always bear the marks.

"You're right," Holly said with a tight smile. "I've got lots of deep cleaning I could be getting done this morning."

"And if I don't go relieve the night nurse of her duties in the next five minutes, she might refuse to come in early the next time I beg," Amy said.

Only Georgia didn't seem to be in a hurry to jump when he barked, but that was probably because she hadn't stopped working the entire time he'd been present. She leaped from the stove and brushed her hands on the seat of her coveralls.

"I'll walk you out, shall I?" she said cheerfully. "I'm about to head to the garden shed to clean the gutters. The glamorous life of a handywoman never ends."

He couldn't think of a polite way to demur, so he waited while she gathered up her toolbox and provided some parting advice to Holly about changing the filters before accompanying her out the doors.

"I'm glad to catch you this morning," Georgia said, as though there was nothing odd about the two of them chatting as they moved through the maze of hallways. Just two people, one of whom apparently harbored table-rocking sexual fantasies about the other, their footsteps so long they were practically running. What could be weird about that? "I wanted to ask you again whether you'd be willing to help out with Homeward Bound."

"Homeward Bound?"

"Yeah." When he didn't say anything right away, she supplied more information. "The charity that builds houses for families in need? The one I've been volunteering for since I was eighteen? I got put in charge of the local Chapter last year when I finally got my contractor's license."

THE NAME AND premise were well-known enough to strike a chord, but that was where the familiarity ended. Thousands of grant applications crossed Monty's desk every week, and it was impossible to keep track of all the organizations that needed funding and were turned down. Once upon a time, he'd tried to keep a more accurate personal count, but he'd learned that if he wanted to preserve his sanity, it was better to focus on the people he *could* help, rather than the ones he couldn't.

"What is it you want?" he asked warily.

Her face fell, cheeks heavy with the weight of her disappointment. "Oh. You don't remember our conversation?"

"No, I..." *Shoot.* There was no way to pretend he had any idea what she was talking about. It seemed that unless this woman was rating his sexual prowess, he didn't pay attention to what she had to say. How charming of him. "I'm so sorry. It's not ringing a bell."

"Never mind. I figured getting you to participate would be a long shot anyway." She waved him off with an attempt at a smile. "Forget I said anything. It's not a problem."

But it *was* a problem, and he felt that fact more keenly than he might have a few hours ago. Not only was it remiss of him to forget about Georgia's charity work in the first place—his dad would never overlook that sort of detail about anyone on his staff—but he was in the bizarre position of wanting to impress her. This woman, a woman he rarely saw and barely knew, thought his personality sucked.

Well, it *did* suck, but he didn't care for people to actually know that. Or discuss it amongst themselves in the family kitchens.

"Have you applied to the Montgomery Foundation through the traditional channels?" he asked. "It's not exactly sanctioned, but I'm sure we could expedite the proposal given your years of service to the family."

He passed a hand over his eyes, barely stifling a groan at the familiar drone of his voice. He was doing it again, speaking as if he'd swallowed a business report and was doomed to a lifetime of churning it out piece by piece. "If it's something you'd like, that is," he added lamely.

"Oh, no. We're a local Chapter of a state organization, so the money's already taken care of." She spoke loudly—more so than usual, obviously hiding her disappointment. "It's not a big deal. I always seem to be running short on able-bodied young men to do the heavy lifting, and you look like you know your way around the free weights. I thought you might be able to lend some muscle, that's all."

"YOU WANT ME to help you build houses?" An oddly sweeping pleasure took over. Not only did Georgia think he was a ten in the looks department, but she also considered him a bastion of strength. His spine straightened, naturally puffing his chest out a few extra inches.

She promptly deflated it. "I've already hit up everyone else around here. Ryan and Alex stop by occasionally, but they're busy most weekends."

"I see," he said dryly. "How gratifying."

"I *did* ask you a few months ago," she pointed out.

Again, he found himself at a loss. Chances were she was telling the truth, and her request, like so many others, had become part of the monument of missed opportunities that loomed over his day-to-day life. If only happiness could be measured in parties unattended, people unentertained, friendships untenanted. He'd be euphoric.

"I can understand why you might have blocked it out," she said. "It's a lot of hard work, and I think we've acquired a total of eighty-seven stitches all told."

"How…tempting?"

"Well, since all the work we do is unpaid, we try to have a good time while we're out there. Stitches are the price we pay, but it's fun."

Fun?

He must have done a poor job of hiding his disbelief,

because she continued with that same deep-velvet laugh from before. "But it's also a big commitment, and I know how busy you are. Some other time, maybe."

They reached a breakaway point in the hall, two paths laid out so clearly they might as well have been memorialized in verse. Monty would head upstairs to once again pick up the reins of industry while Georgia journeyed outside, where birds chirped and the sun shone and manual labor was considered a source of entertainment rather than a means to an end.

Unaware of how deeply he felt the differences between them, Georgia stuck her hand out and held it inches from his own. Her palm bore every appearance of being strong and callused, an extension of a woman who could only be described with the exact same terms. "I wish there was something I could do," he said, and since there didn't seem any way around it, he slipped his palm into hers. Predictably, her skin was rough and coarse, but it was also hotter than expected, as if proximity to her hammer gave her excess energy, rendering her a Thor in blue coveralls. "Unfortunately, my schedule doesn't leave me much room for extracurriculars."

"I won't mention it again." She didn't let go of his hand right away, and he had to wonder at what possessed her to keep it going so long.

He found out a few seconds later.

"We were just blowing off steam in there, by the way. I don't know how much you overheard—that ventilation hood magnifies sound like whoa, damn—but we didn't mean anything by it."

"I don't know what you're talking about," he said, snatching his hand back.

"You didn't pick up on any of our conversation? Maybe a little something about numbers?"

"I was only a few steps ahead of Amy the whole time."

"Okay." She nodded, but the smirk lifting her lips marred what would have been an otherwise perfect getaway moment. "Then it's probably safe for me to tell you I changed my mind. Plus one for being such a good sport about it."

Despite his determination not to admit he'd overheard anything untoward, he smiled. "Only one?"

"For now." She winked. Like old men who smelled of licorice and sea captains everywhere, she was oddly able to pull it off. "Maybe you could swing by some time and earn a few more. We could admire your arms together."

Admire my arms? He blinked. Surely she wasn't suggesting what he thought she was suggesting. Despite her earlier revelations, there was nothing about this woman that belonged in the sexual portion of his thoughts. She worked for his father. She carried a hammer in her back pocket. And the most attractive thing about her was the fact that he didn't find her the least bit attractive.

So why was he suddenly picturing her naked?

She waved and headed for the outer door, her not-naked form moving with a confident swagger, rendering him a fool. "See you around, Monty. Those gutters aren't going to clean themselves." She paused and winked again. "Bow-chicka-bow-wow."

ALL OF GEORGIA'S best Monty fantasies involved an apocryphal rescue of some sort.

Even though this part of Connecticut was protected from every natural disaster known to mankind—barring the occasional winter snowstorm—her imagination seethed with volcano eruptions, tornadoes and devastating floods that should have made her ashamed of herself. But she wasn't. She wasn't ashamed at all. She gleefully killed off everyone within a hundred-mile radius so that in the midst of the rubble and devastation, only two souls remained.

Her favorite scenario was an earthquake that trapped Monty inside his office, where he always had some sort of body part pinned and unable to get free. Through diligence and the use of her trusty hammer, Georgia broke through the giant pile of boards and rocks only to suffer an aftershock that buried them together.

She always got them out, of course, but only after they'd given up hope and decided to make the most of their last twenty minutes on earth. With sex. Lots of sex. Sex that was desperate and seedy and could only be the action of two people for all intents and purposes alone in the world.

Inside her head, Monty was exceptionally skilled at that kind of desperate, seedy sex.

Inside her head, so was she.

Georgia continued her assault on the minor ecosystem that had developed inside the garden shed gutter, lying prone on the roof as she basked in the double glow of the morning sun and her imagination. There weren't many situations in which the unattractive, unkempt handywoman in coveralls was able to land the six-foot-two gorgeous mountain of a millionaire, and that she was required to concoct elaborate doomsday scenarios to make it happen would come as no surprise to anyone. In a doomsday scenario, it didn't matter whether your underwear came in the form of tiny scraps of lace from Victoria's Secret or enormous cotton briefs from the bargain bin at the grocery store.

In fact, giant bargain bin underwear was probably preferred. If it came down to it, they could turn the briefs into a slingshot and use them for hunting.

"And this is why we don't proposition the man of the Manor, Georgia," she muttered. "Because we probably *could* kill grouse with our panties, should the situation call for it."

To convince herself that she wasn't hurt by the day's interaction—that rejection from a man like Monty wasn't only likely, but carved in stone—she shoved her gloved hand deep in the gutter, scooping out slimy bits of decaying leaves and what looked like a slug colony. She heaved the handful into the plastic bucket propped next to her and scooped again, finding the repetitive motions soothing.

Although most people wrinkled their noses and looked down at her when she mentioned what she did for a living, she'd always found that manual labor had a way of bringing clarity, of stripping everything else away so she could just breathe. She'd tried to get the same kind of focus through yoga once, but it had been impossible to concentrate when her ass was in the air and the spandex pants she'd bought for the occasion were riding.

Some women might be skilled at daintily extracting fabric from between their butt cheeks, but Georgia Lennox wasn't one of them. Which was fine. Whatever. She'd had her Girl Card taken away from her much too long ago to regret its loss.

Well, she didn't regret it *much*. There were times—times that coincided with a chance encounter with the well-groomed, well-packed millionaire she'd somewhat

unwisely chosen as her ideal physical specimen of man—
when she wished she were better at being a woman.

As if to prove how far from femininity a human being
could reside, a sleek black sports car pulled up the cob-
bled drive, coming to a stop a few feet below Georgia and
her bucket o' muck. The woman who emerged from the
driver's side door was *exactly* who belonged on the arm of
a man like Monty. Even from a good ten feet above, Georgia could see the sleek lines of a pair of legs straight out
of a forties film. Everything about her was Hollywood-
glamour perfect. Bouncy hair, perfectly painted lips, the
way you could tell she had a throaty laugh and drank
alcoholic beverages inexplicably made with vegetables.

And Georgia couldn't even find it in her to hate the
woman, because when her perilously high heel lodged
between two of the cobblestones, the woman let out a
"for motherfucking Pete's sake" like a real champ. She
swore even louder when she lifted her foot only to keep
the shoe and leave the heel behind.

Since this was as close to a rescue scenario as Georgia was going to get anytime soon, she set her bucket
aside and rose to her feet. Skipping the hassle of climbing down the ladder set against the back side of the shed,
she gripped the edge of the roof and swung herself down.

"Jesus H. Christ!" The woman screamed as Georgia
fell in a neat crouch a few feet from where she stood.
"Where did you come from?"

She pointed straight up. "I was doing maintenance."

"In the sky?"

"Close. The roof." She laughed. "Sorry to scare you
like that. I should have called down first. I'm Georgia."

She could feel the weight of the other woman's scrutiny as she cast her initial judgments. It was a weight—a

burden—Georgia knew well, and she didn't take it amiss when the woman didn't appear to be impressed with the outcome. It was cool. Few people were.

Still, as she stuck her hand out, waiting for the other woman to shake, she couldn't help but note the differences between them. The woman's hand was nicely formed, the sort of limb that could be described with phrases like *soft* and *silky*. Nothing about Georgia was silky. She spent so much time out of doors she was practically sheathed in leather.

But the woman took her hand anyway. "Ashleigh. Are you some sort of staff member? Perhaps you can help me. I seem to have broken my shoe on the walkway."

Georgia reached down and plucked the rogue heel from between the flagstones. "Not a problem. I don't suppose you have any superglue on you? Or chewing gum?" At Ashleigh's blank stare, Georgia sighed. "I'm not surprised. No one does anymore. I blame four out of five dentists."

She didn't wait for Ashleigh to muster up a polite response—it was one of Georgia's many curses to be unable to interact with the rich in any way that approached sanity—before she dipped into the tool belt strapped around her waist. Although her oversized white truck had a more comprehensive array of tools and fasteners, there was a double-sided nail in a side pouch that would do the trick. With a few efficient movements, she managed to wedge the nail into the heel portion. From there, she only had to flip the shoe over and jam the broken part in.

See? Easy-peasy. She didn't even need to pull her hammer out.

"Voilà." She gave the heel a wiggle before handing it over. "It's not perfect, but it'll hold."

Ashleigh looked at the shoe and back at Georgia, her brows pulled together in obvious concern for her footwear. "Oh. Um. Thank you?"

"You're welcome. It shouldn't stab through to your foot, but if it does, you may want to hunt down some of that chewing gum after all. You can use it to pad your heel."

Ashleigh gave a reluctant laugh, and Georgia couldn't help but feel smug at the sound of it. She'd totally called it—that was the very definition of throaty.

"Do you *really* work here?" she asked.

"As in, am I a vetted professional, or am I the cheerful homeless lady who wanders the grounds? Strange though it may seem, it's the first one."

"I didn't mean—"

"And I'm sorry if I scared you before," Georgia added, interrupting Ashleigh before she bothered with a half-hearted attempt at backtracking. There was no need. Of all the insults Georgia had withstood in her lifetime, being looked upon as a cheerful homeless lady was quite nice. Because of her work with Homeward Bound, she'd known quite a few such women and counted them among her personal heroes. "I saw your heel break off and figured I could help. Can I point you where you need to go?"

"Oh, not me. I know my way." Ashleigh turned her leg and slipped the heel back on, a smile curving her lips as she tested it with her weight. "Hey—that's not bad. I can't even tell it was broken. What did you say your name was again? I'll be sure and tell Monty about your assistance. Maybe he can work you in a raise."

Georgia felt a whoosh of air leave her lungs before she immediately sucked it all back in where it belonged. She was *not* wasting perfectly good oxygen on this situation.

Of course this woman was here to see Monty—Georgia had surmised as much the second she'd seen those legs emerge from the car. And of course she looked at Georgia as the help.

Georgia might technically own her own company, but she *was* the help. The slightly eccentric, ungainly help. The slightly eccentric, ungainly help who harbored an unhealthy crush on the drop-dead-gorgeous scion of the household.

The chasm between the two of them couldn't have been wider if it was the Grand Canyon.

Still… "My name is Holly," she lied. "Holly Santos. I work in the kitchen."

"Are you sure that's what you said before?"

Georgia didn't lose her wide and slightly crazed smile. "Absolutely."

Though she couldn't quite say why, she didn't want Monty to know she'd served his girlfriend in a menial capacity. It was one thing to look at him and feel her own lack of worth, but it was another to have that belief reflected back at her. She was always on the lookout for ways to feel *more* equal to him, not less—it was why she kind of liked that he was such a clod in the conversation department. It leveled the playing field. The Bore and the Beast had a much better chance of success than that other silly story.

Ashleigh thanked her again for the shoe repair and turned to go into the house, and even Georgia had to admire the way she walked, a film vixen right down to the sway of her hips.

She tried to give a little sway herself, but there was gutter goo under her boot and she almost lost her footing. With a sigh, she hopped up the ladder and made her way back to the garden shed roof instead.

At least she had a pretty good view of the grounds from here. She might never own a place like Montgomery Manor, with its sixty sprawling acres and enough room to stretch her legs, but she did get to visit whenever she felt like it.

It was a lot like having your Girl Card revoked but retaining the body parts, now that she thought about it. She might not get to be an active member of the club, but at least she got to stop by from time to time.

Some days, that was even enough.

TWO

"THERE'S NO NEED to announce me. The last time I checked, there weren't any emergency escape routes in there, so he's trapped whether he likes it or not."

Monty's grip on the phone tightened at the sound of the light, melodic voice outside his door, startled to find himself scanning for an alternate exit despite Ashleigh's assertion that none existed. If his office hadn't been located on the fourth floor, he might have actually jumped out the window.

"Hey, Thomas—can I call you back?" Even though he looked forward to these conversations every week with an enthusiasm he'd have been ashamed to admit to out loud, he held the phone away from his ear, as if Thomas might somehow be able to feel his sudden recoil of horror. "Something has just, ah, come up."

"Uh-oh. Everything cool?"

"Um, yes. Cool. The coolest."

Thomas laughed, the same way he always did whenever Monty tried to sound more age-appropriate. Working with *teenagers*—even levelheaded ones—was a constant reminder of how painfully old he was. "No problem, Mr. Montgomery. I know you're busy, and I've got classes. The last grant application isn't due for a few weeks anyway."

Monty nodded before he hung up, even though Thomas couldn't see him. It was the most he could manage as

Ashleigh's voice once again worked its way through the door. "I'll take full blame for barging my way in. No—don't get up. I insist."

As if Katie, whose desk was stationed outside the suite of rooms where he and his father kept their offices, could have stopped her. Few people were able to withstand the force of Ashleigh Bridgerton when she had her mind set on something.

He certainly never had been.

"Well, Monty?" Ashleigh was, as always, a vision in business casual. He wasn't sure how much time passed while he shifted out of work mode, but he suspected it was long enough that he should have spoken up. "Aren't you at least going to say hello?"

He didn't particularly want to, but corporeal restrictions made it impossible for him to retreat into the woodwork as he'd have preferred, so he gave in. "Hello."

She laughed as though he'd made a hilarious joke, and for a moment, he got caught up in remembering what it was like. To feel he was witty and worth getting to know. To enter a room confident that one person, at least, was happy to see him.

It was a mistake, letting his guard down like that. Ashleigh sensed his momentary weakness, and he found himself being embraced and air-kissed before he had time to blink.

"God, Monty. You look more fantastic than I remember." Her arms around him made a sweeping perusal of his torso, and he let her continue much longer than a gentleman should have. It was easy to get caught up in remembering what that was like too. "You also feel more fantastic than I remember. You've been working out."

I'm a ten, he wanted to say, but didn't.

"How is it fair that men get better-looking as they age, but we women slowly decay before society's eyes?" She shook her hair and arched a brow. "That was an easy segue for you to tell me how wrong I am, and that I've never looked better. There's no hurry. I'll wait."

He had to smile. There was no denying that the past twelve months had been good to her. She'd been beautiful when he knew her before, always pulled-together and dressed to impress, and none of that had changed in the interim. She was lean and elegant, dressed in a business suit that probably came straight from Paris. Her hair was swept neatly to one side, the wide set of her lips parted in an enticing smile. And if there were a *few* tiny wrinkles around the corners of her eyes, they only added to her appeal, forced a man to recognize that she was real and had lived—and that both these things were to her advantage.

She was, in a word, perfect. Perfect for him, perfect for his family, perfect for the cattle brand of a gate out front.

"It's good to see you again, Ashleigh," he finally said. He didn't see the point in indulging either one of them in pointing out her more obvious attributes. Ashleigh had always known her own worth. "Come in. Sit down."

"Thank you. I intend to."

He waited until she had arranged herself in the seat opposite his desk before settling in his own chair, unable to miss how nicely she blended in here, this room full of his favorite books and paintings, a room he'd refused to let anyone touch since he'd taken it over at the age of sixteen. The furniture was worn, the book spines were broken, and the coating of dust drove the family housekeeper crazy, but this was one of the few places on the Montgomery Manor grounds where he felt truly at ease.

There was comfort in knowing that the one woman with whom he'd ever felt at ease fit in too.

"Penny for your thoughts?" Ashleigh asked.

He could hardly tell her about the swirl of longing and regret currently taking up residence in his gut, so he settled for a tight smile. "I was just wondering what it is that brings you all this way."

She laughed again, flashing him her neat rows of teeth. "God, I forgot how much fun it is talking to you."

"And by fun, you of course mean painful?"

"By fun, I mean if I want anything personal, I'll have to dig in and pry it out of you syllable by syllable."

"I'm not sure what it is you want to hear." Surely not an outpouring of affection. She'd been the one to break up with him, her sentiments of a year ago not as forgiving of his reticence. He harbored very distinct, very clear memories of that day. She'd said talking to him was like looking for a foothold in a sheet of black ice.

She wasn't wrong.

"Why don't we start with pleasantries?" She shifted so that she leaned over the desk, her expression eager, her favorite jasmine scent stronger. "What have you been up to this past year? I heard Jake got married. I was sorry to miss the wedding."

"Yes, it was a nice service." A bit of a media circus, if you asked him, but no one had. Since it seemed Ashleigh wanted more from him, he added, "I like his wife quite a lot. She's been good for settling him down."

"There, now. That was something. Details and an opinion and everything."

"I believe your brother was present, yes? He came to represent your family in your absence."

Her eyes narrowed in a familiar warning, and an

equally familiar constriction in his chest reminded him that not all of the memories he shared with this woman were pleasant ones. "No one was *representing* anyone. My brother came because he likes Jake and wanted to share in his big day. It was a celebration, not a business arrangement."

"That's what I meant."

"No, it wasn't. To you, all social gatherings have to be part of a master plan or you consider them a waste of your time."

That was because they usually *were* a waste of his time, and nothing he was able to say or do would convince this woman—or anyone, really—otherwise. He didn't enjoy himself at parties, and the vast majority of people didn't enjoy having him there either. Most maxed out after two attempts at conversation, then studiously avoided him from there on out. He'd once caught a woman hiding behind a potted ficus so she wouldn't have to go in to dinner with him.

It had seemed more unfair than painful at the time. He was too big to use a plant as a shield.

Because he spent enough of his time working with figures to appreciate that a zero percent return on his investment was a clear sign he was better off staying home, that was what he did from there on out. Stayed home. Kept company with a fern. Everyone was happier that way.

As this was an argument he and Ashleigh had shared countless times in the past, he didn't bother reiterating it now. There was no reason to.

"Some people enjoy the company of others," she said pointedly. "It makes them happy."

"I understand that."

"I'm not so sure you do." Her eyes narrowed again, but

she stifled the emotion with a shake of her head. "Since we're on the topic of weddings, I might as well tell you what I came here for."

She reached across his desk and held her hand out, palm up. Those long, elegant fingers had once held so much of him, but he found it difficult to initiate the contact she so clearly sought now. He extended his hand so slowly he barely moved at all.

"I wanted you to hear it from me first, Monty." She squeezed, and it felt as if she were applying the pressure to his heart rather than his hand. "I always thought you were going to be the one for me—you know that—and breaking up with you last summer was one of the most difficult things I've ever done."

He *didn't* know that, and he wasn't at all sure he cared to hear more.

"It took me a long time and a lot of soul-searching to get over you, but I finally did it. And a lot of that is thanks to the man I met in Nepal."

"You went to Nepal?"

She ignored him. "His name is Martin, and we're getting married."

Monty jerked his hand back and dropped it into his lap so she wouldn't see the way it shook. *Nepal. Martin. Married.* He recognized the words, but they seemed to be making little impression on his brain.

"Did you hear me? I said I'm getting married."

"Of course. Of course I heard you." He must have taken longer to process her news than he realized, and to cover his discomfiture, he got to his feet with a start. The only thing he could think right now was that he needed time and space—a moment of privacy to gather his thoughts. Why were there always people around when he least wanted them? "Congratulations, Ashleigh. I wish you both well."

"Sit down, Monty."

"I'm very busy—"

"*Sit down.*"

He remained standing. Ashleigh didn't get to tell him what to do anymore. He'd done what he was supposed to where she was concerned—loved her, cared for her, made room for her in his life to the best of his ability— and it hadn't mattered in the end. None of it was enough to overcome the tedium so deeply rooted in his personality he suspected it arose from his soul.

"Fine." She sighed and rose. "We'll do this your way. I didn't come here to be cruel or to rub my happiness in your face, but the wedding is next month, and I didn't want you to find out when the invitation arrives. You deserve better from me."

"Thank you," he said tightly, hoping it would be the last word on the subject.

It wasn't.

"That was supposed to be us," she said softly.

"But it's not," he returned. "You said no."

And there it was. Words he barely allowed himself to think, let alone say. He'd asked this woman to be his wife. He'd gotten down on one knee and said the words that never came easily to him. Love. Adoration. A desire to share his life and his heart with her.

But she'd walked away. The price of his love had been lifelong companionship with Drudgery John—and it had been too high of a price for her to pay.

"Surely you see by now that we'd have been terrible together," she said. He could tell she wanted to take his hand again, but he kept them pinned firmly behind his back. "The look on your face when I walked through this door was evidence of that. You'd have welcomed Medusa with more enthusiasm."

That was untrue and unfair, and they both knew it. He hated snakes.

Her expression softened. "You're such a good man, Monty. You're the best man I know."

Not good enough, he didn't say.

"But for the love of all that is holy, you have *got* to learn to let go sometimes," she said.

"I did let you go."

"Not me. Yourself." She gestured around her, skimming over the familiar objects, the windows overlooking the grounds of a home that would one day belong to him. His things. His place. "There's an entire world beyond these four walls. Things to do that aren't related to work or the Montgomery legacy. When was the last time you did something for no other reason than to have fun?"

Was that a trick question? He worked fifty hours a week running the Montgomery Foundation. At least thirty more helping his father with his hotels. He barely had time to eat, let alone play.

"I can't regret the time I spend helping others." A lot of lives had been changed for the better because of his commitment to these four walls, boys and girls like Thomas offered a chance to say "I've got classes" without hesitation. Maybe it made him a proud man to claim those successes as his own, but those successes were often the only things that kept him going.

"No one is asking you to." Ashleigh lifted her hands in a motion of despair. "And that's why I couldn't agree to marry you. Not then, and not now, not even if you fell to your knees and begged me. I didn't want to have to martyr myself to *your* duties in order to be with you. With Martin, there's no question I come first."

He had the feeling he was supposed to offer his congratulations again, but he wasn't sure how.

"I wish you realized how hard it was for me to walk away like I did," she said. "I think there will always be a part of me that never stops loving you."

"I'm happy for you, Ashleigh." His voice felt raspy, dry, the words so long stifled they fought against the air. "I mean that."

"You don't. You want to call your security guard and have him forcibly remove me." She gave a watery laugh. "It's okay. I didn't expect you to be overjoyed at the news."

She came in for another hug, and he had no choice but to give it. He felt stiff and awkward, unsure where to put his hands. In another lifetime, he might have buried one in her hair and allowed the other to fall gently to her waist, held her until the rest of the world fell away, if only for a few minutes.

But that lifetime was over. She'd come to hand-deliver the message, just in case he didn't get it the first time around. Ashleigh had always been very thorough.

"Your family is getting an invitation, of course, but I don't want you to feel like you have to come." She pulled away and straightened her skirt, a slight swipe of her fingers under her eyes the only indication she was anything but in control of herself. "It would be great if you did, but I understand if it's too much."

He nodded. He had a strong suspicion he'd be working that day.

She grabbed her purse and headed for the door, pausing long enough to look back at him. "Oh! I almost forgot.

One of the women who works here—Holly something?—was really nice about fixing my shoe on the way in. She found me stranded in the front drive and literally swooped to my rescue. I swear, your family always has the best luck with staff."

It wasn't luck so much as his father's exceptional skill in finding and hiring people, but Monty accepted the compliment as it was intended. "Are you sure it was Holly? She's not much of a one for swooping."

"Well, that's what she told me, but I thought she said a different name the first time. She was strange, dressed kind of like an escapee mechanic or something. A person fitting that description *does* work here, right?"

He smiled, his mind immediately flying to Georgia and the almost texturized laugh from this morning he couldn't seem to shake. Escapee mechanic sounded about right. "That was probably the handywoman my dad hires to help out a few days a week. Did she have a hammer strapped to her waist?"

"Among other barbaric things. I wonder why she lied about her name."

"Maybe you heard her wrong."

"Maybe." Ashleigh tilted her head at the open door. "I should get going. I've got an appointment, and I know you have work you'd rather be doing right now. It was good to see you again, Monty."

He wanted to return the sentiment, but it would have been too much of a stretch, so he settled for a nod. It was inadequate, as so many of his responses were, but some things would never change.

"And try to have some fun for once, okay? It's not healthy to live the way you do."

Now he *really* didn't trust himself to speak, so he

merely watched as Ashleigh let herself out. He wished he could attribute the feelings taking over to the wedding news, but that would have been a lie. While the pangs of heartache were present, heavy where they settled in his chest, the reality was that he'd now been called boring by a grand total of four women.

Four separate, vibrant, interesting women who would rather do anything than face a prolonged amount of time in his company. Four separate, vibrant, interesting women who looked at him in the space of one morning and saw little more than a block of wood.

That had to be some kind of record—even for him.

THE LAST PERSON Georgia expected to see as she hauled her equipment into her truck was Monty, bearing down on her with a frown so intense he could have buried them both underneath it.

Well, hell. She hoped she hadn't misjudged the depth of that nail and stabbed his poor lady friend in the heel after all. It was a fairly clean nail, when all was said and done, but rich people were so sensitive about things like that. One pinprick, and they were suddenly sure they had tetanus.

"Hey, there," she said as casually as she could. "Some weather we're having today, huh?"

"What?"

"A summer storm is my guess. I broke my wrist a few years ago, and now I can feel the oncoming rain in my scaphoid. No joke. I almost hope I have arthritis when I'm old so I can extend my radar as far as Vermont."

He blinked at her in confusion, which gave her a moment to appraise him. For what had to be the first time in all the years she'd been working for the family, he wasn't wearing a suit jacket, and he even had the top two buttons of his shirt open and slightly askew. That tiny flash of skin was like cracking open the gates to heaven—dazzling and illicit and somehow all the more compelling because of it.

Monty was never anything but completely pulled together. She was alarmed almost as much as she was aroused at his dishevelment, especially when he leaned closer, dismissing her small talk with a tightly controlled, "This morning, did you mean what you said? About me?"

She stopped, wholly unprepared for that question and the sudden burst of butterflies it released in her stomach—and it took a lot to stump her. She was a killer at Thursday night trivia down at Wings 'n' Brew, rolling off sports statistics and incredibly dated pop culture references like she was born knowing them.

So much for the blonde bombshell being a girlfriend of some sort.

"Um, yes?" she said when he didn't back away. "I guess so."

"You don't sound sure."

Of course she didn't sound sure. She didn't know how many times he'd had an attractive and strapping young man demanding an opinion of his virility, but this shit was hard. What did he want?

Yes, Monty, I think you're a ten. I look at the way your shoulders span massive distances and wonder how it might feel to have your arms crushing me against your chest.

Yes, Monty, I wish you would challenge me to an arm-wrestling match.

If you beat me, I'll perform any sexual act you want.

Yes, Monty, I do dream of you between my legs every night.

In fact, it's pretty much the only way I can get myself off, thanks for asking.

Yeah…no. She wasn't saying any of those things out loud. Especially since he'd just keep looking at her in that intently assessing way of his. Conversations with this man would be greatly improved if he'd stop falling into the habit of ominous silence every few seconds. Or if the earth opened up and threatened to swallow them both. In all her apocryphal longings, the conversation with Monty never flagged. Probably because they were too busy repopulating the earth to bother with niceties.

He cleared his throat, as if waiting for her to respond.

Girding her loins—in probably the most literal way a woman could gird them—she took a deep breath and said, "I'm still sure."

"Yeah?"

"Yeah. Nothing has changed in the—" she scanned the sky, "—eight hours since I've seen you last."

He followed the path of her gaze with a frown. Once again, he took a few extra moments to formulate a question, but this time she was happy to let him. It was enough to have an uninhibited opportunity to gaze at the chiseled outline of his profile. There was a sameness to all the Montgomerys—a kind of glistening ginger goodness that culminated in the most unfairly attractive crop of auburn hair ever to grace the human head—but she hadn't been kidding when she said she preferred this man. It wasn't only that Monty was taller and more robust than his brother. There was a dormant quality to him, as if he'd spent an entire lifetime building up tension and was merely waiting for an opportunity to let it go.

Oh, how she wished he'd let it go. She wished he'd let it go all over her.

Monty raised his brows in a controlled expression, clearly not ready to release all that latent power yet. "Did you just tell the time by looking at the sun?"

"Um, yes?"

"You can do that?"

"Sure." She looked up at the sun again to make sure she hadn't misjudged. She'd lived in this part of Connecticut for so long—spent so much time on these grounds in particular—that she was able to track the sun's path no matter what the time of year. "It's been eight hours and about fifteen minutes, if I'm not mistaken."

He pulled out a pocket watch to check her accuracy, even going so far as to shake the miniature clockwork piece when she turned out to be right. Although she appreciated that he carried a pocket watch in lieu of a more modern timepiece, she wasn't sure shaking it was the best way of demanding precision.

"That's incredible," he said. "How long have you been able to do that?"

"Since those calculator watches were invented."

He stared at her.

"Calculator watches. Remember them? With those tiny buttons you had to use a pencil to push?"

"I'm familiar with the technology, yes."

"Well, I didn't trust them when I was a kid. I still don't, to be honest. If those strap-on computers weren't proof the government was laying the groundwork to track our every movement, then I don't know how else they could have spelled it out for us."

Now he wasn't just staring at her—he was goggling. And making it look good too, his glittering blue eyes wide, the strong hinge of his jaw open enough to allow her a glimpse of how well-crafted his molars were.

What? She liked a man with strong, healthy teeth.

"You're very strange, do you know that?"

She did. Oddity wasn't the sort of attribute that snuck up on you, like depression or a receding hairline. She'd been made aware of her outsider status a long time ago—and by enough people that she'd stopped trying to fight it. Like accepting her inability to pitch a softball faster than sixty-five miles an hour, there were limits to what she could legitimately accomplish in this world.

Normalcy included.

"I'm just saying. Computers we inadvertently carry around with us everywhere we go? Sounds like the start of a conspiracy to me." She whistled the theme song from the *X-Files* and was rewarded with a low chuckle. It seemed Monty was good at incredibly dated pop culture references too.

But his laughter turned off as quickly as it had flashed on, and he leaned close once again. "I'm glad I caught you before you left. I wanted to let you know that I changed my mind, and I'm interested in your offer."

She kept shaking her head, even though he hadn't asked a question and she was getting a little dizzy. Fortunately, Monty seemed to accept her insanity as a matter of course. A reputation for eccentricity came in handy sometimes.

"Is it something you can follow up on today?" he asked, lifting a hand to stop her head from its incessant back-and-forth movement.

And that was it. That was all it took—his fingers gripping her chin with an easy strength she could have broken free of in a second, but didn't. She didn't want to. She wanted him to keep holding her until his gaze softened just enough for her to feel beautiful.

She could wait.

"Georgia? Did you hear me?"

Or maybe not.

Even though she could have taken a few more minutes—hours, days—of that intense staring, there was no need for such lengthy preparations. Desire was overtaking all other sensations—and at a rate that would probably alarm him, were he privy to the inner workings of her inner thighs. Her heart pounded, her body flooded with heat and her breasts grew heavy with anticipation. It was almost infuriating the way her body jumped at the chance to make preparations for the act of love and then refused to cooperate once she finally got there.

It was the ultimate in Girl Card mockery. Of the exactly six sexual partners she'd had in her life, a total of zero of them had managed to rock her world. And by rock her world, she meant basically anything other than a minor fizzle downstairs. She could have orgasms—she had them just fine when it was only her, a rotating showerhead and whatever Monty fantasy she decided to conjure up for the day—but the moment she tried to do anything with an actual human being, it was as if everything went into lockdown mode. Dry it up, pack it in and call it a day—her body became a fortress. A *penetrable* fortress, sure, but a fortress all the same.

It was as though her vagina recognized the futility of even trying. *Sorry, Georgia*, it said. *Maybe it's best if we sit this one out. Wouldn't want you to get unrealistic expectations, eh?*

Frankly, she could do with a lot more unrealistic expectations in her life, which was the excuse she was clinging to for practically accosting Monty in the hallway earlier. Maybe it was foolish to reach for such exalted heights, but she couldn't think of a better way to break the spell than with the man who inspired so many of her dirtiest thoughts.

Not even her body would be so cruel as to deny her pleasure at the hands of John Montgomery the Third. Not when it already worked so hard to make her life difficult.

"Is this a bad time?" he asked, an anxious knit to his brows.

"No, no—this is fantastic," she practically shouted, fearful that the longer they stood in the direct sunlight together, the greater the chance he'd notice who he was talking to and change his mind. "What were you thinking?"

"Well, I'm not quite sure, but I'd like to get my hands in there as soon as possible."

She glanced down at her coveralls with surprise. There weren't many men who looked at pants so baggy she could fit a puppy in there and then chomped at the bit to get inside, but she was flexible.

"Um. Do you want to go somewhere more private first?" The garden shed would probably work, but she wasn't sure he'd be comfortable in there, what with the discarded shears and lawnmower parts and enough insecticides to invade a small country. Also, she was sweaty. And had gutter slime in her hair. She definitely needed a shower first. "Or I guess you could stop by my place later tonight. That's probably best."

He dropped his hand and stepped back, all business once again. She tried not to feel bereft at the loss of his touch, at how quickly the wooing stopped once he got a confirmed yes, but the sensation was there all the same. It seemed Monty was an ordinary man after all.

They all were, once you got down to it.

"That works. Is your address in the employee files?"

She wrinkled her nose, finding that idea more distasteful than all the rest of the seedy arrangements currently underway. It was one thing to make an assignation when moved by the flesh. It was another to pull his dad's billing records into the process.

"Here—I'll jot it down for you instead. Does sevenish work? I've got kind of an early morning tomorrow, so I can't be up too late."

He nodded, accepting her kick-him-out-early excuse as easily as it was offered, and she couldn't decide if that made things better or worse. On the one hand, she didn't relish the idea of forcing more of this one-sided conversation in the heady afterglow. On the other, he could at least *pretend* to want to get to know her better.

"I've got an early day, as well," he said. "I can't thank you enough for letting me squeeze in like this."

"Well, you haven't done any squeezing yet. Maybe you should wait and thank me later."

He laughed stiffly, as if unsure whether or not she'd been joking. "Is there anything in particular I should wear?"

Okay, now things were getting weird. Did he think she had some kind of fetish? Did *he* have some kind of fetish? Maybe he was expecting her to pull out all the stops with a sparkly thong or even a bridle. The bridle she could probably pull off on such short notice. The thong, not so much.

"Whatever you're most comfortable in is fine," she said. "I'm pretty open-minded."

He nodded, apparently satisfied with that answer. She thought maybe she should ask if he had any special requests of his own, but he checked his watch again and glanced anxiously back up at the house. "I should get back to work. I'll see you tonight?"

"I'm looking forward to it."

He leaned in, as if he maybe—possibly?—wanted to kiss her cheek, but thought better of it at the last minute. Before she could decide this whole thing was way too bizarre and change her mind, he turned and made his way back toward the house. She indulged in watching him go, his ass roundly encased in expensive slacks that suddenly seemed a touch too form-fitting to be worn in public.

She was going to get to see that ass. That ass could theoretically be plowing into her less than three hours from now. *Holy shit.*

She slid along the side of her truck until she hit the paved ground, her back resting against the tire, pebbles pressing into her butt. Oddly enough, the sensation brought more comfort than pain, forced her mind to accept the moment as reality. For all her secret longings and inappropriate remarks, she'd never actually thought something like this could happen to her. Fairy tales were for other women, girly women, women who believed in happy endings and magic wishes and dresses made of tulle.

But John Freaking Montgomery the Third made a sex date with *her*, of all people. John Freaking Montgomery the Third said he couldn't wait to get in her pants.

And she, for all her tulle-free, Girl-Card-less ways, couldn't wait to let him.

THREE

THERE WAS NOTHING in Georgia's closet even remotely appropriate for a pre-arranged sex date with one of the most attractive men in the state of Connecticut.

Since Monty seemed rather fond of her coveralls, she almost put them back on after she emerged from the shower all pink and steamy clean. Unfortunately, they were already bundled up at the bottom of her laundry basket, steeping in their own filth, which probably lowered the sex appeal overall.

She stood, wrapped in an ancient bathrobe that was one loose string away from falling apart altogether, and surveyed her closet's contents. Jeans, jeans, frayed coveralls, jeans—oh, look, her favorite green sweatshirt, which she thought she'd lost at the lake last year—jeans and enough sarcastic shirts to open her own novelty shop. She'd long ago made it a habit to sleep in men's T-shirts, which were way more comfortable than those strappy, slippery concoctions designers expected women to wrangle themselves into, and as such, her wardrobe had followed similar lines for years.

She didn't even have a cute bra to put on. Most of hers had become the same generic shade of gray-beige that all undergarments became when washed on the same cold water cycle as everything else.

The idea of lounging on the bed in the nude popped into mind when the sound of the back door opening had her heart thumping in overdrive. Oh, dear God. This was a mistake. She wasn't the kind of woman who had booty calls. She wasn't the kind of woman that rich, powerful men sought for illicit affairs.

She had stomach pudge. Her natural scent was an alluring mixture of Bactine and WD-40. Monty was either coming to murder her and stuff her body into the trunk of his car, or this was some elaborate prank she'd never be able to live down.

She prayed fervently for the first.

"Georgia?" The low, familiar voice of her brother Danny came from the back, flooding her with a relief crested by annoyance. "Are you home? I'm in the mud room."

Technically, the tiny alcove-like spot near the back door was her bedroom, but the layout of her above-garage apartment was small and weird, and she had a lot more mud than she did a need for a separate bedroom. When she'd moved in ten years ago, she'd wedged a bed in her living room, hung her giant flat-screen television on the wall and called it a day. Decoration complete.

"Georgia?" Unfortunately, Danny had a tendency to get more obnoxious the longer you ignored him. "Hello?"

"Go away," she yelled back. "I'm busy."

"No, you're not. You're probably sitting in your sweatpants eating nachos. I need to borrow a wrench."

"Then borrow one and go away."

"I can't find one. Where do you keep your toolbox?"

"The same place it's been for a decade."

A clatter and a rumble indicated her directions weren't proving as helpful as she might have hoped. Danny was the youngest of her three older brothers and the one closest to her in age, but he was also the most useless in a crisis. She could remember all too clearly the year they'd had an infestation of yellow jackets in the backyard. They were both highly allergic, but Georgia had somehow been the one equipped with two layers of snowpants, a discarded fencing mask and a hose to rid them of the plague.

Resigned to helping him before he decided to make himself some popcorn and pull up a chair—which, yes, had been his sole contribution to Yellowjacketgate— she cinched her robe tighter and followed the sound of his voice.

Like her, Danny maintained pathetically tenuous ties to their mother's house, having taken up residence in the basement as soon as he graduated from high school. When he'd learned that their mom meant to give Georgia the above-garage apartment upon reaching a similar educational achievement, he'd thrown a fit. Not only was the apartment a good basketball court's length away from the house—therefore affording some much-needed privacy—but it had its own kitchen. Not that either of them could cook, of course, but when you couldn't afford to move away from home, every illusion of independence was worth its weight in gold.

In the end, Georgia had been forced to play Danny an epically long game of Monopoly for the keys. The game lasted two weeks and ended in bloodshed, and she still had the scar along her upper right eyelid to showcase her victory. Those green houses were sharp little suckers.

"How many times do I have to tell you to knock first, dumbass? This is my apartment. My *home*. What if I was getting ready to entertain a male caller?"

Danny didn't bother to look up from where he dug through her toolbox. "Ha. That's a good one."

"I'm serious. You have to stop coming in whenever you feel like it."

"Then lock your door for a change." He pulled a wrench out with a flourish. "Here it is! And clean up your tools, for chrissakes. How you can find anything in this pit is beyond me."

"I have a system. It's not my fault your pea-brain can't comprehend it."

Danny finally looked up and saw her standing there in her ratty robe, his expression moving from triumph to suspicion in less time than it took her to blink. He had the same mop of curly brown hair the entire Lennox clan favored, and his features were similarly arranged—a bit too large, a bit too weathered, a bit too forceful. But while the combination made Georgia feel as if she needed four-and-twenty blackbirds to come peck off the most prominent parts, he looked comfortably masculine and at home in his skin. All her brothers did.

The bastards.

"Hey." He frowned. "You don't really have a gentleman caller coming over, do you?"

"As a matter of fact, I do." She tossed her head, heedless of the wet whip of her hair as it swung across her back. She needed to get a haircut, but she was trying to grow it out enough to donate to one of those wig-making charities. "Not that it's any of your business, but I do sometimes like to live beyond the scope of cleaning out gutters and playing Halo with you in Mom's basement."

"Who is he?" The sharp note in Danny's voice was impossible to ignore.

"None of your business."

"Is it that dickhead Carl again? Because we told him that if he ever tries to come near you again…"

"Oh, don't worry. You guys did a good job putting the fear of Lennox in him. He wouldn't want me back even if I plated my vagina in solid gold."

"Ew, Georgia. Don't say *vagina*."

"You're the one with no boundaries. Carl wasn't that bad."

She'd actually liked Carl. The softball coach for a rival league team, he'd been impressed by her pitching drive-through, and said as much after a tournament a few months ago. That kind of compliment was exactly what a lady liked to hear during the wooing stages, and she hadn't been immune to his prematurely balding charm.

Unfortunately, he hadn't returned the compliment— and all of his admiration for her pitching disappeared when her brothers descended on him during their second date.

Never mind, he'd said after spending five minutes in the company of the Testosterone Trio. He hadn't even offered to pay for his own beer before he got up and stalked away. *You're not worth this kind of hassle.*

Okay. Maybe Carl had been kind of a dickhead.

"Don't worry so much," she said. Monty wasn't like Carl. There was no pretense of dating or attraction or even much in the way of small talk. This was the simple tale of a peasant girl and her quest for an orgasm with a peer of the realm. "It's no one important."

"If he's not important, then why did you shave your legs?"

Georgia tucked one of her legs behind the other, as if that might erase her obvious overture at seduction. Of course the brother who lived at home would have to be the one who noticed things like her grooming habits. Adam and Charlie probably didn't even realize she *had* legs.

"Oh, go take my wrench and hit yourself with it," she said. Then, because repairs at the main house were supposed to be her domain, she asked, "What do you want it for, anyway?"

"There's a leak in the laundry room. I can hear it dripdripping all night long, and it's driving me crazy. I feel like I'm in an Edgar Allen Poe story."

"Is it that pipe leading through the back wall drain?"

"I think so. I haven't taken too close a look yet."

"This is the wrong-sized wrench." She sighed when Danny sent her a confused glance. Danny was excellent at unfolding the mysteries of his computer—she was ninety-nine percent sure he was part of that Anonymous vigilante group—but his ability to handle anything in a real world capacity was laughable. "Wrenches come in different sizes, because you can only open the jaw as far as the nut… You know what? Forget it. It's like trying to explain brain surgery to, well, you. I'll do it myself."

"I could probably handle brain surgery."

"Only if the goal is death." She shoved her feet into the pair of bright orange knee-high rain boots she kept by the door and cinched her robe tighter. "This was your plan all along, wasn't it, to force me into helping with your ineptitude?"

"I can do it," he grumbled, but not very convincingly. Danny wasn't a subtle creature. None of the Lennoxes were. They sort of barreled in and did their thing, consequences be damned. Sometimes their actions were met with approval. As was more often the case, they scared people away and made enemies of perfectly respectable human beings.

"Make yourself useful and tidy up the kitchen, won't you?" she asked. "I'll be back in five minutes, tops." Five minutes would leave her plenty of time to get dressed and make herself—if not pretty, then at least slightly closer to it. She could also swipe a box of wine from her mom's fridge to help ease the awkwardness of the upcoming evening.

A nice cardboardeaux always did the trick.

AS EXPECTED, THE back door was unlocked at the main house—the open-door policy Georgia favored was a family habit, and probably not a very good one when you thought about it. Fortunately, theirs was a small town, and none of her family members took kindly to intruders. She almost pitied the burglar who might someday wander inside to make off with the paper plates and sports memorabilia. It'd be like falling into a honey badger's lair.

The laundry room was set off from the main basement area, so she bypassed the pit where Danny nested to get right to work. It wasn't that big of a job—a few twists of the wrench and some tightening of the joints—and she was done before too many of the spiders building a web-based colony underneath crawled into her hair.

As time was running short, she tucked the wrench into her robe's belt tie and ran up the stairs, calling out as she did, "Mom—I'm stealing your good boxed wine. You just have to stab those to open them, right? You don't need a corkscrew?"

"I'm in the living room, honey."

Of course she was. Her mom was *always* in the living room at this time of night. An ER nurse by day, she took her downtime very seriously. She was also highly addicted to television cop dramas—she said she liked the procedural stuff, but it was really the bloodshed that drew her in.

"I know where you are," Georgia said. "I was trying to pretend you weren't home so I wouldn't have to come talk to you. Oh. Hello."

She stopped in the doorway, her hands tangled in her hair as she continued picking the worst of the cobwebs out. For reasons it was difficult to determine at that exact moment, Monty was sitting in the living room next to her mom, perched uncomfortably on the edge of a vintage floral chair in what had to be a thousand-dollar suit.

Although there were plenty of questions she could have asked in that moment— What are you doing here? Has my mom shown you the naked baby pictures yet? Do you think my fancy orange boots go well with this robe?—the first words to cross her lips weren't the most ideal ones.

"*That's* what you're most comfortable in?" From the way he sat on that chair, as if contact with the ancient upholstery might cause the yellow flowers to transfer to his slacks, *comfortable* was the last word she'd used to describe him. Gorgeous, yes. Flashy, sure. The embodiment of all her longings in primal male form, obviously. But she couldn't serve him boxed wine dressed like that. That was a full-cork outfit. Twist-top, at the very least.

"Georgia!" her mom said, a rebuke in her tone. She hadn't raised a house full of rambunctious children to semi-successful adulthood without the ability to fell them with a sharp word. "That's no way to speak to your company."

"No, ma'am."

"I hope you're more respectful than that when you're at work."

"Yes, ma'am."

Her mom turned to Monty with a sweet smile. "I'm sorry, John. I don't know what's come over her."

John? She was calling him John already? In all the years Georgia had been working at the Manor, the only person who'd ever dared invoke Monty's legal first name was his father. Of course, in terms of scary parental figures, her mom could probably beat Mr. Montgomery with her hands and feet trussed up like a stuck pig, so it kind of made sense. You didn't mess with that scarily efficient five-foot-two scrap of woman. She made Georgia's brothers look like bunny rabbits.

Monty cleared his throat. "It's fine. She requested casual wear. I guess I didn't realize how literally she took that phrase."

Then, and only then, did Georgia realize what kind of a picture she presented. It wasn't a pretty one, what with her semi-open robe and clunky boots and hair crawling with spiders, but if she'd learned one thing growing up with three older brothers, it was that showing weakness was the worst possible approach in situations of extreme mortification. If you accidentally overslept one day and your brothers drew penises all over your face in permanent marker, you sat across from them at breakfast and chewed your Cheerios as if you didn't have a care in the world. If your brothers photobombed your graduation pictures wearing Village People costumes, you blew the picture up to ten times its size and hung it on the living room wall.

Okay. So she had a wrench tucked into her belt and was wearing no underwear. She could make this work.

"I *do* find this outfit comfortable for lounging around the house, thank you," she said, only a few extra degrees of heat rushing to her cheeks as she spoke. "People think rubber boots make it hard for your feet to breathe, but I find this brand to be exceptionally well-ventilated. There's virtually no toe sweat."

"I'm happy to hear it," he said, but it wasn't her feet he was looking at. He'd fixated on the wide open vee of her robe instead. She wanted to add that there was no sweat on the rest of her either, but her mouth was no longer capable of forming coherent sounds. Toe sweat was her limit.

"I was just telling John you don't technically live in the house. I was going to walk him over to the apartment, but now that you're here..." Her mother trailed off, her gaze pointed. Her mom didn't know *everything* about Georgia's little problem downstairs, but she knew enough to make this moment even more uncomfortable than it already was. "I assume you two have some kind of work project to sort through?"

Not for the first time, Georgia wished she were a more ambitious woman, that her life goals extended beyond finally paying off her work truck and keeping enough volunteers to meet Homeward Bound's housing goals. Ambitious women went to college and got desk jobs. They moved away from home and escaped the extreme mortification of sharing a driveway with one's mother.

"Yes. A project." Georgia uncleaved her tongue long enough to create an escape plan. "And we both have an early morning, so we should get going."

"Didn't you say something about wine, dear?" Her mother's voice dripped with false innocence. "Don't forget to take some glasses with you. I doubt you have any clean ones."

"Oh, I don't drink," Monty said politely.

Well, shit. There went that plan. The awkwardness would have nowhere to go but between them, where it could breed with the toe sweat.

"But please don't let me stop you from enjoying a glass. I don't mind when other people drink. Especially since you, ah, look like maybe you've had a difficult evening." Monty got to his feet and plucked a giant spiderweb from her hair. Even though his hand barely brushed the still-damp strands, she felt the intimacy of the gesture reverberate through her. She wanted to do all kinds of indecent things with that hand. *To* that hand.

She mumbled something about not being thirsty.

"Are the spiders and the wrench connected, by any chance?" he asked.

It took her a moment to realize what he was talking about, since his proximity was constricting her lungs. "Pipes," she managed. "Water. Arachnids."

He nodded as if her string of words made perfect sense. One benefit she hadn't realized to a man famous for his stiff reserve—she could say pretty much anything and his reaction would always be the same. Shakespeare or inane syllables, all she'd ever get out of him was that disconcerting stare.

He tilted his head toward the door. "Shall we?"

Dazed, aroused and aware that her mother was watching, Georgia led the way out. "I should have mentioned it's an above-garage apartment," she apologized as they descended the front steps. "Does being twenty-nine and living at home make me a total loser?"

"I don't know. I live at home, and I'm thirty-five. Would you consider me a total loser?"

Something about the night air—darkly enveloping and cold against her exposed legs—added weight to his question, but her opinions of this man's living arrangements meant nothing. Less than nothing. Nothing times infinity.

"Of course not," she said. "It's not the same situation at all. You're…" Wealthy? Living in a palatial manor? Exempt from the rules that bound her fellow bottom-feeders?

He grunted, misconstruing her silence as an assent. "That's exactly what I was afraid of."

MONTY WASN'T SURE what he expected when he walked into Georgia's apartment, but a young man cursing at an ancient desktop computer hadn't figured into his imagination.

Of course, his imagination hadn't accounted for how profoundly the sight of her bare legs would affect him either. There was no way he could have known that underneath those coveralls, Georgia was hiding what had to be the shapeliest pair of thighs he'd ever seen in his life, strong and firm in ways that defied every law of nature he'd ever encountered. He'd known she was a muscular woman—if the fact that she could hoist and carry logs like they were twigs hadn't tipped him off, then her general swagger would have eventually done the job—but this was more than protein and tissue. Even though she wasn't in motion right now, he could see the delineation of her musculature, overlaid with delicately tanned skin that seemed to go on forever.

She could crush things between those thighs. Basketballs. Hearts. Men.

"Oh, hell, Danny." She returned to motion and used one of those legs to kick at the desk chair. "I forgot you were here. Get out, would you?"

The man didn't look up from where he was clicking.

"Hang on a sec. I'm fixing your computer. You've got like three trojans on this thing. Have you been downloading porn again? I told you to double-check your firewall before you visit those sites."

Georgia's eyes widened, and she shot Monty an alarmed look. He wanted to tell her he had no objections to the occasional enjoyment of internet pornography, but gorgeous legs aside, they weren't close enough to make that a comfortable conversation. He stared at the wall above her head instead.

"Stop it," she hissed, and kicked the chair again. "You know I only did that as a joke. You have to leave now. My company's here."

"Oh, really? Do introduce us." The man turned in the desk chair, steepling his fingers under his chin. His movements were purposefully slow, as if he were reenacting a cartoon villain moment. "Well, well, well. And so we meet again."

"Ignore him. He's leaving."

There was no doubt in Monty's mind that he was facing a brother of Georgia's. As Danny rose smoothly to his feet, it was possible to not only see the similarities between the siblings, but *feel* them. In addition to the same general features, there was a kind of overly aggressive confidence about the whole family that made him feel like a bear being led to the ring, blindfolded and baited. He had no idea what they were talking about half the time, but he was pretty sure he was serving as the butt of a joke only they were in on.

"You're awfully overdressed to be one of Georgia's admirers. Are you sure you're not an insurance salesman?"

"I mean it, Danny. I'll take my wire clippers to your entire cyber complex when you're sleeping."

"Or a mortician. Have you come to sell Georgia a casket? I should probably warn you—she's already made her own. It's that bookshelf over there."

Although determined not to give any of his sensation of groundlessness away, Monty glanced where Danny pointed. Sure enough, a wooden bookshelf rested against one wall, two side panels holding up a series of shelves, a strangely casket-like shape to it overall. It held, among a multitude of odd items, an impressive array of trophies with baseballs on them.

"It's a very nice bookshelf," he said honestly. Simple and practical, its design fusing function and strength to create its own kind of appeal. It reminded him a lot of Georgia, actually.

Especially those legs.

"I told you—it's not a bookshelf. It's a casket. It's attached by notches, so you can take it apart and refit it for burial. Here. I'll show you."

"Oh, my God. You are not showing him my casket shelf. We have things to do."

"But it's cool. You think it's cool, don't you? You totally like my sister's box."

He did, but he had the feeling he was being challenged on some unknown point. "Maybe you can show it to me next time."

"Sure. Maybe at her funeral—*or perhaps your own.*"

"Don't even think about it." Georgia turned to Monty, her lips twisted in an apologetic grimace. "I'm so sorry about this. My family isn't usually this intrusive in my personal life. I swear."

"Yes, we are." Her brother stuck out his hand. "Daniel Lennox. Older than Georgia by eleven months and smarter by thirty IQ points. That's documented, by the way. Mensa."

Although the aggressive way Danny offered his credentials took Monty aback, he accepted the other man's outstretched hand with a semblance of ease. At least this family made conversation simple. He was lucky to get a word in edgewise.

"I'm John. John Montgomery, but most people call me Monty."

The man's eyes widened in an expression similar to Georgia's, and he looked back and forth between them without dropping Monty's hand. "Seriously? As in, the real John Montgomery? Here? With my sister?"

He wasn't quite sure how to respond to that, but was saved from having to when Georgia pulled the wrench from her belt tie and waved it menacingly at her brother. "Out. I mean it."

The threat of physical violence finally did the trick. With a long-suffering sigh, Danny finally released Monty's hand and made for the door. He offered some last-minute porn-access tips as he went, and ducked just in time to miss the wrench that sailed over his head and out the door.

Monty assumed Georgia would want to put on some clothes before they got down to business, so he turned and studied the trophies on the casket bookcase with feigned interest—though his interest didn't stay feigned for long. The trophies weren't for baseball, as it turned out, but softball. And there were a lot of them. State champion, regional champion, national champion... There was even a kids' trophy dated last fall, with a propped-up handmade card containing about twenty signatures and a liberally crayoned "Your The Bestest Coach."

He wasn't sure why, but the fact that Georgia ran a handyman service, coached softball, played softball *and* spent her free time building houses for the underprivileged made him feel like the biggest slacker in the world. Never mind that he was standing inside an apartment so small the bed was literally five feet away from the front door, or that he'd been up since four that morning hard at work of his own. Georgia was a woman who *lived*.

Ashleigh was right. He never had fun, never even left the house without an agenda inside an itinerary wrapped up in a responsibility. No wonder she'd run as far and fast from him as she could get.

He was a vacuum of excitement. A black hole of entertainment. Basically, he sucked.

"So. That was awkward." Georgia hadn't, as he'd hoped, changed into something slightly less revealing—and the absence of anyone else in the room only made her legs that much more noticeable. The apartment, which was already small to begin with, started closing in around him, but he forced himself to stand firm.

He *needed* to do this. Maybe using Georgia's hammer to break out of his shell was a bad idea, but he didn't know where else to turn. He didn't have friends or acquaintances except for work contacts. His family had given up on him years ago. And the one woman in the world he'd opened his heart to was getting married.

There was no way he could ignore it anymore. Everyone around him was building lives, throwing themselves into activities they loved, creating the kinds of memories that mattered. Except him. Alone at his desk. A conversational bore. A hulk of nothing that no one would miss should he disappear from the face of the earth tomorrow.

Georgia might not have intended it, but she'd thrown

him a lifeline that morning. Now he found himself gripping at it almost desperately, fearful lest she take it back again.

"It's my own fault," he said. "I shouldn't have barged in on you like this, but your offer came at the perfect time."

She swallowed, her eyes flicking over him in a way that felt offensive and pleasant at the same time. Or maybe it was just him, his awareness prickling awake after a long period of dormancy.

"I wish I could have taken advantage before, but…" He trailed off. There was no good excuse. He *never* had a good excuse—and that was the problem. In order to have an excuse, a man had to have a life first. "I'm sorry. You deserve better than halfhearted apologies. But I'm here now, and I'd like to know what I can do to serve you most."

Georgia shook her head, unsure if her hearing was accurate, or if she was imagining the entire conversation. No way was Monty standing in her apartment, all six feet two inches of him devouring the oxygen and transforming it into heat, asking how he could serve her. There were impossible dreams—for instance, that she'd be crowned Miss America after showing off her birdhouse-making skills in the talent competition—and then there were dreams so ridiculous she might as well wish for the moon.

This moment was about two galaxies away from the moon.

She pinched the inner skin of her forearm—right where it hurt the most, a location she and her brothers had made the subject of intense study over the years. It hurt, but not enough to convince her, so she did it again. *Ouch.*

Monty watched her with a perplexed frown, but didn't comment. She was coming to appreciate that about him.

"Do you mind if I sit?" he asked, indicating the bed.

"Oh. Um. Sure. Make yourself comfortable. Should I go…" She eyed a chair across the room and decided it would be safer. Now that she had this man in her apartment, the enormity of what she was about to do hit her on several different levels—only half of them related to the throbbing spot between her legs.

She slipped off her rubber boots and curled up in the seat, hoping the appearance of relaxation would force the reality upon her. Unfortunately, her movements only served as a reminder that she had nothing on underneath her robe. She was pretty sure Monty had just gotten an eyeful.

"So," he said, politely keeping his gaze trained above her neck. "What exactly does the job entail?"

"Um…the usual, I imagine."

"*The usual* being, what, exactly?"

Surely it wasn't that difficult for him to work out on his own. "To be honest, I was sort of assuming you'd take the lead here."

"O-kay. But maybe you could be more specific, at least for this initial meeting? This is all new territory for me."

"*All* of it?" Did he mean the casual nature of the affair, or the act of insertion? Because that second one could be a major problem.

A twitch near his eye was the only visible sign of his distress, but Georgia knew it for distress all the same. If she wasn't careful, she was going to scare him away before they shared so much as a kiss.

She at least wanted a kiss. Oh, God, how she wanted a kiss.

"I'm sorry," she said, licking her lips in anticipation of his mouth on top of hers. "I didn't mean to make that sound so judgmental, but I'm counting on you a lot more than I probably should. You're my last chance."

"I think you might be overestimating my abilities a little."

"God, I hope not. No man has been able to get me even close to an orgasm before. I figure if the most gorgeous, eligible man in the state of Connecticut can't get me off, I might as well roll over and give up."

If Monty had been eating something at that exact moment, Georgia had no doubt he would have died. The rate at which air moved into his lungs as he shot up off the bed would have worked to lodge even the tiniest crumb into his trachea, thereby forcing her to pull out the bookshelf coffin way earlier than she'd planned.

"I beg your pardon?"

"It's not that I mean to put too much pressure on you, of course." Her words came fast and frantic. Dammit—she'd been too direct. She was *always* too direct. She possessed no feminine arts. She was unable to flirt or bat her eyelashes. She could hit the bull's-eye on a dartboard with her eyes closed and one hand tied behind her back, but coy mating rituals were beyond her. "You wouldn't be the first man to have tried and failed, but you're, you know, *you*."

He didn't respond, opting instead to stare at her as if she might go up in flames at any moment. Which, given the rate at which her blood was coursing through her veins right now, seemed entirely possible.

"But I totally understand if you'd rather not now," she said. "I don't want you to feel obligated."

"You want to have sex with me?"

Well, obviously.

"Yes?"

"Because you…? You haven't…?"

"Had an orgasm?" she supplied. "Oh, I've had them. Just not with a man."

She stopped short of telling him that the primary way in which she *had* been able to seal the deal was by imagining him in various states of undress—and distress. Even she had a limit when it came to embarrassing herself.

"And, um." He continued staring. "I'm sorry. I'm not used to this kind of plain speaking. Are you trying to tell me that you normally have them with women?"

"With women?"

He nodded.

"Yeah… No. Sorry. There's no trading on this team."

If he looked slightly disappointed at that confession, she was willing to ignore it in the name of self-interest. The chances of this situation repeating itself anytime in the near future were slim, and she wasn't about to throw him out for acting like a hot-blooded man.

In fact, if he didn't start acting like a hot-blooded man anytime soon, she was going to have to take matters into her own hands anyway.

No hot blood emerged in the next thirty seconds. Neither did any cold blood. He just kept staring at her with that same concerned pucker to his brow, as if he was trying to work out a particularly difficult puzzle. Georgia had an inkling what would happen when he did—and that she wouldn't like the outcome—so she gave herself permission to attack.

It was now or never, and never seemed like an awfully long time to spend alone.

There was only a short distance between them, and she covered the ground quickly, her arms out and ready to embrace him. As she'd hoped—dreamed, imagined, prayed for—he was a hard rock of a man, warm and stalwart. Not even when she threw the full force of her body against him did he falter, and although his arms didn't come up to hold her tight, he didn't push her away either.

She brought her lips to his in a gesture that was more experiment than kiss. She wanted to know if he would kiss her back, if he *could* kiss her back.

The answer, as it turned out, was yes.

It took a good ten seconds of pressure before he responded, but she knew the moment the press of her mouth against his transformed from assault to reciprocation. He sighed and softened just enough for her to slip in some tongue, and that was all it took to move into a full-blown embrace. He wasn't *quite* as firm as she'd been hoping, and he didn't grip her by the back of her neck and throw her to the bed to ravage all her senses, but he did drop a hand to her waist, resting it naturally where her hip flared out.

There was a tender possession to the gesture that tingled through her pelvis, and she deepened the kiss without thought.

Monty tasted, inexplicably, of almonds. It took her a moment to realize she wasn't tasting him, but smelling, her senses so jumbled she couldn't discern between the two. His lips grew increasingly warm and responsive, and when his tongue rubbed against hers with a delicious sense of urgency, she felt the pull of it deep in her belly.

This might work. This might actually freaking work.

But then he groaned and pulled away before the kiss started to get *really* good, and she stood there—in her robe, turned on and aware that something was terribly wrong.

"What are you doing?" he asked, his hands falling heavily to his sides. "You can't do that."

"Kiss you? Why not?" The terribly wrong part of the situation only grew more insistent, a warning flashing in the periphery. "Isn't that what you came here for?"

"Isn't that what I…" He shook his head, his frown directed in and out and all over the room. "No. Georgia. *No.* Is this what you thought I invited myself over to do?"

She heard his words. She registered them. They made some sort of indentation on her ability to process thought—but not enough to actually bring any of the wheels to a grinding halt. "Does it matter? That kiss was incredible. Don't you want to do it again?"

"No. I most certainly do not."

She didn't have time for the familiar crush of disappointment to hit, because she was pulled up against his chest once again—and not of her own volition. This time, he didn't hold himself back, and he was every bit as firm as a woman could wish.

No. *Firmer.*

While she'd always assumed Monty was strong, there was no way she could have known he'd use quite so much of his arms to wrap around her and press her body next to his. She didn't know that her limbs would react quite so overwhelmingly either, clinging to him like some kind of wilting vine. Georgia had always prided herself on being able to stand on her own two feet, but in Monty's arms, she was a swooning, dainty scrap of a woman.

Georgia had never been dainty in her life. Not even as a baby. She'd cracked her mom's pelvis on the way through the birth canal.

Monty's mouth moved over hers again, tongue rough and teeth engaged, and she felt herself being backed toward the bed. Her body ached for that bed, for him to crush her to it, and she gripped his shoulders in anticipation of the fall.

And then, all of a sudden, he wasn't kissing her anymore.

"This can't be happening." He pushed her away, and she lost her balance, falling to the mattress with her robe askew. She could see him gaping at where her breasts almost escaped from the material, but her hands were shaking too much to close herself off from view. "Georgia—when I told you I wanted to take you up on your offer, did you think I meant the offer of *sex?*"

"I…"

Oh. Oh, no. This couldn't be happening. She looked down at her cleavage—unimpressive as it was—and back at him. Monty was the most disheveled she'd ever seen him, his skin flushed with color, his tie crooked, a spark of life to him she'd never known existed before. But even in an obviously flustered state, it was impossible to miss the signs. The business suit. The calm way he'd talked to her mother. The fact that before she'd made the somewhat clumsy offer for him to sleep with her, she'd also asked him to volunteer for Homeward Bound.

"You came here about the construction stuff," she said, shock rendering her voice hollow. "You want to build houses with me."

Just like that, the pieces came crashing down. They hit like golf-ball-sized hail, and she had nowhere to hide. All she could do was sit there and take it.

There would be no sex. No plowing. No orgasm. Nothing even remotely approaching desire.

"It's my fault," Monty said. "After the incident in the kitchen this morning, it was my responsibility to be more upfront about setting boundaries—"

"No." If Georgia was clear on one thing right now, it was that she had to be the stupidest woman on the face of the planet. Of course Monty hadn't come here to ravish her. If he was a ten with a somewhat stilted personality, she was a three whose personality bordered on the slightly manic. On no planet did those two combine. "I don't know why I was ever deluded enough to think you might have wanted...well. Me."

"Georgia."

She shook her head, hoping the rapid movement might drown out the sound of pity in his voice. "I have a mirror. I know how these things work."

"Of course it's not that."

"You don't have to be nice. It's okay."

He took her at her word and said nothing—all that was needed to tie up this moment in a tidy bow of humiliation. He could have been *a little* nice.

"I think maybe you should leave now," she said, feeling sick to her stomach.

"Do you, ah, want to talk about it first?"

Talk? There was nothing that Monty—this taciturn, sexily rumpled, oh-so-uninterested-in-her man—could say that would render this situation acceptable. Even if he were a golden-tongued wordsmith, there were only so many combinations of letters in the English language.

"Not really."

"But maybe we should—"

"No." Humiliation had sharpened her mood, honing it into something dangerous, and she pointed it outward in a familiar gesture. Attack or be attacked. Defend at all costs. She might not have ever been any good at making the boys on the playground like her, but she'd been damned successful at making them respect her. "If you overheard everything from earlier today, I think you'd realize that conversation is the last thing anyone wants from you. Please go."

She regretted the words—cruel and unforgiveable—the moment they crossed her lips, but she couldn't regret how effective they were in helping her achieve her goal. With a hurt look, penetrating in how deeply it touched her, Monty nodded once.

Then he was gone.

FOUR

"I'M SORRY, JOHN, but it's not optional. We can't afford for the world to think there's any bad blood between us and the Bridgertons. You're going to that wedding."

Monty clutched his hands firmly behind his back, using the pressure of intertwined fingers to save himself from saying something he'd regret later. It wasn't often that he had to fight to keep the words at bay, but this had been a week of rare and unnerving circumstances.

"I think you'll come to realize it's best for all of us," his dad added. "You need to at least give the appearance of having moved on."

"I don't see why I should have to humiliate myself so you can save face with your golfing buddies."

"You'll humiliate yourself because I'm asking you to."

"And if I refuse?"

His dad locked eyes with him over the family coat of arms that hung in the main foyer. They normally wouldn't lower themselves to have this kind of conversation in a room where anyone could overhear—especially since sound carried through the black-and-white granite entryway the same way it did the ventilation hood of a stove—but Monty had hardly been able to credit his ears when his dad casually mentioned having their tuxedos sent out to be cleaned.

The tuxedos only came out for galas and weddings. As galas were officially off Monty's plate now that Jake had offered to do the schmoozing for him, that could only mean one thing.

"You won't refuse, so spare me the theatrics, please." His dad scrubbed a hand over his face. Given the advanced state of wrinkles on his beige suit—a wardrobe staple for as long as Monty could remember—his father had probably slept at his desk last night. "I'm sorry if it pains you to see Ashleigh getting married to another man, but there's no way around it. We've been struggling to repair the damages of your breakup all year. We have to put a good face on this."

The face Monty gave his dad was anything but good.

He'd known, from the outset, that his relationship with Ashleigh Bridgerton had full family approval. Bridgerton Luxury Spas could be found in several of the Montgomery hotels nationwide, and his dad was nothing if not mercenary when it came to strengthening personal and business relationships. It was part of the reason Monty and Ashleigh had gotten together in the first place. There were only so many times two people could be blatantly seated next to one another at dinner parties before they eventually discovered something in common.

Theirs had been a dislike of salmon puffs.

Fish pastries might not have been a memorable start to romance, but it had been push enough to set the relationship wheels in motion. Unfortunately, his father seemed to have a difficult time understanding that there was a difference between being nudged toward appetizers and being forced to don a tuxedo in the ultimate act of self-immolation.

"I know Jake's marriage to Rebecca filled some deep-seated need of yours to monetize your children's love lives," he said carefully, "and I wish I'd been able to do the same with Ashleigh, but I wasn't. I'm not sure what else you want from me."

"I always thought you gave up on her too easily."

Monty set his jaw. "Would you like me to break up her engagement? Is that what you're asking?"

"Please don't be dramatic, John. I was merely stating an opinion about your lack of social ambition."

That was as good as a declaration that Monty was a failure. His dad spoke and acted in subtleties—he was the sort of man who would never say an unkind word about anyone to their face—but he retained the ability to crush a man under his heel all the same. Monty hadn't closed the deal with Ashleigh Bridgerton, and the disgrace of it would follow him for the rest of his life.

"I'm sorry to let you down, Dad, but this isn't up for negotiation."

"You're right. It's not." His dad held up a hand before Monty had a chance to say more. "I don't want to argue about this. It's already decided. Will you be working on the Hamilton account later today?"

Monty wanted to tell him no. Even though he had more than enough of his own foundation work to last a lifetime, the plans to acquire a smaller chain of New Hampshire inns for his father had been his primary focus for the past few months. He ate, drank and slept those hotels. He dreamed of them. He also occasionally fantasized about burning the lot of them to the ground, so complicated had the negotiations become. The idea of telling his dad exactly where he could shove the proposal was one that filled him with untoward glee.

But he didn't. He never said no—at least, not since he was eleven years old and he'd once mentioned an urge to ride his bicycle instead of alphabetizing the filing cabinet.

From the way his dad had reacted at the time, you'd have thought he requested a room full of hookers and blow.

"I'll put the finishing touches on it tonight and have it on your desk by Friday," he promised. Then, because his eleven-year-old self mourned for a bike—and because his thirty-five-year-old self mourned for hookers and blow—he added, "But I'm taking this weekend off, so any follow-up you need will have to wait for Monday."

His dad's heavy white brows came up in surprise, but he nodded, accepting this unprecedented weekend off as the price for obedience.

"And all weekends this month, actually," he added, feeling reckless. It was the same impulse that had driven him to kiss Georgia the other night. The second kiss, *his* kiss, the one he'd been unable to prevent and couldn't find it in him to regret.

He hardly knew how to credit it, but it had something to do with the way Georgia had responded to him, as if he were a Tarzan warrior claiming his bride. No woman had ever acted like that when he'd kissed her before. With Ashleigh and his handful of previous girlfriends, kissing had been a slow mating dance, the embraces quiet and deep and meaningful—the way he assumed they were supposed to be. Sex had always been a transcendental experience to him, more important than the mere fusing of two bodies.

But kissing Georgia had been barbaric. He wasn't sure how else to explain it. He felt no emotional connection to her, couldn't imagine taking her on a romantic sunset dinner for two, yet he'd wanted to rip her robe off with his teeth, leaving only those ridiculous orange rubber boots while he sank into her.

What is wrong with me?

"Is there something wrong with you?" his father asked, echoing his sentiments.

"No. Nothing wrong," he said, and resolved himself to believe it. When a man had gone through a week like his, he was allowed a little leeway in the sanity department. "It's just that I'm going to be working with Georgia's charity for the foreseeable future."

"Georgia…?"

"Lennox," he supplied. "Our handywoman. Apparently she runs the local Homeward Bound chapter. Did you know that?"

"Of course I know that. I'm the one who suggested she volunteer in the first place. I've been very proud of her progress."

Monty wasn't the least bit surprised to hear his father had a hand in shaping her life. He had a hand in shaping the lives of *everyone* who lived or worked at Montgomery Manor—himself included. Himself especially.

"Well, it seems her progress could use a little boost," Monty said. "Her volunteer numbers are low, so she asked if I could step in and help. I figured it couldn't hurt for me to get out more. And who knows? It might be fun."

"Fun?"

Monty stifled his laugh. "I know. It sounded strange to me too. But she made a compelling argument."

And by compelling, he meant naked. Naked and looking at him with those flashing tawny eyes of hers, calmly asking him to be the first man to give her an orgasm—and for no reason other than that he was John Montgomery the Third. As if by might of his name and birth alone, he was some kind of sex god.

He wasn't. He wasn't even close.

But for the first time in his life, it didn't seem like too much of a stretch.

He stood straighter, forcing his blood to move in its regular cyclical pattern instead of a relentless downward spiral. It wasn't as if he was planning on taking her up on the offer of sex anyway. It wasn't as if the offer still existed in the first place. He was going to have a hard enough time convincing her to let him on the job site at all.

"I do like the idea of you getting out into the community more." His dad didn't look entirely pleased at the idea, but Monty didn't care. He wasn't asking permission. "As long as you're comfortable adding it to your regular duties."

Monty felt a twitch in his temple, a flare that was equal parts anger and frustration. Of all the thousands of people who worked for his father, none of them—not a single one—was treated like a machine the way he was, forced to carry the burden of ten men. And he'd seen people work hard before. The Montgomery Foundation funded over a hundred nonprofit campaigns—most of them concentrated in childhood education and foster care advocacy—and the men and women who worked at the grassroots level were some of the most dedicated people he knew. Thomas was unquestionably his favorite, the recently emancipated eighteen-year-old serving as a spokesperson for many of Monty's projects with an enthusiasm that never flagged, but even he took the occasional weekend off—and without anyone questioning his audacity at such selfishness.

It sometimes felt as if the entire world was allowed to enjoy life at the expense of Monty's own. Their vacations were his vacations. Their celebrations were his celebrations.

Unfortunately, their happiness had never been quite so easy to pretend was his own.

"I can manage it," he said tightly.

His dad nodded, accepting Monty at his word. "Oh, and John?"

He was almost afraid to ask, but in this, as in all things, he had little say in the matter. "Yes?"

"It would be better for all of us if you could manage to find a date in time for that wedding. A pining man is rarely good for business. It makes us appear weak."

GEORGIA SPENT THE week doing every conceivable task on her to-do list before finally giving up and heading out to Montgomery Manor. Handywoman Express currently served three dozen clients, but most of them only needed her a few days out of the year. Gutters and plumbing disasters, the occasional spackle or loose roof shingle— she liked to think she could make a good living if she bothered to spend time and money on marketing. As it was, the most she managed was to slap her name on the back of the jerseys of a dozen six-year-old softball players and hope for the best.

More often than not, *the best* meant relying on the Montgomerys to fill in the financial gaps.

"That's probably why it was a bad idea to proposition and then insult the oldest son," she muttered as she hoisted her toolbox out of the back of her truck.

Forget the personal mortification she'd suffered at Monty's rejection—she must have been crazy to put her livelihood in jeopardy for the sake of a roll between the sheets. Montgomery Manor wasn't just a place where she occasionally pieced together a few wooden boards and called it a day. She freaking *loved* it here. She loved the house, a sound piece of architecture riddled with woodworking details she'd never tire of studying, and she loved the expansive setting of the surrounding countryside. She also loved the people—and not only the ones she fantasized about naked. Not once, in all her time working at the Manor, had she been made to feel out of place or as if her oddities outweighed her value.

That level of acceptance—unequivocal, unquestioning, hers from the moment she'd arrived—wasn't something she got very often. It had been stupid to risk throwing all that away for a few seconds of bodily fluids and muscle contractions.

"Here. Let me give you a hand with that."

She felt the full forty pounds of her toolbox being lifted from her hand and clutched her fingers more firmly. "No, thanks. I've got it."

Her forceful tone was due primarily to the fact that she was suddenly standing so close to Monty she could smell him. Almonds again—except this time, she found the scent less of a heady intoxication and more like maybe he was steeped in cyanide.

"Let go," she repeated when he made no move to relinquish his grasp. She used to go weeks at a time without a glimpse of this man, and now he was everywhere. "I don't need help with my own toolbox."

"It's heavy."

"Of course it's heavy. It's full of metal." When not even that got Monty to back away, she tugged as hard as she could. He let go so suddenly she almost lost her balance and sent hundreds of dollars' worth of socket wrenches flying, but she was saved from hitting the ground ass-first by his stabilizing hand on her wrist.

Dammit. She could feel the strength and heat radiating through him as he held her firm. Why couldn't he have spindly T-Rex forearms? Making a fool of herself wouldn't be such a guarantee that way.

"I'm sorry. I was just trying to help."

She shook his grip off and brushed nonexistent dirt from her coveralls. As usual, she was dressed to impress absolutely no one in her standard work uniform, while Monty had been poured into a dark suit perfectly molded to his shoulders. She latched on to that—to how unfairly handsome he looked for nothing more than sitting at his desk for hours—and scowled. What kind of a man dressed up if he never planned on leaving the house?

"The day I'm too weak to carry my own tools is the day I give up on life and start crocheting doilies. Did I pronounce that right? Crotcheting. Crooshaying." She sighed. "Sewing shit with hooked needles."

"You like doilies?"

"Of course not. No one likes doilies. They're the tattered remnants of a patriarchal society that doesn't believe in allowing women to be idle."

He smiled at that, at her irritation and the unjustness of a world that believed women and yarn were good for nothing but decoration. "First calculator watches, now this. Do you have conspiracy theories for every inanimate object you don't care for?"

"Yes."

He laughed and showed his teeth in a rare demonstration of enjoyment. "I believe you do. I look forward to hearing more of them."

His words were overly formal and slightly ridiculous—no one wanted to listen to her rant about how Tamagotchis had inadvertently trained a generation of neglectful parents—but they were sincere, and that was enough. Even though she didn't say so out loud, she forgave him for everything. For being so unfairly attractive. For turning her down. For causing her extreme embarrassment and several sleepless nights.

But mostly for kissing her as though she were worth being kissed.

"I owe you an apology," he said.

"Please don't. If you do, then *I'll* have to, and I hate apologizing. Can we pretend the other night never happened instead?"

"I'm afraid that would be impossible for me, Georgia. Even if I wanted to." The way he said her name, all rumbling and deep, made her loins quiver. As in *actual* quivering loins. She whimpered and pressed her thighs together, but that only made the wobbly sensation worse.

Wobbles were not good for business.

"There must be *some* way we can make the other night disappear," she pleaded, feeling desperate. "I could try swinging my toolbox at your head in hopes of causing amnesia. Ooh, or I could try swinging it at my own head. You wouldn't worry about apologizing if I was unconscious, would you?"

Nothing. Not even a twitch to acknowledge that she spoke at all.

"I'm not going to be here long anyway. Apparently, there are a few paving stones loose in the garden. I'll be out of here in half an hour."

Still nothing.

"Okay, fine," she said, and dropped her toolbox with a clang. She didn't know if he was doing it on purpose or not, but she couldn't take much more of this intense staring. As an intimidation tactic, it was right up there with needles to the eyeball. "You win. I'll apologize. I'm sorry for saying I didn't want to talk to you, and I'm sorry for throwing myself at you practically naked, and I'm especially sorry for telling you way more information about my personal life than you could ever want to know. My grasp on reality has always been a cause for concern."

The reward for her apology was one more of those half smiles, resulting in yet another overwhelming rush of forgiveness moving through her. *Forgiveness*. Right. As if that was the sentiment currently puckering her nipples.

"I can see why you hate apologizing. You're terrible at it." Monty took a step forward, his arms out as if he wanted to embrace her. But the very idea was ridiculous, and her momentary distraction gave him enough time to clasp her hands in front of her and hold her in place. *Doubly* in place, because she was also unable to look away as his gaze bore down into hers. She was trapped. "Besides—none of those are anything you should be ashamed of."

"You only think that because you've never thrown yourself naked at someone before," she said. Then, since that night wasn't a topic she wanted to dwell on for all of eternity, she added a sincere, "And I *am* sorry about what I said right before you left. I was hurt and I lashed out. That's what I do. Sometimes I say mean things. Other times I throw a wrench. Fistfights are also a distinct possibility."

"You have anger management issues?"

"No. I have brothers."

His lips turned up at the corner, stopping her heart. "Fair enough. Apology accepted. Now it's my turn."

"You really don't have to—" She tried to pull away, but he held her fast, his thumbs rubbing a soothing pattern onto the backs of her hands. There wasn't anything romantic about the gesture, and she was sure he didn't mean to send sparks of sexual awareness up her arms, but what her mind knew and her body longed for had always been two vastly different things.

Hence her current predicament.

"I didn't handle myself well the other night, and I'm sorry for it." He spoke in the same careful manner that gave him his reputation for solemnity, but there was such an intimacy about the combined physical and emotional connection—a thoughtfulness so often lacking in her life—that she fell spellbound. "I shouldn't have been so shocked by what happened. I shouldn't have taken advantage of your vulnerable situation. And I *really* shouldn't have enjoyed myself as much as I did. If it's not too much of an imposition, I'd appreciate another chance to volunteer with you this weekend. That's to build houses, in case there's any confusion."

She blinked as he released her hands, her vision blurred with red dots as if she'd spent too long staring at the sun. Her whole body felt the same sense of dazed bewilderment. She honestly had no idea if she'd just been insulted, propositioned or crowned queen.

"Would that be okay? I normally wouldn't push so hard, but your request for help came at the perfect time." He reached up and adjusted his already impeccable dark green tie in a gesture of nervousness. "I'm no expert at manual labor, but I've always been a fast learner and I promise to work hard."

Even though it had been her intention to spend the rest of her life pretending Monty was nothing more than a figment of her dirty, irrepressible imagination, she felt herself weakening toward him.

It wasn't her fault. He was just so freaking *nice*. Men weren't supposed to be nice when she revealed her inability to behave according to proper female norms. They were supposed to run as fast as their legs could take them. It was what they'd always done in the past.

"Please don't say no," he said. "I don't get very many opportunities like this, and it's rare for me to be looked at as anything other than a suit. I can help you with this, Georgia. I know I can. I just need you to give me a chance."

Well, hell. She found herself nodding along, her empathy feelers tingling in all the right places. If someone were to walk up to her right now and offer her the opportunity to be looked at as more than a pair of coveralls, she'd jump up and hold her hammer against their throat until they made it happen.

People didn't like looking past the surface of things—no one knew that better than she did. A suit was confidence, an unattractive woman was worthless, a homeless family was trash. End of story.

"Of course you can help," she said, resigned. She'd no more turn down Monty's plea for help than she would shut the door on a friend. "Just show up Saturday around seven, and I'll put you to work. I wasn't kidding about needing all the hands I can get."

There was a gleam in Monty's eye that had her immediately regretting her choice of words.

"I mean hands for building. *For building.*" That was it. She was throwing herself into the old mill pond the next chance she got.

"I wouldn't dare presume anything else," he said, his

voice laced with laughter, clearly enjoying himself at her expense.

She took back what she said about him being nice. He was horrible.

And maybe a little funny. And sweet. And possibly more gorgeous than she remembered, the sun playing with shadows in his hair until it was gold and red and brown all at once.

She bit back a sigh and hoisted her toolbox once again, glad to have a concrete task to provide a temporary distraction. For all that she was pleased to have Monty's offer of assistance for the weekend, it was difficult to decide if his presence would make things better or worse.

Better, because if she didn't do something about her volunteer numbers soon, there was every chance she'd lose the one job that meant even more to her than Montgomery Manor.

Worse, because she knew now what happened when Monty held her in his arms.

He became real.

FIVE

"GOOD MORNING, SIS!" Adam breezed through the diner door with the confidence only a man in possession of the world's largest ego could manage. Never mind that old men were quietly lingering over their coffee, or that the raccoon-eyed waitress bearing a plate of French toast clearly had one of the biggest hangovers known to mankind. Adam had exactly one volume level. On. "I'm not too late, am I?"

"For breakfast?" She scanned the table where she and Danny had demolished most of a stack of pancakes, half of a pig and enough eggs to start their own farm. "Yes. It's all gone. The diner is officially out of food."

"Ha-ha." In addition to conversing at devastating decibel levels, her oldest brother also had the habit of speaking laughter instead of making the sounds. "Not even you two could eat an entire restaurant's contents."

"Want to bet?" Georgia asked. She'd always thought she'd make an excellent competitive eater. It was the incongruously svelte women who won those contests every time. "Put your money where your mouth is. I'm just getting started."

Adam ignored her with a wave of his hand, which was only to be expected. He hated parting with his earnings unless he absolutely had to. It was a good thing she hadn't had to play *him* in Monopoly for the rights to the above-garage apartment, because he was impossible to beat. He hoarded play cash like it was the real thing.

"Seriously, Adam. Sit. Eat. You're making the other patrons nervous standing there."

He obliged her in the sitting portion of events but pushed the plates away from his side of the table. "Thanks, but I'm not hungry. I already ate—Nancy has us on this gluten-free thing."

"Gluten-free?" Danny asked, horrified. "Why would you do something like that to yourself?"

"Some of us aren't as young as we used to be," Adam said. Which was preposterous, because he was only five years older than Georgia. Their parents had been very busy during their procreative years. "In fact, Nancy is pushing me to start working out more—she's worried about my heart. That's why I'm here. I'm not too late, right?"

Georgia felt an impending sense of doom taking up residence alongside the gallon of maple syrup in her stomach. Until the day treadmills were used to generate electricity and cut back on utility bills, she couldn't imagine him willingly stepping on one.

"Too late for what, Adam?" she asked.

"To help you with your house-building stuff." He didn't make eye contact. "You're always on our backs about how little we pitch in. I thought I might join you today."

She dropped her fork with a clatter. Not once, in her entire twelve months of serving as a contractor for Homeward Bound, had Adam expressed the slightest interest in helping. As the oldest sibling and the only one to remember their father before he died, he'd stepped into his role as male figurehead early on and with a tenacity that was neither warranted nor welcomed. He dominated, he instigated stupid rules and he'd made quite a name for himself as a personal injury lawyer. But he didn't *pitch in.*

And from the way Danny was squirming uncomfortably in the seat across from her, she had a good idea why he was here today.

"You're too late. Danny has already selflessly arisen from his bed before the ungodly hour of five to lend a hand. We're all full up."

"But you're always trying to get us to come," Adam protested. He gave in to the lure of her last remaining pancake, ripping pieces off and shoving them in his mouth. "Last month you told me volunteering was my duty as a community leader and as a man whose career was equal to that of bottom-feeding lampreys."

"It still is. But not this weekend."

Adam looked at Danny, who shrugged and slumped further in his seat. "You have to take me. Nancy rescheduled her cycling class to stay with the kids, and she'll kill me if I ask her to undo it now."

"You made him drag poor Nancy into this?" Georgia shoved Danny in the arm. "You asshole. What did you say?"

"I didn't say anything!"

"So help me, if I see Charlie walk through that door next…"

She did. Her favorite brother, a levelheaded chemistry teacher she'd *thought* she could count on to behave like a normal human being, was the next to enter the chiming diner door. He, like Danny, at least had the decency to look ashamed of himself.

"Hey, George," he said, and plopped next to her. He was the only one who got away with calling her that.

There had been a brief period in her teens when she'd insisted everyone call her by the more masculine nickname, but the phase hadn't lasted long. When a girl had three older brothers, a bowl cut and a mean left hook, it was wise to hold on to what scraps of femininity she could. "I guess you're on to us by now, huh?"

"I thought better of you, Charlie," she accused, ignoring the other two. The Testosterone Trio was together once again. "How could you?"

"Danny said it was bad. He said you shaved your legs."

"Does it strike anyone else at this table as odd that my depilatory habits are a regular topic of family discussion?"

Three male voices mumbled an incoherent response, and Georgia was filled with an alternate urge to murder and hug each of her brothers in succession. This situation—the four of them sitting over the demolished remains of breakfast as they debated her love life—wasn't as bizarre as it looked to the outside world.

From her earliest memories, Georgia had been the possessor of not one, but three protectors willing to stand up for her, no matter what. At a time when other kids struggled to understand their place among their peers, she'd known exactly who she was. She was Georgia Lennox, one of four, beloved in her family, able to fight and climb and scrap as well as any boy, and don't you forget it.

Although that period of her life held sad memories too—the loss of their father to a quick and painful cancer, a single mother working double shifts to pay the lingering medical bills while supporting her family—it was contentment that stood out most in her mind. It had been impossible to hurt for long when you had three built-in companions so wholly and unquestionably devoted to your happiness.

Unfortunately, the idyll of her isolation lasted only until the day she entered kindergarten, when classroom walls separated her from her brothers. Without their shielding presence, she became aware of a vulnerability that hadn't existed before, an *otherness* she was too young to understand at the time. She could still remember the day Adam caught her crying during recess because Bobby Strom kicked her in the shin and called her ugly.

With the blustering anger that characterized him even today, Adam told her that being ugly was better than being stupid, and then he'd promptly gone over to Bobby's house and punched him in the nose.

That day had become the foundation for pretty much all of her adult dating life. And she couldn't blame them for it—even if she'd wanted to—because their intentions were one hundred percent honorable. This was what happened when the ugly duckling didn't grow into a beautiful swan. The brother ducks formed a mallard army and dared anyone to mess with her.

They were her best friends in the entire world. God, she hated them sometimes.

"We want to meet the guy, that's all, George." Charlie pushed his wire-rimmed glasses farther up the bridge of his nose. "He's a bit of a high-flyer, don't you think? John Montgomery isn't the type you normally go for."

"I'm not *going* for anyone. We had a business meeting the other night, that's all. Danny was misinformed."

"Mom corroborated," Adam said. "She mentioned wine."

Goddammit. She knew asking for the wine had been a bad idea. With alcohol and shaved legs on the table, there was no way she could legitimately deny her interest in Monty. It was a rare day when she pulled out all the stops in her efforts to woo a man, and her brothers knew it.

"And it's not like we're going to do anything to him," Charlie added, his expression earnest. He had these wide-set eyes that made him look innocent, but he was the most dangerous of the bunch. Chemistry teachers knew sneaky things. "Not physically or anything. We're going to make sure he checks out, that's all."

"He checks out," Georgia said firmly. "I've known him for over half of my life."

"And that's another problem." Adam polished off the pancake and moved on to hungrily eyeing the bowl of flavored creamers. "There's a tricky ethical issue at play here. He's your boss. How do you know he's not using his position of power to take advantage of you?"

"He's not my boss. *I'm* my boss. You know that. You're the one who helped me file all the small business paperwork."

"So you're really not going to let us come?" Charlie asked. Since there were no more forks left on the table, he plucked the spoon from her coffee cup and used it to start poaching the last of her sausage crumble. From the way her brothers acted, you'd think no one had ever fed them before. "Is this an official veto?"

She sighed, feeling the walls of her predicament closing in on her. As much as she'd have loved to order her brothers to sit this one out, she could hardly turn down the offer to add three semi-willing volunteers to her ranks. Not only was it unfair to the people who needed roofs over their heads, but every passing week propelled her closer and closer to failure as it was.

Failure wasn't an option—not in this arena. Yes, Georgia sucked at being a woman. Okay, she was even worse at relationships. And her softball skills deteriorated with every passing year. But she was a *good* contractor. She'd prove it even if she had to sneak out to the build site every day and hammer each nail with her own two hands.

Which, given the current state of affairs, was a likely possibility.

"Of course you can still come," she said, resigned. If she had to choose between being relieved of her position and being saddled with the Testosterone Trio, she'd pick unnecessary machismo every time. "But you have to promise you'll be nice to him."

"Ha-ha, that's a good one," Adam said, and sobered once he realized Georgia had no intention of backing down. "Wait—you're serious?"

"No ganging up."

"We don't gang up."

"No scaring him away with threats of violence."

"Threats aren't prosecutable."

"And no dropping hints about our relationship—I'm begging you. It's not romantic between us, and you'll only make things weird if you mention it. We're just friends. I get the feeling he's a lot more lonely up there at the Manor than he lets on."

"Lonely?" All three of her brothers stopped gnawing on their various breakfast items to stare at her. *Lonely* wasn't a word that figured in their collective vocabulary. They'd climbed over one another growing up, they continued climbing over one another now that they were all grown, and there was never a shortage of Lennox support to go around.

At least, that was how it worked for the male Lennoxes. None of her brothers had ever lacked for female admirers, and between their family, friends and lady loves, their lives had been a continual onslaught of attention.

Georgia had the family and friends, of course, but not the love. She sometimes thought they didn't realize how much one missing piece could hurt—that the constant, gnawing ache was so much a part of her she wasn't sure it would ever go away—but then they looked at her with that combination of pity and affection, and she knew they knew.

They wanted her to find love and acceptance almost as much as she did. It was why they fought so hard on her behalf.

It was also why she let them.

"And I want each of you to behave like the professional adult I know you have hidden somewhere inside you. Yes, Adam, that includes you. You're all going to be assigned to a different area, and you won't be given walkie-talkies to play with."

"Come on, Georgia—"

"My site. My rules. It's for the safety of everyone involved."

Charlie sent her a wheedling smile. "Not even me? I promise only to communicate for the betterment of mankind."

"Especially not you," she said. "Don't think I haven't forgotten that time you taught Adam and Danny how to speak in Morse code so you could have dirty conversations about my friends through the bedroom wall. There will be no clandestine signaling. You'll be nice to Monty. You'll work hard. And don't you dare undermine my authority in front of my team, or I'll tell Mom."

All three men straightened in their seats, nodding their

solemn vow. The threat of maternal intervention was one
they'd all learned to make in only the most extreme circumstances. If people thought Georgia was tough, that
was only because they'd never had to face the woman
who'd raised her.

"It's a deal," Adam said, and stuck out his hand. "But
you're buying lunch."

She shook. As if there'd ever been a question otherwise.

SIX

"THAT DIDN'T COUNT. You started before I was ready." The man who'd taken up the spot alongside Monty on the angled rooftop dropped his nailer with a clang, and they both narrowly escaped the resulting projectile. "Ahem. Sorry. That was a lawsuit waiting to happen."

For reasons Monty couldn't quite understand, the man assigned as his partner for the day—he'd introduced himself as Adam—voiced his exclamations rather than made them. He was also strangely combative, to the point where Monty found himself evading the roof's edge and any sudden movements in that direction. He wasn't afraid of death, per se, but it seemed a shame to go before he had a chance to enjoy himself a little.

Yes. That was right. He was going to enjoy himself. Despite thirty-five years of convention and obedience—or perhaps because of it—Monty was ready to throw caution and roofing nailers to the wind. He was going to have fun even if it killed him.

Which, given the current expression on Adam's face, was a distinct possibility.

"I went on your mark," he pointed out, holding his own nail gun close. He could use it as a weapon if it came down to hand-to-hand combat. "You're the one who counted that round down."

"You had your shingles laid out already. It was an unfair head start."

Monty eyed Adam wordlessly. At first, the man's request to go head-to-head and see how fast they could respectively nail down their rows of roofing tiles had seemed like a joke. After all, they were two men working toward a common goal, covered in tar and sweating under the noonday sun. Surely camaraderie was the more effective way to reach their quota.

But the more time he spent up here, the more he wanted to beat this overly confident jerk. It wasn't uncommon for people to meet him and take him into immediate dislike, but it was rare for them to actually do something about it. His peers were far too polite to ask him to leave, the organizations he served too grateful to hint at the same. Like an unwanted suitor, he sat in on board meetings and attended conferences, invited out of a sense of obligation rather than because anyone actually contemplated accepting his hand.

Adam harbored no such delicacy. The words *clodpole* and *jackass* had been uttered multiple times already, and Monty had no doubts the other man's vocabulary would only grow more violent as the day went on. Since he had no idea how he was supposed to handle this kind of overt aggression, he'd gone with instinct.

Instinct, as it turned out, really wanted him to win.

"I'm no cheater," Monty said. "Should we go again?"

Adam nodded and extended his hand. Monty shook, but only after first bracing his feet against the roof's underlayment in case the man tried to pull him over the edge. He meant it—he wasn't going to die up here today. Georgia had greeted him that morning with a huge smile, transformative in the way it started at her lips and took over her whole expression, softening her from the inside out. Her brother Danny hadn't smiled, but he *had* gone so far as to shake Monty's hand, as had several other of the men and women who were working below, all of them as unimpressed by his presence as they should be.

He felt like he was fourteen and cutting class to hang out with the cool kids—the kids who were good at wood shop and gym and hung out under the bleachers after school. He'd never been one of the cool kids before, and he could see now why so many of them fell into delinquent behavior.

Because it's fun. Because there's more to life than playing by the rules.

Seriously. If someone were to pass him a clove cigarette right now, he'd be all over it. He'd even inhale.

"Oh, we're going again," Adam confirmed with a nod. "But this time, I think we should make it interesting."

"I like interesting things," Monty said carefully. He hoped this guy didn't mean money. The last thing he wanted to intrude on this day was a reminder of the bank account awaiting him at home—and all the responsibilities that came with it. "What did you have in mind?"

"That depends. I've got friends in high places around here. Anything pique your fancy?"

That sounded innocent enough. Monty cast a look around the work site, searching for an item worthy of their competition. The house they were working on was mostly finished already—apparently, they were only doing surface stuff today—so it was all roof shingles and siding on the outside, tile and carpet on the inside. He appreciated that he got to start at the finish line rather than being thrown, hard-hat first, into tasks like foundations and plumbing. He *was* a fast learner, but not that fast. He didn't want the structural integrity of anyone's home depending on him.

And it was clear this would be a home someday soon. The subdivision was filled with just that, *homes*. Most of them bore similar architectural styles—neat and compact, the yards small and the design simple—and Georgia had proudly informed him that many of them had been built with her help.

She had every right to be proud. Monty might help fund projects like these, but she was the one who actually made things happen. Even though he tried to make personal connections by working one-on-one with kids like Thomas, he sometimes forgot that there was a whole other side to philanthropy. An active side. A side where you could emerge in the daylight and shoot nail guns at strangers.

His gaze moved in Georgia's direction, irrevocably drawn toward the woman who managed to pack so much life into each day. There was no denying she was in her element out here. Like the rest of the eight or so volunteers milling around, she'd donned the mandatory yellow hard hat—an interesting complement to her standard coveralls—what looked like a fifty-pound work belt strapped around her waist, and boots so large she could have waded the Amazon in them. On any other woman, the combination would have been too much.

But Georgia wasn't any other woman, and she looked just right.

Monty's fascination with her was more than admiration for her cheerful efficiency and greater than awe at her physical strength. If he had to choose, he'd say it was that so much efficiency and strength could exist inside a person who unabashedly lived in the apartment above her mother's garage. Georgia didn't care about beauty or material gain or what others thought of her. She didn't hide her shortcomings or shy away from her flaws. She said exactly what was on her mind and let the fallout scatter where it may.

No one in his world operated along similar lines. He was surrounded by people—family members, business associates, ex-girlfriends—who did everything they could to hide their weaknesses. Nice clothes, expensive makeup, polite conversation, invitations to weddings that were, in their own way, a mirage of money and happiness...no one ever came out and said what they were thinking.

He wanted to go home and say it. *I'm hurt that Ashleigh is getting married, but the pain isn't nearly as great as the relief.* He wanted to stand up and shout it. *I'm tired of always doing the right thing if it means I have to sit and watch my life pass me by.*

As if feeling Monty's scrutiny from above, Georgia glanced up and waved, her smile bright and honest even from this distance. He waved back. Despite the heat, a combative partner and a blister he could feel forming on the web between his thumb and forefinger, he was enjoying himself for what had to be the first time in years.

"Oh, no. Oh, hell no," Adam said. Monty turned, startled to find that the other man had moved from combative to downright murderous. "You better not say that the thing piquing your interest is my sister, or so help me, I will throw you from this roof. I don't care who you are or how much money you have."

Monty froze, his mistake suddenly so clear he almost laughed out loud. *Of course* this man was related to Georgia—that same pronounced chin and nose, those eyes with an almost yellow ring around the center, the way he would gladly throw Monty to the ground and start wrestling with him right then and there. There was only one line of blood with such a strong compulsion for bodily harm.

"You're her brother."

"One of three. Older by several years and well-connected when it comes to harassment lawsuits, in case you were wondering. I got a three-sixty on the Bar."

This time, Monty really did laugh out loud. "That's impressive, but how does your Mensa score compare to Danny's?"

Adam didn't appear to understand his reference right away, but the longer the pair of them stood at an impasse, the more the other man weakened. "Danny's IQ is no joking matter."

"I'm appropriately in awe of his intellect, I assure you."

"Damn straight you are. He could hack into your entire hotel chain's infrastructure and dismantle you from the inside out by this time tomorrow."

Monty's brows went up in surprise.

"You don't believe me," Adam said. "You think I'm exaggerating."

"No, I'm sure he's quite skilled."

"You corporate CEOs are all the same. You think you're infallible, but that's only until the walls come crashing down and it turns out you've been skimming money off the top all along."

Monty didn't bother correcting him. He was neither a corporate CEO nor a thief, but he doubted anything he said would alter this man's opinion.

"Here—I'll show you what he's capable of." Adam pulled his cell phone out of his pocket and poised his finger above the screen. "Do you have your phone on you right now?"

"Ye-es. Why?"

"Here's my number. Dial it."

Monty didn't make a move to obey.

"I'm not going to do anything to harm you, so you can relax. Georgia made us promise to be nice to you today, which I'm assuming includes not tampering with technological devices or kicking you off the roof when your guard is down. I only want to make sure you understand what you're getting into."

"What I'm getting into," Monty echoed.

"Just dial already, would you? Jesus—I feel like I'm talking to a stone wall."

The insult accomplished what persuasion could not. He wasn't a stone wall and he wasn't a sheet of black ice and he wasn't afraid of Adam Lennox or his brothers. To prove it, he punched in the numbers and hit send.

Five seconds later, the cheerful sounds of "It's a Small World" began emanating from the device in Adam's hand.

"I can't get rid of it," Adam said as he hit cancel, cutting the world off when it was full of fears. "No matter how many times I change the SIM card or take the damn phone back to the store for a replacement, nothing anyone can do will change the ringtone. Danny puts it right back on again. I have no idea how."

Monty released a burst of laughter that surprised them both. "I can see how that might get annoying."

"Ha-ha. Tell me about it. I have two daughters, and they fucking love it. They sit at home all day and call me just to hear me yell. Do you want kids? They're monsters. Take my word for it and cut those tubes while you can."

Since that sounded an awful lot like Adam was approaching acceptance, Monty merely ducked his head in a gesture of agreement. He had a feeling discussing his thoughts regarding procreation probably wasn't a wise step anyway.

"Don't think this means I like you." The bluster was back in Adam's voice. "It was meant to be a warning. Danny knows his shit, and he's not afraid to fling it."

"I'll be sure and keep my electronics to myself at all times."

"If you know what's good for you, that's not all you'll keep to yourself."

Monty didn't pretend to misunderstand him. "I don't mean any offense to you or your brothers, but I think Georgia is fully capable of handling herself." From where they stood, looking down on her as she oversaw the delivery of an enormous roll of beige carpet, she seemed like the most capable person in the world.

"I'm sure it seems that way to someone who doesn't know her very well," Adam said, "but tell me—what do you see when you look at her? What is it about her that appeals to you?"

Monty was startled by the question, direct to the point of bordering on inappropriate. "She's my friend."

"Bullshit. Friends don't give up their Saturdays to build houses in ninety-degree weather when they could easily buy ten houses on their own. What do you see?"

Monty felt himself being pulled into the argument—probably because it *was* ninety degrees and he didn't enjoy having his every motivation questioned. He drew himself up to his full height and answered as honestly as he could. "She's strong."

"And?"

"She's nice."

"And?"

"She doesn't ask annoying questions."

He could have said a few more things—about how he wanted to run his hands over every inch of her legs, or that he liked the way she kissed, without restraint and as if he was the most virile man in the world—but he suspected those answers might result in one of them being carried away on a stretcher.

Adam held up three fingers, ticking off each one as he spoke. "She's strong because she's had to spend the majority of her life defending herself against assholes who can't see her real value. She's nice because she can rarely tell the assholes from the non-assholes until the damage is already done. And she does ask annoying questions. She asks them all the time. You clearly haven't spent any length of time in her company or you'd know that."

"What are you trying to say?"

"I'm saying that if you do anything to hurt her, I *will* come after you. So will Danny. So will Charlie. If I see so much as one tear fall from her eye over John Montgomery the Third, I promise you'll be John Montgomery the Last." He hoisted his roofing nailer. "Now. Are we on for that next row?"

Monty had never felt so strong an urge to nail things in his life. He wanted to nail hard and nail often and kick the ass of the man sharing his roof. Not once, in his entire life, had he made a woman cry. He'd never made *anyone* cry. In order to do that, he'd have had to make an impression on their lives that actually meant something.

People were often disappointed in Monty. They were put off by his reserve. They accepted his offer of marriage and returned a polite *no, thanks* before going off to find their soul mates in Nepal.

But to cry over him, a person would have to care first. Someone, somewhere, would have to feel love.

"Oh, I'm still game," Monty said, simmering with an emotion he barely recognized, let alone understood. "Did we decide what the stakes are?"

"How about this—you win, and I won't grab my brothers and nail you to the wall?"

"That seems dramatic, but okay." Monty didn't much care what the losing stakes were—he had no intention of letting things progress that far. He was more than a lump of inertia in his own life, and he'd labor up here all day to prove it. "And what if you win?"

"Then you leave Georgia alone. Off the job site, out of her life, zero contact. Done."

Again, that seemed a touch dramatic, but Monty was as game as he'd ever be. "I suppose I don't have any other choice."

"Damn straight you don't," Adam replied. "And I have to say, I'm a little disappointed at how easily you caved. I thought you'd push harder, seeing as how you and Georgia are such good *friends*."

"Oh, we're still friends." Monty flexed his hands and got ready for the race. "I just don't have any intention of losing."

GEORGIA KNEW IT hadn't been the best idea to pair Monty and Adam on top of the roof for nail-gun duty, but when she'd called roll to find that the Palecki brothers had once again failed to arrive, her options had been limited.

Staffing shortages had been a problem since the day she'd risen to the position of head contractor for the Ransom Creek Chapter of Homeward Bound—a position she'd been working toward most of her adult and adolescent life, though she hadn't known it at the time. Unpaid, undervalued, impressive to just about no one but herself, this job was the one thing in this world she was unequivocally qualified to do. It was the one thing she had when all the rest of her life seemed to be constantly circling a drain.

OR SO SHE'D thought twelve months ago, when the offer first came in. Armed with her newly minted contractor's license and dewy-eyed with optimism, she'd been prepared for things like grueling physical labor and long hours and the occasional flesh wound. *Fun things.*

What she hadn't been prepared for was the bureaucracy. As it turned out, most volunteers were here to build contacts, not houses. For every five who signed on to the program, only three showed up. Of those three, she was lucky to keep one for longer than a few weeks at a time. The second they figured out that she didn't own a larger construction company with actual paid job openings, and that, yes, she *did* expect them to follow her orders despite being in possession of two X chromosomes and the breasts that went along with them, they were out the unfinished framed wooden door.

It was a confirmation of everything Georgia had ever known about herself. It didn't matter how important the project was, or how good she was at her job, or how hard she tried to create a niche for herself—people didn't respect women who defied traditional gender roles. People didn't respect *her*, period.

And now poor Monty and Adam were the ones paying the price. Mostly Adam, from the looks of it.

"Should I ask why my brother is wearing a sandwich

board inviting everyone to enjoy his hot nuts, or is it better that I not know?"

Monty, more relaxed than she'd ever seen him in a tightly fitting polo shirt and a pair of jeans that looked as if they'd been dipped in tar, laughed. He *laughed*, as in actually opened his mouth wide enough to show signs of human pleasure.

"We found that sign over in the Dumpster when we were cleaning up. Why would someone throw such a gem away?" He glanced over at where Adam stood as the butt of every good testicle joke known to mankind, her brother's face growing increasingly red with each jab. "To be fair, I might not feel the same if I was the one inside it. I almost was. My hands started cramping up at the end."

Georgia just stared at Monty, her mouth agape. She'd broken him. She'd pushed him into proximity with the Testosterone Trio before he was ready, and now he was cracked.

"We did an okay job, right?" He turned to squint into the late afternoon sun, making a survey of the freshly covered roof. "It looks good to me, but I'm not the professional."

It took her a moment to realize that *she* was the professional he referred to. "It's fine. I mean—it's great. An excellent example of a roof. One of the best I've ever seen."

"Are you okay?"

"Am *I* okay?"

"You seem…off." His brows came together anxiously. "I'm sorry if it was cruel to make your brother put that on, but he lost fair and square. And it was his idea to do the challenge in the first place—we were down to all or nothing at that point."

"All or nothing?" she echoed, feeling bewildered.

"We made quite a few bets today."

"And you *won?*" No one won against Adam. Not in anything. If you got too close to his king in chess, he had this way of "accidentally" knocking the board off the table when you weren't looking.

"Not all of them, but I won the ones that mattered." He paused. "Why didn't you tell me your brothers were going to be here today?"

"I didn't know. They cornered me at breakfast and demanded to be let in. I don't know if you spent enough time with them to notice, but the Testosterone Trio is difficult to evade when they come at you all at once."

His lips lifted in a smile, another one of those human manifestations of joy she wasn't sure what to do with. Since when was Monty—*her* Monty, a silently stoic man whose stare could crack stone—such a happy, well-adjusted human being? Her brothers were supposed to bring out the worst in people, not the best. It was the rule.

"Is that what you call them? The Testosterone Trio?"

"It fits, don't you think?"

"I don't know. It seems kind of exclusionary to me. I like Quarrelsome Quartet better."

Georgia felt a spreading warmth move through her, almost as if sunshine had been lodged inside her rib cage. There was no way Monty could know how highly she regarded any comparison that placed her on equal footing with her brothers.

"Hey, what are you doing after this?" she asked, his compliment propelling her toward folly.

A long, penetrating look was his only reply.

"Don't worry. I'm not going to make you stay after and clean gutters or anything." She squirmed as the sunshine ebbed away, leaving only that look. "It's just that it's tradition for the whole crew to go out for drinks after a good day, and today was definitely a good day. You should come."

"Really?"

"Why not? You can spend some more time being attacked by my brothers. They'd love that."

"You're sure I won't be in the way?" He pulled off his hard hat and ran his fingers through his hair in a gesture of self-consciousness. She thought that gesture was for her benefit, that he was trying to find a polite way to decline, but his expression turned inward at the last second. "I already know your brothers hate me, but I don't want to put a damper on everyone else's fun while I'm at it."

"Don't be ridiculous. You won't damper anyone's fun."

"It's not ridiculous. It's a fact. Social gatherings improve more when I go out the door—not when I come in it."

"That's not true…" she began, but bit down on her lip when Monty's frown didn't lift, no glimmer of self-deprecation to lighten the mood.

How many times had she thought that exact same thing? Monty was nice to look at but unpleasant to talk to. Monty was a ten cut down to a five for his personality. Only yesterday, Holly had been teasing her about how industrious her crew would be now that she'd have Monty there to stare everyone into action.

She felt like the biggest asshole in the world. Okay, so Monty wasn't exactly teeming with laughs, and you had to get used to long periods of intense scrutiny if you intended to spend any time with him, but he'd managed to make Adam wear a sandwich board about nuts. That wasn't the work of a man with no personality.

That was the work of a man with a death wish—which just so happened to be a trait she admired the hell out of.

"Listen up, everybody!" She put a finger in either side of her mouth and released a piercing whistle, causing Monty to wince. Her talent at putting men off with loud noises and barbaric gestures knew no bounds. "Excellent work today. If we get this packed up and put to bed in the next thirty minutes, the first round of drinks at the Lager Loghouse is on me."

A rallying cry went up around the site, and Georgia turned to Monty with a triumphant grin. "They aren't a tough crowd to please. If you pick up the second round, I guarantee you'll have half a dozen new best friends."

"Does that figure include your brothers?"

"Well, let's not go crazy here. From the way Adam is glaring at you, I'm pretty sure he's already taken a hit out." When Monty's eyes flared, she laughed and patted him on the arm. It was a good arm, strong and taut where the fabric cut across his biceps. She could have spent hours running her hands over that bulge—her second-favorite kind on a man—but she caught him staring and dropped her hand before she did something awful like mentioning orgasms again.

"What kind of hit are we talking?" Monty asked carefully.

"The traditional kind—but don't worry. He's notoriously tight-fisted. No assassin he hires is going to be very good. He'll probably miss the first time."

"And the second time?"

Georgia just laughed. "I hope you have good reflexes."

SEVEN

"NANCY IS GOING to kill me if I don't go home soon." Adam glanced at the clock above the bartender's head with a grimace. The more time that passed, the more pronounced the grimace grew, and the more often it got pushed Monty's direction. "The kids have to be approaching meltdown mode by now."

"Oh, don't let us stop you," Georgia said. "We don't mean to make any more demands on your time."

Her eyes met Monty's over the top of her beer, sparkling with contagious humor. Although his own inclination had been to clear out before the other man's head had a chance to explode, she was enjoying this power play with a perversity he couldn't help but admire.

"I bet your poor wife is going crazy," Georgia continued with a wink in Monty's direction. "She's going to be really upset you spent all night carousing with the crew. Remember that time she got so mad at you for buying her a dishwasher for her birthday she made you sleep in the garage for two weeks? God, that was funny. You had such a hard time getting rid of the fleas."

Adam released a snort from nostrils so pinched they defied the laws of human anatomy. "There isn't any crew here to carouse with. They all went home."

"I know." Georgia clucked sadly. "Lightweights, every last one of them. I thought for sure Danny would outlast you."

The result of this interchange was a clear stalemate. In any other human pairing, one of the siblings would have given up hours ago. Although Monty didn't drink—most of his workdays started at five in the morning, and a clear head was a must at that hour—he'd purchased Georgia's suggested round and won an alarming amount of camaraderie in the process. There had been laughing and back slapping and all those other manifestations of healthy human interactions. He'd had no idea friendship came so cheap.

But even cheap friends had to go home eventually, which left only the three of them at a sticky table surrounded by empty beer bottles, each one fixated on being the last man standing.

Well, Georgia and Adam wanted to be the last ones standing. Monty was merely enjoying the show, hanging on out of a combination of perversity and curiosity.

And maybe a *small* desire to win. He couldn't help it—the Lennox combativeness was contagious, their determination some kind of game. These were not people who believed in the existence of a middle ground. If Monty's life was a testament to careful decisions and not rocking the boat, Georgia and her brothers preferred kickboxing on the prow.

Of course, Georgia's leg pressed up against his might have had something to do with his resolve. Sometime in the past thirty minutes, she'd scooted close enough that the entire length of her thigh, warm and unyielding, touched his. He was too much a man—and too much aware of what that leg looked like in the flesh—not to feel each movement she made as an ache deep in his groin.

"How long have you been married?" he asked Adam. It was a poor attempt at diverting his attention from his contemplation of Georgia's thighs, but at least he got the conversation going again.

"Not that it's any of your business, but ten years."

"Congratulations."

"Thank you," Adam said thinly. From the contortion on his face, you'd think he never displayed gratitude before.

"He and Nancy were high school sweethearts," Georgia put in. "We love her. She's fantastic."

"She is, isn't she?"

"Much too fantastic for you." Georgia turned to Monty with a wide smile, dazzling him with how assured it was. "It was lucky for all of us that Adam got to her before she realized how much better she could have done for herself. We consider their marriage one of the most successful portrayals of Stockholm Syndrome in existence."

"Ha-ha. Very funny. I'll have you know the women at the firm consider me quite a catch."

"Only if you count the chub they chop up and use as bait."

"Look who's talking. At least I found a woman willing to marry me. You're the one who can't interest a man for more than twenty-four hours before he decides he'd rather upgrade to his hand."

A stunned silence fell over the table. Monty would have been hard-pressed to say who was horrified the most by Adam's comment, but he suspected it was himself. He was the one who saw the flash of pain cross Georgia's face before she quickly snuffed it out. He was the one who felt how rigid her leg grew against his, every muscle in her body contracting at once. And he was the one who felt an almost overpowering urge to reach across the table and throttle the bastard she called brother.

"Oh, fuck. Georgia—I'm sorry. That came out wrong. I didn't mean it."

"I know," she said brightly. Too brightly, her speech almost brittle as she struggled to keep it from shattering. "It's okay."

"No, it's not okay. It was a shitty thing to say."

"Shitty, but true." Georgia wished she could unlock her arms enough to reach across the table and take the hand Adam held out to her in a gesture of apology, but every bit of her concentration was taken up in not falling apart in front of Monty.

For a few minutes there, she'd felt an almost giddy rush at how well the evening was going. She was witty, Monty was charming, and he hadn't run away at the first opportunity to afford itself. He'd even *touched* her, playing his foot against hers in what she could have sworn was a deliberate motion while her brother scowled at them from across the table.

But of course reality intruded—it always did, and she refused to be anything but grateful for it. Georgia wasn't built for romance and affection. She wasn't the sort of woman who married the love of her life and floated into a blissful happily ever after.

The sooner she accepted that truth, the better it would be for everyone at this table.

She lifted a shaking hand, hoping she could make it to Adam's without breaking down.

"I once got dumped by a girlfriend who announced she'd rather spend the holiday weekend among department store mannequins than with me."

Georgia swiveled her head to stare at the man next to her. So did Adam, the pair of them gaping in open-mouthed wonder as Monty tore at the damp label on his untouched bottle of beer.

"Another woman I took on a few dates admitted she only went out with me as a way to get to my brother."

"I don't think that's—"

Monty met Adam's eyes across the table, locking him in place. "That actually happened more than once, though I didn't find out about the other times until a few months after the fact. Usually because a tabloid reported seeing them together."

"I don't see how—"

"I know you don't," Monty said with that somber firmness of his. "But I doubt anyone who's been with his wife since high school realizes how difficult it is to find someone, whether it's for twenty-four hours or twenty-four years. You'll have to forgive me for thinking your opinion on the matter is one hundred percent irrelevant."

Georgia couldn't tell if she felt a stronger compulsion to laugh or to cry. Adam's natural response to being verbally smacked down—and by a man like John Montgomery—was to puff up like a gorilla and start thumping his chest, and she could tell that was exactly what he wanted to do.

But he couldn't. Not without shoving his foot any further inside his mouth than it already was.

She could have kissed Monty. She almost did. But before she could do much more than wonder what could have compelled him to make a romantic confession like that in public, Adam was rising to his feet, his movements jerky.

"I should be getting home to my family," he said, his face red.

Personal experience told her that the bluster in his

voice was due primarily to shame—there was no doubt in her mind he was sorry for what he'd said—but it probably looked more like anger to a man like Monty.

Monty didn't let it derail him. In a single, well-practiced move, he also stood, his hand outstretched. "It was nice to meet you, Adam," he said, his words formal and polite. "As strange as it sounds, I enjoyed your company on the roof today—and I can promise you I won't forget what we talked about."

"Good. Because despite what happened just now, it still stands. It will never *not* stand."

And like that, it was over. No more standoff. No more belligerence. Adam was actually dropping a twenty dollar bill on the table to cover his share of the tab.

"Wait—you're paying for your own drinks?" Georgia could handle the rest—the insult, the humiliation, the vaguely offensive way she wasn't being included in their manly goodbyes—but the day Adam willingly parted with cash was the day she started scanning the skies for four shiny white horses. "What just happened here? What'd I miss?"

"Ha-ha, Georgia." Adam leaned in and dropped a brotherly kiss on her forehead. It was the same way she'd seen him tuck her nieces Abby and Emma in at night, and she felt a surge of affection for him despite the situation. He tried so hard to take care of them all, even if he didn't always succeed at it. "Have a good night. I'll see you at family dinner on Wednesday."

"I know you didn't mean it," she said, since it seemed like her turn for a peace offering. "Thanks for helping out today."

"Anytime," he said gruffly, but he didn't meet her eye as he headed for the door.

THERE WERE A thousand things Georgia wanted to ask Monty after Adam finally left—about his dating past, about his relationship with his brother, about why he was being so persistently nice to her—but once they were alone together she settled for "How the hell did you do that?"

"How did I do what?" he asked, not the least put off by her swearing. She appreciated how even though he was so patently a gentleman, he didn't seem to care that she was no lady. Ladylike behavior was as much an enigma to her as a pushup bra.

"How did you get rid of him so easily? No one can handle Adam when he's in a mood like that—not even Nancy. He actually spends quite a bit of time sleeping in the garage, if you want the truth."

Monty chuckled, but didn't make a move to divulge any of his secrets.

"I'm serious. When Adam gets into his overprotective mode, he could scare away the pope. I've never known anyone to get him to walk away like that when he's itching for a fight. Here—arm wrestle me."

"What?" He dropped his hands under the table before she could get a grip on him. "I'm not arm wrestling you. What does that have to do with anything?"

"It has everything to do with everything." She reached under the table and grabbed his hand, but she couldn't move it to the top of the table. There was a power to him—a tenacity—she was coming to appreciate.

That wasn't all she was appreciating. The texture of his skin was that perfect combination of rough and soft, and even though she was trying her serious best to outmuscle him, her only result was the hot press of his palm against hers. He was that strong.

"Come on. I want to see if you can beat me."

His hand moved to the tabletop, taking hers with it, but instead of propping their elbows so they could enjoy a quick competition, he held her fingers firmly entwined in his own. *Oh, dear God.* He was holding her hand. By force.

"What are you doing?" she asked, staring at where their hands met.

"If I confess something, will you promise not to hit me over the head with your beer bottle?"

"It's actually a lot harder to break a bottle that way than you think," she said, her voice thick. He was still force-holding her hand. How could she think straight if he was still force-holding her hand? "The bottles are manufactured more compactly than they used to be. It's so companies can make you think you're getting more beer than you actually are."

Monty's lips lifted in a half smile. "Alcohol distributors are part of the mass conspiracy?"

"Who better to gain people's trust? Polls show that people put more trust in their local breweries than they do their politicians. If I had plans to take over the world, I know where I'd start."

"If you had plans to take over the world, I have no doubt you'd have accomplished it by now." His smile lingered. "It's better for all of us that your ambitions run to more altruistic channels."

Monty's compliments—if that was what they were—had a way of yanking the ground out from under her feet. If he'd have called her beautiful or darling or, God forbid, feisty, she'd have known in a second he was lying. But like comparing her to her brothers, altruistic was a sneaky one to slip in there, and the idea that she could take over the world pandered to her vanity in ways he couldn't possibly understand.

"I won't hit you over the head no matter how strong the provocation," she promised. "I think I might owe you one for getting rid of Adam anyway."

"I'm afraid the provocation might be stronger than you think." He didn't look up when he spoke, busy instead running his fingertip over the jagged edges of her nails. If he wasn't careful, he was going to slice himself open. "This isn't easy for me to say, but I want you to know I've been giving your problem some thought."

She swallowed. "My problem?"

"Yes. Your problem."

The doors were wide open for interpretation. There were so many problems in her life that he could have been talking about *anything*. Her ungainly appearance and pathetic income level. Being almost thirty and still living at home. The fact that every week, she fell a little bit more behind in her building schedule.

And, of course, there was the tiny matter of her having blurted out her sexual inadequacies while half-dressed and in his arms. Chances were pretty good it was that one.

"I thought we already decided we were going to erase that conversation from the annals of space and time." Heat flushed all the way up to her eyeballs. "It's not exactly my favorite memory of us."

"But it is one of my favorite memories of us."

A jolt of alarm moved through her, so fast it felt like lightning. Even the hair on her arm retained an upright tingle, as if the storm had no intention of blowing over. Monty couldn't possibly be serious right now.

"Because…you enjoy watching women make fools out of themselves?" she guessed.

"No. Because I like to think there might be something I can do about it."

Sex. He was talking about sex. He was talking about his penis and her vagina and the act of inserting the one into the other. Or so she assumed.

Since the last assumption she'd made where this man was concerned hadn't ended well, she decided it would be better to lay it all out there. "And by doing *something*, you mean…?"

"I, uh…" He coughed and had to clear his throat by taking a drink of lukewarm beer—his first in the more than two hours they'd been inside this bar. "Well, if it's not too late to take you up on your offer, I'd like to be the first man to make you experience an orgasm."

She laughed.

Laughter was the absolute wrong response when a gorgeous man was looking at you with his piercing blue eyes and offering to rock your world sideways, but she couldn't help it. He was so solemnly earnest, his language chosen with the same kind of care he probably used when buying a car or picking out a necktie.

He frowned. "I thought that was what you wanted?"

"It is—I swear. I do. I really do." More laughter emerged, this time breathless and higher-pitched, the sounds of a woman nearing the edge. "I'm just not used to men saying things like that to me. I promise, it's not you. I'm basically twelve years old and ill-equipped to deal with this sort of thing."

"You don't like it?" He nodded once, as if checking something off an internal checklist. "That's okay—it's good to know, actually. Dirty talk is off the table."

She was even closer to careening over the cliffs of insanity now. This had to be the most surreal conversation of her life. "What exactly *is* on the table?"

"I don't know," he said, his sincerity almost as palpable as the sexual tension between them. "I was hoping you could tell me. I've never been the kind of man people go to for a good time—not for sex, not for anything. I wasn't kidding when I said those things to your brother about my dating life. They really happened."

"Those women are idiots," she said fiercely.

"Maybe." He looked away. "But it's been that way for as long as I can remember. Even as a kid. Growing up, Jake was the fun one, Jenna was the adventurous one and I was the responsible one."

"That doesn't make you responsible for my problems," Georgia said in some confusion. Volunteering to build houses with her was one thing. Volunteering to stick vital portions of his anatomy inside her was an entirely different one. "I appreciate the offer, I do, but—"

"I *want* to do this, Georgia. More than anything. And if today has proven one thing to me, it's that I'm capable of enjoying a good challenge."

She stopped, and her mouth fell open, though it didn't stay that way for long. As if aware that she needed only a slight push to be sent reeling, Monty lifted a finger to the bottom of her chin and forced her lips closed.

"I overheard the entire conversation you had with Holly in the kitchen that morning. I know you're not interested in me as a person—that the attraction you feel is physical only." He shushed her before she had a chance to object. "That's okay. It's probably better that way."

"You're serious about this?"

"I'm serious about *everything*. That's the problem. At least this way, I figure I can use my powers for good."

He lifted her hand to his lips and bestowed a light, gentle kiss on its surface. Her poor, weathered hand with a Band-Aid on the thumb where a blister had opened up and the fingernails that had been bitten down until they were all as sharp as razors and some kind of sticky substance that had probably been transferred there from her steering wheel.

Oh, dear God. She let out a whimper.

"Excellent." His smile was so self-indulgently charming it slayed her. "Hand kissing is something you like. I'll add it to the list."

Her voice, when she finally found it, came out strangled. "I wouldn't rule the dirty talk out either. That was my first time hearing it."

He dropped her hand and stared at her, his expression so intent she thought she might combust on the spot. Was there a time when she'd lamented his propensity to stare? She took it back—she took it all back. He could sit there forever if he promised never to blink again. "How interesting. It was my first time saying it."

She swallowed. "Maybe you should try again. For research purposes."

"I want to be the first man to make you experience an orgasm." He repeated the words with the exact same intonation as before, but this time, her compulsion to laugh had been relegated to a galaxy far, far away. All she wanted to do was moan and fall off the sticky vinyl seat. "Should I keep going?"

"Yes, please."

"Well, um, ever since we kissed the other night, I

can't stop thinking about you in those ridiculous orange galoshes."

Okay. That was a little weird, but she could go with it.

"And I liked the way you made me feel when you were in my arms."

"Oh, yeah?" She licked her lips. This was more like it. "And how was that?"

He paused, as if he needed a moment to gather his thoughts. "Powerful, I guess? You made me feel physically strong, but also as if I were a man worthy of your time and attention and affection—as if I mattered. I liked feeling that way. I don't feel that way very often."

Wait a minute. That wasn't dirty talk. That was sad talk. That was really fucking depressing talk.

"And even though I can't promise you much," he continued, "I can say with absolute certainty that no man will work harder or more diligently to get you to climax. I'm good at hard work. It's pretty much the only thing I'm good at, to be honest."

Georgia couldn't tell if she was more turned on than she'd ever been in her life, or if she wanted to cradle Monty to her bosom and hand him a tissue. That was *not* how dirty talked worked in the movies.

"Was that okay?" he asked anxiously.

"It was…" She wasn't quite sure how to put this delicately. "It wasn't *bad*, but I think you're supposed to use more four-letter words."

He blinked. "You mean like *fuck?*"

"Well, yes. Like *fuck*. And *cunt* and *cock* and *hard*… You know, body parts and stuff. And you can be more specific about all the things you're going to do to me, if you want. I wouldn't mind." In fact, she'd kind of love it. In double fact, she kind of wished he'd do it right now.

But as one who had been on the receiving end of sex feed-back before—*not* her favorite post-coital moment—she ended with a compliment instead. "That part about the boots was nice."

"Oh, good. I was hoping I might get you to wear them for me later." He held up his hand and drew a deep breath. "No. Wait. I can do better than that. Give me a second. How about… The thought of you wearing nothing but those orange boots gets me hard?"

She almost laughed again, but thankfully pulled her-self back before she ruined all of her chances—and his self-esteem. "I think maybe you shouldn't phrase it as a question."

"Georgia." He leaned close and ran his thumb along the line of her cheek, stopping only when he reached her lips. "The thought of you wearing nothing but those or-ange boots gets me hard. Will you put them on for me?"

"Yes." She'd wear them. She'd wear them every day for the rest of her life. If he kept looking at her like that—almost hungrily—she'd glue the damn things to her feet. She made a motion to rise. "I'll put them on right now."

He swallowed so heavily she could see the outline of his Adam's apple as it worked up and down. Oh, how she wanted to lick him right there, where his pulse beat and the scrape of a beard began. Was licking on the table?

"*Right now*, right now?" he asked.

"Give or take an hour? I'm girlish enough to want to take a shower, and I'm pretty sure there are like six pizza boxes in my apartment I want to hide under the bed first."

"Okay."

"Okay? Just like that? You'll show up in an hour and pleasure me six ways to Sunday?"

"Okay," he said firmly. "Just like that. I'm going to show up in an hour and pleasure you six ways to Sunday."

A shiver worked through her. "You're getting better already. I really felt it that time."

His lips twitched enough for her to know her joke didn't go unrecognized. "To be perfectly frank, I'm hoping you'll feel it a hell of a lot more than that."

"That's the first time you've ever said *hell* before, isn't it?"

His blush was a delightful thing, so out of place on a man of his years and stature it was almost like viewing a mirage. "No, but it's not often that I find myself saying it to women I intend to sleep with."

"Women you intend to fuck," she supplied helpfully.

He blushed even more. "Women I intend to—*ahem*—fuck."

EIGHT

"Before we get started, I think we should clear a few things up first."

"Things?" Georgia stopped in the middle of pulling open her apartment door, her expression guarded. "What kind of things?"

As Monty had requested—however inelegantly—she wore nothing but the robe from before and the orange rubber galoshes he couldn't seem to shake from his memory. He wasn't sure what it was about those boots that got to him, but he suspected it was how perfectly they suited her. These heavy, functional, whimsical pieces of footwear—boots no woman he'd dated before would be caught dead wearing—and she sauntered around like she was born in them.

"General housekeeping issues," he said, forcing his gaze upward. "A few concerns I have about moving forward."

"Do you mean my brothers?" She pulled the door open the rest of the way to usher him inside. Thankfully, she didn't seem the least bit put off that he was discussing intercourse as though he'd just walked into a business meeting. The poor woman was probably coming to expect it from him. "So help me, if Adam called or is hiding out there in the bushes, he's getting socks every birthday for the rest of his life."

He laughed, relaxing as he took in the now-familiar

sight of her apartment—the simple four walls that some-how managed to keep this woman contained. "No, I didn't see him on my way up."

"I swear on my Cracker Jack prize collection they don't dictate every aspect of my sex life. It just looks that way. Whatever it is, I'll take care of it. No low-rent assassins, I promise."

"Thank you," he said calmly, "but I'm not worried about them. Dealing with people who don't like me is a fairly typical day in my world."

"They don't dislike you."

He leveled her with a careful stare.

"They don't want to bear your children or anything, but believe me when I say they're warming to you. You should have seen what they did to Carl."

"Who's Carl?"

She nodded knowingly. "Exactly."

Monty had no idea what Georgia was talking about. He had no idea what she was talking about at least half the time, but that was hardly a new thing for him. He was almost always a few steps behind in fast-paced conver-sations, and he could only be grateful she didn't seem to take it as a sign of his deficient personality the way everyone else did.

"Well, if it's not the Testosterone Trio, what is it? Have you changed your mind? Should I not have mentioned the pizza boxes? I threw them away, in case you're won-dering. They're not really under the bed."

He wished there was some sort of guide for this—or that he'd had a little more time to prepare. A *real* sex god would have swooped in here with his erection already primed and ready to go. A *real* sex god wouldn't bother with conversation at all. It'd be all tongues and sweat, a woman crying his name as if her life depended on it.

Unfortunately, he wasn't anyone but himself, slow and plodding, a stickler for prep work. There was no use pretending he could change now.

He took a seat at her computer desk, waiting until she settled on the bed before speaking. "I don't mean to put you on the spot, and you don't have to answer if you don't want to, but I'd like to get a better understanding of what we're dealing with here. Is it an anatomical problem?"

Her mouth fell open as his meaning sank in.

I'm sorry, he wanted to say. *So far from plying you with four-letter words and detailed descriptions of carnal activities, I want to talk anatomy first. Aren't you so glad you picked me?*

But she didn't run away. At least, not yet.

"O-kay," she said slowly. "You really want to know? It's not…off-putting?"

He shook his head. "I think it will help."

"Then it's not anatomical. Not to my knowledge, anyway. The doctors I've seen have been more than happy with the size and shape of all my parts. One even told me I have a lovely cervix."

"Congratulations?"

"I know. I had no idea how to respond either. Like, was I supposed to thank her?"

Some of Monty's uncertainty sloughed away at the sound of her rich laughter, unchecked and rapidly becoming one of his favorite sounds in the world. Her laugh boosted him the same way her kisses had, inflating him with confidence and propelling his forward motion. Which was good, because the questions only got more difficult from here.

"If it's not physical, do you think it's a mental issue?"

"I haven't seen a shrink about it or anything, if that's what you're asking. I did take a quiz once on WebMD to see if they had any insight, but they said my problem stems from the six different types of cancer I apparently have. To be fair, there *is* a questionable mole on my lower back."

Now it was his turn to laugh—and also to pin his gaze on the robe that currently covered her. He liked the idea that there were things like moles and freckles to explore under there, that she was merely waiting for him to make a survey of her body. He liked the idea enough to feel the sex god rising.

"If everything else is in working order, are you saying it's a question of opportunity?"

"What do you mean, opportunity?"

He hesitated. A man didn't have to be a Lothario to know when he was about to insult a woman in the worst possible way. "Well, if you don't have much experience with men, I thought that might be why—"

Georgia shot up, her spine straightening like an arrow. "I'm not a virgin or anything."

"I didn't think you were."

"I'm perfectly capable of finding willing partners."

"I'm sure you are."

"It's never been a question of quantity. It's the *quality* that concerns me."

"Georgia, I think you might be misunderstanding me."

It was the wrong thing to say, as usual. She crossed her arms and glared at him. "Oh, I understand you fine. You're as bad as Adam. You think I can't get laid. You think a man has to be desperate to descend to my level."

"I don't think that."

"I'm not very good at it, okay? Is that what you want to hear? I'm terrible at sex, and then I get self-conscious about being terrible at it, and then it becomes an embarrassing mess of bodily fluids. I just need to get someone in there who knows what he's doing, that's all."

He felt like a jerk. He *was* a jerk. He should have gone with his first instinct and swept in here, commanding her to disrobe and then laying her flat with four-letter profanities. He should have forgotten the lifetime of training and education that compelled him to move slowly and cautiously, to always weigh risks before taking action.

He should have remembered what he came here to do. To give Georgia what she wanted, yes, but also to have fun. When Ashleigh told him to step outside his office and enjoy himself, she'd probably hoped he'd take up racquetball or start building wooden ships inside bottles—not begin a course of sexual exploration with his family's oddly compelling handywoman.

But this was what he wanted. A tactile experience, a torrid experience. A chance to be the Monty no one believed existed—the one who could get in there and know what he was doing for once.

He made for the door without a moment's hesitation. It would have been better to provide Georgia with some kind of explanation before he left, but he didn't want to slow down or lose his momentum—like most large, immovable objects, Monty needed to stay in motion to keep going.

And he was going to keep going. Now that he'd made the first step, he wasn't sure he ever wanted to stop again.

THE LAST TIME Georgia cried, she'd been hit in the thigh by a softball coming off the bat at roughly eighty miles per hour.

At the time, when it felt as if someone had reached inside her leg and manually extracted her femur bone, the tears had been an automatic response. She couldn't help her leaking eyes any more than she could stop herself from sinking to the ground, her legs no longer capable of holding her up.

She'd have been ashamed of those tears later, if not for the vibrantly red and purple bruise that colored most of her thigh for the next few weeks. She'd worn shorts every day, practically daring people to look away from her pain.

It was the Lennox way. Tears were only acceptable when your body looked like a house of horrors afterward. Tears were only allowed when physical pain was the motivating factor. Since the day of the infamous Bobby Strom incident, Georgia had never allowed anyone—male or female—to give her a reason to break down. Until now.

"Fuck him," she said, jumping to her feet and dashing an angry hand across her face. Technically, the water in her eyes hadn't formed droplets yet. Until that point, they were just excess moisture. "Holly was right about him all along. He's probably terrible in bed. Chances are he'd want to consult a map before he went in search of my clit."

She didn't have a chance to work her tantrum up any further. With a crash that rattled the photobombed graduation picture on the wall, Monty pushed the door to her apartment back open. He was large enough to fill the entire doorway, nothing but shoulders and smoldering eyes as far as she could see.

"What are you—?" she began, but he slammed the door and crossed her tiny apartment in three strides, the floor shaking with each movement.

"I thought I told you I wanted to see you in *only* the boots."

There was no time to process his statement or the fact that the man who'd exited the building seconds ago wasn't the same one who reentered it. Gone were the questions and concerns, eliminated was that look of pity in his eyes as he tried to better understand the wasteland that was Georgia's sexual history. Instead, she found herself facing a man who exuded power—and who was exuding it in her direction.

"You came back," she said.

His response was a kiss. It was the sort of kiss most women only dreamed about—one of those embraces that rendered the knees into a useless set of joints and made a girl feel as if she could be swept off her feet in the manner of romantic movies everywhere. Although she might have harbored doubts about his sincerity a few seconds ago, every bit of hesitation fled as his lips moved over hers again and again.

Monty didn't ask to embrace her, didn't tentatively express his regard. He took, and his mouth said what words could not. Yes, she was wanted. Yes, she was desired. Yes, he would make this happen for her if he had to devour her from the inside out to do it.

"Of course I came back," he said. "I just needed to hit Reset."

She wanted to laugh at how seriously he spoke, as if passion could come at the click of a button and the determination of a man who'd only ever known hard work, but he distracted her by tugging her robe open and slipping a hand inside.

She wasn't ready for the shift from kissing to actual skin-on-skin contact, and she stiffened, her hands locked in place where she clung to his shirtfront. She wasn't sure what she expected to happen, but he didn't balk or slow down as he ran his touch over the less-than-perfect mid-section that awaited him. She could have kissed him for that. She *was* kissing him for that.

It wasn't as though she was *ashamed* of her body—her arms and legs weren't half bad, and her boobs were small enough that the term perky still applied—but unless she gave up on beer and nachos and a humane daily caloric intake, she wasn't likely to get that daintily tapered waist everyone considered such a hallmark of female beauty.

She was a woman built to work hard and work often, with a stockpile of calories stored around her abdomen for the lean times that never came. No man would ever sweep her into his arms and call her beautiful, but it was enough to be swept away and considered fuckable every now and then.

And that was precisely what Monty was doing. Although she felt an overwhelming urge to cover herself back up again, Monty lifted both his hands, running them along her shoulders and down her arms, taking the robe with him. His movements were deft and sure—and it was a good thing too, because she might have stopped him otherwise. She wasn't sure she'd ever been entirely nude with a man before. She'd been in states of partial undress, sure, but this standing stock-still, on display, all the glories—or lack thereof—of her body there for the taking was new.

And a little bit exhilarating, if she was being honest.

"Okay." He reached up and undid the top button of his shirt, a gesture that shouldn't have affected a woman standing stark naked so deeply, but there it was. That tiny measure of intent was the sexiest thing she'd ever seen in her life. "Tell me, Georgia. What do you like?"

The question caught her off guard—all the more so because he continued loosening the various accessories that held him together. Laces untied but shoes not all the way off. Belt unbuckled but not pulled open. Shirt untucked but still covering his chest. He was a werewolf getting ready to transform into a beast.

Her mouth puckered and grew dry. "I'm not so sure I understand the question."

"The goal here is your satisfaction, yes?"

Yes.

Oh, yes. She nodded.

"As much as I'd like to read your mind and make it magically happen, that's probably not a realistic goal for either of us. It'll be better if you tell me what you prefer." Monty spoke in a careful, even tone, though he felt anything but as he continued disrobing before Georgia's feasting eyes.

If she kept looking at him like that—as if he could leap mountains in a single bound—she was likely to get tossed to the bed and taken without remorse. Never, in his years of careful, considerate relationships with women, had he felt so much like a sexual object. Never, in his years of careful, considerate relationships with women, would he have wanted to. For all that he avoided communication in every other aspect of his life, he liked the parts that came before and after sex—the intimacy and the low-murmured conversations, physical affection in various states of urgency. He liked them almost as much as the act itself.

But what Georgia was demanding of him was different. Not emotional satisfaction—that tricky, elusive thing he desired but could never quite attain—but physical satisfaction. Body parts and body fluids and the rough act of combining the two.

"I don't… I'm not…" She blinked. "I'm not sure I know what I prefer. No one has ever asked me before."

"Would it help if I gave you a few options?" Monty asked.

"I don't think I can handle options right now. I'm too overwhelmed."

He felt a smile lift his lips. No one had ever claimed being *overwhelmed* by him before, though he was rapidly coming to embrace the sensation himself.

It was the sight of her standing naked in front of him that did it. Her upturned pink nipples—so lush on this rough-edged woman—had drawn tight against the air, and he saw now that the muscular legs he'd admired before echoed throughout the rest of her body, strong and solid everywhere his gaze landed.

That strength was his undoing. Georgia's curves were implied rather than flaunted, her body more of a testament to hard work than vanity, but the overall effect was staggering. The gentle flare of her hips, the attractively jutting breasts, the way her skin moved over the top of her musculature like delicately wrapped steel—it was as if she were two people. Coveralls Georgia of the mighty hammer, and Naked Georgia, who was doing a good job of making his own hammer feel mighty.

"Can't you just…" She waved a hand over the tops of her legs, where the thighs he loved came together in a neat vee. "Do your thing?"

My thing? He had no thing. There was no signature Monty move. He didn't have a magic formula for success. But the way her eyes looked trustingly up into his… *Hell.* He'd make it up as he went along.

Dispensing with further preliminaries, he gripped the back of her neck and brought her in for another kiss. It didn't take long for her tongue to begin sliding across his, her determination impossible to ignore. Whatever her lack of success in the sex department, she was more than proficient at this. A little greedy, perhaps, and kind of hurting him where she tugged so hard at his hair, but he didn't dare get in her way. He'd let her bite him on the neck and wrap him up in chains if that was what it took to get her off.

Since she seemed more than happy to continue climbing him like a tree—and as he had no objection to that sensation himself—he used his free hand to explore the body laid bare to him. He enjoyed the ripple of her skin, incongruously soft under his fingertips, but he was also committing the contours to memory, making a mental note of how she reacted to each touch.

She shrank when he touched her waist or attempted to trace the outline of her form. She moaned into his mouth when he cupped the weight of her breast with his hand, practically screamed when he tweaked a nipple. And when he dipped a hand lower, grazing the tip of his forefinger against the wet divide of her thighs, she all but grabbed him around the neck and slammed him into the nearest wall.

Right, then. She seemed ready. Best to get on with things.

He backed them toward the bed, not stopping until Georgia's legs hit the mattress and she fell to the unmade sheets below. Everything about her as she landed was parted—lips, legs, the glistening sheen of her womanhood. It hadn't been his intention to dive headfirst between her legs like this, but seeing her so open had him falling to his knees. Literally.

He tugged on her booted ankle, pulling her to the end

of the bed until her ass rested on the edge. Licking his lips in anticipation of what was to come, he took a moment to confirm with Georgia that this was okay.

It wasn't. Not if the wary look in her eyes was anything to go by.

"You don't like it?" he asked, dropping her ankle with a start.

"Let's just say it doesn't like *me*," she replied. "And it probably won't like you either. I've tried it a few times, and the outcome wasn't pretty. For either me or my partner."

"What did you do to him?"

"A fat lip and crushing disappointment."

He eyed her open legs again, taking in the delicate pink folds with renewed interest. *Another challenge*. He wasn't sure he'd ever encountered a hostile vagina before.

She clamped her legs shut, nearly snapping his head off in the process. "Don't even think about it, Montgomery. It's going to be hard enough for you to do this the old-fashioned way. Why don't you just climb on and show me what you can do?"

Her crude words jolted him back to a sense of his responsibility. Somewhere in the midst of all that kissing, he'd forgotten what he came here to do. The fantasy wasn't a man who carefully questioned her about preferences or pressed his mouth against her body for the most intimate kind of lovemaking. The fantasy was him bending her over a table and proving his might with his not-so-spindly forearms.

There was no table nearby, but he had a bed and a raging hard-on. Clearly, he could improvise.

"You have to open up at least a little," he said with a growl, and ran a hand up the outside of her leg. As he'd hoped, his touch worked in getting her to relax, and he even managed to slip his other hand between her thighs as he lowered himself on top of her.

He dropped his mouth to hers for another deep kiss as his fingers hit her sweet spot, slippery with desire and warm to the touch. It seemed like the perfect time to say something about how good she felt, but phrases like "nice cunt" and "tight and hot" weren't as easy to speak out in the moment as one might hope.

"Condoms are in the bedside drawer," Georgia said, just as he was clearing his throat and steeling his resolve.

He tried not to let his relief show as he nodded. Since he didn't want to give her an opportunity to lose the rapid breathing and undulations that indicated he was on the right track, he made quick work of ripping open the silver square and slipping a condom over his length.

It had been too long since he'd been with a woman, longer still since he'd felt this kind of pressure and anticipation to perform well. Each sensation of his own hand on his erection pulled at a spring deep within him, and he prayed—actually cast up a few words to whatever voyeuristic deity might be listening in—that he wouldn't disappoint her.

Once again, he thought a few words might be incumbent, but he settled for a long, leisurely glance down at her instead. She wouldn't believe him if he said so, but there was something beautiful about the way she lay there, eager yet wary, exposed yet not at all open. She wanted him, there was no question of that, but a man would have to prove himself to Georgia before he earned her true respect.

He had a feeling that kind of thing would be more difficult to elicit than a mere orgasm.

She opened her knees wider in a gesture of invitation, and he proved powerless against those incredible legs. He dropped to the bed once again and pressed his erection against her entrance, able to feel the heat of her body even through the latex.

"I'm so glad it's big," she said with a moan, and that was the end of him. Bracing his hands on her hips, he tilted her pelvis up from the bed and sank in her.

An explosion of sensation lifted him away from himself and more fully into her than he thought possible, considering the depth—or lack thereof—of their relationship. He didn't care who he was or who she was or even that he'd never been this intimate with a woman he didn't love before. All that seemed to matter was that her body was tight and eager around his, and her legs wound themselves around his hips as he plunged in again. And again. And again.

The strength of her was apparent as he moved his hands around to cup her bottom, and she needed no help to hold herself firmly against him. Her thighs were like some kind of gift from heaven, crafted of steel and satin, and he basked in it.

So did she.

Her soft cries of ecstasy were enough to make any man feel like a master of the universe—but knowing he was the first man to take her this far only added to his feeling of omnipotence. He was John Montgomery the Third. Sex god. A solid ten who was finally taking steps to correct his five personality.

He was also a mere man, and he felt his balls growing tighter as he neared release. He slowed down to better pace himself, and it was only then he realized she'd stopped moving against him. Or with him. Or at all, really.

"Is something wrong?" He made a motion as if to withdraw, but her legs were still clamped around him, holding him tight. He groaned, since her legs clamping also meant her vagina was clamping, but managed to hold himself firm. "What is it?"

"It's not working."

"It's not?" It was sure as hell working for him. "Here, maybe if we change the angle."

She obliged, but only in a way that gave meaning to the word—as if it were an *obligation*. On her side, her legs scissoring him, she should have noticed some kind of change, whether positive or negative, but all he got was the same lack of response.

He slid a hand between them, hoping he could at least massage her clit while he moved against her, but the sizzle or the chemistry or whatever you wanted to call it was gone. She even let out a hiss as he touched the wet space where their bodies met.

"Hmm. What else?" he mused. "We could try—"

She shook her head and released her hold, almost kicking him away in the process. As she rolled away from the edge of the bed and sat up, everything about her posture signaled defeat. Her shoulders were slumped and her head was down, and Monty thought for one horrified minute that she was crying.

He'd never claimed to be a fantastic lover, but he'd never made a woman *cry* before.

But when she turned to face him, she wore a tight smile, and he could tell she had no intention of shedding a single tear. "I'm sorry. It was stupid of me to think it was going to be any different just because you—" She cut herself off and took a deep breath. "I'm okay if you still want to finish."

He could hardly credit the words coming out of her mouth, but as he took a moment to process them, her expression didn't change. In addition to the tight smile, she wore a look of fierce determination, as if daring him to comment on how quickly the mood had plummeted.

He wasn't that brave.

"Is that what you think I'd like?" he asked carefully. "To have you lie there and take it while I get myself off?"

She cast a look at his erection, which hadn't subsided in the slightest. "Yes."

He felt suddenly exposed, his desire defiant and almost obscene given the recent turn of events. In haste, he turned away and stripped off the condom, giving himself time to cool and will his blood flow back to normal.

He was still semi-erect as he extracted his boxer briefs from the pile of clothes on the floor and pulled them on. It wasn't his most elegant moment, but at least he wasn't pointing at her anymore, mocking in how able he was to close the deal regardless of her feelings on the subject.

When he turned around, she was sitting up on the bed, her robe on and the boots off. The clothes—when matched with her look of utter dejection—made her appear younger and more vulnerable than before, and he felt a pang for having failed so spectacularly.

You had one job, John. One freaking job.

"I'm sorry," she said as she tucked a strand of hair behind her ear. "I didn't mean for that to come out so harshly. I wanted this to be good for you too."

"It was good for me."

She snorted, an inelegant, unapologetic, not-at-all-ladylike sound that captured everything he liked about her.

"I mean it," he insisted. "I don't know what kind of a life it is you think I lead up there at the Manor, but it's not often that I get to spend the day playing with nail guns, going out to bars and kissing naked women. I call today a win."

"Really?"

"Really." He sat on the bed, his weight causing the poorly sprung mattress to sink and propel Georgia closer to him. They weren't quite touching, but he could feel the heat and tension rising from her body. "I'm sorry this was such a disaster—I guess I was overly confident I could make it work. I'll come better prepared next time."

"There isn't going to be a next time."

He reached up and laid his hand against her cheek. Considering how close their bodies had been only moments before, it barely counted as a touch. But the way she turned into it, a sunflower following the sun, made him feel as if all wasn't lost.

Please don't let it all be lost.

"I wish you'd have told me I only had one shot," he said. "I would have pulled out some of my more creative moves."

She was startled into a laugh, and when she looked up at him, her expression had softened. "I'm sorry. I didn't mean to mislead you—I should have been clearer about how much of a lost cause I am where this sort of thing is concerned. Thank you for trying. It means a lot to me that you were willing to give it a go."

"So that's it? I know it's probably not proper etiquette to press my case, but I honestly believe we might have better luck next time." Now that he thought about it, he'd rarely had a stellar performance with any woman the first few times. Like most things worth doing, sex took work, diligence and regular practice to do it really well.

At least, that was what he'd always believed. It was

the Montgomery way. If at first you don't succeed, get up two hours early and try again tomorrow.

"It takes time to get to know someone else's body," he said. "What works, what doesn't work. What makes you scream, what makes you laugh, what makes you get a leg cramp." His joke fell sadly flat, as they so often did.

"I don't think I can. Once was weird enough. I work at Montgomery Manor, you've seen me naked, I know your fetish for rubber footwear..."

Her joke hit perfectly, and his amusement compelled him to lean down and place a kiss on her startled lips. "I also work at Montgomery Manor, you've seen *me* naked, and I don't have a fetish. Yellow or red boots wouldn't do it for me—it's that particular pair and the woman who fills them."

Her lips remained startled.

"You don't have to answer right away," he said as he rose from the bed. This had to mark the first time in his life he had the upper hand over someone in conversation, and he intended to use it to his advantage. He'd flee before she had a chance to turn him down flat—it wasn't cowardice when it could be considered strategy. "But I *would* like to give this another try. I've never been a quitter, and you never struck me as one either."

"Accepting the inevitable isn't the same as quitting," she said, her voice sullen.

"Are you sure about that?" he asked. "It looks an awful lot like quitting to me."

He scooped up his clothes and ran for the bathroom before she could grab the wrench on the bedside table to throw at him. He made it in time.

Thunk.

But just barely.

NINE

"I'M GOING TO fuck you like an animal. Spread it wide for me. I'd like to lick your glorious—" Monty's voice dropped to indistinguishable levels, "—cunt."

He clicked the record function on his phone and tossed it to the desk, feeling as foolish as he was sure he sounded. Taping himself and playing back the recording had *seemed* like a good enough idea at the time. He'd done the same thing a few years ago on the recommendation of his family's publicist when he had to give a series of speeches to drum up donor interest.

But this wasn't too-long pauses over shuffled note cards or a meeting full of people he couldn't picture naked even if he wanted to. He was attempting to seduce an empty room here.

The room didn't much care for it. The room was as dry as the Sahara.

"Come on," he growled, and reached for the phone again. This time, he also grabbed a notepad and the earbuds he normally kept plugged into his iPod for workouts. "How hard can this possibly be? Other men do it all the time."

He forced his eyes closed as he played back what he had so far. Even he had to admit there was something particularly unsettling about the way he paused and cleared his throat before any of the words Georgia had recommended—the ones containing four letters and harsh syllables and a wealth of crude meanings. It was like listening to a parent give the worst birds-and-bees talk of all time. "Okay now, Georgia. This is what we call the..." Snicker. Pause. Hesitate. Avoid eye contact. "Penis."

It was that bad. Twelve-year-olds would flee in fear.

Practice swearing more, he scrawled in his neat hand. It would be a challenge—he'd never been particularly good at it the way other boys were, the way he imagined Georgia's brothers were. It was the sort of thing that arose from tussles in fields and scraped knees and the constant one-upmanship that resulted from high spirits and not enough adult supervision. In other words, all those things Monty had never enjoyed.

Look up synonyms for vagina, he added as he heard himself struggle over a particularly painful mention of Georgia's pussy. He hated that word. Their cook growing up—Patrick, a man as cheerful as he'd been clueless— had always used *pussy* when talking about the beloved tabby he'd rescued from a local shelter. Jake used to ask him pointed questions about the cat just to see how many times he could get Patrick to say the word in one sitting.

Hmm. Maybe he should ask Jake about this. Jake was probably excellent at coming up with crude yet sophisticated ways to talk to women. Jake was the epitome of crude sophistication.

Call Jake, he wrote at the bottom of his list. That would be the most difficult of the bunch. If there was one thing his brother liked most in this world, it was humiliating Monty. Admitting he needed help in the seduction department would give his brother fodder for the rest of their lives.

He switched over to the voice function. "Well, it's too damn bad." There. He got that one out okay. "I'll master the art of verbal foreplay even if I have to lower myself to ask my younger brother for help to accomplish it."

"I'm sorry, John—am I interrupting something?"

He glanced up, nearly hurtling the phone through the nearest window, to find his dad poking his head into the office. The older man's brows were drawn tight as if he was working over a question in his mind—something along the lines of whether or not he'd remembered to take his blood pressure medication that morning, or if foreign relations with Russia would impact his hotel chain's expansion, or if his oldest son was possibly nearing an emotional break.

"No, Dad. It's fine. Come in."

He did, and with a greater agility than Monty anticipated. "Who were you talking to just now?" he asked.

"No one. It's nothing." In his flustered state, Monty tugged the earbuds out and shoved the entire package—phone and notepad and all—into the top drawer of his desk. His fingers hit the screen while he did, and he noticed an arrow move across the screen before he managed to close the drawer all the way.

What was that arrow? His heart pounded as he mentally scanned all the functions of the voice recording app he'd downloaded earlier that morning. Record and playback. Store and delete. He really hoped that arrow meant delete.

His dad stared at him for a long, thoughtful moment before finally speaking. "You've been acting strange lately."

Monty disagreed, albeit silently. This was probably the *least* strange he'd ever acted in his life—especially when compared to the rest of the world's population. So he had a secret lover and took an entire weekend off of work to swagger around with a hammer. So he turned to Google for advice in pleasing women. If the answers that popped up in the search bar were any indication, he was far from the first—or the most disturbed—man to try that.

Perhaps it was all the fresh air and socialization clouding his brain, but those things seemed far more ordinary to him right now than a lifetime spent shackled to his duties. And his dad, he suspected, knew it.

It was dangerous, this freedom thing. Once you gave your prisoner a taste of the real world, he started to get all kinds of ideas.

Prisoners and shackles. Hmm. Maybe that was what Georgia liked.

His father cleared his throat over the course of twenty painful seconds before extracting an envelope from his interior pocket. He held it just out of Monty's reach—a tactic he often used when the document was a particularly distasteful one.

"Is that for me?" he asked, playing his father's game as one born to the rules.

"Since you don't seem to be making any steps toward finding a date to the Bridgerton wedding, I've taken the liberty of compiling a short list."

"A short list?"

"Now, I don't want you to think I've exhausted all my resources yet. These are my top picks—women I know you'll be comfortable with, and who will lend enough authenticity to show your genuine happiness for Ashleigh and her betrothed."

"Martin."

"Excuse me?"

"Her betrothed's name is Martin. They met in Nepal."

"I know they met in Nepal. What does that have to say to anything?"

"I've never been to Nepal." Monty pushed back from his desk and strode to the window overlooking the back of the grounds. He normally loved this view, enjoyed the way the entire family legacy spread out before his eyes. The formal gardens gave way to the rolling hills of the surrounding countryside in a seamless line of green, and even though it was nothing to some of the estates he'd seen in England or Italy, Montgomery Manor had one advantage none of the others could touch—of being home.

He loved it here. His work was here. His life was here. But in that moment, he would have traded it all for a chance at finding love in Nepal.

"You wouldn't like it. It's teeming with tourists."

Monty clasped his hands behind his back and didn't bother turning around, though he'd stopped seeing much beyond his own wavering reflection in the windowpane. "I've also never been to Iceland or Tahiti or South Dakota."

"You want to go to South Dakota?"

"Not particularly, no. But if I did—so what? It's not as if it would happen. In all the years you've had me working by your side, I've never traveled anywhere that wasn't part of a business trip."

"Then we'll open a hotel in South Dakota for you so you have a reason to go. Will that make you happy?"

"Probably not." Monty sighed. He wasn't even sure what he was asking for anyway. Two weeks away so he could visit a monument to four dead presidents all by himself was hardly the stuff of fantasies. At least here at the Manor, he got to enjoy the novelty of being the only stony face. "Let's see the list."

His dad handed it over with some reluctance. "Like I said, I can come up with another ten if none of these suit you."

Monty sliced the envelope with the letter opener on his desk and extracted the document, neatly typed on monogrammed paper, which meant it had also passed through the hands of Katie. Wonderful. By now, the entire staff would know he was being set up by his father—the information would probably even reach Georgia before the week was through.

No worries. He was just a grown man who couldn't get a woman off or find his own dates. Somewhere, on this planet of seven billion people, there was a sadder specimen than he. Though probably not any who vacationed in Nepal.

"Willa Trentwood?" He stopped and blinked. "She's sixty years old, Dad. And didn't Lupita Hall's husband die just last month?"

He shoved the list back toward his father, too traumatized to keep going. If these were his top picks, Monty had no desire to see what kind of alternatives he'd come up with.

"Willa has always been remarkably well-preserved for her age, and she loves early British history. And, yes, maybe it's a bit too soon for romance with Lupita, but she doesn't have any children, so I assumed she'd be preferable to Maddie Balmore."

Monty's head spun—and not only because his dad was an alarmingly well-informed matchmaker. "Early British history?"

"She's written some incredible papers on the Roman aqueducts. You love aqueducts."

No. He *had* loved aqueducts. When he was seventeen.

For a whole two weeks there, he'd even considered majoring in something like engineering or history in hopes of increasing his love affair with the principles of irrigation. But that, like all manifestations of independence, had been swiftly quashed under the wheels of the hospitality trade.

"And Lupita's childless state?"

"I know how uncomfortable you get around children. You visibly cringe whenever Lily and Evan enter the room."

"I do?" As far as he was aware, he was rarely in the same room with his half siblings in the first place. Like most adults, they found his company stilting, and therefore avoided it whenever possible.

"Hold on to the list. Think it over." His dad began backing toward the door, his hands up to keep Monty from making any sudden movements. "I think you'll like some of the options I came up with. Nice and well-connected women, but not overpowering ones. They won't pull you away from your work, but could still be pleasant company."

Monty didn't trust himself to speak as his dad continued his retreat, waiting only until the door clicked shut before wadding the paper into a ball and dropping it in the wastebasket under his desk. It was too close to his feet there, though, and he could feel the names marching close to his toes.

He didn't like those names. They were the names of serious women, intent women, women he'd choose for a man whose interests ran to the dreary and desiccated.

This was how his father saw him. A man so far gone he needed to take a grandmother or a new widow to an ex's wedding. A man whose love of aqueducts eighteen years ago was the most memorable thing about him. A man who could only date women who didn't get in the way of his duty.

Never mind that all those things were technically true. Truth had an uncomfortable way of stripping a man down to his barest parts—and Monty's barest parts were pretty grim.

With a growl of frustration, he reached again for the phone in his desk. "Fuck him, fuck his list and fuck that wedding," he said, the curse words practically tripping off his tongue. He was going to channel his anger into something productive, like coming up with inventive ways to tell a woman how it felt to be inside her.

But the moment his hand grasped the phone, he remembered that ominous arrow, and it was with less rage and more fear that he scrolled down. Next to the wav file he'd created, he noticed a cheerful green check mark and Georgia's name, as well as a message that his recording had been sent to her number.

It wasn't possible. He'd never asked Georgia for her number. He'd just showed up at her house and her job site, slowly taking over her life because he didn't have one of his own.

Except you had Katie sync all the Montgomery Manor records after you updated the system last month. Don't forget how painfully efficient you are when it comes to things like this.

Painful was right. Unless he was very much mistaken, he'd just sent the entire thirty-seven minutes of him belaboring over cocks and cunts to the woman he was trying to impress with them.

Oh, fuck. Maybe he'd end up relocating to South Dakota after all.

TEN

"GEORGIA, CAN I see you in the living room for a minute?"

Georgia froze, a milk carton pressed to her lips as she stood near the open refrigerator door. That woman had eyes like a radioactive eagle. "I was going to put it in a glass, Mom—I swear."

Silence filled the house, and she tucked the milk guiltily back into its place on the top shelf. She was always ravenous after softball practice, but her own fridge contained nothing but Chinese takeout of indeterminable age and origin. A slight detour to her favorite restaurant—Chez Mom—was necessary before she snuck out to the build site to lay some off-the-clock kitchen flooring.

"There's a package of Girl Scout cookies hiding under the lettuce." This time, her mom's voice sounded at her back. "The coconut ones. Don't tell Danny."

"I could have sworn I looked under there!" Georgia pulled the crisper drawer open and probed deeper. Sure enough, the familiar purple box was neatly tucked away behind an array of untouched leafy greens.

She ripped open the package and grabbed two cookies before offering the box to her mom, the pair of them bonding over a moment of nostalgic triumph. It probably wasn't necessary to use such clandestine cookie measures anymore, but old habits died hard. Growing up, Georgia used to hide her favorite snacks in empty tampon boxes under the bathroom sink. She and her mom had shared many a secret Toblerone that way.

Unfortunately, their system had only worked until the day Charlie took a football to the nose and landed on the brilliant idea to shove tampons up his nostrils to stop the bleeding. He'd discovered her treasure trove of contraband junk food, and she'd had a hard time even holding on to maxi pads after that.

"One of these days, you're going to have to learn how to shop and cook for yourself." Her mom took a seat at the retro table and chairs that had been stationed in the kitchen for as long as she could remember. "Either that or marry rich."

Georgia almost crushed the cookie in her hand. "Marry rich?"

Her mom's expression, always serene, gave nothing away. "How'd it go this weekend with your brothers?"

Aware that the conversation about to take place was unavoidable, Georgia fell to the chair opposite her mom, working her cleats off her feet and peeling away her knee-high socks—which they both knew full well she wouldn't be washing for herself later. Georgia was useless both as a woman and as an adult. Domesticity made her twitch.

"Surprisingly well, actually. They didn't break anything."

"Or anyone?"

"No. They might have been tempted, but they didn't act up. Not enough to cause problems."

In all honesty, it was *she* whose behavior was suspect. She was the one who brought a man home for sex afterward. She was the one who then failed at said sex. She was also the one studiously avoiding all thoughts related to the upcoming weekend, when the cycle could theoretically start over again.

For the first time in her life, she hoped they got rained out.

"I'm glad to hear it. I liked your young man."

"Mom." She squirreled an entire cookie away in her cheek to avoid having to make eye contact. "He's not my young man."

"Oh? Are you just using him, then?"

It was a wonder more squirrels didn't choke to death. By the time Georgia managed to clear the cookie from her trachea and wash down the crumbs with the glass of milk her mom poured for her, she'd regained some measure of calm.

"I think it's a good idea, to be honest," her mom said, as though they'd never lost the thread of conversation. There was a reason Georgia's brothers were such evil geniuses. The apples clung perversely to the tree. "It's about time you cashed in on some of your fancy connections to start seeing results. I never understood the point of laboring so hard for those people if they won't give you anything in return."

"Mom!"

"They have money, Georgia. And power. It's not wrong to be attracted to those things."

"It's not the money or the power I'm attracted to," she muttered. It was everything else she'd been lusting after. *Still* lusted after, if she was being honest.

Maybe it had been foolish to put all her metaphorical eggs in Monty's strong, capable, oh-so-big basket, but it was too late now. All the eggs were broken, just like her. He'd been this perfect, attentive lover—a gift from the gods, molded to survive any apocalyptic scenario—

and she'd fizzled out. One second, he'd been filling her, his body driving her closer and closer to release, and the next…well. He'd still been filling her, but her body had reared up from the edge and was beating a hasty retreat.

It was too much. *He* was too much.

Everything inside her had clamped up at once, a familiar feeling of detachment taking over as her fifth grade Sex Ed teacher's voice filled her head.

When a man and a woman love each other very much, they get together and create a baby. Sometimes, though, they don't want a baby. But they still get together, because that's how strong their love is.

To this day, it had to be one of the worst explanations for intercourse she'd ever heard—and with three older brothers, she'd heard plenty—but it was the one that had always stuck with her the most. Probably because it had been a crock of shit.

Real sex—the grown-up kind, the modern kind—had little to do with love or babies. It was friction and fluid. It was a moment of mutual desire too quickly gone.

"It's not wrong to ask for help every now and then, you know," her mom said softly. "Especially since John seems like the perfect solution to your problem."

Georgia's gaze snapped up. How could her mom possibly know that? She'd never told anyone how deep her fantasies were rooted.

"If anyone can get you the volunteers you need, it's going to be that man and that family. What did he say when you approached him?"

Oh, God. She bit back a groan. She'd done it again—confused business with sex, assumed everyone was as obsessed with orgasms as her. "I don't know. I didn't ask."

"That *is* what you invited him for, though, right?"

Her mom's eyes narrowed, scanning Georgia's face as if reading a book. "You told him they might replace you if you can't get your numbers up?"

She didn't answer, not trusting herself to speak—and this from a woman who brazenly invited millionaires to share her bed. She almost wished her mom *had* been talking about sex. At least then she could pretend outrage and stomp away.

"Georgia?" her mom echoed.

She shoved another cookie into her mouth, unsure where to look or what she could say to make this conversation come to an end. It was one thing to admit she was defective in the sexual arena, to go to bed every night aware that she was warming no one's thoughts, traipsing through no one's dreams. Loneliness wasn't her favorite thing, but she could handle it. She'd been handling it her entire life.

But Homeward Bound wasn't just a feeling of gnawing regret in the pit of her stomach, warning her that her best years were passing her by. It was the foundation of everything she did and everything she was.

When she'd first signed up as a volunteer after Mr. Montgomery dropped a casual hint about how suited she was for the task, she'd had no idea what she was getting into. Building houses had seemed like a good way to hone her skills for the future, meet other people who shared her interests, pass the time—the usual things eighteen-year-olds were concerned with and didn't give a second thought to.

What she found, however, was so much more.

It wasn't acceptance, and it wasn't enjoyment, though those things certainly played a role. It wasn't professional success either, since the work continued unpaid and would for the foreseeable future. More than anything, it was the chance to lose her sense of self for a few hours of the day that drove her. All her problems, her desires, her shortcomings, the catastrophic crater that was her personal life—everything became secondary when she faced the pile of two-by-fours that would someday be a home.

No one's happiness depended on Georgia Lennox— this strange, awkward, unattractive human being she'd become—and she doubted it ever would. But for the space of a few months, she got to be an important part of some family's story.

That meant something. Maybe not much, but something.

"I can fix this on my own, Mom." She spoke firmly, willing the words into fact. "I don't need to wave a magic Montgomery wand to make everything better. I just need to work a little bit harder, that's all."

Her mom sighed. "Georgia, I have never known a person to fight the wrong battles with as much tenacity as you."

"What's that supposed to mean?"

Her mom reached across the table and gave her hand a squeeze. "I *love* that you chose volunteer work over a career, and I couldn't be prouder of all the things you've accomplished, but you don't have to prove yourself by struggling all the time. You're not your brothers."

Georgia slipped her hand out from under her mother's and grabbed another cookie, but for once, she'd lost her appetite. She toyed with the coconut, breaking pieces between her fingers.

"It's also time you got a separate landline for your apartment," her mom added. "There's a message for you

on the answering machine. I highly suggest you listen to
it and delete it before Danny gets home."

Georgia never got phone calls that weren't work related. That would require a social life first. "Who's it
from?"

"He didn't say. But don't worry—I think you'll be
able to figure it out."

"I WANT YOU to ask me what I'm wearing right now."

Monty groaned into the phone, pressing his free hand
to his eyes, as if obscuring his vision might somehow
also obscure his shame. "Hello, Georgia."

"It doesn't have to be all that detailed. Just a quick,
'What color are your panties?' will do."

"I take it my recording went through."

"Recordings aren't sexy. Don't ask me about recordings. Ask me about my panties."

"It was an accident. I pushed the wrong button. My
phone must have seen your name on the file and assumed
I meant to send it to you."

"Okay, fine. What are *you* wearing right now?"

As he was already in his room for the night, he'd gone
far enough to dress down in pajama pants and an undershirt, but neither one of those sounded all that thrilling
to put into words. Neither did the fact that he'd sunk into
his favorite armchair with a stack of legal documents to
go over. He *could* have gone downstairs to join the rest
of the family, but his father—in a fit of either cunning
or madness—had invited Willa Trentwood for dinner.

A man had his limits when it came to how much he
was willing to let others dictate his life. And for the first
time in his, Monty finally realized where that limit was.

Right here. Right now. With a woman twenty-five

years his senior sharing her treatise on ancient Roman irrigation techniques.

"If you could erase that recording so your brother Danny can never get his hands on it and ruin me socially, financially and emotionally, I'd really appreciate it."

Georgia laughed, filling his ears and the room with a comforting aura. He hadn't been aware until this moment just how much the sound of her voice affected him, like swimming in a pool of warm honey. *What a nice way to wind down after a long day of work.*

"I'm not deleting that masterpiece," she said. "I'm keeping it forever. I'm going to burn it on a CD so I can take it with me and listen while I work."

"You still listen to CDs? What decade are you living in?"

"A smart one. Mp3s are nothing but a conspiracy that forces consumers to rely on downloadable content."

He tossed the stack of legal documents to the side, settling deeper into his armchair as Georgia explained how easy it was for corporations to sneak code into the online files that consumers were being encouraged to grow dependent upon. Considering what her brother was capable of, Monty had to admit there was a certain amount of logic to her argument.

"Yet you have a computer and know how to download porn on it."

"I'm telling you—Danny meant that as a joke. A *joke*." She paused. "But speaking of pornographic materials…"

"Remember that time I came over to your house and you were dressed in nothing but a robe, and I was really nice about not making fun of you for it?"

"You liar. You totally made fun of me."

"I did no such thing." He sat up straighter. "I was a gentleman through and through."

"That day when you came to talk to me by my truck, you were totally mocking me with your eyes. Mockizing? Mizing? You twinkled, you asshole."

"I didn't know I *could* twinkle." He turned his head to examine his reflection in the mirror on the side wall, but all he could see was the same man who'd always stared back at him—firm and tense, unsmiling. Dull. But there was something else there too, a subtle transformation that started—yes—in his eyes, making everything seem less bleak by proximity.

Well, look at that. That might actually be a twinkle.

"Take my word for it. You can. But since I intend to be an *actual* gentleman through and through, I promise not to make fun of you for the dirty tape."

He noticed she didn't compliment him either. "Was it bad?"

"Well…" She hesitated, as if weighing her next words carefully. "You didn't sound like you were enjoying it very much. It's probably one of those things that's more fun when you've got an appreciative audience."

He couldn't argue with that.

"I might be willing to appreciate you. If that's something you want, I mean."

He didn't answer right away. While he wouldn't object to the occasional instructional moment from Georgia—especially as it related to what she liked in bed—he didn't particularly relish the thought of highlighting his inadequacies. Especially not in an arena that already made him feel so far out of his depth. Who'd decided verbal communication was the most important thing, anyway?

Georgia, apparently. "If you want to get better at talk-ing dirty, you have to practice."

"And if you want to get better at having orgasms, you have to practice too," he replied.

He could hear her shuffling in the background, hope-fully in her apartment and far away from her brothers' prying ears. "You think we should try again?"

"I do."

"And you *want* to try again?"

"More than anything in the world."

She let out a strangled gurgle, which he was famil-iar enough with by now to take as a good sign. Georgia made very strange, difficult-to-interpret sounds some-times, but that one he knew.

See? He *was* a fast learner.

"And you'll let me help you in return?" she asked. "I'll feel a lot less weird about this if I can also do some-thing for you."

He wanted to tell her that she'd already done enough—given him tangible goals, sex god confidence, a spark in an otherwise dreary existence—but he doubted she'd count those as anything worth having. Georgia was very much a physical woman, capable and grounded, and she put a lot more stock in the ability to arm wrestle than she did a less substantial kind of strength.

That was probably why it was so frustrating for her not to have mastery over her body in bed. He was no expert in sexual relations, but it seemed to him that she valued physical intimacy far more than emotional inti-macy. And that maybe she hadn't yet learned the two were often intertwined.

"It's a deal," he promised.

"Excellent. Now ask me what I'm wearing."

He sighed and gave in, torn between amusement at her determination and apprehension about the efficacy of this plan. "What color is your underwear?"

"Don't call it underwear. It has too many syllables and makes me feel like I'm either nine or ninety years old."

"I don't like the other word."

"Panties."

"Yes. That one."

Her laughter filled the phone again, this time accompanied by a cellophane crinkle. He could almost picture her, sitting on her bed and casually eating snack foods while he struggled to say the most rudimentary of words. She was probably recording this for her CD too. "Can I offer some advice?"

"I doubt I can stop you," he said.

"Don't think so much about what you're going to say." Georgia moved the phone handset to a more comfortable crook in her neck as she settled against her headboard. She hadn't been prepared for a lengthy conversation— she'd almost expected Monty to hang up on her, to be honest—so it took a minute before she found a comfortable spot. "No offense, but when I listened to that recording earlier, I could almost hear your thought process unfolding."

She'd also laughed herself silly. Wondered how long her mother had plugged in. And been so touched by Monty's diligence she'd stared at the wall for an hour instead of going to the build site as she'd planned. With the exception of her family, she couldn't think of anyone who'd ever worked that hard on her behalf. He'd said *cunt* for her.

"Just push it out. Whatever you're feeling, whatever you're thinking. Don't filter it first."

He paused, clearly filtering. "What should I say?"

"Why don't you start with something easy? How was your day?" A good ten seconds passed without a sound, compelling her to laugh. "It's only going to get harder from here, Monty. That one was supposed to be a gimme."

"I don't mean to take so long to respond to things," he said. "It's always been this way for me. By the time I understand all the facts and come up with a response that values the conversation the way I feel it deserves, everyone else has moved on. I've never been one for flippancy."

Georgia dropped the potato chip that had been making its way into her mouth, and she didn't even care when it left crumbs on her favorite sweatpants. Monty made his confession without pride or pity, his words as matter-of-fact as almost everything else that came out of his mouth, and she felt like an ass for not realizing it sooner. *Of course* he wasn't one for flippancy. He didn't always join the repartee around him—not because he didn't want to or because he thought himself above it—but because he wasn't the sort of man to speak without first weighing the risks to both himself and his company.

Monty wasn't boring. He was careful. He was *kind*.

What the hell kind of world did they live in where that distinction was almost impossible to make?

"Then I'll wait," she said, and even went so far as to push the chips away to give him her full attention. Anyone who knew her dietary habits would realize what a sacrifice that was. "As long as you need, for as many pauses as you want. How was your day today?"

This time, as she anticipated his reply, she didn't allow herself to dwell on anything except how nice it felt to have a strong, handsome, considerate man on the other end of the line—a man whose conversation she *did* value, even if she hadn't realized it before. His conversation was probably the most valuable thing in her life right now, because unlike most people she talked to, he meant every word.

"I didn't love the parts where I got into an argument with my father or accidentally sent you that recording, but I'm feeling much better now that I'm talking to you. Relaxed."

She was about to ask him what kind of argument he'd had when it dawned on her that talking about his family wasn't going to help them get to the dirty part of the conversation. "*How* relaxed?"

He chuckled, tickling her ear. "Relaxed enough to understand your meaning on my first try."

"And what sorts of things do you like to do when you're relaxed?"

"Do you want me to answer that honestly, or am I supposed to sex it up?"

Well, hell. She wasn't going to be nearly as good of a teacher at this as she thought. Even the word *sex* from his lips had her thighs trembling—which was the overall goal, she supposed, so she shouldn't complain. "Sex it up, my friend. As much as you're comfortable doing."

"Let me see…" He took a slow, careful breath. "If I'm relaxed and I've got some time on my hands, I might try jumping into the shower."

She froze, the phone a brick in her hand. They were going to *do* this, then. "Showers are nice. Would you be wearing all your clothes in it?"

"Probably not. I tend to shower following the same general process as every other sober human being."

"So you're naked?"

"For the sake of this scenario? Yes."

She bit her lip to keep from laughing out loud at his painstaking accuracy. "I don't suppose you want to glance in the steamed-up mirror and tell me what you see, do you?"

"Not really, no. I doubt my own reflection would be of much interest to me right now."

Fair enough. She'd have to use her imagination—and that overactive beast was already filling the gaps in with powerful shoulders and a chiseled body tapering down to...*ahem*.

"Okay, you're naked. The towel is pooled on the floor, and you're about to step inside. Tell me, what's the temperature of the shower?"

"Hot," he answered almost immediately. "Scalding hot. So hot I can barely stand it."

Mmm. That was a fast answer—and a great answer. Maybe inanimate objects were easier for him to describe than body parts and sex acts. "And how does the water feel as it cascades over you?" she prodded.

"Wet. Slippery. It makes me wish someone was in here with me, to be honest."

She was feeling wet and slippery enough herself to question the propriety of dropping her free hand down the elastic waistband of her sweats, but that would be inappropriate unless he was doing it too, right?

She settled for dropping her hand to her thigh instead, a few inches shy of brushing against any vital parts. "Is your shower *big* enough for more than one person?"

There was his chuckle again, though this time it held a long, continued rumble that made her clamp her thighs together with a whimper. "Yes, Georgia. It's quite large—

and growing larger by the second." He paused. "This doesn't really count, you know. I haven't used any of your four letter words yet."

"Your words are doing the trick just fine," she managed.

"Are they?" He sounded inordinately pleased with himself. But the next part didn't come out quite so easily. "Do you want to— That is, can I—"

"Yes," she gasped. "I want to, and you can."

There was a pause long enough for Monty to have extracted himself from his clothes or otherwise made himself comfortable enough to begin stroking. She desperately wanted to ask him if that was what he was doing, but despite the fact that she was playing teacher to his pupil here, she was no phone-sex expert. She was no expert on anything related to men. Or women, for that matter.

"So what happens now?" he asked, his voice rough.

"I'm not sure. We could go back to talking about the shower if you want."

"Is that how you normally do this?"

She made a gurgling sound that might, from a generous listener, be termed a laugh. "Are you kidding? You've met me. Do you really think I've done this before?"

"You're the one who set yourself up as my guide. I was merely following your lead."

They were veering dangerously off topic here, but it seemed suddenly important that she speak up. No, she wasn't any good at sex. No, she didn't have much experience with all the other things sex entailed—lolling in bed, drowsily basking in the afterglow, sharing laughter and kisses long into the night. *The relationship stuff.*

And that was fine. She might be the last woman on

earth a man would consider a fitting receptacle for all his love and affection, but if there was one thing she'd mastered through time and extensive longing, it was how to survive on sexual fantasy and sexual fantasy alone.

"Fuck the rules," she said.

"I beg your pardon?"

"Fuck the rules—I think that's how this is supposed to work. There's no right or wrong way to talk dirty to me, and you can say and do whatever you want. You're not John Montgomery the Third. I'm not Georgia Lennox. We're just two people trapped on an iceberg who have to share body heat or risk dying adrift at sea."

Pause. "Icebergs are cold."

"I know."

"And they might have polar bears."

"The increased danger only heightens the moment. Don't worry—I'll protect you. I'm an expert at bear wrestling."

He laughed, another one of those semi-restrained, oh-so-warm sounds that pulled her in like quicksand. "I believe you. But it's not really bears I'm interested in wrestling right now. What I'd like to do is wrestle *you*."

That got her free hand under her waistband in a flash. There was no way Monty could know that the two of them being forced to fight under the lustful eyes of the Roman Empire had been last night's feature—but she sure as hell didn't mind revisiting it now. Despite their temporary derailment, she was still very much primed and ready to go, and she reveled in the familiar warmth of her own body.

"What would you do if you managed to get me pinned?" Georgia asked. "And that's a pretty big *if*, by the way. Probably about as big as your shower."

Monty tilted back against the headrest of his chair and enjoyed a moment of laughter and mounting desire—a combination he wasn't sure he'd ever experienced before. Although he would have infinitely preferred to have Georgia's strong hand—or even better, her strong body—working up and down his erection, her rapid breathing was doing an excellent job of keeping his movements going.

"It won't be easy," he said with a hitch in his voice, "subduing you."

"Of course it won't."

"You'll struggle to get free."

"Good for me."

"But I'll manage to calm you with kisses."

"Cheater."

"And I'll eventually get you exactly where I want you—underneath me."

Her low moan tugged at his insides. "What do you demand, Monty? Now that you have me exactly where you want me?"

"Not much. I plan to hold you there and make you tell me a story."

She released a growl of frustration that set him laughing again.

"Don't worry. I also plan to satisfy all your bodily desires." It would have been a good time to segue into cocks and balls, but even though his cock and his balls were very much on his mind—and in his hand—right now, he didn't plan on introducing them into the conversation. "But I want to hear your stories too, Georgia. I enjoy the sound of your voice. I enjoy it almost as much as I do the sight of your bare legs."

"My legs?" she said in a hoarse voice.

He hoped that was a sign she was close to coming, because he had to clench his hand over his own length to keep from shooting off before she was ready.

"Your legs," he confirmed. "If you let me, I think I could spend hours between them."

He interpreted the cry that greeted him on the other end of the line as a confirmation of Georgia's release. Giving himself up to that sound—softer and sweeter than he could have ever imagined—he closed his eyes and allowed the moment to sweep him away.

And what a moment it was, out of control and expansive, so much more than a man and his hand.

He'd had sex using nothing but words. *Him.* Monotonous Montgomery. Drudgery John. The man no one wanted to converse with unless they absolutely had to.

"I told you I wasn't broken," Georgia said a few seconds later. "Defective, maybe, but not without hope."

"I never doubted you." He didn't move, his limbs heavy with satisfaction. There was something incredibly inelegant about this situation—sitting here sticky and sated—but he found it difficult to care. Elegance was overrated. "It would be a strange thing to lie about."

"Yes, well as you've pointed out before, *I'm* strange."

"You're also an excellent teacher. Thank you. I feel much more proficient now."

She didn't respond right away, and a sudden burst of panic seized him. *This* was why he preferred the moments after sex, when all the uncertainties and questions that arose between two people could be answered with an embrace. He didn't possess the words to reassure her the way she deserved, and without the ability to wrap his arms around her and hold her tight, he didn't know how to make sure she didn't run scared.

Because he wanted to do this again. He wanted Georgia to trust him enough to see this thing through to the end. Sex, friendship, a strange and exciting place where the two intertwined—whatever it was they were doing made him feel good. Happy.

Alive.

"Will you do me a favor and stop by my office tomorrow?" he asked, hoping his desperation didn't show. If anything, he'd veered too far in the opposite direction, his request more of a gruff command.

"Why?"

"Because I want to give you something."

He could practically see her dig in her heels. "Nuh-uh. No way. If you think I'm bad at apologies, you should see how I am with gifts."

"It's not that kind of gift, Georgia. I promise."

She ignored him. "And I think we should make it a point not to see each other at the Manor unless we absolutely have to. It's better if we make this a strictly-after-work-hours arrangement."

His voice became even gruffer, though it was a rising sense of anger and not desperation that drove it this time. "Why? Because you're ashamed of what we're doing?"

"No. Because if anything goes wrong, I'm the one who has to walk away from a valuable client." She hesitated. "I've worked with your family for eighteen years, Monty. I'm not afraid of losing your dad's business if it comes down to it, but it's not something I'm going to seek out either."

He held himself perfectly still, her meaning settling over him like a weighted blanket. "You'd give up Montgomery Manor, just like that?"

"Well, yes." He could hear the surprise in her voice. "Better me than you, wouldn't you say?"

He couldn't say. He couldn't even breathe. The idea that Georgia would give this place up for him—that giving this place up was even an option—filled him with an inexplicable feeling of warmth. And cold. And warmth.

That weighted blanket refused to make up its damn mind.

"I'll tell you what—if I find I have a few extra minutes tomorrow, I'll make a special trip up to your office," she said. "But I'm not making any promises. And I'm serious about the no presents thing. I hate presents."

He struggled to find his voice, eventually forced to settle for: "No one hates presents."

"I do. And I hate surprises even more. My brothers tried throwing me a surprise birthday party once. I don't think you want to know how it ended."

"Stitches?" he guessed.

"Casts."

ELEVEN

GEORGIA'S FAMILIARITY WITH the fourth floor of Montgomery Manor stemmed primarily from duty. As a teenager, she'd removed the molding in both Monty's and his father's offices to gouge out a space behind the trim to run the necessary cables. She'd also refinished the floors a few years back, and once had to get in the crawlspace above a storage room to clear out the family of bats that had taken up residence inside.

The bats had actually been quite cute, and she still sometimes felt a pang at having so mercilessly ousted them. All they'd wanted was a nice, dark hole where they could hide from the vagaries of a world that looked at them and felt only horror. They'd probably never see such luxury accommodations again.

She felt like a bat herself, flitting through the familiar halls only after she was absolutely sure she couldn't hear any movement around each corner.

This was a mistake. These gorgeous wood-paneled halls, the stately quiet of wealth hard at work, her own gnarled hand pulling open the outer office door—it didn't make sense. Maybe she should have made an effort to dress up for this. Or at least put on something other than the blue coveralls that made her feel, for what had to be the first time, like an intruder under this roof.

"Oh, hi, Georgia." Katie looked up from her desk, her glasses perched daintily on the end of her nose. Like

Georgia, Katie had been working at the Manor since she was a young woman, but they couldn't be less alike as human beings if they tried. The other woman's quiet efficiency and pertly uplifted nose were pretty much the opposite of everything Georgia stood for—loud efficiency and a heavily robust nose. Katie probably loved yoga and baked cupcakes too. "I think Monty's on a conference call right now, but he asked me to interrupt with some fake urgent business if it runs past two o'clock. I'll give him five more minutes, and then you can be my fake urgent business."

"Oh, I don't want to interrupt—" Georgia began, but *real* urgent business rang in, and Katie gestured to one of the fluffy brown leather chairs while she took the call. Unless Georgia wanted to stand there gawping like an ogre who'd never been taught manners, she had no choice but to sit and wait patiently for the man of the Manor to see her.

She sat, but not patiently.

It would have been unfair to accuse Monty of doing this on purpose—reinforcing their social differences, making her feel uncomfortable in a place she'd never once felt uncomfortable before—but she did anyway. This was his fault, with his promises and presents and perfection. He did this, with the sound of his *I think I could spend hours between your legs* filling her ears as she came.

And she couldn't even pick up one of the magazines on the table to distract herself, because the options were *The Journal of Philanthropy*, showcasing a beaming blonde woman in a power suit, or *National Geographic*, discussing the evolutionary trends of bedbugs.

Which are you, Georgia? those magazines asked.

A well-coiffed MBA bringing light to the world, or a woman who should probably be worried about the cleanliness of her bedding?

It was the sheets, okay? Her mother was right. Since marrying rich was a joke of cosmic proportions, she should probably get better at doing laundry. And vacuuming. And all adult responsibilities, really. She couldn't even make toast.

She slouched further in the chair, feeling petulant, when the door directly opposite her swung open. Her heart lifted as if on a string, but the man who appeared didn't boast the broad shoulders or carefully chiseled jawline that made her shiver in delight.

He did, however, possess a pair of those same, all-seeing blue eyes.

"Mr. Montgomery!" Georgia stiffened, that string winding itself around her heart until she thought the organ might stop. She'd never had one of those get-caught-making-out-with-a-boy moments in high school, but she was pretty sure this had to be a similar experience. "I didn't know you were going to be here. I stopped by to…"

Oh, hell. What did girls who got caught with boys shoving their tongues down their throats say in this sort of situation? Girl Card members probably knew. They probably had a whole secret list to memorize.

"John mentioned you might be by today," Mr. Montgomery said pleasantly, no more dismayed to find her sitting in his office reception area than if he'd come outside to find her repairing fence posts. He lowered himself into the chair next to her, his linen suit riding high enough that she could see the tops of his argyle socks and an inch of hairy white leg above that.

She stared at that patch of hairy leg, clung to it like it was a beacon of hope. His hairy leg was a reminder that even though this man could throw her out on her ass and bar her from ever crossing his threshold again, his follicles functioned the same way as everyone else's.

Or something like that. Mostly she was finding it difficult to meet his eyes.

"We don't see enough of you upstairs," he continued. "We don't see enough of you, period. I hope all is going well with your Homeward Bound project?"

She cast her eyes up, jolted to attention.

"John mentioned your volunteer shortages. I hope you don't mind."

She did. She minded quite a lot, actually. It was bad enough that she'd become so desperate she had to beg her family and friends to help dig her out of her hole—a lady wailing in distress of her own making—but it was also weird to think of Monty and his dad kicking back and discussing her over lunch.

Oh, yeah. Georgia's great with a hammer. She's also got this weirdly shaped belly button that looks like an old woman screaming obscenities. I kissed it once.

"So it's true?" Mr. Montgomery prodded gently. "You're struggling?"

"Oh, it's not so bad," she said, the rock in her stomach due more to the reality of her situation than the lie. "I underestimated how much of my time it would take to deal with things like recruitment and retention, but hard work has never scared me."

"No." He smiled, the creases of his face folding in well-traveled lines. "No one could ever say that about you. You aren't scared of much."

It seemed silly to continue being scared of *him* after

a statement like that, so she forced herself to relax. Mr. Montgomery might be rich and all-powerful, but it wasn't as if he could make her Homeward Bound situation worse than it already was.

"I go over to the build site when I have a free evening to try and pick up some of the slack, but there's still an enormous amount of work to do to meet our annual quota," she said, keeping her voice's wobble to a minimum. "I only have two hands, you know?"

"It's never fun to feel impotent in these situations," he agreed.

Impotent?

"I know John has often struggled with the same feelings, especially when it comes to the Montgomery Foundation. There's always one more project to fund, one more kid on the street who needs his help. He'd work twenty hours a day if I let him."

Impotent?

"In fact, I'm a little worried that taking on another charitable project—even one as worthwhile as yours— might be a bit much for him. Especially at this time."

Impotent? Georgia begged to differ. What she suffered from wasn't impotence. It was situational. A question of quality. She'd like to see Mr. Montgomery stay on schedule if all he had to rely on were the Palecki brothers of the world.

"I'm sure you can understand my concerns."

"No, not really," she said, and forced her concentration into place. They *were* still talking about Homeward Bound, right?

Mr. Montgomery didn't enlighten her. Nor did he lose the smile on his face. All he did was change positions, resulting in the drop of his hem over that safe patch of skin. "How long would you say you've been with us now, Georgia?"

She wanted the hairy leg back. "Um…eighteen years? Give or take a few months?"

"That's a long time."

"It is."

"And you enjoy it?"

Oh, dear. This sounded an awful lot like a precursor to the dissolution of a contract. Unemployment better not be Monty's idea of a present. Even something horrific like jewelry was preferable to that.

She turned to Mr. Montgomery with a gulp. She hadn't been kidding when she told Monty she'd walk away from this place with her head held high before she'd do anything that would bring actual harm to him or his family, but that didn't mean she'd like it.

"Of course I enjoy working here," she said, her voice only slightly wobbly. Who wouldn't? Nice people, good pay, incredible phone sex… "I sometimes think walking through the gates of Montgomery Manor is like walking into a hug. It just feels so *safe* here, you know?"

"I do know, and I'm happy to hear you confirm it." Mr. Montgomery smiled, his eyes crinkling in that same way Monty's did when the sentiment was real. "We'd hate to lose you for any reason. *Any* reason whatsoever. You know that, don't you?"

She gulped. "Yes, sir."

"We consider you one of us, Georgia. We always have."

She swallowed heavily, fearful that to show her panic would give it justification. He knew. He knew that his fancy millionaire son had put his penis inside her plain hundredaire vagina, and now it was all over.

"Which is why I feel comfortable admitting that I wish

you'd come to me first. If you needed more volunteers, I'd have been happy to talk to my builders to see what kind of arrangement we could come up with. There's no shortage of skill on the Montgomery crew."

Alarm bubbled in her throat, followed quickly by the constriction of rage, making her choke. Mr. Montgomery wasn't sitting here talking to her because he was concerned about her ability to tempt his son away with her questionable female charms. Oh, no. He was concerned because he thought she couldn't hack it as a contractor.

Just like my mother. Just like everyone else.

It wouldn't be so terrible if it wasn't so true.

"Thank you, but no," she said, and shook her head. Pride rendered her movements stiff, anger made them jerky. "I'm more than capable of seeing to my own team. There have been a few setbacks, but nothing I can't handle on my own."

Mr. Montgomery opened his mouth as if he wanted to object, but he changed his mind and closed it again.

"Is that everything?" she asked tightly.

"For now, yes." Mr. Montgomery was on his feet again, his smile back in place. "But if you change your mind, please let me know—I'm open to suggestion. If you don't want to use my crew, perhaps there's another solution we haven't discovered yet."

She thought that was the end of it, but he had yet to move away, his wide form casting a shadow over her, making her feel small.

"I'd like to see more of you, my dear. I know you get your work orders through Sarge, but I think you should pop upstairs every once in a while to let me know how things are getting on. My doors are always open to you—I hope you know that."

It was a kind thing to say, but Georgia couldn't help feel uneasy as Mr. Montgomery politely bowed back into his office. Her uneasiness didn't get a chance to abate, either, as the moment one man withdrew, the other appeared as if by magic.

Magicians—that was what they were, the whole lot of them. Master manipulators trying to pull quarters out of her ears and orgasms from between her legs. She wasn't getting anywhere near a box or a saw without writing her will first.

"You came." Monty beamed from the doorway, full of all the broad shoulders and piercing blue eyes a girl could hope for. And he probably didn't have argyle socks to offset them, either. "I didn't think you would, to be honest. I figured you'd chicken out."

She pulled a face and stalked into his office without waiting for an invitation.

"Please. I don't chicken out of anything," she said, even as her legs longed to send her running as fast—and as far—in the opposite direction they could go.

"WHAT ARE YOU DOING? You can't touch me. Your father is two doors down."

Monty knew it wasn't nice of him to laugh at Georgia when she wore such a panicked look, her fight-or-flight reflexes kicking in and visible on every line of her face. He also knew it wasn't nice of him to enjoy the sight of those lines. *Too bad.*

When she wasn't moving, Georgia's features were just that—features. A nose and lips, eyes and cheeks, each one easily labeled by its constituent parts. It was when emotion took over—for good or for bad—that all her features came together, working as one. As was the case with her other strengths, it was the combined force that held the potential to fell civilizations.

Georgia in motion was a beautiful thing.

"I mean it. He had me cornered out there—it was like he was waiting for me to get upstairs and out of my element so he could pounce."

"My father is occasionally a wise man."

Monty inched closer, cornering her against a bookcase, enjoying the incongruity of the bedraggled woman in coveralls surrounded by all that expensively bound leather. If he liked the way this room set Ashleigh off to advantage, showcasing her at ease among his belongings, he loved what it did to Georgia. She was a square peg firmly wedged in a round hole, as oblivious to any and all things related to the laws of geometry as she was to the rest of society's rules.

"I'll scream," she warned.

"Go ahead. I'm sure security can be here in under a minute. Alex would probably love you for it. I think he gets bored."

Georgia braced her legs shoulder-width apart and tensed her arms at her sides. "I don't need Alex to fight for me. I'm serious, Monty. You are *not* giving me that kind of present. Not in your family's house."

He slowed but didn't stop. "You aren't going to make me wrestle you for real, are you?"

The glare in her eyes turned into a flash, and he found himself grinning deeper. He had no idea what it was about these Lennoxes, but they stripped him of almost all his self-consciousness, replacing every emotion with a simple urge to fight—and to win.

"What is this about?"

"I'm going to do exactly what I threatened to do." He

drew close enough to kiss her, though he didn't dare make contact. Bracing his arms on either side of her head, he leaned close, locking her in place. "I'm going to trap you underneath me."

"You're going to *try* to trap me underneath you."

"And I'm going to make you tell me a story."

Knowing she could easily kick him in the groin and render all his future offspring null and void, he nonetheless brought his arms around her and pulled her body against his. She didn't fight—at least not yet—but she held herself stiff, her cheek pressed flat against his shoulder.

"Relax." He gave her a jiggle. "Five minutes is all I ask. Just let me hold you for five minutes."

"Why?"

"Because I want to."

"Why?"

"Because I like you."

"Why?"

"Your brother was right. You do ask a lot of annoying questions." He loosened his grip enough to peer down at her. As he'd hoped, she looked more annoyed than upset. "Given how tense your muscles are right now, I'm guessing you aren't used to this kind of thing."

"People touch me. People touch me all the time." She made a face. "They just don't touch me in a place where I do business, because that would be inappropriate. And weird."

His response was to run his hands up and down her arms, enjoying the contours hidden underneath the thick fabric.

"Relax," he commanded again. "I'm not going to take things any further than a hug. I want you to get used to my touch."

"Oh, nice. Because I'm like the mangy dog in the corner of the animal shelter everyone is afraid to approach because it might decide to bite?"

"Yes."

She laughed, shaking them both, and finally relaxed against him. Her own arms came up and manacled around his waist—adding a quick and almost painful squeeze as if to prove she could end this embrace whenever she felt like it.

He didn't mind. She *could* end the embrace whenever she felt like it. But he hoped the sensation of his heart beating against hers, the warmth of their bodies working like a kind of thermal massage, would do for her what it always did for him. Build comfort, make her feel more at home in her skin. Allow herself a chance to feel what it was like to belong, if only while the moment lasted. He never felt more alive than he did in the arms of a woman he cared about.

He wasn't sure if that made him the most pathetic man alive or merely human, but he liked to think it was the second one. There was life in this boring old soul yet.

"This feels strange," Georgia said, her voice muffled by his chest.

"It's only strange because you're not used to it."

"Monty, I've hugged men before. Not in my coveralls, obviously, and not because I was threatened to get wrestled to the ground otherwise, but it's not as if I've lived in a cave for the past twenty-nine years."

"You've had boyfriends."

As Monty phrased his words as neither a statement nor a question, Georgia couldn't decide whether or not to take offense. She was leaning toward yes, but it was hard when she was drowning in the scent of warm almonds and a pair of strong arms.

Monty, as it turned out, was a crazy good hugger. *It's because he hugs the way he kisses. Like he means it.*

"Define what you mean by boyfriend," she said, breathing him in. Five minutes of this wouldn't kill her. Five minutes of this might actually be nice.

"Is there more than one definition?"

"I have lots of friends who are boys. Dozens of them, in fact. I've slept with a few, but as Adam so kindly pointed out the other night, it never goes much beyond that."

He didn't loosen his hold on her, but his breathing slowed. It was the standard response she'd come to expect when conversing with this man. This moment of suspension—of stillness—was him taking the time to craft a careful response. She enjoyed it the same way she might the first plunge underwater at the lake, the quiet of a winter morning untouched by footsteps in the snow.

"Is it that your brothers scare them away?" he eventually asked.

"No."

"Really?" His surprise was clear. "I thought for sure they were part of the problem—not letting anyone through, the princess up in the tower sort of thing."

The idea of Georgia being some kind of dainty fairy-tale maiden was so laughable it made her snort. As in, actually create a pig-like sound with her nose. Here was Monty, being gallant and romantic and holding her in his arms, and she was wearing her coveralls and acting like a barnyard animal.

"They're the exact opposite, if you want the truth,"

she said. "They're constantly trying to set me up with their friends."

While her brothers might gleefully chase away the Carls and Montys of the world—men they suspected of using her or being insincere in their pursuit—they didn't balk at making their own love connections. In fact, she suspected they downright loved it. Her early twenties had been the worst, a blur of blind dates and chance encounters she cringed to look back on. Not a single weekend went by without some meet-cute at a bar with one of Adam's law school cronies or Charlie's teacher friends—guys who liked her fine as a drinking buddy, but who had no interest in candlelight dinners or meditations on her downy complexion.

She could sense Monty's incredulity, so she elaborated. "You have to understand how my brothers function. They see the world only through their own eyes, and refuse to consider there might be other realities in existence. Because *they* love me so much and without question, it's hard for them to understand why other men don't feel the same way."

Monty's whole body tensed where it curved around hers. "What's that supposed to mean?"

"Exactly what it sounds like. Look, I know you're being really nice and patient with me, and I appreciate it more than you'll ever realize, but since we're being so honest with one another, why not come out and say it? Men aren't interested in me like that."

"I am," he growled. "Don't I count?"

"I already told you I don't have any problems getting sex—with you or with anyone. A one-night stand is different." She didn't wait for him to make that angry noise again. "I'm not seeking pity or compliments here.

I'm stating a fact. Looks aren't everything, and maybe if I wasn't so off-putting in every other aspect of my life, I'd have a chance. But let's face it. I'm not pretty. I don't have nice clothes or a comfortable retirement account. I can't clean or cook or even promise that I'd be any good at raising kids someday. I work with my hands and smell like it most of the time. I can beat men at almost every sport out there and refuse to strike out to make them feel better about it."

She could tell he wanted to argue with each fact she threw out, so she saved the best one for last. "And none of that might matter if I was even remotely good at sex. Men will forgive a lot if it turns out you're a wildcat between the sheets. But as you've experienced for yourself, I'm not exactly setting hearts and reproductive organs aflame. So what's left?"

He didn't say anything, and it wasn't because he was crafting a careful response this time. She'd stumped him. There was no answer. Pot roast, perfume or pole dancing—you had to give men *something* to brag to their friends about. The most any of them could say about her was that she was handy for fixing things around the house. Hardly the start of a lifelong romance, and hardly good for their egos. Once you unclogged a man's plumbing for him, there was no turning back.

She thought that was going to be the end of it, but Monty nodded. *Nodded.* As if everything she'd said made perfect sense.

But he surprised her, as he so often did. "I'm not very good at relationships either," he said. "Not for the same reasons as you, obviously, but there's something about my combination of features that puts women off in a similar way."

She wanted to protest or laugh or personally hunt down every female stupid enough to consider Monty anything but a catch, but something about his long pause had her reconsidering. "What do you mean?"

He smiled sadly. "You already know. You guessed it the day I came down to the kitchen."

Goddammit. She wished she'd never said that thing about him being boring. Not only was it patently untrue, but it was a horrible thing for someone to have overheard. She knew better than to underestimate the cruelty of carelessly spoken words. "I don't think that anymore, Monty. Not now that I know you better."

"But it's true," he said, no touch of malice in his tone. "I never took the time to cultivate interests outside of work. I don't have any hobbies except for the occasional pulp detective novel. I don't enjoy long walks on the beach or drink alcohol to excess or secretly rescue puppies in my spare time. I'll never care for small talk or spend fewer than ten hours a day at my desk. And even though I travel for work, I've never gone anywhere just for fun. My entire world is the size of my office, and it shows."

She knew better than to try and argue this time. He wouldn't believe her if she did—and with good reason. She wouldn't believe *him* if he all of a sudden changed his tune and started slinging compliments on her supple curves and fine eyes. So she settled instead for, "Lots of workaholics have perfectly happy married lives. Your dad does."

"There's a difference between being a workaholic and being an automaton. No one falls in love with a machine." His arms fell away from around her, but although there was a tightness to his jaw, he didn't appear upset. "There. That wasn't so bad, was it?"

"You really called me all the way up here to give me a hug?"

"Yes." He ran a finger along the outside of her lips. The action was as intimate as a kiss, and she couldn't help herself from nipping softly when he got too close to her teeth. "I have a pretty hectic schedule, so I won't be able to see you until this weekend, but I wanted to make sure we maintained physical contact in the meantime. Meet me out behind the garden shed tomorrow at noon?"

"Are you serious?"

He placed a hand over his heart. "I never joke about clandestine meetings with my lover."

"Is that what I am?" she asked, flushed with pleasure. It was a silly, giddy reaction, but she couldn't help it. No one had ever called her that before. "Your lover?"

"My *secret* lover," he said with a grin. Then he flushed too, as if surprised by his own audacity. "I've never had one of those. It's fun, isn't it?"

She nodded, unable to stop herself. It *was* fun. It was new and strange and probably a bad idea, but she was also enjoying herself. She was having sex—sort of—and it wasn't a disaster. But then she heard movement outside Monty's office door and jumped away, her motion so abrupt she almost upended a globe. She met his eyes with a guilty start.

Well, at least it wasn't a disaster *yet*.

"What have you been working on today?"

Monty's arms stiffened around her, transforming their clandestine hug into a death threat. Georgia thought for a second they'd been exposed, one of the gardeners or security guards stumbling upon the room in the summerhouse they'd discovered was perfect for a daily five-minute embrace, but the willful way in which Monty slowly relaxed again put her at ease.

Apparently, that had been a self-imposed freak out.

"You don't do well when people ask you how your day is going, do you?" She didn't look up from where her head nestled against his shoulder. She liked that shoulder—not just touching it, but talking to it. It was warm and comforting and the perfect height for conversation. "There's no double meaning, if that's what you're afraid of. I'm not a spy for a rival hotel chain, sent here to seduce you into giving up trade secrets."

Monty laughed softly, shaking them both. As this was their third hugging adventure so far, they'd reached a nice balance of desire and relaxation. Mostly she just wanted to push him to the wicker couch and kiss him until their lips lost all sensation, but the feeling of his hand running slowly through her hair, catching tangles and pulling stubbornly through, was almost as good.

If his goal with all this not-exactly-innocent hugging had been to build sexual tension until she thought she could come on willpower alone, it was working.

"I'm just not used to people caring about what I do," he said. "Do you really want to hear the answer?"

The sudden constriction in her chest hurt a thousand times worse than the snarl he tugged with his fingers. It wasn't his words so much as the way he uttered them, as if no one caring was simply the way of things, a truth so deeply rooted it didn't even occur to him to question it.

"Absolutely," she said. "So much of your job is still a mystery to me."

He narrowed his eyes at her, as if trying to make out

whether or not she was mocking him, but she must have passed the test, because he placed his chin on the top of her head and answered. "It's not a mystery. It's boring."

"Tell me anyway."

"Don't say I didn't warn you." He took a deep breath that might have been a sigh. "Right now, I'm trying to convince a few other foundations to go in with us on a new foster care project, since the funding is too high for the Montgomery Foundation to bear alone. The goal is to increase post-secondary education options for older kids, the ones transitioning out of care."

Georgia nodded, her movements inhibited by the press of her face against his shoulder. "I read about that. College classes and skills training and stuff for teenagers being kicked out of the system before they're ready, right?"

"You read about it?"

"I have the internet. I can type at an impressive twenty words per minute. I know how these things work. It's a really good idea. How'd you come up with it?"

"I didn't. There's this kid, Thomas Escobar, who brought the issue to my attention a few years ago when he applied to the foundation for help with college tuition. We don't do scholarships, but something about his story struck me. He has no family, no long-term foster parents, no support network, period. More than money, he just needed someone to believe in him enough to see the whole process through." He sobered. "I know how it feels to be adrift like that, believing no one cares. As it turns out, thousands of other kids do too."

Even though she wanted to ask more questions, probe harder, something about the way he held himself so stiffly had her backing off. This wasn't just a project for him, the same way Homeward Bound wasn't just a job for her. "He sounds like a great kid. What other kinds of things do you have to do to get things going?"

He laughed softly. "Even more boring things, I'm afraid. There's a lot of groundwork that goes into this sort of thing. Because we're dealing with higher education and the state care system, my job requires a lot of coordination with politicians and people in positions of power. I basically drop my name and get results. It's shameful, really."

"And what happens once you're done with this project?"

"I'm never done." He sighed and narrowed his eyes again, as if to make sure she was still interested. This man had some *serious* self-esteem issues if he thought helping kids and name-dropping and political power plays were the stuff of ordinary men. "I started off in education because it seemed like the easiest place to get the most results. But Jake has us funding arts programs now, and I've been looking into extending the domestic education work to an international level. You might actually like that one. It would require us to train and commission local craftsmen to build schools in third-world countries—with nail guns and everything."

"I like *all* of them, Monty."

He grunted, a sound she interpreted to mean disbelief. "It's not as glamorous as it sounds. Most of my work is done from behind a desk."

"And most of my work is done on my hands and knees. So what?"

His laughter was far too robust and protracted for the situation—at least, until Georgia realized what she'd just said.

"Oh, God. That's not what I meant." She buried her

head even more into the side of his neck, where his pulse leaped and the scent of almonds threatened to overtake her. She should probably make more of an effort to be all dainty and floral-scented herself, but she wouldn't know where to start. "I just crawl under a lot of sinks, that's all. Maybe I should go find one right now."

"Don't you dare. I like you out here where I can see you." He dropped a kiss on her forehead as the hug came to an abrupt end. "And as much as I hate to bore you and run, I have a conference call this afternoon. I should go."

A sigh escaped before she could prevent it—as did the look of longing she sent to the wicker couch. It was a good make-out spot. You could tell from the way the flowers on the fabric frolicked, all winding tendrils and unfurling petals.

"I'm sorry, Georgia." Monty lifted a finger to her cheek. "I promise we'll pick back up where we left off. I just need to wait until I have enough time to devote myself to the task."

"I know," she said, and was surprised at how much she believed it. For the first time in her life, she felt it might actually be a possibility—that sex could feel normal, that she might be capable of achieving an orgasm through the traditional avenues.

It's because I trust him. The fact that Monty was handsome and strong and willing were nice perks, but those qualities were less important right now than the fact that she genuinely liked this man. He wouldn't hurt her. He wouldn't take advantage of her. He wouldn't promise her anything he didn't intend to follow through with.

"You don't mind that I'm making you wait?" he asked. "I feel like the least attentive secret lover of all time."

"Of course I don't mind, Monty. I've got other shit

I should be working on too." His eyebrows rose at her crude language but she just shrugged. "I told you—there's a reason I've never managed to pull off that whole 'girlfriend' thing. I can't even muster up a jealous, clinging need to be by a man's side at all hours of the day and night. I'm the worst."

"The absolute worst," he confirmed, but there was something about the way he looked back through the doorway—as if she were the beams holding the summerhouse roof aloft—that made her feel like the absolute best. "I'll see you tomorrow at the build site?"

"I'm never anywhere else," she said, and waved him off. In fact, she was headed there right now. A few hours of stapling would do wonders for working off her sexual frustration.

And for helping her catch up—but she wasn't going to admit that part out loud.

TWELVE

MONTY WASN'T SURE when he became aware of the tension on Georgia's job site, but it was probably a good three hours after he arrived.

As a general rule, he wasn't great at picking up on the moods and tempers of those around him. His default assumption was that people weren't enjoying themselves—which often turned out to be the case—so he operated in a kind of emergency mode by default. Head down, keep conversation to a minimum, eyes on the prize.

So even though he started out the morning taping off the windows somewhat amicably next to one of his hey-I-bought-you-a-beer friends, he failed to notice when the cheerful shouts of the rest of the crew became subdued. At least, he failed to notice right away. But when Adam picked up a roller and began slapping paint on the living room wall next to him without a single snide comment, he realized something was amiss.

Adam had grunted when he'd seen Monty pull up in his Lexus. He'd grunted even louder when Georgia winked at him. And the noise he'd made when he caught Monty watching her hand out the day's assignments barely qualified as a human sound.

That last one hadn't been his fault. Watching Georgia bark out orders had to be one of the sexiest things he'd ever seen. Tough and callused and determined, everything about her should have been off-putting to a man accustomed to the opposite.

But he *knew.* He knew how smooth her skin was underneath those stiff coveralls, how pliable she became when his mouth touched hers, how her velvety voice turned liquid when she was aroused. Harboring that knowledge felt like carrying secret missives to the king or bearing a hidden treasure map in a tattoo on his back. No one else realized that when they shook her weathered hand, they were touching something precious.

"What's going on?" Monty asked when Adam actually stood politely by and let him pour more of the paint into the tray. He was half-afraid he had a Kick Me sign on his back, or that Adam had covert plans to paint him from head to toe in Sandstone 0554. "Did I miss something?"

Adam firmed his mouth and shook his head. In any other man, that show of submissiveness would have been a welcome change of pace. In a relative of Georgia's, that show of submissiveness made him nervous.

"Did Georgia tell you to be nice to me again? You don't have to take her so literally. I can handle myself."

"Dip the roller in the paint and put it on the wall. It's not complicated."

"Is this about the other night?"

"Would you stop talking and get to work? Sigh." Even Adam's frustration had its own word. "I think I preferred it when you stood around and stared at me. We need to look industrious for the next few hours. Georgia's out there getting ripped a new one by her project manager."

"She's what?"

"Getting ripped a new one. Figurative for tearing open a second asshole. Literal for being screamed at by a dickwad who's never lifted a hammer a day in his life. Now move, would you? You're getting paint all over the drop cloth."

Monty went back to standing around and staring. How could a man who'd threatened to murder him if he made his little sister cry be so blithe about the literal and figurative act of creating ancillary bodily orifices?

Adam lifted his hand in an obvious up and down movement. "Like this. Paint. Wall. Pretty. See how it works?"

Monty shook his head and dropped his paint things instead. The large front window to the house had been propped open to allow for ventilation, and he made his way over there now, hoping to find that Adam had exaggerated in this, as in all things.

He hadn't.

Georgia stood some distance off, a clipboard in hand, staring into the face of a man who was waving furiously around him. Monty strained to catch some of the words flying out of the man's mouth, but the sound of tiles being cut screeched from the kitchen, making it impossible.

He turned back to Adam with a frown. "What's he so mad about?"

"Productivity, I imagine. This house was supposed to be done weeks ago."

"And she's going to stand there and let him yell?"

Adam shrugged. "She probably feels it's warranted. She's been worrying about being behind for months."

Although the sight of Georgia being reprimanded got Monty's blood boiling in ways he typically reserved for his own father's strictures, it was Adam's blasé comment that almost pushed him over the edge. "I don't understand. That's all you have to say?" He wiped his hands on the cloth he'd tucked into his back pocket. "Clearly, there's been a miscommunication somewhere if he feels he can treat a volunteer like that. She's subject to weather and staffing restrictions like anyone else. One of us should explain—"

Adam laughed outright. "You go right ahead, Montgomery. I dare you."

"What are we daring him to do?" Danny pushed his way through the hanging plastic separating the rooms, lengths of white molding in hand. "I want in. You guys are having all the fun in here."

"Hey, Danny. You're just in time. Mr. High and Mighty here thinks he ought to go bail Georgia out by speaking to her boss on her behalf."

"Oh, dude. No." Danny dropped the molding with a clatter. "Just no. I wouldn't do that if I were you."

"I'm not going to say anything bad." Monty couldn't understand. Not only were Adam and Danny clearly unconcerned with their sister's well-being, but they were laughing at him. *This* was the Testosterone Trio? *These* were the men who cared about Georgia so much they'd protect her against any man who dared to hurt her? "Getting bureaucratic middlemen to fall in line is what I do for a living."

"Yeah, but Georgia—"

Adam slapped a hand in the middle of his brother's chest. "You heard him. He's an expert at bureaucratic middlemen. He can smooth things over in a second."

Danny clamped his mouth shut, though he retained some of the worry around the lines of his eyes. As if they were all connected by an invisible umbilicus, Charlie also chose that moment to enter the room, a hammer in hand and his eyes wide.

"Did you guys hear some of the stuff that man is accusing Georgia of?" He let out a low whistle. "I haven't heard someone in a suit swear like that since the time Adam ran his car into a field of dairy cows. Remember how close you came to hitting that Guernsey?"

"Oh, please. That wasn't my fault. You were the one who grabbed the wheel from me."

"Yeah, because you weren't paying attention to the road—"

With a grunt of irritation, Monty turned and walked away. He didn't care to stick around to listen to how narrowly Adam missed charges of cow-slaughter, or to hear another stricture on the wisdom of abandoning Georgia to get ripped a new one all by herself out there. Maybe they thought it was funny to watch their sister being treated like garbage—maybe that was the cause of her low sense of personal value in the first place—but he wasn't about to stand there with his head down and a paint roller in hand.

"What's his problem?" he heard Charlie ask as he stormed through the plastic barrier.

He didn't hear the answer, but the sound of three men chortling at his back was one he wouldn't soon forget.

Nor would he forget that Georgia's brothers weren't the only crew members to abandon their leader in her time of need. Although he'd seen Georgia forcibly send one man home to care for his sick dog and provide breakfast for the rest out of her own pocket that morning, every head within sight was bent to its work, eyes trained as far away from her as possible. Not a single man or woman on the site—all of them volunteers like her—was willing to stand up on her behalf.

The man's yelling hadn't abated any in the time it took Monty to stalk across the yard, and he overheard snippets about "misrepresenting her skill set" and "continued failure to meet unit goals." Both of those were enough to ensure him that this man was a terrible leader. Motivation, not castigation, was how you got results when dealing with people who weren't being paid for their time. It was Philanthropy 101.

"I hope I'm not interrupting anything," Monty said as he approached the duo. He tried to keep his voice level, but it was difficult when he was swirling with so many emotions at once. This would normally be the time when he'd keep his mouth shut and wait for a moment of privacy to work through things on his own, but he felt no such compulsion today.

He wanted to storm and rage. He wanted to put this man in a sandwich board and nailgun him to the wall.

"Who are you? I don't recall seeing you here before." The man flicked his gaze over Monty with a dismissing grunt before returning to berate Georgia. He looked to be in his forties and as if he spent as much time as Monty behind a desk, though with much less diligence to the treadmill during his lunch hour. "And that's another thing, Ms. Lennox. I'm not at all convinced you're getting the proper clearance and liability forms for these new volunteers. You know each one has to complete a background check first, right?"

Monty cleared his throat.

This time, the man gave Monty his full attention, his beady eyes snapping. "Do you need something?"

"Yes, actually, I do. I'd like your name and the name of your supervisor."

The man's brows came together in a crack across his forehead. "I don't see how that's any of your business."

"You wouldn't, would you? That's because you didn't

give me a chance to introduce myself. I'm John." He extended his hand, covered in dried paint splatters and firm with tension. "John Montgomery."

The man stared at his hand for a full twenty seconds before he shot his own out and manacled Monty with his strong grip. He didn't let go right away either, his pumping movements enthusiastic to the point of pain. It was all the confirmation Monty needed to know his name-dropping had its intended effect.

"Mr. Montgomery—I had no idea, no idea at all." He shot an accusing stare at Georgia. "I knew your family was in residence in Ransom Creek, but Georgia failed to mention you were here today. Is this a scouting expedition, or merely a courtesy call? I wasn't aware the Montgomery Foundation had an interest in Homeward Bound."

"Actually, I'm here as one of Georgia's volunteers."

Monty's hand still hadn't been relinquished by this point, so he carefully extracted his fingers, shooting a wry grimace at Georgia as he did. To his surprise, she didn't share his humor in the situation or even appear grateful for the interruption. In fact, she didn't appear anywhere near the grateful spectrum. She looked...

Uh-oh. She looked furious.

"One of her volunteers?" The man—Monty still didn't know his name—looked back and forth between them. "You're here working?"

Even though he could see Georgia's lips firmed into a tight line and was able to read the warning in the expanding yellow flecks of her eyes, he was determined to commit to the path he was on. Georgia might not want his help, but he was here, and he was happy to offer it. It was a rare day when he got to take advantage of the perks of his position—if he couldn't throw his weight around when a friend needed it most, what was the point of having it in the first place?

"Of course. When I heard there were volunteer shortages, I naturally stepped up to lend whatever help I could. It's important to lead through action, don't you think?" He smiled tightly. "We can hardly expect the community to heed a call to arms if we aren't willing to do the work ourselves."

"Naturally," the man agreed, though Monty was pretty sure he missed the point. "Say, do you have a few minutes to spare? I'd love to talk to you about some of the opportunities that might exist within—"

"He can't." Georgia's voice, flat and dry, broke in.

"I'm sure you can spare him for a few minutes," the man said with a forced laugh.

"I wish I could, but you were absolutely right about me wasting resources and using this build site as a personal playground. If I'm going to uphold the Homeward Bound mission, we need to buckle down and get to work. And that means *all* of us."

Monty knew when he was being dismissed. He would have liked to push things a little further—walked the man through the neighborhood so he could see for himself how far things had come, discuss ideas for increasing interest in the project—but he had to settle for handing over one of his business cards, which only made Georgia's face grow red and give him a moment's concern for his personal safety. That was not a happy red.

He didn't look back as he returned to the house, where the Testosterone Trio stood watching and laughing from their safe distance. Adam, Charlie and Danny burst out in applause as soon as he walked through the plastic, Adam going so far as to throw in a wolf whistle.

"Oh, man. You are in for it now." Charlie slapped a hand on his back—the friendliest overture any of them had made toward him thus far.

"It was nice knowing you," Danny agreed. "I hope you remembered to tell your loved ones goodbye this morning."

"I'll say this for you, Montgomery," Adam added as he handed him the roller he'd abandoned earlier. "You've got balls. There aren't many men who'd walk into that situation unarmed. I may not like you, but you've got my respect."

Monty accepted the roller, but not without first checking each man's face. All three bore the same knowing smirk. "What aren't you guys telling me?"

"Oh, I tried to tell you," Danny said cheerfully. "You don't want to undermine Georgia's authority. Not if you value your life."

"But you do it. All three of you—you've done nothing but try to tell her what to do since I walked into her life."

Adam laughed and rubbed his hands greedily. "That's relationship stuff. Relationship stuff is nothing. We're talking about the job."

"You don't stand between Georgia and the job."

"You *never* stand between Georgia and the job."

Like that, the conversation was over. As if a lunch bell sounded, all three men returned to their work, laughter on their lips and malicious gleams in their eyes.

GEORGIA FOUND MONTY in the downstairs hallway, painting the ceiling as if he hadn't a care in the world. The second she stormed through the door, the room cleared, her brothers—the chicken-hearted bastards that they were—taking themselves away without so much as a grunt of acknowledgment. Two of the other crew members fled with them.

Good. It was better this way. There would be no witnesses to the upcoming slaughter.

"Do you have any idea what you did out there?" she said.

Monty didn't turn right away. He took his time putting his roller down and wiping his hands, his movements as slow and methodical as always. Since he'd once again decided that work clothes meant the tightest-fitting shirt known to mankind, she could see the bunch and pull of his muscles as he moved.

Instead of turning her on—or perhaps in addition to it—those muscles made her seethe with annoyance. *It's not fair.* Monty could make even painting seem like some kind of erotic dance. He could swagger around job sites in his too-tight shirt, speaking in his rich baritone, pulling out business cards and his family name like magic.

And because he was so careful, so methodical, she couldn't even rant and rave like she wanted. She had to stand here at his leisure until he was finally ready to turn her way—which he did, a sincere twist to his smile.

"I'm sorry, Georgia," he said simply. "I had to do something."

There was no trace of arrogance as he spoke, nothing cocky or smug she could latch on to and beat him over the head with, and instead of assuaging her anger, his apology only fueled it. Goddammit—any self-respecting man would at least give her something to vent at. Her brothers would have wasted no time in provoking her ire.

"Do something?" she echoed.

"Yes."

"Like pulling rank?"

"Yes."

"And humiliating me in front of my entire crew?"

"Not on purpose."

"That doesn't make it better."

He hesitated. "I couldn't help myself. I didn't appreciate the way that man was talking to you."

That had to be the sweetest thing anyone ever said to her, grandparents and greeting cards included. There were so many implications behind his statement—that she was a woman who deserved to be treated well, that he would stand up and be the one to do it, that he cared, period.

So of course she exploded.

"No one likes the way Meecham talks to me. No one likes the way Meecham talks to anyone. He's an asshole." She'd somehow crossed the room and got up in Monty's face. Proximity to this man always unsettled her, but she buried the feelings of longing and desire, allowing the more easily managed anger to the forefront. "But he's *my* asshole, and you don't get to mess with that without my permission first."

Monty kept a perfectly straight face, but she realized what she said about two seconds later.

"You know what I mean," she muttered, her cheeks aflame. "I get that you're all-powerful and can swoop in here to fix things with your big words and fancy name, but I spent years earning my spot on this team. Do you know how many licensed female contractors there are in the state of Connecticut? Do you have any idea how much crap I've had to wade through to get to this point?"

He didn't answer, because he couldn't possibly know. No one did—not even her brothers, the people closest to her in the entire world.

The construction world was a shitstorm of misogyny, and she'd been standing in the middle of it for as long as she could remember. She'd stopped keeping track of how many slurs on her femininity she'd suffered, of how many times her appearance was used as an invitation for insult, but she knew to the exact number how many volunteers she'd had to kick off the team because they refused to take orders from a woman. It was thirteen men over the course of one year. Thirteen hardworking, desperately needed men who'd put everyone in danger by not being able to tuck their dicks away for eight hours a week in order to help people in need.

Meecham blamed her for it—and rightly so. A male contractor wouldn't have suffered the same staffing shortages she did. A male contractor would have been happy to slap his compatriots on the back and tell Georgia it was a good thing she had a decent ass, because no man would ever want to fuck her from the front.

But what Meecham didn't understand, and what each of the men she'd banned from the project didn't understand, was that their doubt and cruelty didn't make her want to quit. It only made her want to try harder. No one was going to kick her in the shin and call her ugly and make her cry.

Not if she had anything to say about it.

"This is *my* crew and *my* project," she said, her voice dangerous. "And if being in charge means I have to let Meecham spit all over me once a month so he can go back to his funders with his head held high, then I'll do it. I'm tough. I can take it."

"But you shouldn't have to take it, Georgia. That's the thing."

The last of her patience snapped at the sound of his

voice, so earnest, so outraged on her behalf she couldn't bear it. She didn't need Monty's pity or his munificence. She didn't need him to speak down to small men on her behalf. What she needed was to tackle the deep, systemic issues that had plagued her since birth. She was too much of a woman to succeed in this business, but not enough of one to succeed in her own life. Somewhere, somehow, there had to be a middle ground.

There *had* to.

"What is it about you and your father that makes you both think I can't handle this? I know I'm up against a wall, and I'm trying to tear it down." She felt hot tears prick at her eyes, which only fed her anger. She was *not* going to cry. Not over this, and not in front of a man she was supposed to be using only for sex. "This isn't something that money or power can fix, and I'd appreciate it if you'd let me do this on my own terms."

He reached out to her. "Georgia, I'm sorry—"

"You need to go." She dashed a hand across her eyes, furious with herself for letting things get this far. Monty had not only demeaned her in front of Meecham, but now she was demeaning herself by letting her emotions win. How typical. How *female*.

"Thank you for your help with the construction—with everything—but I think it's better if you leave now."

"Leave?" His brow came down heavily, his eyes hurt. "You can't mean that."

"I do mean it."

"Georgia. Please." He reached, this time coming perilously close to pulling her into a hug. A week of training had prepared her for it, forced her body to curl into his embrace as if it were the only thing it wanted. His strong arms, that wide chest, the way he was able to make her feel desired without even kissing her—those things were dangerous out here. More so than falling beams and asshole supervisors.

"No." She jumped back. "Not *now*, Monty. Can't you see I need you to go?"

Monty's troubled gaze didn't lift, and she thought for a moment the tears were going to win, that she was going to break down before this mountain of a man moved an inch. But she heard the shuffle of feet from the rear, the tread of three quietly approaching allies.

They arrayed herself alongside her—Charlie and Danny to her left, Adam to her right—her brothers, her best friends, her favorite people in the world.

"I warned you, Montgomery," Adam said. "I told you what would happen if you hurt her."

Monty opened his mouth as if he wanted to speak, but he clamped it shut without allowing any words to cross his lips.

Georgia felt more relief at the sight of Monty's slowly retreating form than she could possibly express. If it had been the two of them alone in the house, she would have caved. She would have thrown herself at him, begged him to hold her tight and—horror of all horrors—cried in his arms.

If she thought she had problems earning respect now, she couldn't imagine what would happen if her crew found her sobbing because one man yelled at her and another one cared.

A Lennox didn't cry, dammit. Not without a bruise to show for it first.

THIRTEEN

"IF I ASK you for advice about something, can you promise not to laugh, criticize or otherwise humiliate me?"

"No."

The speed with which Jake responded had Monty pressing his fingers firmly into his eye sockets. He wasn't sure what the direct pressure on his ocular nerves was supposed to accomplish, but at least it stopped him from hanging up the phone in a fit of irritation.

"Is that a no to the advice, or a no to the humiliation?"

Jake paused long enough to think about it—or at least to give the appearance of thinking about it. Monty's brother had always been excellent at manipulating conversations so that he was the one in charge. "The latter. You know I'm against getting involved in your problems as a general rule, but this one sounds like too much fun to pass up. How can I help humiliate you?"

Monty sighed and sat back in his office chair. He had a thousand and one things he should have been working on, but so far all he'd managed to do was make a sex recording, delete it before he got up the nerve to send it to Georgia, order flowers and then hastily cancel the order once he remembered who the intended recipient was, and plot various ways in which he could get Georgia's supervisor fired without her knowing about it.

He was a mess—and not just because he'd spent the better part of his morning staring moonily out the window. He had no framework for this sort of thing. Ninety percent of his inability to successfully navigate inter-personal relationships was due to not extending himself enough. He didn't leave his desk, he didn't go to parties, he didn't get involved—these weren't exactly the type of qualities a woman looked for in a lifelong mate.

But if anything, Georgia preferred those things about him. She was the one reluctant to give up five minutes of her workday for a hug. Her idea of a party was beer and a dartboard. And she wanted him to be less involved in her life, not more. The fact that she'd banned him from her work site—literally banned him, her brothers forming a barricade daring him to try and come back on Sunday—proved how little his presence mattered to her overall happiness.

He wanted to matter, dammit. He wanted Georgia to be sitting at home right now, feeling as adrift as he was.

"If I tell you what I need help with," Monty said, "this doesn't go any further than the two of us."

"Unfair. I reserve the right to tell Becca. You know how much she loves a good humiliation."

She didn't—Jake's wife was actually one of the nicest people Monty knew, but he doubted he'd get his brother's help any other way. "Okay, you can tell Rebecca, but she's the only one. I mean it, Jake. This is serious."

"No. You? My dearest, most foolhardy brother? You intend to be serious for once?"

Jake clearly had no intention of making this easy on him, but Monty couldn't say he was surprised. Since boyhood, Monty had been the one to make the rules, set the boundaries, infuse his siblings with the dignity they were so sorely lacking. As one who hated rules, boundaries and dignity in equal proportions, Jake relished any opportunity to gain the upper hand.

"You're good with women," Monty said. "Or you used to be, anyway."

"I beg your pardon—I still *am* good with them. Do you have any idea how many married women I flirted with at the Eaglewood gala last night? I had to be in visible raptures over no fewer than a dozen new gowns. Becca signals me the name of the designer from across the room. One blink is Valentino. Two is Badgely Mischka. You don't want to know what she does for Dior."

Monty felt his skin growing hot. "You know what I mean."

"I do, but you make it so easy." Jake paused. "By the way, you should get a call from Winifred sometime this week. She wants to hear all about your foster care initiative."

"*Our* foster care initiative," Monty corrected him, but allowed the subject to drop from there. His brother didn't like to admit how much a part of the Montgomery Foundation he was now, but there was no way Monty could have accomplished as much on his own. Jake was so *good* at people. With one charming smile and a flick of his wrist, he opened doors that had been closed to Monty for years.

"So…you're calling me about lady advice?" Jake asked.

"Well, I wouldn't call her a lady."

"Even better. What can we call her?"

Monty almost said her name out loud. *Georgia. My secret lover. Our family handywoman. A person you used to make fun of for being the only female in a hundred-mile radius you didn't care to see naked.* "A friend."

"That's boring. Pick something else."

"There is nothing else." She wasn't his girlfriend, but she wasn't some random stranger he was willing to walk away from either. In Monty's limited vocabulary, there was no phrase large enough—or small enough—to contain what she meant to him.

"Are you sleeping with her?"

"In a manner of speaking."

"*Should* you be sleeping with her?"

"Probably not."

"Well, now. Things are starting to get interesting." Jake made a humming sound in the back of his throat. "I don't suppose this is why Jenna was called back to the lair to find you a love life, is it?"

"What?" Monty planted his feet more firmly on the ground. "Jenna's coming home?"

"That's what she told me. She wanted to know if it was just her being recruited to help you get over your melancholia, or if it had become a family affair. Are you feeling melancholy, Monty? Do you gnash your teeth and beat at your breast in despair?"

"Fuck!" There was no need to force the profanity out. It came all of its own accord. "This better not have anything to do with Willa Trentwood."

This time, Jake's humming sound became a startled shout of laughter. "Oh, Monty. Please tell me the illicit love affair you called to talk to me about is with Willa Trentwood. She's practically Dad's age. I'll give you anything you want—money, fame, the future rights to my firstborn child."

"I'm not sleeping with Willa," he said, and kicked his desk. He didn't feel much better, so he tried again. "Laugh all you want, Jake, but you're not the one Dad is trying to set up on dates. He thinks I'm pining over Ashleigh."

"Are you pining over her?"

"No." Monty didn't even have to stop and think about it. "I mean, I might have been upset when she first came to tell me she was getting married, but I never *pined*. And now that I have…"

"A fuck buddy?" Jake prompted.

"Is that what it's called?" Monty asked, slightly taken aback. That sounded so much cooler than anything he'd ever had before.

Jake laughed. "Yes, Monty. That's what the kids are saying these days."

Okay, then. He could accept that. "Well, now that I have one of *those*, I don't care what Ashleigh does with her life. Or Willa. Or Jenna, for that matter."

He could hear the sound of clapping on the other end of the extension, slow at first and then picking up speed. He didn't have to see Jake's face to imagine the ironic smile he probably wore to accompany it.

"Very funny," Monty muttered. "It's not as if anything is going to come of it anyway. I think I screwed things up."

"Aha." Jake extended the two syllables into about sixteen. "So you're calling your resident Don Juan for advice?"

"I refuse to refer to you as my resident Don Juan."

"What'd you do wrong?"

Monty still wasn't entirely sure. Meddled where he wasn't wanted and undermined Georgia's authority, yes, but there had been more to her anger than that. If he wasn't mistaken, it was the apology that set her off more than his interference.

That was when he remembered—she didn't like apologies. Or doilies. Or presents. Or hugs. His list of things to avoid was growing quite long.

"It's complicated," he eventually said.

"Bored-her-to-death complicated or acted-like-an-idiot complicated?"

"Acted-like-an-idiot complicated."

"Really? You surprise me. I thought for sure it'd be the first one."

"So far, you're a really terrible Don Juan. I hope you realize that."

Jake laughed. Normally, his brother's ridicule would set Monty's back up, but it had the opposite effect on him now. He didn't care if Jake mocked him as long as it meant he could fix things with Georgia. He'd give almost anything to hear her laugh again.

"It's probably not as dramatic as you're making it out to be," Jake said. "What's the one thing she values most in this world?"

Softball. Tools. Phone sex. Fixing things. "Her family."

"I'm ninety-nine percent convinced you're making this person up. No one likes their family that much."

"Jake."

"Okay, okay." He paused. "In my experience, fuck buddies and families rarely mix, but if you're serious about wooing this non-lady friend of yours, it's best to hit her where you can have the most impact. It'd be a hell of a lot easier if her favorite thing was jewelry or international travel, but you've never been very good at picking women. Maybe you can buy her family the jewelry instead. How do they feel about diamonds?"

Monty smiled at the image of him getting down on

bended knee and offering Adam a pair of earrings. "They probably crush them between their teeth at night."

"Seriously, Monty. Is she even human?"

Monty just smiled. Jake talked big, but his wife was a bit of an oddity herself—and he knew for a fact his brother wouldn't have it any other way. "Thank you for the advice. I'll admit it's not a terrible idea."

"Of course it's not. It came from me." Jake released a soft chuff. "I hate to say this, but I'm a little jealous of Jenna now. It's almost worth coming home to watch if you've got a diamond-crunching fuck buddy and Dad is wooing Willa Trentwood for you."

"Does this mean you'll fly out and save me?"

"Not a chance, brother dear. But I'll be calling in to see how things progress. Some things are too good to pass up."

MONTY HAD NEVER crashed a party in his life.

He'd seen Jake do it countless times in the past, sauntering through the front doors of clubs and ballrooms, sweet-talking his way past bouncers who could crush his head between forefinger and thumb. If he had to pinpoint how Jake managed to pull off his daring entrances, he'd say it was his brother's monumental arrogance. Doors had a way of opening to a man when he acted as though the key to the universe dangled from his fingertips.

But Jake had never faced this particular door before. White. Well-worn. A hook at the top for holiday decorations, a dent at punching level for any number of reasons it was all too easy to imagine. Monty could hear sounds of life going on behind the walls—there must always be life going on behind these walls—and knew his initial assumption had been correct. Wednesday night family dinners at the Lennox house. This aggressive, contradictory, combative family literally couldn't go a week without seeing one another.

And he was going to force his way inside to take part in it.

The way he figured it, there was a fifty percent chance he was making it through that door alive. The other fifty percent held a multitude of colorful deaths.

It's worth it. Without waiting for his damnable caution to kick in with second thoughts and third thoughts and thoughts so far removed they could legally marry, he knocked. As no one in the Lennox family moved slowly or quietly, he could hear the thump of heavy feet and the voices of incredulous men on the other side of the peephole.

"Oh, hell no. You will not believe who's standing on our front porch right now."

"He's got some nerve, showing up uninvited. Does he think he owns the whole fucking town?"

"Ha-ha. I'm almost glad to see him again. Now we can show him what it means to turn on a Lennox."

Monty shifted from one foot to another, unsure what was supposed to happen next. He'd hardly expected a warm welcome, but he hadn't thought they'd leave him out here either. He'd at least hoped to make it inside.

"You know I can hear you, right?" Monty called back. "I'm standing right here."

"Get out of my way, you idiots," a feminine voice interrupted. It wasn't the sexy rumble of Georgia's voice or the somewhat softer timbre that belonged to her mother. He barely had time to puzzle it through when the door swung open to reveal an attractive brunette dressed in a pink sweater set topped with a strand of pearls.

He relaxed almost immediately. Women in sweater sets and pearls were his kind of people.

"I'm so sorry," she said, and shoved her back against the door so hard it caused several grunts to emerge from behind it. "They have no manners and even fewer brain cells. It's not so bad if you can keep them separated, but the second they're all under one roof, it's as if their intellect implodes."

Monty smiled, relaxing further. This woman wasn't just his kind of people. She was an ally.

"I'm Nancy." She extended her hand. "Adam's wife. It's so lovely to finally meet you."

The moment she stopped bracing the door, it gained enough momentum to start swinging back in Monty's direction. He barely had time to stop it with his free hand when Georgia entered the living room.

The sight of her marked the first time in the past decade he'd encountered her in neither coveralls nor robe. While she could hardly be said to have dressed up for dinner with her family, he couldn't help but notice how different she looked—how much softer and more approachable. Simple jean shorts showcased her legs and made the most out of her athletic form. An oversized maroon softball jersey and tennis shoes gave her a relaxed, youthful appearance. And her hair was pulled back in the ponytail she never went without. While he could have enjoyed the sight of her like that—at home in her skin and around her family—for hours, he'd have been lying to say that he was drawn to anything but the expression on her face. It held more surprise than anger, more joy than pain.

Whatever else he might read into the way she stormed

across the room to join her brothers behind the door, he knew, in that moment, she didn't hate him.

Non-hatred was good. In his world, non-hatred was practically love.

"Adam-Charlie-Danny-Georgia." Mrs. Lennox said their names in one breath and with a well-practiced air. "If you don't get out from behind that door and offer our guest something to drink, I won't hesitate to make you eat at the kids' table tonight."

The sudden lack of pressure pitched Nancy into Monty's arms. She crushed the flowers he'd brought against his chest, filling his nostrils with the scent of bluebells, and for a horrified second while he righted the pair of them, he thought he was about to be accused of accosting Adam's wife on top of everything else. But Nancy brought her lips to his ear and whispered, "Don't worry— I'll get you to neutral ground. Just play along."

Play along with what? he wanted to ask, but Nancy released a howl and sank to her knees, clutching her wrist as though she were in pain. Since her wrist had been perfectly fine two seconds ago, he felt only a mild fear as Adam dashed to her side.

"Oh, hell, Nan. Did we hurt you?" He sank to his knees. "You weren't supposed to get in the way. We had him right where we wanted him."

"I'm okay," she said, her voice small. She looked up at Monty and winked, her oversized brown eyes holding nothing but laughter. He stepped back to allow her and Adam a wide berth. "It's nothing. I may need some ice, that's all."

The other three siblings emerged, looking sheepish and guilty—which Monty was sure was the point. He had no idea whether to applaud Nancy or be horrified at the lengths she had to go to stop a physical brawl with this crowd. She'd married into this family on purpose?

"We didn't mean it, Nancy." Charlie rubbed the back of his neck in concern. "It was only a bit of fun."

"I'll get the ice," Danny offered.

Monty waited to hear what Georgia would say, but she watched Nancy with less concern and more amusement. When she glanced up to meet Monty's eye with a yellow-ringed twinkle, he realized this kind of antic was probably common.

In times of extreme physical violence, feign an injury. Somehow, he thought that might not work as well for him as it did for the delicately mischievous woman in pearls.

"Nancy has weak wrists," Georgia supplied as her sister-in-law was led carefully to the couch. "And ankles. And head—the slightest bit of bickering gives her a migraine. It's funny how her pain tolerance comes and goes. She gave birth two times with no anesthetic, and I once saw her take a baseball to the eye without so much as a whimper."

Monty's eyes widened in alarm. "Did one of *you* throw the baseball at her?"

Georgia laughed, unable to repress her inexplicable feeling of joy any longer. "No, we're not that bad. It was at Adam's lawyer league. A corporate defense attorney at a rival firm did it. You should have seen Adam demolish him in court the next week."

Monty shook his head, but Georgia could tell he wasn't nearly as horrified by her family as he let on. She'd seen people be horrified by her family before. She'd seen people be horrified by her family so often she'd lost track. Sometimes, they pulled a Carl and ran out the door as fast as they could. Other times, they remembered a last-minute appointment or a grandmother on her deathbed. Still others went to the bathroom and never returned.

Not one had ever stood on the other side of the door and pushed back.

Until now.

"These were for you." Monty held out a sadly crushed bouquet of flowers. They were a kind of bluish purple, probably pretty once. Nancy might even know what they were called. "Or, if you weren't speaking to me, I was going to give them to your mom."

"That was sweet of you," her mom said firmly, coming forward to take them. "Wasn't that sweet of him, Georgia?"

"Yes, ma'am. Very sweet."

"It's not a big deal," Monty said. "You can throw them out."

"Nonsense. I'm going to put them in a vase on the center of the table for dinner. They'll serve as a reminder about what happens when good manners enter this household."

Monty released a sound that had equal chances of being a laugh or a choke.

"I hope you're planning on joining us for dinner, John. There's plenty to go around, and we'd love to have you."

"Oh, please say you'll stay," Nancy called from her position on the couch. She added a groan and clutched her wrist when Adam opened his mouth to contradict her. If that injury wasn't going to be milked all night as a means of passive-aggressive manipulation, Georgia would eat those flowers. "It'll be lovely having the extra company for a change. I hate being the only non-Lennox around here."

"You're a Lennox," Adam said fiercely.

"You know what I mean."

"You're a Lennox," Charlie and Danny echoed.

"Then it's settled," her mom said, and bustled off into the kitchen before anyone could argue with her.

The sound Monty released this time was one hundred percent a laugh, and it reminded Georgia that she was still angry with this man. If anything, the fact that he'd showed up at her mom's house like this, uninvited and bearing apology plants, was further proof of how justified her anger the other day was. The whole point of having a secret lover who worked a zillion hours a week was that he wasn't supposed to intrude on workplace issues or family drama. He could rescue her from a zombie invasion or shark attack, should the need arise, but not from real life.

Zombie invasions weren't real. Shark attacks were pretend. They were safe and neutral territory, because once the danger subsided and the lights came back on, she could go back to being herself again. Georgia Lennox. One of four, beloved in her family, able to fight and climb and scrap as well as any boy, and don't you forget it.

But Monty was ruining things. Monty was swinging his handsome millionaire might and blurring the lines between fantasy and reality.

"Laugh all you want, but she means it about the flowers." Georgia affixed a frown on her lips. "We'll probably each have a broken petal arranged on our plate as a warning. I think she learned a lot of her parenting techniques from *The Godfather*."

He wasn't dismayed. "I like her."

"That's because you don't believe me about the cautionary garnish."

"But why would I get one? I didn't do anything wrong."

"Are you sure about that?"

Monty's face fell as her meaning settled in. "Can we go somewhere more private to talk?"

Oh, hell. She couldn't let him derail her with chivalry and that sad-eyed look. She needed to throw him to the Testosterone Trio, who were quickly catching on that Nancy was faking her injury. As experience was proving, Georgia was worthless when it came to setting up walls to protect herself against this man, but her brothers could build faster than any crew she'd ever overseen. They'd have the Great Wall of China erected by the time the salad course rolled around.

"No."

"It doesn't have to take long. You dismissed me so summarily on Saturday, I didn't get a chance—"

"No." Georgia crossed her arms and stepped back, forcing distance between their bodies. She didn't regret asking him to leave on Saturday, and if she were given an opportunity to do the day over, she'd make the exact same choices. Distance had been necessary for her to regather and regroup, but if he kept looking at her like that—like a puppy she'd kicked and then banished to the cold—she might do something terrible like forgive him.

Monty's lips turned down even more, but the flash of her two nieces running by saved her from saying anything. She reached down and grabbed each one by the collar to halt their forward progression.

"Emma, Abby—you're just in time. I'd like you to meet my friend Monty."

Monty's look of pain flew immediately to panic, and Georgia had to halt the laugh that filled her throat. At eight and six and dressed in matching pink dresses, Adam's daughters looked like cardboard angel cutouts who'd drifted down from heaven to play with rainbows and kittens. In reality, they had no use for rainbows or kittens or any other cliché that might prance across a young girl's imagination. They had Adam's ruthless cruelty and Nancy's ability to manipulate any situation.

Georgia adored them.

"Is he going to work?" Emma asked, her big brown eyes narrowed in suspicion.

"No. He's joining us for dinner."

"Is he the president?"

"No. Not of a country, anyway."

"He looks like the president."

Monty squatted to face Emma—the older of the two and by far the most outspoken. "Thank you. I think that's a very nice compliment."

"Whatever." Emma shrugged. "But you should probably know that presidents lie."

Georgia laughed at the incredulous look Monty shot her way. "She's precocious. We're very proud." She gestured at where the girls had come in. "Why don't you two show my friend your doll demolition factory? Maybe he can help you take off the heads of those tricky ones you were telling me about."

"Oh, no, you don't." Her mom emerged from the kitchen to come to Monty's rescue. "I'm taking him in here to help me finish dinner."

"But, Mom—" Georgia began, but she caught the martial look in her mother's eye and stopped. She knew that look. She respected that look.

"Thank you, Mrs. Lennox," Monty said politely. "I'd love to help."

Vanquished by good manners, Georgia had no choice but to let him go. And Abby and Emma, buoyed by the

idea of finally getting to the stuffing of the vintage Cab-
bage Patch Dolls, dragged Georgia off to the beheading
in his stead.

THE COMFORTING SMELLS of pasta and garlic bread as-
sailed Monty's nose as he followed Georgia's mother
into the kitchen. Gluten had been all but banned up at
the Manor—his stepmother, Serena, was a health nut
of the highest order—and he could practically hear his
stomach rumbling at the prospect of filling up with de-
liciously bland carbohydrates for once.

"I don't really need much in the way of help," Mrs.
Lennox said as soon as he stepped into the green-tiled
kitchen, worn from use and somehow more comforting
than all the rooms in his own house combined. "You can
stir if you want to, but I won't tell anyone if you take a
seat and relax."

"Do I look that tense?"

"Yes. You do." She turned to him with a smile. Although she was considerably shorter than her children,
leading Monty to wonder just how tall her husband must
have been, he could see pieces of them in her. The yellow ring around the eyes, the unruly hair, a certain set
around the mouth that dared anyone to mess with her.
And while she had a softer, more feminine look than her
daughter—she had jewelry and makeup on, for one—he
found he preferred Georgia's transformative smile and
belligerent air.

He preferred them so much he wasn't sure what to do
about it. Jake's idea of getting in here and making nice
with the family was a great first step, but it was just that.
A step. Short of cutting himself open with one of the but-

ter knives set out in front of him, he wasn't sure how to get these people to like him.

He didn't know how to get *anyone* to like him. That was the problem. He could fix Georgia's staffing issues in under an hour flat—and had almost made the call to do it—but it wasn't what she wanted. Nor did she want what all the other women in his life had asked for, which was for him to put down the spreadsheet and mingle at cocktail parties.

Those two things were all he knew. Those two things were all he had to offer.

"Don't worry about it," Mrs. Lennox said, and dropped a plate of carrot sticks in front of him. He took one out of politeness and began munching. "They can be a bit much, those four. They sometimes forget that they're grown adults and not a band of thugs living out of a tree fort."

And then she turned to the kitchen counter, humming to herself as she grated a bowl of parmesan cheese.

His teeth crunching the carrots sounded overloud to his ears, but he found himself relaxing despite the strangeness of the situation. While she was alive, his own mother had never picked up a fork unless she was eating, and he wouldn't have parked in the kitchen to keep her company if she *had* cooked, but he liked to think that he could still participate in these traditional rituals.

You *could* teach an old dog new tricks. The training period took longer, that was all.

"So, you're the oldest one, right?" Mrs. Lennox asked after a few minutes of companionable silence.

"The oldest in my family? Yes."

"The one who does all the nonprofit stuff? You run the Montgomery Foundation?"

Monty nodded before realizing she couldn't see him.

Aware that she was making an effort to draw him out, he cleared his throat and said, "Among other things, yes. I'd prefer to focus solely on the foundation, but I find my time increasingly taken up with hotel duties. It's been hard trying to strike a balance between what I want to do and what I have to do."

He thought maybe he'd bored her with details—that a simple yes or no had been all she wanted—but she nodded. "Ah. That makes sense."

"It does?"

Mrs. Lennox turned to face him, her smile warm. "I was curious, at first, what it was she might see in you, but I'm starting to understand. You two have quite a lot in common."

"We do?" He was beginning to sound like an unintelligent parrot, so he tried again. "I mean, I realize we have quite a few similarities, but I wasn't sure anyone else saw it. She takes her Homeward Bound duties seriously."

"Very."

"And she doesn't like to ask for help."

"Not if she can possibly avoid it."

"And, uh…" He toyed with a carrot stick. "She doesn't make things easy on a man. If he's interested in her romantically, I mean."

If he was afraid he'd gone too far with that statement, putting into words thoughts best kept to his own counsel, Mrs. Lennox swept away all doubts with her pearly laugh. "That's a nicely phrased way to put it, and I applaud your discretion, but there's no need to tiptoe around me. I'm not the one you need to impress."

"But the only thing Georgia is impressed by is arm wrestling," he said, sounding as petulant as he felt. "I refuse to arm wrestle her for her affection."

"Oh, you dear, sweet man—she's not the one you need to impress either."

Now he was confused. "She's not?"

Mrs. Lennox wiped her hands on her apron and handed him the block of cheese. He accepted wordlessly, picking up the grating where she left off. "It's my own fault, really, but you have to understand what it was like for them as kids. Their father was gone, I was working long hours—you know how it is—and they were left to fend for themselves most of the time."

"They seem close."

"They're not close. They're downright feral." She laughed and showed him how to better angle the cheese grater. "I find it's easiest to imagine them as a pack of wolves. They hunt together, defend their territory together, kill together—they're an all-or-nothing deal, and woe to the outsider who tries to lure one of them away."

He stopped his motions. "I'm not trying to lure her anywhere."

"*I* know that," she said with a smile. "But you have your work cut out for you getting them to see it. They're wolves, John. And as much as I love them, I'm afraid they're not particularly gentle ones."

"You don't have to do this." Georgia stood at the base of the elm in the backyard, a towering beast of a tree that had been earmarked for city removal a decade ago. Every few years like clockwork, an engineer would notice how close it was growing to the power lines and put in a work order for it to be cut down. And every few years like clockwork, Danny hacked into the system and changed the order for a limb trimming only.

They couldn't let the city take Old Hardwood. Old

Hardwood was a legend. Old Hardwood would remain standing until one of them managed to make it all the way to the top to extricate the Frisbee that had been lodged there some twenty-two years ago.

"I mean it, Monty." She broke the touch barrier she'd imposed over dinner and placed a hand on his arm. "They're trying to get you to kill yourself. It's their goal. Murder without all those nasty legal implications."

He smiled, apparently undismayed at the idea of falling from a height likely to kill, paralyze or otherwise maim him.

It was happening again. The Testosterone Trio was bringing out all the whimsical qualities in Monty—the daring and the fun, the determination to win, that latent dormancy she'd *thought* was some kind of sexual potency, but was actually a juvenile need to pee into the snow farther than the other boys.

"Are you worried about me, Georgia?"

"Yes." She refused to be sucked into that smile. That smile might have won over her mom and Nancy, made Charlie unbend enough to talk about complex chemical compounds, but it wasn't going to work on her. He'd actually kept his knife in his right hand the entire time they ate dinner, acting like some kind of English lord while the rest of them shoveled the food in. She couldn't stand up to his fancy English lord eating. She barely knew how to hold a fork. "The same way I'd be worried about any human being facing his demise."

"Since when are you such a chickenshit, Georgia?" Danny came to stand beside them, staring up at the tree. "Damn. I don't remember it being so high up there."

"Oh, come on. It's not that high—" Adam joined them and let out a low whistle. "Did we get shorter? That's sixty feet if it's an inch. Can you even climb trees, Montgomery? Did they teach that at the fancy Swiss boarding school you went to?"

Monty stared at him. "I didn't go to boarding school."

"See what I mean? You can't even do being rich right."

Monty didn't respond, just shrugged out of his suit jacket before handing it off to Georgia. He rolled his shoulders and worked his hands, for all intents and purposes a man preparing for battle.

"This is ridiculous." Georgia had to keep trying. She didn't like Monty meddling in her work stuff—and sure as hell didn't need him to gaze soulfully in her eyes and promise to make men respect her—but she didn't want his blood on her hands either. She'd *really* be out a valuable client then. "You don't have to climb a tree to prove yourself. They were just joking when they dared you to take the Old Hardwood challenge."

"I know. But I saw my brother do something similar last year, and it worked out really well for him." He paused and examined the tree. "He only broke one rib."

That was it. Georgia tossed Monty's jacket to the side and placed her hand in the middle of his chest, doing her best to ignore the firm beat of his heart and the way the hard-packed muscle of his torso elicited indecent thoughts about the tree falling on the house and trapping them both.

"Fine. You win. But if you insist on doing this, I'm invoking Ladies First."

"What? Georgia—no," Danny said.

"You hate Ladies First." Adam pushed his way forward. "You said it makes a mockery of your ovaries."

"Why are we talking about Georgia's ovaries?" Charlie piped up from the rear.

"She's going to try to get the Frisbee so her man friend doesn't hurt himself." Adam scowled. "But she's not doing it. It's too dangerous."

"Oh, nice." Georgia had to bite her lip to keep from smiling. Her brothers were as easy to read as cue cards. "It's not too dangerous for Monty to go up and try, but it's too dangerous for me. What are you trying to say? He's better than me? Stronger?"

"Goddammit." Adam turned to Monty with a finger out. "This is your fault, Montgomery."

"What?" Monty shook his head as if clearing it. "I'm still stuck on the Ladies First thing. You guys seem to make up a lot of arbitrary rules."

This time Georgia had to bite her tongue to keep from laughing. Arbitrary rules were pretty much a Lennox staple. "It's a real thing. If there's ever a competition, the lady gets the option to draw first blood. It's only polite."

"Really?"

Charlie shrugged. "Nancy made us incorporate it a few years back. She's kind of a sore loser about things like this."

"Watch yourself, Charles," Adam warned.

Monty was beginning to understand what Mrs. Lennox meant when she said these four were part of a wolf pack. He was also beginning to understand what Nancy said about the collective intelligence level plummeting when they were in proximity. Taken alone, he was fairly sure each and every one of them was a sane, somewhat ordinary creature capable of rational thought—himself included. But something about the spark of challenge in the air had him forgetting everything except a desire to make his way up that tree and fetch that stupid Frisbee.

They weren't the only ones with canine instincts.

"So, Georgia gets to try first, and then me." Monty stepped back to allow her the playing field. "That's fair."

"Thank you, Monty," Georgia said with a beaming smile he lapped up like honey. Half the reason he was doing this at all was because of all the attention she was giving him. She'd done a decent job of ignoring him through the meal, but ever since talk turned to the post-dinner entertainment, she'd been gradually thawing toward him.

Climbing a tree was nothing. He'd scale Mount Everest if it meant he had another chance.

"For fuck's sake, Montgomery—what's the matter with you?" Adam planted himself in front of the tree, arms crossed. "Georgia, you can't go up there and you know it."

"Don't you remember?" Danny said. "You broke your wrist the last time you tried."

"Scaphoid?" Monty guessed.

"It doesn't feel like any rain is coming," Georgia confirmed, meeting his eyes with a sparkle. "Now get out of my way, Adam. I'm about to bring down Old Hardwood. God, victory is going to taste so good."

"If you want up, you have to go through me first. You're a grown-ass woman, not a monkey. Montgomery, I'll give you one more chance to back me up here."

Oh, no. He wasn't falling for that again. He knew what kind of things happened when he tried to tell Georgia what to do. He might want to throw his body over hers and force her to the ground to prevent her from breaking her neck, but Georgia wouldn't appreciate him for it. He'd known, that first time she opened her legs to him, that gaining her respect would be a tricky, upward path.

He just hadn't realized how literal that upward path would be.

"Not a chance, Lennox," he replied. "I know when I'm being led to the gallows."

Adam pushed off from the tree and stalked a few paces away, his movements jerky. "May I have a word, if you please?"

Monty looked to Georgia in alarm, but she merely shrugged and started stretching. Although her stretches were in and of themselves worthy of his attention, a dance of flexibility and strength he could watch for hours, curiosity compelled him to hear what Adam had to say.

"I'm not sure what it is you want me to do," he said as he approached. "You're the ones who told me to back off."

"From telling her how to do her job," Adam said, biting the words off. "Not from trying to kill herself to flirt with you."

"Flirting? Is that what she's doing?" He glanced back at the tree, where Georgia was circling, looking for a foothold. That didn't look like any flirtation he'd ever encountered.

Adam's scowl only deepened. "I'm going to tell you something, but I don't want you to think it means I approve of you coming here and making nice with my wife and kids, okay?"

In any other man, that could be construed as an olive branch. In this man, it could be construed as an olive branch about to knock him unconscious. "O-kay."

"She likes you. She likes you enough to invite you to her job site, to forgive you for fucking up on said job site and to allow you to break bread with us. You follow?"

Not really, but he did feel a spreading warmth in the region of his chest. She liked him?

"As her brothers, we're allowed a very small amount of control in her life. We can oust the scumbags she dates and back her up when the scumbags don't get the hint the first time around—" Monty received a very pointed stare for that one, "—but our influence stops there."

Monty still didn't follow.

Adam swore under his breath. "I see you're back to being a stone wall. She'll listen to you, okay? I don't like it, and I sure as shit don't understand it, but there it is. You win."

Monty blinked, and blinked again, and blinked once more for good measure. "You want me to prevent her from climbing that tree?"

"Yes."

"Because I'm the only one who can?"

"Yes." Through his teeth this time. "Do you want me to have it notarized, Montgomery? Shit—just go stop her, will you?"

Monty did. Or rather, he attempted to, his feet propelled by the cloud he walked on, his thoughts still somewhat hazy. Had he broken through the Testosterone Trio barrier at last?

"Hey, Georgia?" he called. She was about ten feet up already, her face screwed up in concentration as she searched for a handhold.

"What? Did he convince you I'm likely to fall into a maidenly swoon and come crashing down? Don't listen to him—he's a lawyer, remember? He lies."

Monty hoped not. He wasn't sure he'd heard any words more welcome than the ones Adam had oh-so-begrudgingly imparted. "I won't do it if you don't."

"What?" Her gaze turned sharply his way.

"If you come down and promise not to kill yourself, I promise not to make the attempt either."

"Oh." She dropped her hand from a large knot in the side of the tree. "Okay, then."

And that was it. With a quick and alarmingly agile movement, she let go of the tree and came leaping down in a neat crouch near Monty's feet. In that moment, he almost regretted calling her back. She probably could have made it.

"Should we shake on it?" she asked, and extended her hand. "No more using Old Hardwood to woo my brothers?"

"I wasn't wooing your brothers," he said, but he took her hand in his own. Her touch was still rough and callused—and this time covered in splinters of bark—but he wasn't sure he'd ever felt a more welcome palm against his. There was forgiveness in that handshake. And desire. And a feeling of expansion in his chest that went on for miles.

"Fine." Her voice was low, and he knew she felt it too. "No more using Old Hardwood to woo me."

"I wasn't wooing you either." Even though he knew her entire family was watching—either in the backyard or through the kitchen window where Nancy was washing the dinner dishes—he brought her hand to his lips and dropped a slow and careful kiss on the surface.

Hand kissing, it turned out, was still good. Hand kissing was still great.

"If I was wooing you, I'd try much harder than that tree."

"Harder?" she gasped.

"As hard as you can stand," he said. And didn't falter over the words once.

FOURTEEN

"WHAT ARE YOU doing out here?"

Monty whirled from his contemplation of the tree in his family's orchard, so startled he dropped the rope he'd borrowed from the gardener's shed. "Oh, hi, Dad. I didn't expect to see you out here so early."

His dad consulted his watch, as if the answers to his son's lapse into lunacy might be hiding behind the solid gold Roman numerals. "I can't imagine you expected to see anyone at all. It's six in the morning. Why are you out here with a lasso?"

Monty picked up his rope and twirled it, laughing at the comparison. It *was* kind of like a lasso, now that he thought about it—if cowboys roped Frisbees in their spare time. "I was trying to figure out how difficult it would be to throw this rope to the top of a sixty-foot tree. The answer, in case you were wondering, is very."

"Are you sure you're feeling all right?"

"I've never been better," he said truthfully, and tossed the rope again. It went all of twenty feet before tangling in a branch. "Fuck. I'm going to have to find a better way. Do you know how high those remote-controlled helicopters can go?"

His dad stared at him.

"I doubt it'd have the capacity to lift anything anyway. Maybe it could just jar it?" Monty resumed his perusal of the tree. Even though it wasn't quite as tall as the one in Georgia's backyard, it seemed the closest approximation. There had to be an alternate way up there.

"It's Saturday," his dad stated.

"Yes, it is."

"You're not working?"

Monty looked at him in some surprise. "We already agreed I'm taking weekends off this month."

He'd have preferred to be suiting up to join Georgia and her brothers at the build site this morning, but even though he'd been forgiven for his interference, Georgia had announced with absolute conviction that he was banned from the premises until further notice. The banishment hurt—it hurt a lot more than he cared to admit—but he wasn't about to cross her will.

Her will was wrong. Her will was stubborn and contradictory and tied into some deep-seated need to prove herself by tackling unnecessary challenges. But her will was also one of his favorite parts about her. He was going to have to find some other way to get her to trust him again.

So far, all he had was this rope.

"Yes, we did agree to that—so you could help Georgia with her project." His dad spoke slowly and with an emphasis on each syllable. "Does Georgia's project need you to lasso a tree?"

Monty fell into a burst of laughter—it was too much, the heavy-handed concern, the cautious way he was being watched out of the corner of his father's eyes. If he wasn't careful, the next date he got set up on would be with a psychotherapist. "What Georgia's project needs is a wide-scale infusion of skilled labor, but I'm not brave enough to make the offer. You go ahead if you think you'll have better success, but don't say I didn't warn you."

His dad frowned. "I did offer."

"You did?"

"She turned me down."

Monty laughed again, finding the sound easier with each passing moment. It had been a long time since he'd dared to be amused at his father's expense. Maybe years. Possibly a lifetime. "Why am I not surprised by that?"

His dad looked as if he wanted to say more, but he firmed his lips in a line. "You really plan to spend your whole day off playing outside?"

Monty's amusement fled, and he was back to feeling eleven years old again, squirming under the steely gaze of a man who demanded nothing less than his soul. "Yes, Dad. That's exactly what I plan. I'm going to lasso trees and catch tadpoles in the pond and maybe ride my bike to the store later so I can steal a pack of gum. Do you have a problem with that?"

The iron in his voice dared his dad to contradict him. There was no way he could know Monty was bluffing—that there was an annual report sitting on his desk he intended to go over until his eyes bled, or that he'd promised Thomas he'd confirm his meeting with the Connecticut Board of Regents—and he had no intention of offering enlightenment. This automaton wasn't done working, but he was done following the orders programmed into him since birth.

"If you're looking for plans this evening, I could always call up—"

"No." His hands tightened on the coil of rope. "No more of this. I'm sorry my life choices bring you so much displeasure, but I'm not going to have dinner with Willa. I also found my own date for Ashleigh's wedding, and I'm not going to keep having this discussion with you.

Now if you'll excuse me, I need to find an alternate route to the top of that tree, and then I have a long day of juvenile misbehavior ahead of me."

He could tell his dad wanted to say something—something that would crush Monty under the weight of expectation and obligation, something so he would remain exactly where he'd been for the past thirty-five years of his life. He settled for "You found a date for Ashleigh's wedding?" instead, his tone disbelieving enough to border on outrage. Monty might as well have expressed an interest in necromancy.

"Yes," he said, and resumed his attentions skyward. "She's younger than me, not in mourning for her deceased husband, unlikely to bring any financial prosperity to your future business plans, and quite possibly my favorite person in the whole world."

Not even his dad dared argue with that.

HOURS HAD PASSED since the rest of the crew went home for the day, but Georgia lingered, finding it difficult to walk away from the mounting to-do list in her head. She blamed visions of recessed lighting and drawer pulls for why it took her so long to realize she was being watched by a tall, dark figure near her truck, almost indistinguishable in the twilight air.

She didn't panic, as instinct urged. Palming her trusty hammer instead, she did what any well-armed woman would do alone and at dusk. She strode forward and threatened bodily harm.

"Monty! What are you doing here?" She stopped as soon as she recognized the glint of auburn at the top of his head. That glint was everywhere lately—there were a surprising amount of redheads in this world, once you started to look for them. "I thought I banned you from crossing this threshold."

"You did."

Not very effectively, it would seem. "Do you understand what being banned means?"

"It means I'm exiled. Prohibited. Unwanted." He didn't move. "I think I understand that word better than anyone, Georgia. Don't worry. I promise not to touch anything."

Even me? she wanted to ask, but it wasn't the right moment for flirtation. She and flirtation had always enjoyed a somewhat questionable relationship, but today was worse than usual. Not only was she covered in residual fertilizer from the lawn spray they'd put down earlier, but Monty's words had her stopping in her tracks. Making him feel unwanted had never been her intention, and guilt tore through her for not remembering how keenly he felt his outsider status.

She also felt a swirl of annoyance. She wasn't supposed to feel guilty for this man, what with his incredible looks and huge bank account and high-handed business tactics. He had everything a human being could possibly want, and was therefore untouchable. That was the fantasy, right? A god from up high, gilded in his perfection, his personality a blank slate she could fill in on her own?

Unfortunately, Monty was turning out to be none of those things. He was real and unsure and awkward. He was a man who looked out at the world and wondered just what it was everyone else seemed to know that he didn't.

Goddammit. She blamed the hugs for the weakness in her heart and in her knees. Hugs opened the doors to all kinds of emotional overflow. And now it was flowing all over the place, mucking up her job site and making her question everything.

"I know we didn't make any concrete plans for to-night." He spoke before she had a chance to formulate a response that wasn't a complete sacrifice of everything she was. "And I'm not here to interfere with your work, but I was hoping you might be able to spare me a few hours."

She ignored the way her heart went into overdrive—at how desperately she wanted to launch herself into his arms and allow him to interfere in anything and every-thing he wanted—and gripped her hammer tighter in-stead. It was better this way. Monty might be able to turn her into a swooning, flighty bit of fluff with the touch of his lips on her fingers, and he might possess the ability to hug her into submission, but she still retained a *few* of her faculties.

"That depends on what you intend to do with my hours," she said carefully. "If you want a hug, I should probably warn you I smell like fish. It's the seaweed in the fertilizer we sprayed. It's an organic brand."

"I want a lot more than a hug, if you're up for it."

Faculties. She had faculties, dammit. "But I smell like a mermaid. Did you miss that part?"

His laughter was silent, but she could tell from the way her truck shook at his back that it was real. "I can wait until you shower, Georgia. Unless you *want* to do a mermaid thing, in which case I'll go roll around in the yard until we match."

Her faculties slipped even more, leaving a gaping hole behind. "How do I know you aren't trying to lure me away on false pretenses?"

His shoulders came down. "Is this a bad time? I know you said you were busy, but I thought…"

"No!"

He blinked.

"I mean, yes. Of course yes." She sighed, powerless against the desire she felt for this man—not just in a sexual way, but for the pleasure of his company, period. "No, it's not a bad time. Yes, I'd love to play mermaids with you. I wasn't expecting you, that's all."

"That's okay. I wasn't expecting me either."

His words made no sense either in context or out of it, but she nodded all the same. Truth be told, she could really use one of his strong hugs right about now. Meecham's visit to the site last week had left a rain cloud overhead, and not even the regular raillery of her crew had been enough to dispel it. Emotions, self-doubt, girlish dreams…the floodgates had been opened, and now she was drowning.

And she didn't even have time to grab one last gulp of air before she went under, because Monty chose that moment to stride forward and kiss her. His mouth was as desperate and grasping as she felt inside, pieces of him fitting into the hollows of her heart as if they belonged there.

"Should I drive, or did you want to follow me?" he asked, pulling away only to press his forehead gently against hers.

"Follow you where?" Off the nearest cliff? It might already be too late.

"It's a surprise."

"I thought we already discussed how I feel about surprises."

"You can put me in a cast if you don't like this one—I promise."

"I'll put you in a cast anyway. I'm serious, Monty. You have to tell me."

He didn't look pleased at the idea, but she stood firm. Hugs she could accept with relative grace. Sex was the gift that kept on giving. But this man was capable of too much—had too many resources at his disposal—for her to feel comfortable going in blind.

"I thought it might be easier for you if we had sex somewhere new this time. Somewhere with no negative associations."

Oh.

Okay. That was considerate of him, actually. She'd never thought of location as being part of the problem before. "As long as it isn't anywhere near the Manor, I think I'm okay. My truck can be quite roomy."

Monty looked back at the cab of her Ford with only mild horror. "Uh, maybe some other time? For tonight, I thought we might try something more upscale."

Georgia stopped. "How upscale?"

"Five stars? Recognized by *Upmarket Traveler* as a 'feast for all the senses'?"

"Oh, no." Georgia put her hands up and backed away. "No, no, no. You're not taking me there. Anywhere but there."

Her hesitance only seemed to infuse a childlike joy into his smile. She mistrusted that joy. She mistrusted any joy beamed so directly her way. "But, Georgia—if I can't take my secret lover to my own hotel, what's the point of having one?"

She wasn't falling for it. "The secret lover or the hotel?"

He flashed his teeth. "Both."

THE HARTFORD MONTLUXE afforded an average man the perfect opportunity to woo a woman. From the marbled lobby on the bottom floor to the penthouse at the top, everything about the hotel was designed for romance. Luxury linens, gleaming mirrors, discreetly uninterested staff members who could satisfy any whims that fell within legal confines—all of it could be acquired for a price.

For a not-so-average man—say, the next in line to inherit the entire chain of hotels—it was red carpet treatment from the get-go. Monty had no more ushered Georgia through the revolving doors, his hand clamped firmly over hers so she couldn't run away, than the concierge began trying to ply them with champagne and compliments.

"No, no—we don't want the penthouse," he said for what had to be the tenth time. "A regular room is all we require. Take my card, run it through your system and charge us for every tiny bottle of vodka that disappears from the en-suite bar."

"But, Mr. Montgomery, I'm not authorized to do that."

He looked to Georgia with an apologetic wince. The last thing he wanted to do was scare her away with all of this bowing and scraping—honestly, unless you counted his philanthropic efforts or the other day at the build site, he rarely took advantage of his family name or money—but the yellow ring in her eyes was alit with laughter.

"What if I get the room?" She reached into her pocket to extract a wallet made of Velcro and duct tape. "Would that simplify things?"

She'd squirmed uncomfortably as they came in through the reflective doors, wrinkling her nose at her own appearance beside his. She'd almost made a break for it when he was recognized by several bellhops coming in. But this—him struggling to make the front clerk understand the most basic of requests—had her feeling perfectly at ease.

"I'm not supposed to charge any members of the family." The desk clerk looked ready to cry, but at Monty's attempt at a smile, she gulped and nodded once. "Maybe I can pretend I didn't see him come in with you?"

"Excellent." Georgia tapped a credit card against the marble countertop. "Put the room under my name and on my card, but lock access to the minibar, if you please. I'm not made of money."

Monty laughed, which only seemed to cast the desk clerk further into confusion. "I had no idea it would be so difficult to whisk a woman away for a night of passion. They make it look so easy in the movies."

"Monty," Georgia said, a threat in her voice. It was the "night of passion" bit that did it.

To avoid another attempt at escape, he grabbed her hand and brought it to his lips, loving how the rough texture of her hand was so at odds with the rest of her. He loved even more how powerless she was against that tiny display of affection, rendering him powerful in ways he'd never known existed. It didn't matter that she was still halfway angry with him, or that the Montluxe was the last place she wanted to be seen with him. When he pressed a single kiss on the surface of her hand, he somehow managed to say the thousands of words lodged in his throat.

And she somehow managed to hear them.

"I can't believe you conned me into taking you to the most expensive hotel in Connecticut," she muttered, though her cheeks flushed as he finally relinquished his grip. He would have kept her fingers entwined in his, but the clerk finished processing their request and handed

Georgia the key card. "I take it you must not do this very often."

"Lure a woman upstairs?" he said. "Never."

"Not even when you were younger?" She led the way to the elevators, and he was more than happy to let her. She seemed to prefer it this way—paying for the room, calling the shots, ignoring the fact that he could clear everyone out of this entire building with the snap of his fingers.

His wealth obviously made Georgia uncomfortable, and that was okay. It made *him* uncomfortable most of the time. But it existed, and it was a large part of his identity. If he wanted more from Georgia than an occasional stolen hug—and it was becoming clearer and clearer to him that he did—it was time to start introducing her to his other half.

If Monotonous Montgomery hadn't sent her running for the hills, he could only pray Moneyed Montgomery wouldn't either.

"How is it possible for me to be the first woman you've wooed with luxury?" She stepped into the mirror-paneled elevator. "Did you hatch as a responsible, levelheaded human being? If this were my family's hotel, I'd have been living off room service and pillow mints for years."

"You want the truth? I hate these hotels. I always have."

As the doors closed in front of them and the elevator began its ascent, Monty became aware of how wrong Georgia had been when she claimed to smell like a mermaid—she was an incredibly untrustworthy source when it came to this sort of thing. She smelled not of the sea but of the air and sky, of the peaty topsoil that covered the earth where the two met.

He wanted to bury himself in it. In *her*.

"I don't understand," she said, oblivious to the fanciful notions churning inside him. "How can you hate your family's hotels? They're your whole life."

His whole life, reduced to a pile of overpriced bricks. "It's easy," he said. "You know the saying 'you have to spend money to make money'?"

"Yes."

"Well, where I come from, you have to make money to spend money."

They exited the elevator and approached their room's door. Waiting only for Georgia to swipe the key card through, he pushed it open, taking in the familiar sight of a mid-level room in a high-end hotel with a feeling of discomfort. Plush white sofas, curtains that billowed in a nonexistent breeze, a full lounge area before you got to the French doors leading to the bedroom—everything about the six hundred square feet was luxury at its most accessible.

Georgia crossed the threshold slower than him, and he tried to remember that she was seeing it for the first time. The room was probably impressive to anyone who hadn't spent two months working out a deal with the company who supplied their thousand-thread-count sheets.

Unable to prevent himself from touching her for another second, he wrapped his arms around her waist and pulled her close. She tried to yank herself away, but he buried his head in her neck and inhaled the scent of her like a dying man enjoying his last minutes on earth.

That was what she was becoming for him, and at an alarmingly rapid rate. Earth. Stability. A feeling that maybe he wasn't quite as groundless as he'd always thought.

"It looks to me like you have money enough," she murmured.

"There will never be enough."

"What do you mean? I know where you live, Monty. I see what you accomplish. You guys are loaded." She pulled back, her expression puzzled. He loved how her eyes communicated with him even when she didn't intend to—it was the same with her body, stiff and then yielding and then one hundred percent pliable. She might talk big and swagger large, but in these moments of quiet intimacy, she was just Georgia.

Just Georgia.

"Why do you spend so much of your time and energy on Homeward Bound?" he asked, hoping to help her see through the flash and bang of the Montgomery name to what went on underneath. This room was the flash and bang. He cowered in the layers below.

"Because it's my job."

"Yes, but you have a contractor's license. You could be making good money building houses for pay instead of offering your services pro bono and not even getting appreciated for it."

"Don't you dare start with Meecham again."

"I'm not talking about Meecham. I'm talking about you. Why do you do it?"

"Because I can," she said, appearing almost confused at his insistence.

"So can lots of other people, but they don't. What makes you special?"

For all that Georgia prided herself on being an oddity, she frowned in a way that made him think no one had ever asked her that before. She knew she was different, she hid behind her idiosyncrasies as if they were a shield, but she never once considered that those things might make her nothing short of incredible.

"There's nothing special about me—that's why I can do it." Her frown didn't lift. "I don't have a spouse to make demands on my time. I don't have kids to raise. I don't have much in the way of a social life. I don't even have all that high of a cost of living, thanks to my mom, and your dad has helped too—paying me well and allowing me the flexibility to come and go."

Monty nodded, hearing substantially more in that answer than she was willing to say out loud. He heard it because it was what echoed inside his own heart, day after long, tedious day. She volunteered—not because she felt called to it or because she enjoyed the elation that came from making a real difference in people's lives, but because helping others wasn't even a question.

"It's the same for me, but on a bigger scale," he said. "I don't have the wife or kids, my personal needs are few and I'm in a unique position where I can actually do something worthwhile."

She didn't respond, and any alarm he felt at having put her off dissolved when he realized she was waiting for him to finish. Without drawing attention to his deficiency, without passing judgment, she stood there and allowed him a chance to pull his thoughts into a coherent sentence.

He wasn't sure anyone had done that for him before.

"Unfortunately, my deal with my father is a bit trickier than yours," he continued after a pause. "If I want to make the Montgomery Foundation succeed, then I have to make the Montgomery hotels succeed first. As long as I help his hotels thrive, he'll make sure the money is always there for the projects I care about."

Sometimes, it felt like a deal he'd made with the devil rather than his parent. Not that it mattered. The contracts were signed either way.

Since talking about his dad was the last thing he'd had in mind in bringing Georgia here tonight, he used her momentary distraction to tug at the buttons along the front of her coveralls. She noticed and wrinkled her nose before swatting his hands away.

"Ew, Monty. I'm serious about the shower. I can't feel relaxed enough to have sex if there are grass seeds under my fingernails. It was bad enough walking through the lobby with you. People were staring. And fleeing."

"Nobody fled."

"They fled. They just did it discreetly so you wouldn't be offended."

He thought for sure she was exaggerating, but something about the firm set of her lips had him reconsidering. He tugged on her belt loop to pull her pelvis flush against his own. "So we'll take a shower."

She backed away, her head shaking a distinct and resolute *no*.

"Did I say it wrong?" He'd tried to make it sound sexy, but maybe he'd gone too far. *Dammit*—he never did get any advice from Jake on how to make these things come out easier. "We had such a good time in the fake shower, I thought it might be fun to try—"

"No way." She was still moving backward, close enough now to the bathroom door she could lock herself in. "When I said I wasn't expecting you, I meant it."

He blinked.

"I wasn't *expecting* you, expecting you."

Still nothing. "I have no idea what that means. Are we speaking in code?"

She sighed and threw up her hands. "So much for ladylike mystery. I haven't had a chance to shave my legs, okay? I not only smell like a mermaid, but I look like a yeti underneath all this. I'm a grab bag of mythical creatures over here."

"Get in the bathroom, Georgia."

"See? I told you. I'm disgusting. Men run in fear when they see me coming."

He began unworking the knot of his tie. "Get in the bathroom, Georgia."

"And I hope this fancy hotel of yours stocks safety razors. Cartridge razors are dull on purpose so people have to throw them away after one use."

"Get in the bathroom, Georgia."

"I'm just saying—it's another ploy by big business to increase unnecessary consumerism. You shouldn't encourage them."

He didn't bother repeating himself again. In a quick, lunging attack he didn't know he had in him, he scooped her up and carried her, kicking and screaming and laughing, into the bathroom. It gleamed with marble and brushed nickel—a few more deals he remembered without much fondness—but for the first time in his life, he thought he might rather like it in here.

HE SHAVED HER legs for her.

Georgia lay in the giant whirlpool tub, stark-ass naked, smelling of soap bubbles and lavender body wash, her leg held aloft while Monty concentrated on moving the razor over her calf. From the look of intensity on his face, she figured there was a fifty-fifty chance he'd slice open her veins.

She didn't care if he did. The image of him perched

on the edge of the tub with his collar undone and his sleeves rolled up was one she'd take to the grave with her. It would be the bloody, painful grave of a woman who died from bleeding out in an Italian marble bathtub—but dammit, that woman died happy.

She ducked her head under the bubbles and counted to sixty, using her momentary invisibility as an opportunity to release an underwater scream. It was a scream of ecstasy and confusion, lust and something more. This couldn't possibly be her life right now.

"You know, the more you splash around, the greater the chances I gouge a hole in your knee," Monty said calmly as she resurfaced.

"I'll be still," she promised, but it was impossible when he lifted her leg higher, the razor snaking a path up her inner thigh. He could have been stripping the skin and she wouldn't have noticed. She was that far gone.

"Have I ever mentioned how much I love your legs?" he said, twisting the limb to get a better look at it.

"Once or twice." Her voice came out a sigh. "But you can tell me again."

"It's because they're so strong." He ran his hand over the patch of thigh he'd just shaved—he said it was his way of testing to make sure he didn't miss any spots, but Georgia was pretty sure he was doing it to torment her. "I never really thought about strength being its own kind of beauty before, but it is. When I touch your legs, I'm admiring what's on the surface, but I'm also appreciating the work that goes into shaping them. I'm admiring the woman whose life and livelihood created them."

"They're just legs."

"No. They're *your* legs."

She stared at him, mesmerized by how easily he was

able to quash her inadequacies, almost thirty years of feeling not good enough for anyone—boys, men, herself—wiped away in the space of one luxurious bath. He dipped the razor in the water and made a motion to keep going but she sat up, sloshing water all over the floor.

"I'm ready now."

He seemed startled. "But you said you can't feel sexy until your legs are hair-free. I've got a whole thigh left to go."

"I'm ready, Monty. Now."

He understood without the need for her to explain further. With a nod, he got to his feet and extended an oversized white towel. "I've got a good feeling this time."

She practically came on the power of his piercing gaze alone. "I do too."

FIFTEEN

"GODDAMMIT!" GEORGIA PULLED herself off Monty's lap, leaving him exposed and at full attention. There sat a gorgeous erection with a gorgeous man attached, and it might as well have been a crayon for all it was getting her off. "It's still not working. Why isn't it working?"

He cleared his throat. "Do you really want me to answer that?"

"No." Her voice came out surly and strained, but she refused to apologize for it. Anyone's voice would be surly and strained in this situation. She was naked, she had one-point-five shaved legs, and one of the most generously understanding men in the world was literally sitting there waiting for her command—but she was no nearer an orgasm than if she'd spent the day bowling. "Yes. No. Yes. Final answer."

"Do you promise not to get angry at me?"

"This isn't me being angry. This is me being frustrated beyond belief. If I was angry, you'd be on the floor by now."

He offered a sympathetic smile, puncturing her rage at its center. It was impossible to throw a tantrum in the face of naked commiseration. Naked commiseration was the worst. She sank on the edge of the bed with a sigh, not even caring when her stomach fat folded in on itself like an accordion.

"Okay—you can tell me," she capitulated. "Does it feel crooked inside? I bet it feels crooked inside."

Now he was sympathetic laughing, which was only a small step above the smiling. "It doesn't feel crooked. It feels perfect."

"You're just saying that."

"I'm not. I never lie about anatomy."

She snorted. It was as close to a laugh as he was going to get.

"As someone who recently got some similar advice on his phone sex skills, I'd venture to suggest you're thinking too much about it. There's a point—I'd say about five minutes in—when you stop feeling and start thinking. I can tell your concentration shifts by your expression."

"My expression? Oh, hell. Do I make funny faces on top of everything else?"

"Not funny. *Determined* is a better word for it. It's like you're in the final stretch of a marathon and have no intention of coming in second."

She dropped her head to her hands. "That sounds awful."

The edge of the mattress sank as he took a seat next to her. Monty was so solidly comforting and warm, the intoxicating strength of him at odds with the lavender soap currently making him smell like a bath and body store. His arm fell around her shoulders as he pulled her close. "It's not awful. It's kind of cute, if you want to know the truth."

"I'm not cute."

"You're cute when you want to win the race."

"No, I'm not. I'm maniacal—a fanged beast who'll trip anyone trying to pass me."

"Georgia." His finger came up under her chin, forcing

her head up. His lips touched hers for the barest whisper of a kiss. "You're thinking too much again."

"Never, in all my life, have I been accused of thinking too much. I wouldn't even know what it feels like." Even though her voice grumbled, most of it was for show. No one had ever called her cute before. Beautiful would have set her warning bells off, but she could believe cute. Cute was for sloths and pigeons and all of nature's odd quirks.

"Trust me—overthinking things is a subject I know well. It took me ten minutes to decide on a pair of socks before I came to get you."

"Did it?" She glanced down at his feet, even though they'd been bare for quite some time now. He had perfect feet in addition to perfect everything else, each toe well-proportioned and placed. "What's so hard about socks?"

"Well, first of all, I wanted a pair that would go well with my suit. I thought about something whimsical, maybe a pinstripe, but none of those ones were clean. And then I didn't want something too heavy since you've always been so open about your own lack of toe sweat."

She laughed and relaxed against him, burrowing into his chest like a sloth. Or a pigeon. "I have naturally arid feet. You shouldn't compare yourself to me."

"And *you* shouldn't compare yourself to what you think other women experience. I'm not saying your internet porn is wrong, but sex isn't all moaning and mutual climaxing—there are times when everything goes the way you have it planned, and there are times when it's an awkward fusion of bodies and moisture and air." He paused, but with that suspended breath he adopted when he wasn't through yet. "At another risk to my personal safety, I'd say you haven't spent enough time with one partner to realize that not all sex is good sex, but that all sex can still be good."

Monty was afraid that he'd overstepped his boundaries, but he lowered his hand to Georgia's side and began running his finger along her naked body anyway. He liked how she had this way of merely tolerating it for the first few seconds, like a cat, before finally relaxing enough to actually enjoy it.

"What's the longest you've ever been with someone, since you're so full of wisdom on the subject?" she asked.

He hesitated. Part of him—an admittedly large part—balked at the idea of telling Georgia anything about his past relationships. He didn't like talking about his failures any more than she liked experiencing them, and there was something off-putting about talking about one woman while another curled up naked in his lap.

But he owed her the honesty of a real answer. She was literally laying herself bare for him. The least he could do was return the favor.

"My most recent relationship lasted a little over ten months."

"Oh." Her voice sounded small, but she dropped a hand to his thigh and began absently running her fingers up and down it. As she wasn't one to fall easily into gestures of affection, he took it as a good sign. "Did you love her?"

"I was with her for almost a year, Georgia. Of course I loved her."

Her hand didn't stop moving against his leg, and his body was quick to remind him that the longer she went without satisfaction, the longer he did too. "I'm not jealous, in case you were wondering," she said.

"I wasn't going to suggest it."

"But it does seem unfair. You make it sound so easy."

"It wasn't easy, not by a long shot." It was baffling how a woman who would dig her heels in and do the work of fifteen men without a word of protest also expected relationships and sex to be simple. "But it was worth the effort. At least, I thought so at the time."

"What happened? Or should I not ask? You don't have to talk about it if it's painful."

"It's not painful," he said. "At least, not in the same way it used to be. She's actually getting married in a few weeks, and my dad has all but given me an ultimatum to attend so I can prove to the world how non-painful it is."

"That sounds awful."

He huffed his protest. "Not nearly as awful as the dates he's been trying to secure for me."

Georgia was silent for a moment, and he thought maybe he'd ruined the moment, introduced too many weird factors into what should have been *their* time together. "Is that what you were arguing about the other day?" she eventually asked.

"It's what we've been arguing about for weeks."

"I don't mind." She continued stroking her fingers up and down the length of his thigh, tracing the ligaments as if committing them to memory. "I imagine there are all sorts of high-profile events like weddings you need to attend. It's no fun to go to those things alone—believe me, I've been to enough to know."

"Georgia, if I go to that wedding, you'll be my date."

"You couldn't possibly want to take—"

"Promise me. Don't abandon me to those terrible people."

"And by terrible people, you mean your friends and family?"

"Yes."

She laughed, but he could tell she'd been surprised by his request. "I don't do fancy weddings, Monty. I don't do fancy anything."

"This place is pretty fancy." He smirked. "*I'm* pretty fancy."

Georgia's hand paused near the top of his thigh, her grip tight enough to stop the arterial blood flow. At least, it was tight enough to stop the blood flow to his leg. "That proves my point. Look how well this turned out."

"Who said anything about being done?" He nuzzled the back of his hand against her breast, and her nipple hardened almost immediately at the touch. "The way I figure it, we've got a few more hours of diligent effort in us."

"Diligence isn't required." She gasped as he flicked his thumb over the tip of that enticingly pink nipple. "I can, ah, finish things myself after you leave. It'll probably be faster that way."

"The devil you will." He lifted her out of his lap and tossed her to the bed, covering her body with his own. Once again, she unleashed barbarian tendencies he didn't know he possessed. "Is it really that simple when you do it on your own?"

"Well, kind of." She scrunched her nose as color bloomed across her cheeks. Like most of her gestures, this one was exaggerated, highlighting her already generous features, but he found nothing to fault in it. Her smile was captivating, her eyes flashing, her expressions priceless. It was difficult to remember a time when he'd found her anything less than perfect.

"Would it be like the other day on the phone?" he asked, unwilling to let her rosy cheeks go to waste.

"Um, yes?"

"And will there be icebergs?"

She blushed deeper. "It's not always an iceberg. Sometimes I like to mix things up with other natural disasters."

Unable to resist any longer, he pressed his mouth to hers for a kiss, using the force of gravity to prolong the twining of tongues and the tangle of legs. By the time he pulled away, she was back to wriggling underneath him—and he was back to appreciating her wriggle.

He brushed a strand of damp hair out of her face. "So how does it usually work for you when you take matters into your own hands? Walk me through it, step by step, and leave nothing out. For science."

She buried her head in his shoulder. "I can't. It's too embarrassing."

"Georgia, you straddled me in a chair while I had your nipples in my mouth. I think you can manage it."

"Okay. Fine. But only because you said *nipples* without hesitating."

Now it was his turn to color up. "Start talking," he said, his voice gruff. Damn if he'd ever be able to say *nipples* with a straight face again.

"I usually conjure up one of my favorite fantasies first," she said, her head still buried. She added her hands into the mixture, her fingers stroking lazy circles along his biceps.

"Icebergs and natural disasters?"

"Yes. And before you mention how weird that is, I already know. I watched a lot of disaster movies as a horny, unsatisfied teenager. I think I got confused about which parts were causing all those feelings."

His laughter shook them both. He could readily picture a younger Georgia salivating in equal proportions over Hollywood movie stars and the explosions trying to kill them. "Could you conjure one up right now? Even if it's you and me and a luxury hotel room and not the real deal?"

"Yes. I think I could manage."

"Could you do it while I touch you?"

"I can try."

She closed her eyes, and it was all the invitation he needed. Without waiting for her to overthink things, he slipped a hand between their bodies. He started at the top, his fingers swirling lazy patterns over the tight pucker of her nipples. "Okay," he murmured, fighting the urge to take her breast into his mouth. He didn't want to pull her too far away from her head, so it was probably best to stick to slow movements and low tones. "You're inside your fantasy. What happens next?"

"I need a minute to set the stage. Hang on."

He gave her a minute, and then another, losing himself momentarily in the soft, pale expanse of her skin. She had very clear tan lines on her torso from her work outdoors and her sporting activities, but he loved the juxtaposition of colors, of all that soft skin waiting for his touch. He managed to make his way down from her breasts to the swell of her lower stomach when he realized he'd been at this for quite some time. "Um, how elaborate is this stage of yours?"

"Very. I'll need a bit longer. You're about to be burned alive."

"Wait—your fantasy puts me in mortal danger?"

"Yes. You went inside a burning building to rescue a kitten, but the ceiling fell and you can't get free. I have to come rescue you."

She *sounded* serious, and the serene expression hadn't

left her face, so he decided to roll with it. If he had to die to close this deal, then into the flames he went. "It's nice of you to come get me. What am I wearing?"

"Mmm, good question." Her sleepy voice had him daring to move his hand lower, brushing lightly over the top of her mons. "You went in with a suit, but you had to take the jacket off to bundle up the kitten, and you used your regular shirt to cover your mouth. You're stripped to the waist and sweating like a beast."

"I usually wear an undershirt too," he pointed out.

She opened one eye. "It's *my* fantasy."

"Fair enough. What are you wearing?"

"It's not important. All that matters is that I get to you before you succumb to the smoke. You're terribly weak."

He paused. "This isn't what you normally fantasize about, is it? Me facing death?"

"Always. You wouldn't believe the horrors I've had you up against. Does it bother you?"

He wasn't sure yet. He'd always assumed there were people out there who wished him dead—certainly ones who wished him into a dark hole where they wouldn't have to interact with him—but this was different.

"Is it that you like it when I'm powerless?" he ventured.

"No. I like it when you need me. I like it when I'm the only one who can save you."

Without stopping to think or agonize over words or wonder if he was doing things wrong, he lifted her hand and placed it on his erection. The pressure of her fingertips was an agony, and he felt a tightening in his testicles that strung his entire body like a live wire. "I do need you, Georgia."

This time, when her eyes flew open, they stayed that way.

"What happens once it becomes clear you're my only

recourse?" he asked, his breath coming hard and fast. He would have liked to say he was asking out of motives of pure chivalry, but she'd started moving her hand up and down his length, and it was all he could do not to rut against her hand. "What then?"

"Showerhead, vibrator, fingers," she murmured. "Whatever's closest."

"Would you let me watch?"

"Right now?"

"I'm here. You're here. I'm already nearing an untimely demise. It seems like a waste of a perfectly good kitten otherwise."

"You'd like that?" She sounded hesitant.

He lifted her hand from his erection and placed it between her legs, gently nudging one of her fingers between the damp folds. Her moan was a shock through both their systems. "I wouldn't *like* that. I *need* that."

She nodded and opened her legs, giving him a glimpse of her wide-open sex, pink and enticing. His view was almost immediately impeded by the movement of her hand. Two fingers slipped neatly along the line of her opening, and she bucked her hips to gain more traction. He would have liked to rub his own aching dick in time to her movements, but he was too busy studying, watching, learning.

True to form, she was efficient and focused. She didn't tarry long over the task, her fingers deft and sure as they moved in what had to be a familiar pattern to her by now. In this, as in all things, she knew what she was doing, and she did it well. He wouldn't have had time to take notes even if he wanted to.

When her cries became more pronounced, he slipped a fresh condom over his length. She moaned and her movements became jerky, and he could tell when she peaked by the way her whole body stilled, arching against the bed, before moving back down into a posture of rest.

He wasted no time in moving over her, bracing himself with his arms so as not to crush her with his weight. His erection nudged at her hand, and he paused only long enough to ask, "May I?"

She nodded and helped guide him inside, where the ebbing contractions of her vagina pulled him in and made him feel immediately at home. It wasn't the same—it wouldn't be the motions of *his* ocean bringing her over the edge, and her satisfaction was only a lingering memory as he took his own—but at least she could get used to equating this glowing purr of contentment with his body inside her.

"Is this okay?" he asked as he moved against her. Orgasm had given her body a pliability it lacked before, and she smiled dreamily as she opened her legs to allow him better access.

"It's fantastic."

It *was* fantastic. Georgia felt so right and so comfortable, and he felt a kind of power at having helped bring that smile to her face, even if he wasn't quite up to traditional sex god standards. He was just sex god enough—and that was enough for him.

He came quickly and without ceremony, too busy enjoying her pleasure to linger on his own. And he refused to let her go as he rolled them both to the side. *This* moment—these few minutes of liquid, languid intimacy—was what he'd really been waiting for.

"Well, now I feel kind of bad," he said, speaking directly in her ear as he wrapped his arms under her breasts and pulled her close.

"Don't feel bad. I can't remember the last time I felt so happy. That was almost like the real thing, wasn't it?"

"It *was* the real thing," he said firmly, and planted a kiss on her neck. "But that's not what I was talking about. I was actually wondering what happened to the kitten while we were busy working off all that adrenaline from the rescue."

She slapped a hand over her mouth. "Oh, the poor kitten. I totally forgot about him. He probably burned up."

He made the motion of the cross over Georgia's chest. "May he rest in peace."

"I wonder if what I needed all along wasn't a strapping hero to save, but an animal sacrifice. Maybe next time you should try to rescue a goat. Imagine the possibilities with a goat."

He just shook his head and relaxed further into the pillow, listening as Georgia outlined all the animals she was willing to burn at the altar of ecstasy. There were quite a few.

Although it hadn't been his intention to stay overnight, he found himself sinking into the mattress with heavy limbs and heavier eyelids. It was dark and warm, and he felt more at home in this hotel room than he'd ever thought possible.

A few hours of sleep wouldn't kill him. A few hours of Georgia in his arms wasn't the worst thing that could happen.

"I thought you were going to have to get back to work," she said, her words reaching him almost as he was about to drift off.

"Fuck work," he said, and held her tight.

Work had never done anything but fuck him right back.

SIXTEEN

GEORGIA WOKE TO a plate of breakfast meat, a clean pair of coveralls on her pillow and a kiss from her knight in shining armor.

Okay, that last one was a touch melodramatic, but she'd have knighted any man who ordered her a double side order of bacon. With sausage, he could be king.

"I wasn't sure whether or not I should wake you before I leave." Monty looked an apology down at her before gesturing at the bedside clock, which warned her it was rapidly approaching six. "I had your clothes sent down to be cleaned, and there's coffee and food. I wasn't sure what else you might need."

"Oh, shit. Is it that late already?" She bolted upright, flashing her bare torso and only feeling mildly embarrassed by it. She wasn't normally the saunter-around-nonchalantly-naked sort, but she also wasn't the snuggle-through-the-night sort either, and that had worked out pretty well in her favor. "I can't believe I slept in."

Somehow unable to recognize that this was a genuine emergency, Monty remained standing and staring. "You think six o'clock is sleeping in?"

"Judge not, my friend. I don't see you lolling about in bed either." She threw back the rest of the covers and grabbed her clothes. Gone were all traces of green, ocean-smelling muck. Gone was the oil stain that had stubbornly persisted on the knee area. In its place were creases. Someone had actually ironed her coveralls. "Wow. I could get used to this kind of thing."

And then she realized how much of a long shot something like that was—magical nights of cuddling while tiny elves pressed her clothes—so she ducked her head and ran to the bathroom to change. There was no need to let Monty see how badly she wanted this, how painfully aware she was that it could never be.

She wasn't sure whether to expect him to be around when she emerged five minutes later, but he was waiting on the other side of the bathroom door, his hand extended.

The fact that he waited for her was enough to weaken her knees, but he'd also managed to wedge most of the bacon inside a biscuit and was holding it out. "For the road," he said, and watched as she jammed it in her mouth while she pulled her hair back in a ponytail. She'd fallen asleep with the strands still damp from the shower, so she looked an awful lot like she'd been caught in a wind tunnel, but time was running short. Wind-tunnel hair would have to do.

"I'm sorry for not waking you," he said, still watching. "It didn't occur to me that you probably start your day as early as me."

"I do." She bit off a large chunk of the bacon biscuit and swallowed. God, she could get used to that too. A lifetime of meat and affection and laundry—she was that easy. "I've got inspectors coming out today to see how things are coming along. I need time to hide all the exposed wires and shoddy craftsmanship on the roof." She saw the look of guilt that statement caused and laughed. "That was a joke, by the way. The roof is great."

He flushed and lifted his chin a fraction. "Is my tie straight?"

She reached up and tugged the knot—with three older brothers, tying a tie was one of the few fashion-related things she was good at—and took a moment to smooth his lapel. She didn't realize, until his eyes met hers with an almost shocked look, how nauseatingly domestic this whole situation had become.

"Sorry," she mumbled, and dropped her hand.

He caught it. "Don't be. This is kind of nice, isn't it? Having someone to see you off in the morning?"

"Yeah," she agreed, though she didn't care to dwell on how nice it felt. Because this *was* nice. This was wonderful. This was what people meant when they talked about being in love.

Unfortunately, it was starting to appear as though there was no magic penis cure for what ailed her, which meant that as soon as this thing with Monty was over, she'd be right back to square one. Alone and sexually defunct. Making her own breakfast. Maybe even investing in an iron.

"Come on. I'll walk you down." Monty released her hand. With one careful perusal of the room to make sure they hadn't left anything behind, they were out the door and on their way back to reality.

GEORGIA SAW THEM FIRST.

She wasn't sure what compelled her to look toward the fireplace, where a couple stood quietly conversing over a coffee cart, but she and Monty only made it halfway through the lobby before she almost toppled over a marble end table.

Maybe it would have been better if she had. Maybe she

would have knocked herself unconscious so she didn't have to see the contorted grimace that passed over Mr. Montgomery's features before he plastered on a familiar smile and strode their way.

Georgia didn't believe in fainting—a few deep breaths and a slap to the face were every woman's best friend—but she would forever be grateful for the way Monty placed his hand under her arm and moved closer to her side. He was allying himself. He was choosing her.

Thank God. They were both going to need it.

"John, Georgia—I'm so glad I caught you before you left for the day." From Mr. Montgomery's pleasant voice and easy smile, you'd think he was happy to discover his son and heir escorting a handywoman in neatly pressed coveralls through the lobby of his hotel. "I was afraid you might have checked out already."

"No, you weren't. I'm sure you already confirmed everything with the front desk clerk." Monty turned to the woman with a tight smile. "You must have wrapped up your business quickly, Jenna. I didn't expect to see you for a few more days."

Georgia knew Monty's sister, Jenna, of course. They couldn't have shared more than a dozen conversations in the past decade—Jenna was in charge of the hotel chain's international operations, so she rarely in residence at the Manor—but it was impossible not to recognize the gorgeous redhead. If Georgia and her brothers looked like hot-off-the-presses facsimiles of one another, Jenna and her brothers were more like opposite sides of the same coin. They were all crafted of the same gilded metal, but her side contained nothing except perfect curves and delicately formed features.

"You knew I was coming? Damn. I was hoping to

make an entrance." Jenna leaned in and kissed Monty on either cheek before turning to Georgia to do the same. Georgia wasn't proud of herself, but she cowered behind Monty to keep those ruby red lips away. Air kisses freaked her out.

Unperturbed, Jenna quirked a brow and stepped back, a smile playing on her lips.

"It was nice of you both to see us off, but Georgia and I were hoping to get out of here sooner rather than later. Duty, as you know, waits for no man." Monty took his role as protector seriously and planted himself even more firmly in front of her. It was alarmingly gratifying to have a wall of man between her and the rest of the Montgomerys.

What a wimp she was turning out to be.

"Oh, we won't keep you, Georgia." Mr. Montgomery smiled even deeper, the creases of his face folding up on one another. "Did you want me to have your truck brought around?"

"No. That's okay. I—"

"Dad, I'm perfectly capable of seeing my girlfriend out on my own. Thank you."

The first sign of stress cracked in Mr. Montgomery's brow at the sound of that word. *Girlfriend.* Such a silly way to describe a woman of her years and yet somehow the best thing she'd ever heard.

Wait. *Girlfriend?*

"John, I'm not sure if you're aware what kind of a statement this is sending—"

Again, Monty interrupted. "I know, Dad. I know exactly what kind of statement I'm sending. It's the same kind of statement you made by calling my little sister home to manage my love life for me. No offense, Jenna."

"None taken." If the way her eyes were lighting up was any indication, offense was the furthest thing from her mind. She was enjoying this.

Too bad no one bothered to ask Georgia how she was feeling right about now. She couldn't make any definitive statements, but she was bordering on a bewildering kind of panic-rage. Surely Monty hadn't intended for them to be caught red-handed like this. Surely he would have talked to her before deciding to announce to his father—and her employer—that they were an item.

"Georgia, you look like you could use some coffee," Jenna said brightly. "Preferably with a touch of Irish in it. What say we find our way to the bar?"

"They're not open yet."

"They'll open for me." She extended her arm. Georgia looked at that arm—elegantly crooked and offering her booze before seven in the morning—and shook her head.

She wasn't some polished businesswoman who could drink Irish coffees and mimosas for breakfast. She wasn't dressed for lounging around in a hotel lobby while the rest of this conversation took place. And she definitely wasn't going to continue hiding behind Monty while she had two perfectly good legs to stand on.

She was a—most likely—unemployed handywoman who had inspectors coming by her build site in less than an hour. And that was fine. As she'd so elegantly told Monty before, she'd never be the type of woman to latch on to a man and wilt. She had shit to do.

"Thanks, but I really need to get going."

Life hadn't prepared her to bid goodbye in a situation like this, but she felt it would be rude to stalk away without showing Monty *some* kind of support. Unfortunately, kissing was out of the question while his dad stood there watching, and hugging seemed forced. The most she could handle was a handshake.

It was ridiculous—a handshake, after murdering imaginary kittens together—but it was all she could come up with. Monty took her hand in his own, a troubled frown pulling at his face. "I'll call you later?"

"Sure. When you can. You know where to find me." Even though she wanted to be mad at him—she *was* kind of mad at him—she squeezed his fingers in a show of solidarity.

"I'm sorry, Georgia," he said, but it was hard to tell which part of the situation he was apologizing for.

She'd hoped to make it outdoors without having to look back, but the clatter of heels after her had her turning around as she reached the revolving glass doors.

"Take me with you." Jenna snaked her arm through Georgia's. "Or at least let me pretend to be going with you. You can't leave me in there with those two. Cross fire always leaves such a nasty residue behind."

Georgia wasn't sure how to respond, so she kept walking, her steps long. Despite enormously spiked high heels, Jenna matched her stride for stride.

"I wouldn't worry about it, if I were you," Jenna said conversationally as they passed into the early morning sunshine. She neither seemed to notice or care that Georgia had yet to say a word to her. "It looks scary when Monty and my dad go head-to-head, but they're both far too dignified to make a scene. They'll argue politely through their teeth and shake hands and then sit down to dinner tonight as if nothing happened."

"I wasn't worried," Georgia said. At least, not about making a scene. Embarrassing herself in public was just another day in her regular life. But the more she thought about the way Monty had greeted his family—coldly, calmly, as if he'd been expecting them—the more worry that settled on her shoulders.

Monty wasn't just some nice guy who was willing to tackle her orgasm problem. He was John Montgomery the Third. He had wealth. He had responsibilities. He had a very public family who didn't take it lightly when he diddled the help.

This is what happens when you fly too close to the sun, Georgia. Somewhere in the midst of all this grandeur, she'd lost track of her flight path and singed off her eyebrows.

"And their argument isn't about you." Jenna laughed at her own comment, painting herself as another one of those throaty film vixens Georgia could never be. "Okay, maybe it's a little about you—but only as a secondary complaint, I promise. Where are you parked?"

Georgia stopped walking. "I can manage, thanks."

Jenna took her animosity in stride, and in an extreme violation of the rules of personal space, reached up and tugged the elastic out of her hair. Georgia had to use a mega-grip version to keep the band from slipping out, so it took a firm tug, but Jenna didn't let that deter her. She even went so far as to spread the strands of her hair like a fan, holding the boring brown color up to the sun as if it might catch a sparkle.

It wouldn't. Georgia absorbed all light and glitter.

"There's just so much of it," Jenna said, mostly to herself.

Georgia held herself perfectly still, as though confronting wildlife in its natural habitat, hoping the other woman would eventually move on.

She didn't.

"And the uniform is probably fine for work, but you should carry something lighter in your car for afterward. Or you could layer. How do you feel about layers?"

"I like them in cake?"

Jenna pressed her hand against Georgia's shoulder, twirling her so that she faced the parking lot. Without asking for permission, she tugged her head back and began doing something to her hair. It hurt, but Georgia wasn't about to say so, so she stood there and let Jenna finish whatever it was she was attempting.

"Perfect. It's still out of your face but infinitely more attractive."

Georgia noticed a fat braid fall over one shoulder.

"And here. It's better if you're not quite so tightly packaged." Jenna reached up and undid the top two buttons of her coveralls. Since cleavage was the last thing any woman needed in a construction zone where every ounce of respect had to be wrested out of belligerent masculine grips, Georgia waited until the other woman was done and then promptly did them back up again.

"Fine," Jenna said with a sigh. "I can see I have my work cut out for me on more than one front. You get to work. I better go inside and deflate the tension."

Georgia was still feeling bewildered and uncomfortable enough to want to flee, but she waited until the other woman waggled her fingers in farewell before letting out a long, soul-deep breath—and then she looked at the sky and realized she was going to be late.

Fan-freaking-tastic. The day had started out so well too.

With bacon and everything.

"I'M SURE I don't have to tell you how you've opened us up to public outcry." Monty's dad spoke in the calm,

level tone of a calm, level man—though anyone familiar with the tight press of his lips would know that the
older man was rapidly reaching his limit. "Never mind
the legal ramifications. How would it look to the community if they knew you were sneaking out with our
handywoman?"

"Her name is Georgia." Monty didn't move as he
spoke. Jenna—in a perverse fit of good humor—had
poured him a coffee from the cart and set it at his elbow,
but he didn't dare lift the china to his lips. There was a
good chance one of the three of them would end up wearing the beverage.

"I know her name. Stop saying that."

"Then stop referring to her as *our handywoman*. She's
not a bogeyman. You won't accidentally summon her."

Jenna snickered and covered her indiscretion by taking a sip of coffee. A decent sister would go find something to entertain herself, but Jenna had never been the
decent sort. She loved a good family drama too much.

"I know I've been putting a lot of stress on you lately,
especially regarding this wedding, but you have to understand—"

"I don't feel stress regarding Ashleigh's wedding."
Monty interrupted his father yet again. He was finding
it surprisingly easy to conjure the words he wanted to
say. Anger had a way of loosening the tongue. "I already
told you I found my own date. If I decide to attend, I'll
take Georgia, not some monochrome robot of a woman
whose bank account you admire. Sorry you wasted your
time in coming all this way, Jenna."

"Oh, time enjoyed isn't time wasted," Jenna said, holding her cup up in a mock toast.

"So, what? This is part of your newfound adolescent

rebellion? This is you trifling with a woman who's been a part of our family for almost twenty years?" His father's words grew tighter and more controlled. "I have to say—I might have expected this sort of thing from Jake before he got married, but not you. Never you."

His dad might grow more contained as his anger took over, but Monty felt the exact opposite. His emotions had grown to proportions equal to the hotel lobby, threatened to spill out over sidewalks and into the streets.

"No." He got to his feet, done with this pretense of a family discussion over a breakfast table. "This is me making my own goddamned decisions for once. This is me putting my desires before the family's for once. Think about what you just said, Dad. You'd have forgiven Jake for sleeping with one of your retainers. You'd have slapped him on the wrist and made a show of your disappointment, but you'd have ultimately forgiven him."

"And I'll forgive you too, as long as you stop acting like a child who's had his toy taken away."

"Georgia isn't a toy."

"I'm glad you recognize that."

"And she isn't going anywhere."

"John, you can't—"

"I can't what? Continue seeing a woman I care about? Make my own decisions regarding an ex-girlfriend's wedding? Go to South Dakota if I feel like it?" Monty gave up on the pretense of caring. He didn't care that he'd wasted an hour sitting here in a hotel lobby instead of making headway on his morning email. He didn't care that several people had stopped what they were doing to listen in. And he didn't care that both his father and Jenna were staring at him with their mouths open and shocked looks on their faces.

No—scratch that. He did care about those shocked looks. Those shocked looks said much more about him than they did the people wearing them. He'd become so predictable, so dependable, so much a cog in the wheel that it never occurred to his closest relatives that he might want more out of life.

And he wanted more. He *deserved* more.

"I'm done," he said, and tossed his napkin to the floor. It fluttered underneath the chair, that white square of defiance, and they all watched as it came to rest. "I'm going to head back to the office and make sure my files are in order, and then I'm done."

His dad also got to his feet, his movements not quite so self-assured. "What do you mean, you're done?"

"Done. Finished. No longer willing to agree to your terms of employment." Monty felt an unexpected burst of excitement flood through him, lifting both his shoulders and his spirits. He'd had no idea that even the act of declaring his freedom would be its own kind of release. "Don't worry—I'll write you up an official resignation letter before I go. I'll even say whatever you want so you don't have to lose face or appear weak. I know how much you hate that."

"But you can't—"

"Yes," Monty said firmly. "I can. I'm not Jake, Dad. You don't have any financial control over me. You did too good of a job training me to always make the responsible choice. I probably have more liquid assets than you do at this point."

There were many things he could have added—several things he probably *should* have added, a few parting words for the little boy who never did get his bike ride—but he didn't feel like explaining himself to this man anymore.

And as he turned to leave, he realized this was the first time he'd ever taken steps as a Montgomery in name only. He was walking away. He'd cast off the shackles.

For good or for bad, he was finally free.

SEVENTEEN

MONTY HAD BEEN sitting in his car for ten minutes before he realized he had company.

All the lights were off at Georgia's apartment and the accompanying house, so he'd relaxed enough to push his seat back and unknot the tie at his neck, which had been feeling more and more like a noose as the day wore on. He sat up now, peering closer at the empty back porch. If he wasn't mistaken, there was a dark figure folded up on those stairs, a curly wisp of smoke rising from fingers and lips and fingers again.

A shadowy hand lifted in greeting, and Monty realized he'd been made some time ago. With a sigh, he shut his phone and got out of the car. It would have been preferable to talk to Georgia before he spoke to her family, but short of backing out of the drive and pretending he was invisible, it was too late now.

"I didn't know you smoked," Monty said as he approached the back door.

It was a stupid comment to make—he didn't know much about the man other than that he was good with computers and liked garlic bread—but he needed something to break the ice. Besides, it felt kind of nice to be back to the conversational wasteland he'd inhabited for most of his life. It was the only familiar ground he had right now.

"I don't." Danny unfolded himself from the stoop and

crushed the butt underneath the heel of his heavy black boot before kicking it into the bushes. "And if you're smart, you won't tell anyone otherwise."

Monty sighed. *More threats, more antagonism, more people to hate me.* At some point in the past decade or so, every person on the planet must have gotten together and decided he was their mortal enemy—standing up against fun and pleasure and justice everywhere.

"You think I'm going to go running to your mom or sister?" he asked. "Really? You look at me and the first thing that comes to mind is, 'I bet that guy loves a good tattle'?"

Danny's face broke into the wide, crooked smile Monty was coming to associate with all of the Lennoxes. "Okay, maybe that was unfair, but you never know with you straight and narrow guys."

"I'm not a straight and narrow guy."

"Oh, you're straight. You're the Washington Monument of upright citizenry."

Monty had no idea what that meant, but he suspected it wasn't a compliment.

"Georgia's not here," Danny said, anticipating his next question. "We got back from the build site around six, but she was called away for an emergency flood at Mrs. Peabody's place. She could be hours."

"Oh." Disappointment pinged in his chest. After the way Georgia had left the hotel this morning, upset and determined not to let it show, he'd wanted nothing more than to reach out and reassure her, so he'd made her house his first stop.

But maybe it was himself he'd wanted to reassure all along. She was the one hard at work on a twelve-hour day when he was suddenly facing nothing but open air.

"Do you think I should head over and see if she wants help?" he asked.

Danny laughed and slapped an arm over Monty's shoulder. "No. Georgia most definitely does not want your help. One of these days, you'll figure that out. Care to come in and wait for her?"

Monty bristled, alarmed at this sudden show of hospitality. He also touched his hand to his pocket to make sure his phone hadn't been lifted.

"I can't offer much. Frozen burritos and a Halo marathon is all I've got, but it's better than sitting in your car. Less obvious too. I thought you were a really bad FBI agent at first."

"If I were an FBI agent, I would've parked under that tree a few houses down."

Danny pushed through the door. "If you were an FBI agent, you'd lease the house across the street and pretend to be a blond married couple with a Yorkie. Come on. I'll take you to my lair."

"I can't find the rocket launcher. Are you sure this is where you saw it?"

"It's next to the boulder. Hurry up—I can't hold this bastard back forever."

"Oh, here it is. Extra ammo too. I'm on my way."

Georgia rubbed her eyes and blinked, certain that exhaustion was playing tricks with her mind. That was *not* Monty sitting in a gaming chair next to Danny, rocking back and forth as he navigated his way through Blood Gulch. He was a mirage. A manifestation of three hours spent wading through a basement with a sump pump dragging behind her.

"Oh, hey, Georgia," Danny said, not looking up from

the screen as he and his not-Monty guest played video games.

"Hey, Georgia," not-Monty echoed.

Not-Monty sounded an awful lot like the real thing. He looked familiar too, what with the various suit components covering his body. It looked as if his tie and jacket had been discarded and cast to the side, and he'd kicked off his shoes to reveal—oh, dear God, were those pinstriped socks?—underneath.

No one but the real Monty would wear such adorably upscale socks. Until last night, she hadn't even known pinstriped socks were a thing.

"Please tell me there's a perfectly logical explanation for this. Did I hit my head on the crossbeam on the way down? Did I drown in Mrs. Peabody's flooded basement and wind up in hell?"

"Just a second—we're almost done."

It was a command Georgia knew well. She'd spent far too much time down here with Danny and his friends not to recognize that men in the throes of a blood battle saw nothing but the pixels in front of them. She settled herself in the computer chair and waited for her boys to come home from war.

Fortunately for her sanity and mounting curiosity, it only took about five minutes before the rankings flashed on the screen and both men were able to start blinking again. Danny offered a quirk of a smile in greeting, but Monty got to his feet, looking flushed and ashamed of himself.

As well he should.

She might have spent the day working the worst of her aggression off, but traces of it remained. She struggled to hold on to those traces now, grasping at them like will-o'-the-wisps. She'd been used this morning. Monty had suspected his family would find them out at the hotel but had taken her anyway. Jenna had braided her hair against her will.

Screw it. Unable to resist the quiet, hesitant way Monty kept staring down at her, she gave in. She could yell at him later. Right now, all she wanted was to recapture the feeling of complete and utter acceptance she felt in his arms.

It wasn't her fault. Grown men playing video games in dark, smelly basements were her weakness.

"Oh, gross," Danny said as she flew across the distance and raised her lips to Monty's. Monty was still slightly dazed from the video game, which gave his kiss a sleepy, gentle quality she found potent. "Take your disgusting display of affection elsewhere. This is a blood and guts and guns only zone."

"You're the one who stole my…" Hmm. She had no idea what to call him. That *girlfriend* from this morning was still suspect, but she could hardly pretend he was nothing more than a friend anymore—not that her family had believed her in the first place. She settled for "My Monty. If you can lure him underground with video games, then I can lure him back to the surface with promises of the flesh."

"Please don't ever say *promises of the flesh* within my range of hearing again. I thought we talked about this."

Georgia sneered at her brother. That was what he got for dragging Adam and Charlie into her business in the first place.

"Thanks for the company, Montgomery," Danny said, ignoring her. "You weren't as terrible at Halo as I thought you'd be."

Monty hadn't lost his look of utter bewilderment. "You're welcome?"

"Take it and run," Georgia advised as she led him toward the stairs. "It's as close to a compliment as you'll ever get from him. How long have you been here?"

"I have no idea. What time is it?"

Since the sun had gone down hours ago, Georgia had to resort to the old-fashioned rooster clock hanging above the stove. "Almost ten."

Monty blinked at her. "Are you serious?"

"Did you have to go already? I'm sorry I was so late, but Mrs. Peabody's washing machine pipe burst, and she had all her family heirlooms stored in her basement. She called me in tears. I would have let you know, but after the, ah, altercation in the lobby this morning, I figured it'd be a few days before you'd have time to see me."

Or a few weeks. Months. A lifetime, even. In fact—what was he doing here at all?

"No, it's fine. I didn't realize I was down there for so long, that's all." He held open the door and ushered her through. "Video games are kind of addicting, aren't they?"

She laughed. He sounded as though he'd never even played Tetris as a kid. "Yes, they are. It might have been bad sex and poor relationship skills that kept me single all these years, but it'll be video games that keep me that way for the rest of my life. By now, all the good men are either taken or married to their Xboxes."

He stopped, holding her in place in the middle of the basketball court. "But you're not single anymore."

Their hands remained interlocked, but their bodies were separated by the half court line. "I'm not?"

"Maybe you didn't hear what I said to my dad this morning, but—"

"I heard."

He didn't move, not even a flutter of his lashes to indicate that he was composed of anything but stone. "You didn't like it?"

"I liked it."

He swept Georgia into his arms. "Good," he said, and kissed her again. This kiss was neither sleepy nor distracted, and Georgia sagged into his chest, grateful to have so many of her questions answered in such a hot and pressing embrace. Was she wanted? Were they okay? Could they keep pursuing the ever-fleeting vision of a perfect orgasm?

Yes. Yes. Oh, God, yes.

All questions should be answered this way whenever possible—with needy tongues and strong arms, with hands moving downward until her ass was clasped and held in place.

"Maybe we should take this to my apartment," Georgia suggested when her legs became incapable of holding her weight any longer.

A troubled look flashed through Monty's eyes.

"What? What is it?"

"There are a few things we should talk about first."

She dropped her arms, and her knees locked. She knew this was too easy, too perfect. Easy and perfect things didn't happen in real life. Not to her. "It's your dad, isn't it? He was furious."

"Do you want to go inside where we can talk privately?"

"Is it that bad?"

Monty rubbed a hand over the back of his neck. "I'm

inclined to think it's a good thing—but that depends on how you react."

She swallowed, bracing herself for the worst. She'd been fired. Her name would be blacklisted from every handyman service in Ransom Creek. Monty was bearing her secret love child and his father had cut him off without a penny.

"Remember the day you said that if anything goes wrong with this thing of ours, you'd be the one to lose a valuable client?"

Oh, hell. She sagged with a combination of relief and disappointment. Monty's news came as no surprise— she'd spent most of her time at Mrs. Peabody's doing mental calculations to figure out how long she could survive on her savings and the stale rice cakes in her mom's cupboards that not even her brothers would touch. It wasn't ideal to be banned from Montgomery Manor, but she was a big girl wearing big girl pants, and she'd known the risks of entangling herself with Monty.

All that mattered was that he was *here.* Even though she knew it was wrong to keep holding on to this man when it was the last thing his family wanted for him, she was too selfish to care.

Much.

"It's not a big deal," she said, pushing her fears and doubts to the side. Between Monty and Homeward Bound, it was getting awfully crowded over there. "Please don't feel bad on my account. I'll rally. I always do."

"No, you don't understand." He took her hand. "*You* aren't out a valuable client. I am."

Georgia shook her head, not sure she understood. As he had that first day at the Manor, Monty lifted a hand to her chin to halt the relentless back-and-forth movement.

And as he had that first day at the Manor, he stripped her of everything but the desire to maintain that contact through whatever means necessary.

"You don't have to leave the Manor. That was never an option, at least not as far as I was concerned." He dropped his hand. "I tendered my resignation today. As of about five hours ago, I'm no longer employed by the Montgomery Foundation or any of its affiliated companies."

"What!?"

"I finally did it, Georgia. I'm out. And I'm all yours."

EIGHTEEN

As it turned out, Georgia had no idea what to do with Monty now that he was in her possession.

"Do I need to feed you?" she asked as she watched him bring in a suitcase and set it by the front door to her apartment. That was it—*one* suitcase. An entire lifetime packed up in a neat square the size of her pillow. Her softball trophies alone would take up more space than that. "Or water you? Are we going to have to take regular walks and play fetch together?"

Monty laughed and tossed himself on her bed, his hands behind his head as he stretched out. He'd always been so carefully and quietly controlled before—she didn't realize how much of that bed he took up once he let himself go. If he put his arms out, his fingers would probably extend over the edges.

"Only if you also promise to pet me and bathe me," he said. He was acting so much like a normal human male she almost wanted to check for signs of possession. But then he sat up, an anxious twist to his smile. "This is okay, right? I don't have to stay here tonight—or ever, if you don't want. There are a hundred hotels not owned by my father where I could easily put up."

"No, it's great. It's perfect." And it was great. It was perfect.

As far as she was concerned, this was the dream. Not only had she somehow managed to woo Monty into her bed, but he was so happy there he wanted to stay. Indefinitely. As her official boyfriend, with all the perks the title entailed.

She reached to the inside of her forearm and pinched. *Yep.* Still hurt.

"Do you want to talk about it?" She moved to her closet to extract some kind of nightwear. Once again, this was a situation in which something strappy and slippery would come in handy—and once again, she was faced with rows of T-shirts emblazoned with various lewd slogans.

"I'm not sure what there is to say, in all honesty. He got mad. I quit. He got madder."

Georgia gave up and grabbed the nearest T-shirt, which vowed Pants Are Overrated. With any luck, she wouldn't be wearing it long anyway. That was the point of cohabitation, right? Nudity and endless sexcapades?

"Did you quit because of me?"

"Yes."

She stopped breathing.

"No."

She started again.

"Well, maybe." He reached for her, and she was so deprived of oxygen, she had no choice but to fall to the bed in his arms. He took his time settling her into a comfortable position, a horizontal full-body hug. "You didn't *cause* this, if that's what you're asking. The trouble between me and my father has been brewing for a lot longer than either of us was willing to admit. You were the tipping point, nothing more."

Was that supposed to make her feel better? "So you took me to that hotel knowing your dad would hear about it? To tip things?"

"No. I took you because I was trying, in my ineffective way, to tell you how much you mean to me. I know we joked about being secret lovers, but I'm not ashamed of what we're doing. I never have been. And I refuse to apologize for wanting to be with you."

He sounded so *sure* of himself—of her, and of them. Everywhere she turned, people seemed to accept Monty's presence in her life without even a ripple of apprehension. Her mom handed over sex recordings and sage advice on marrying rich. Danny wrinkled his nose and told her to take their kissing elsewhere. Even Monty's sister had acted all chummy.

She kind of wanted to call up Mr. Montgomery just so she'd have someone on her side. *My son has clearly lost his mind, taking up with an unattractive, undersexed handywoman like you*, he'd say. *I know, right?* she'd reply. Then they could compare notes on the inherent wrongness of this whole situation and come up with a plan to save Monty from her evil clutches.

"Maybe I wanted to keep it a secret," she said. "Did you ever think about that?"

His arms around her became a vise, though she couldn't tell if he was insulted or afraid she might leave him. "Yes. I thought about it."

Well, that wasn't the answer she was expecting. "And you figured it didn't matter what I wanted?"

"I figured I'd try to change your mind." He rolled her underneath him, looking down with such tenderness she almost had to pinch her arm again. If things continued like this for much longer, she'd become one giant bruise. "I know I'm not an ideal boyfriend, Georgia. I'm too serious and set in my ways. I'll probably bore your family and friends until they start hiding behind plants to avoid me. But I can change. I *am* changing. And now that I don't have to spend nine-tenths of my day working, I can put you first, where you belong."

"That sounds…great," she said, dazed—and not only because he was unbuttoning the top of her coveralls and laying a trail of kisses along her collarbone. "But don't you think quitting your job was a bit drastic?"

"I don't like to think of it as quitting." He continued pushing fabric down her arms. "I like to think of it as switching careers."

"Are you going to take up race car driving or writing the Great American Novel, like any man in the throes of a good midlife crisis?"

He laughed against her breast, where his mouth was snaking downward, licking and grazing its way to the lining of her—sadly, still grey-beige—bra. "Nope. My mission is simple. I'm not going to rest until you've had all the orgasms you can handle."

"Hmm. The pay is crappy."

His response was to take her nipple into his mouth and suckle deeply.

"And the hours are long."

This time he used teeth, causing a jolt of surprised satisfaction to move through her.

"And there's no guarantee the product will ever work the way it's supposed to."

He lifted his head enough to smile at her. "It sure will be fun testing it, though, don't you think?"

She moaned and gave herself over to his tongue, determined to enjoy it while it lasted. She gave this thing of theirs a week, tops. Monty didn't belong to her. He belonged to the people who needed him most—and it was only a matter of time before they rallied up their pitchforks and came looking for him.

"QUICK, HOLLY—YOU HAVE to hide me." Georgia burst through the kitchen doors and scanned for the best hiding place. The fridge was probably too full, and the heat emanating from the stove rendered that option less than ideal, but the pantry was fairly large. She might be able to squeeze on the bottom shelf. "You can't let her find out I'm here."

Holly waved a wooden spoon at her in greeting. "What's wrong? Who's hunting you?"

"Jenna." Georgia spoke the other woman's name in hushed tones, fearful of bringing a curse down upon her head. "I hear the click of her heels now. Do you think I'll fit in the dumbwaiter?"

Holly laughed—*laughed*—at her distress and continued stirring. "You're more than welcome to try. Let me know if you want some cooking grease to ease your passage."

"This isn't funny." Georgia realized now her error in choosing the kitchen as her hiding spot. Although Jenna rarely made an appearance down here, this was one of the few rooms without a back entrance unless she wanted to trigger the fire alarm. She was trapped.

"It's kind of funny."

"I saw Mr. Montgomery earlier and literally ran the opposite direction. I almost fell down the stairs."

"Still funny."

"But what am I supposed to say to her?" Georgia wailed. "Sorry I enslaved your brother and toppled your family dynasty—here, let me fix that broken bit of plaster in your bedroom to make up for it?"

"*Have* you enslaved him?" Jenna's voice, a cloying pool of doom washing over her, arose from the doorway. "I'd love to know how you did it."

You could have warned me, she mouthed to Holly, but the other woman merely pressed her lips together in a suppressed smile. She was loving this. Every staff member at the Manor was loving this—in less than one week, Georgia had become the best joke this place had ever seen. She'd caught the gardening crew affixing empty paint cans to the back of her truck in some kind of mock bridal salute.

"Don't worry." Jenna extended her hand. "I'm a peace-bearing messenger."

"I'd really rather not get in the middle of your family stuff." Georgia eyed the long, elegant hand reaching out to her with trepidation. "If you want to talk to Monty, you'll have to call him yourself."

"But I don't want to talk *to* Monty," she said, waggling her fingers in a beckoning gesture. "I want to talk *about* him. I always like my brothers better via proxy."

Holly snickered while Georgia contemplated murder.

"Let me put it this way," Jenna added. "If you don't talk to me, then I'm under strict orders to gag you, bind you and haul you upstairs to meet with my father. Alex is on standby to help. You're not leaving here without talking to one of us."

"I suggest you go with Jenna," Holly said. "Mr. Montgomery hasn't been in the best mood lately. He sent back the eggs this morning. Twice."

Georgia groaned. It was no more than she'd expected. Mr. Montgomery wanted to eat her spleen instead of more traditional breakfast foods. Jenna wanted to braid her hair to a bedpost so she could never escape again. She didn't even want to think about what must be going on at the Montgomery Foundation right now. The thought of the upheaval caused by Monty's defection tied her stomach up in knots.

"You're sure I can't try and convince Monty to give you a call instead?"

"I'm sure." Jenna waggled her fingers again, this time with impatience. "I won't eat you, Gigi. I promise."

Georgia swiveled her head to stare at the other woman. "What did you just say?"

"Gigi. It's what I've decided to call you. All the best society hostesses use repetitive, vowel-heavy nicknames. Now come *on*."

There was no gainsaying her. If asked a few months ago which of the family offspring was most like Mr. Montgomery, Georgia would have said Monty without a moment's hesitation. The commitment to work, the quietly domineering way of leading, yes, even the wooden personality—they all spoke to a strong tie between father and son.

But she'd have been wrong.

Monty was nothing like his father. He was gentle and quiet and *good*. He cared about other people so much he'd dedicated his entire life to helping them, even though ninety-nine percent of the population would never take the time to appreciate him the way he deserved.

This sister of his, though… Georgia narrowed her eyes at Jenna. There was no telling what she might do, but Georgia suspected a new nickname was the least of her worries.

"So, tell me," Jenna said as she led her through the swinging double doors and down the hall. Georgia had no idea where they were headed, but she didn't dare ask.

It seemed like one of those situations where it was better if the hostage went in blindfolded. She wouldn't have to be silenced later. "What's that brother of mine been doing with his newfound freedom?"

If Georgia was startled at how closely Jenna's words echoed Monty's—that leaving this family was a kind of release from servitude—she didn't have the courage to say so out loud.

"No—don't answer me. I can guess. He's organized your taxes, come up with a more efficient way for you to store your canned goods, anticipated your mailman's arrival time so he can be out there to meet him every day to save him the trip up the drive, and looked over your retirement plan to come up with ways you can diversify." Jenna rattled off the items without batting an eyelash. "Am I close? Three out of four?"

Georgia couldn't help it—she laughed. "Only two. I haven't told him where the tax or retirement information is yet."

"But he asked, right?"

"Yes. He asked."

He'd also spent an alarming amount of time playing with Danny in the backyard. They *said* they were trying to invent a way to get the Frisbee out of Old Hardwood without climbing the tree, but so far, all Georgia had seen was a really long series of sticks duct-taped together. Which was ridiculous—as if they hadn't tried that at least eight times before.

"If you want my advice, it's best if you give him a project to work on."

"A project? What do you mean?"

"You know how you can't leave a new puppy alone

for the first few months without coming home to find all your shoes chewed to pieces?"

"Yeah, I guess so." Georgia was more of a cat person herself, but Charlie had a pair of chocolate labs who'd devoured his college textbooks when they were young. Personally, she'd thought it was the best way to treat the table of elements, but Charlie hadn't been quite so understanding.

"It's kind of like that," Jenna said. "Monty has always needed more chew toys than other men—he needs thousands of them. If you aren't careful, he's going to destroy your house."

"Wait. Where are you taking me?" Georgia's head was reeling, so she'd somehow failed to take note that they were now on the third floor of the Manor and moving persistently down the hall.

"My room. I want you to try something on."

"Like…a hat?"

Jenna laughed, filling the empty hallway with her mirth. "Yes, Gigi. Like a hat, except you wear it on your body. I told you to start thinking about layers. Did you assume I was kidding? This whole blue-collar-working-woman thing you've got going on is fine when you're actually working, but you can't expect to blend into life upstairs without at least a few day dresses."

"Whoa, whoa, whoa." Georgia took a page from Adam's book and voiced her complaints so there could be no mistaking her. "I'm not here for anything but work. I have no desire to *blend in* upstairs."

"Maybe you should have thought about that before you enslaved my brother." Jenna's glance was pointed but not cruel. "Like it or not, things like image matter to this family. Meetings, dinners, parties, weddings—

it's a never-ending whirl of social obligations. Or didn't you know?"

"I…" She knew, of course, in that vague, hazy way one was always aware of things going on in and around the Manor. Over the years, she'd done her fair share helping Holly and Sarge prepare for a big party or society tea, but she'd never stuck around long enough to watch the guests arrive.

And why would she? They weren't her guests. They weren't Monty's guests, either—especially not now that he'd renounced all ties to the family name and fortune.

"Of course you know—you've been here longer than almost anyone." Jenna squeezed her hand. "Since it's become clear Monty has every intention of keeping you around, I've been assigned the monumental task of making you look the part."

Look the part? Georgia didn't know whether to laugh or cry. She wasn't the sort of woman you dolled up and dragged to social gatherings to show off. She was more the type you locked in the closet until polite company left.

"I think you're missing one important thing in all this," Georgia said, feeling trapped. "He left. He quit. He doesn't want to be part of this anymore."

She might as well have been talking to a rock for all her words made an impression on the scarily composed redhead.

"It's not often that I receive a summons from my dad, Gigi. He and I deal together best when we're thousands of miles apart from one another, but I dropped everything the second he called. Did it occur to you to wonder why?"

Jenna didn't wait for a response as she opened the door to her room and ushered her inside. Georgia couldn't recall ever receiving a work order for the room before, but she doubted it would've made a lasting impression on her either way. It was a functional bedroom in blond woods and pale peach linens, the only sign of adornment a mirror opposite the bed.

"It wasn't just to find Monty a love life, if that's what you're thinking. My dad has been worried about him for months now." She appraised Georgia through narrowed eyes. "You're, what? A size ten?"

Georgia nodded before she realized she was playing into Jenna's twisted mind games. "I think I'd better go. I'm not comfortable doing all this behind Monty's back."

"Sit. Calm down. No one is going to ask you to do anything against your will." She softened, her already gorgeous features relaxing into a look of sympathy. Jenna was unquestionably a striking woman under any and all circumstances, but in that moment of genuine human emotion, Georgia found her breathtaking. "He won't last out there on his own for much longer. He can't. He's physically and mentally incapable of separating himself from work for that long."

"You can't be sure of that," Georgia said, but it was a halfhearted protest. Poor Monty was already showing signs of wear. She loved having him around, there was no question of that—and they'd managed so far to get her off by escaping an alien invasion, withstanding a heat wave and avoiding a particularly devastating meteor strike—but he'd been growing increasingly tense as the days wore on.

Like a puppy in desperate need of something to chew.

"The Montgomery empire can't exist without my brother—you know that, right?"

Georgia felt sick. There was nothing Jenna could say that she hadn't already told herself a thousand times.

"Maybe it's not fair for all the pressure to rest on his shoulders, but he put most of it there himself. He lives this place. He breathes it. He always has."

Georgia steeled herself, determined to take Monty's side. Even if she agreed with everything Jenna was saying, he deserved to have at least one person on his side. Family was supposed to take your side. It was what her own family had always done.

"You guys might have a hard time seeing it, but there's still a person underneath all that deadline-meeting efficiency. There's only so much he can take before he cracks." Georgia paused. "I think he was closer to cracking than you realize."

"We *know*," Jenna said. "Why do you think I dropped everything to come to Monty's rescue? He wasn't so bad a few years ago—I mean, he's never been good at finding a work-life balance, but at least he went out occasionally. After he and his girlfriend broke up last year, he all but locked himself away out here."

Georgia grew unnaturally still. She wasn't jealous— *she wasn't*—but she couldn't help remembering the way he'd so casually admitted to loving that woman, as if there was never any question otherwise. Of course he was struggling to get over a love like that.

"Was he devastated?" Georgia asked quietly.

"No, no—don't misunderstand me. *Devastation* is too strong a word. It was more as if he decided not to bother anymore, like he finally had the excuse he'd been searching for. Dates, romance, a social life—he wrote it all off and started working twice as many hours as he used to." Jenna offered her a wry smile. "My dad thought maybe he could strong-arm Monty into putting himself out there again, or that he could entice him out on low-obligation dates with some of the women he knows, but you can see how well that turned out. And when he found out about you, well, he panicked. He thought Monty finally *had* cracked—and that he cracked in your general direction."

"He's not mad at me?"

"No—God, no. Half of him is convinced Monty is holding you against your will, and the other half thinks you're a godsend. He's not…holding you against your will, is he?"

Despite the revelations of the past twenty minutes, Georgia laughed. She blamed it on the relief of not being held responsible for corrupting the Montgomery family scion—at least, for not being held completely responsible for it. "No, and I doubt he'd have any luck if he tried. I have a very overprotective, overinvolved family."

Jenna shuddered. "My deepest sympathies."

"I'm still not trying on your clothes."

"You will," Jenna said with a confidence so substantial it could have shaken floors. "If there's one thing I know about my brother, it's that he can't exist for very long without the Montgomery Foundation. It's his whole life—and if you intend to be a part of that life, you're going to have to start thinking about where you fit in."

Georgia's urge to be violently ill only intensified. Not because Jenna was mean or wrong, but because she was *right*. For other people, the idea that one's entire life could be wrapped around a job might sound pathetic or exaggerated, but Georgia wasn't other people. If someone took away her Handywoman Express and Homeward Bound in the same day, she wouldn't know how to function anymore. Fixing things, building things—it was more than a job, more than a hobby. It was everything.

Jenna smiled. "You might even like it. Dresses are quite freeing."

Georgia shook her head, unwilling to commit to anything that involved ingratiating herself into the family without Monty's knowledge. It was too much. He'd made the decision to leave Montgomery Manor, and he could make the decision to come back. He was a grown man, not a puppy.

But Jenna's smile only deepened. "I'll let you go this time, Gigi, but when you change your mind, you come straight to me."

MONTY HAD NEVER been so bored in his life.

"What are your plans for the day?" Georgia entered her tiny kitchen with her coveralls on and her work boots clomping. The sight of those coveralls filled him with an unaccountable surge of jealousy. What once had been his favorite outfit—a sign of Georgia's industriousness, of her lack of concern for outward appearance—was now the last thing he looked forward to in the morning.

Those coveralls meant she had work to do, a big project ahead, people who counted on her to get things done. Like the suits he wore regardless of the day of week, it was less about wearing clothes and more about making a promise to herself about what the day contained.

As his current attire of jeans attested.

"Oh, you know," he hedged. "This and that."

"*This* meaning playing video games with Danny and *that* meaning organizing my sock drawer?" she teased.

That had been his task list on Monday. Her socks could hardly be that much of a mess already.

"Actually, I thought I might look over the Homeward Bound contracts and proposals to see if I can come up with a marketing angle you might be missing." He spoke casually, his attention focused on the eggs he was stirring to give an appearance of ease. "I've got a few ideas about how you can boost local interest."

"Ideas?"

"One in particular. I've found that for a lot of the smaller grassroots organizations, all that's needed to garner interest and funding is the right publicity. Have you considered asking one of the families if they'd do an interview to tell their story?"

The silence that greeted him wasn't a good sign. Of all the things he'd come to learn about Georgia—that ever-growing list of things to avoid—being pushed out of her comfort zone was the most distasteful to her. Challenges were welcomed as long as they included feats of physical strength, but the second anyone called into question her other capabilities, she shut down.

The idea that she might put too much emphasis on orgasms and not enough on enjoying the act of love for what it was? Unacceptable.

The idea that her lack of success with relationships had less to do with her looks and more to do with her inability to accept her own value as a human being? Not a chance.

And the idea that she might be driving her own organization into the ground by refusing to accept assistance? She wouldn't even consider it.

But that didn't make it any less true.

"It doesn't have to be a big publicity push," he continued without losing his casual air. "In fact, smaller is usually better. I've found that when you give people a face—someone to sympathize with, someone to root for—they tend to take a more vested interest in the outcome. There's a similar phenomenon in disaster relief.

You can report that five thousand people died in an earthquake and no one will lift a finger. But show one picture of a mother holding her deceased son, and the whole country mourns his loss."

"You wouldn't dare."

There went the appearance of ease. He abandoned the eggs and turned to face her—this woman he cared about so much it overwhelmed him, this woman who was driving him absolutely insane. It had been easy to pretend her stubbornness wasn't a prohibiting factor when he didn't encounter it every day, but now that he was here, he saw for himself how she was her own worst enemy where Homeward Bound was concerned.

"This is ridiculous, and you know it." He crossed his arms, determined to out-glare her. "There's no reason for you to continue struggling when you don't have to. I have time on my hands and I have the expertise to do something about your staffing problems. Why won't you take advantage of that?"

"Because I don't need to. I'm *fine*. I've got this."

"I'm not trying to take your project over, if that's what you're afraid of. All I'm trying to do is find a way for you to keep doing what you love."

"Dammit, Monty. You promised you wouldn't get involved."

He hadn't promised that. He hadn't promised Georgia anything. In order to do so, she'd have to admit to *needing* something first. So far from needing him, he'd become an accessory in her life, the shiny toy she played with at night. The sexual objectification that had seemed so fun at first was now a painful reminder that he still hadn't earned the elusive respect she reserved solely for her brothers.

"You're the most infuriating woman I've ever met. Why do you insist on making it so hard for people to help you?"

"You're the most infuriating man I've ever met. Why do you have to be helping someone all the time?"

"I don't want to help *someone*, Georgia. I want to help you."

"And when I want your help, I'll be sure to ask for it."

The eggs started smoking. With a grunt of frustration, Monty clicked off the stove and tossed the ruined breakfast pan under running water. The interruption gave him a moment to collect himself, and he could only be grateful for it. Arguing with Georgia wouldn't get him anywhere—as a woman born to obstinacy, it gave her the home-field advantage. He needed to find another way in.

"I'm sorry," he said, and pulled her into a hug. As he expected, she fought for a good ten seconds before she finally yielded. "I didn't mean to start the day off with a fight—I'm usually better at timing my battles than this."

"That's not really apologizing," she said, her voice muffled. "It's rescheduling."

He laughed and held her tighter, loving how warm she felt against him. "I don't hear you offering any apologies in return. How's this? I know you hate it when I make suggestions about Homeward Bound, but I can't help it. Solving problems like these has been my job for years, and I haven't been able to turn that part of myself off yet. It's been a lot more difficult than I thought to transition away from life at the Manor."

That was an understatement of epic proportions. For years, he'd operated under the impression that the world outside his office was a seething, swirling orgy of entertainment. People had fun and did what they wanted and answered to no one but themselves—while he and he alone remained bent over his desk. It was a truth he saw reinforced by Jake's never-ending pursuit of enjoyment, in Jenna's jet-setting to places he'd only ever seen in pictures, in families like Georgia's gathering for weekly dinners.

As it turned out, there weren't any entertainment orgies. Fun was being had and memories were being made, but people also went to work. They answered to their bosses and their obligations. They put on their coveralls and labored under the sun. And still only he remained—not bent over a desk this time, but somehow just as chained down as before.

Freedom was an illusion. A boring, mind-numbing, never-ending illusion.

"You miss it, don't you?" Georgia asked softly.

He nodded, not trusting himself to speak. He missed it more than he ever thought possible.

"Maybe it's time for you to think about returning." Georgia spoke carefully, and he could tell she was striving for the same detached tone that had failed him before. "The foundation needs you a lot more than I do. We could go back to our daily meetings in the summerhouse. Those were fun."

"I don't want to have to sneak out to see you, Georgia. You deserve better than that."

She stiffened again. "Please don't make this about me. Make it about your dad, or your sister, or the job, but don't make it about me."

Silly woman. It could never not be about her—not anymore.

"Your family has been nothing but kind to me since you moved out," she said, almost pleading. "I'm sure you could find a way to strike a deal for fewer hours or more free time if you ask. They miss you more than you realize."

"No." He strengthened his grip on Georgia, fearful that to let her go would be to lose the only remaining part of himself. That part was small and growing infinitesimally smaller by the day. "I can't go home—not like this, not on my knees. It's what he wants."

"And what do you want, Monty?" she asked.

He didn't answer, because he didn't know.

THE CALL CAME in the middle of the night.

Never a heavy sleeper to begin with, Monty hadn't gotten a good night's rest since he'd left Montgomery Manor. He loved having Georgia nestled against him, and they certainly wore themselves out in an attempt to find innovative rescue scenarios, but wakefulness never truly left him.

He blamed his cell phone, eerily silent now that he'd stopped work calls and emails from coming in. Like a ticking bomb, it sat heavily by his side, more ominous in its silence than it had ever been when active.

The sound of it ringing now was almost a comfort. The crisis had arrived, the company was collapsed, a lifetime of hard work had come to a grinding halt. At least now he didn't have to pretend he didn't care what happened anymore.

"Hello?" He rolled out of bed and tried to speak softly, but Georgia's apartment was so small there was no way to even sneeze without disturbing the peace. "What's wrong?"

"Mr. Montgomery?" The relief in Thomas's voice was

impossible to ignore. "Finally! I've been trying to get hold of you for days."

Monty's grip on the phone tightened so much he was afraid he crushed the delicate electronics. "You have?"

"Is it okay that I'm calling your emergency number? They told me you were in Hong Kong, and I checked online first. It's like the middle of the day there, right?"

Monty didn't have to do the mental calculation. Hong Kong was twelve hours opposite East Coast time. If his family wanted to pretend he was out of reach, they'd gravitate as far away as they could possibly get. All the way to the other side of the globe.

"A gorgeous afternoon," he lied. The room was dark save for the glow of Georgia's face. She was sitting up in the bed, watching him with a cloaked expression. "What's up?"

"They canceled my meeting with the Board of Regents, and no one will tell me why." The relief that had lowered Thomas's voice rose to an urgent pitch. "I know you're hella busy, and it's not part of your job to deal with my personal shit…"

Monty cleared his throat, more out of habit than anything else.

"I mean, I know you're busy, sir, and you've already done so much for me, but I had my presentation ready to go and everything. Why won't they even see me now?"

Monty swore. He tried to keep the sound under his breath, but he was sure Thomas heard him. Getting Thomas in to see the Connecticut Higher Education Board had been something he'd wanted right from the start. There was only so much Monty could do by standing around talking about a need for change—he was just one more dried-up rich guy with privilege oozing out of his pores. It was kids like Thomas who would lead the real change.

It had taken him *months* to get that meeting set up, dozens of favors called in. There was no reason why it shouldn't have gone through.

If it was possible to transcend the confines of space and time, Monty would reach out and strangle his father right now. If step one was to pretend that he was in an extended business trip in Hong Kong, then step two was to start cutting down all the projects that mattered to him. It was slash and burn, with Monty as the fall guy.

"I'll fix this, Thomas. I swear. There's been some restructuring going on, and…" Who was he kidding? This wasn't restructuring. This was a collapse of everything he'd been working toward. "This isn't your fault. This is on me. I dropped the ball."

Monty felt rather than heard Georgia approach from behind. She moved silently, pushing him to her computer chair before he could apologize for interrupting her sleep.

Coffee? she mouthed.

He nodded gratefully and grabbed the nearest pen, jotting down notes regarding all the ways his desertion had impacted this kid's life and all the things he'd need to do to make up for it.

It was a long list.

"I'm so sorry, Georgia," he said later, when streaks of sunlight were beginning to touch the sky and he'd finished off an entire pot of coffee. "I could have taken that to my car."

"Don't be ridiculous. An emergency is an emergency." She spoke brightly, but there were lines of anxiety around her mouth he knew he'd put there himself. "What was the emergency, if you don't mind my asking?"

"Lingering Montgomery Foundation issues," he said.

"That was Thomas? The kid you've been helping?"

He nodded. The kid who'd been helping him. The kid who would be the walking dead today, exhausted from staying up all hours of the night to call on Hong Kong time, determined not to inconvenience Monty any more than he had to.

"Is it going to be okay?" she asked.

"Yes. No. Yes." He took a deep breath, willing the last of his anger to ebb away. He had the capacity to get Thomas his meeting back, but without the full Montgomery might behind the foster care initiative, it was like propping up a single log to take the place of an entire dam. "Thomas will be fine—he's the sort who'll always find a way to land on his feet. It's the rest of the kids I'm not so sure about."

If he didn't know any better, he'd say she brightened at his words. "Does this mean you're going back to work?"

He firmed his lips in a line it would take a thousand crowbars to crack. "No. It means nothing short of a miracle will ever get me to work for my father again."

NINETEEN

"OKAY, JENNA. I'M IN."

It took Monty's sister a few seconds for realization to settle in, but it was clear from the way her face lit up that she hadn't been one hundred percent convinced Georgia would be back.

"How in are we talking?" Jenna asked, not yet rising from the desk in her bedroom where she sat studying her laptop. Georgia wasn't sure if Monty's resignation had increased the other woman's workload or if she was merely as much of a workhorse as he was, but these Montgomerys sure knew how to be productive.

She almost wanted to steal the laptop and smuggle it out to Monty later. He could hide it under his pillow and dream in email, access the files he needed to fix whatever catastrophe had arisen in the middle of the night. Maybe it would erase some of the look of devastation that fell over him whenever he thought she wasn't looking. He called *her* stubborn and infuriating, but she wasn't the one who refused to admit how much her work meant to her.

She *knew* she was a crazily obsessed contractor who busted balls and then had to stay up all hours to make up lost time. At least she was willing to own it.

"All in." Georgia took a deep breath. Her entire body balked at the idea of standing here, plotting and planning and agreeing to let this woman be her guide, but she didn't know what else to do. Monty was miserable. She'd never seen a man so near tears as he'd been on the phone with this kid who obviously meant the world to him. And with nary a bruise in sight. "Whatever it takes to lure him back. Spreadsheets. Hotel chains. Day dresses." *Miracles.*

"Tell me where to go and what to do, and I'll do it."

"Oh, I've got grander plans than that. Have you ever taken dancing lessons?"

Georgia opened her mouth to offer an obliging laugh, but Jenna's thoughtfully puckered lips were one hundred percent serious. "Not unless you count line dancing in gym in middle school. I'm not a good dancer, Jenna. Not even a little."

"You will be by the time I'm done with you. Are you sure you're still in?"

She closed her eyes and nodded, feeling the same way people must when they sold their souls to the devil or financed a vehicle from a used car dealer.

"I promise to be as gentle as possible," Jenna said. "But tell me—how do you feel about Brazilians?"

Georgia blinked. "I don't think I know any. I've never been south of the Equator."

Jenna's laugh cemented the dissolution of Georgia's soul. "Oh, Gigi. This is going to be so fun. You have no idea."

"I'M TAKING YOUR girlfriend shopping, Monty, not to North Korea to start World War III. Please have some faith in my ability to purchase shoes without causing irreparable harm."

Georgia had to bite the tip of her tongue to stop herself from admitting that North Korea held more charm for her than the promised trip to Hartford. She'd prefer to wrestle dictators over shoe salesmen any day.

"Although I should probably warn you that I intend to take her to lunch afterward. Am I allowed to feed her, or is that against the rules too?" Jenna spoke with a light air, but there was no mistaking the steely undercurrent. Georgia knew her family was a force all its own, but Jenna scared her. She had a feeling this woman didn't hear the word no very often.

Monty turned to Georgia, both hands on her shoulders, his palms heavy and warm and comforting in ways that shopping with his sister would never be. Why, oh why, had she agreed to get in the middle like this?

"I'm finding it hard to believe this is the innocent shopping trip she's painting it out to be," he said, his gaze searching hers. Those blue eyes saw everything. "You don't have to do anything you don't want to, Georgia. Not for me. I separated myself from my family for a reason. They don't get a say in what you or I do."

Oh, yeah. That was why. Because Monty was kind and supportive and one hundred percent miserable.

"I need new rain boots," she said, striving for jocularity. "I was thinking of mixing it up a little bit."

"I saw the sweetest pair of studded ankle boots in Prague last month. I bet we can find something similar."

"She's partial to rubber," Monty said tightly. "Something with good aeration."

"I'm going to ignore the words *rubber* and *aeration* in relation to our discussion of ladies' footwear." Jenna shuddered. "I'll be out in the car, Gigi. Don't let him bully you."

Gruffly, he pulled her to him and dropped a kiss on her lips. "Don't let *her* bully you," he said. "She seems nice on the outside, but believe me when I warn you she's as ruthless as they come. She'll send you home with no less than an entire wardrobe overhaul—and none of it will make you even remotely as attractive as you are in coveralls."

"Oh, please," she said, flustered. "No one likes to see me in coveralls."

"I do."

She had no defense against that. It was such a ridiculous compliment it had to be true. She covered her flustered state by saying, "I think it's time for something more upscale, don't you? Now that I'm shacking up with a Montgomery, I feel dowdy in comparison."

His grip on her tightened to the point of pain, and he might have squeezed the life out of a lesser woman, but Georgia was no lesser woman. "You're not dowdy—and I'm not a Montgomery anymore. Not in any way that matters."

It was those comments that really hurt. He would never *not* be a Montgomery the same way she would never *not* be a Lennox. Everyone hated their family sometimes, but you found a way to get over it. That was how families worked.

"You don't have to be nice to her for my sake," Monty added.

"But you're nice to my brothers. You're having lunch with Adam today without a gun being held to your head. How is this any different?"

He didn't answer, because he couldn't. Monty had spent hours in her brothers' company, playing their twisted games, climbing their stupid trees, becoming accepted—no small feat for *anyone*, let alone a man who balked at the idea of overly familiar camaraderie.

He couldn't deny her this same opportunity to fit in his world, even if he didn't think he belonged there anymore.

"Just…don't let her manipulate you. Don't let her change you."

"I'm not so easy to change. If anyone knows that by now, it's you."

And that was that. Georgia looked uneasily back at Monty while she grabbed her ID and shoved it in her pocket, but he'd slapped a determined smile on his face. She recognized that determination. He would continue pretending this was the life he wanted, that he didn't spend restless nights worrying about all the projects he'd dropped and the people he'd let down.

Which meant Georgia had to pretend too. Apparently, she had to pretend all the way to the shoe store and back again.

"THIS IS NOT a shoe store." Georgia stopped her heels on the sidewalk outside the salon. The chemical scent of hair products and nail polish and plutonium wafted out, making her eyes water. "You didn't say anything about…"

"A haircut, Gigi. You can say it. Hairrr cut."

Georgia glared at Jenna, who was smiling at her as though the two of them had been best friends forever.

They weren't. They weren't even close. Jenna was an evil sadist with the stamina of twelve horses. Four hours of trying on skirts and dresses and sweaters and some kind of torture device called Spanx, and Georgia had never been so exhausted in her life. So far, all she'd bought was a pair of shoelaces. They had yellow stars on them.

"You'll like this place, I promise." Jenna pulled open the door, releasing even more plutonium into the atmosphere. "They serve you champagne and strawberries while you wait."

At the mention of food, Georgia's stomach rumbled a warning. Apparently, this level of shopping was a marathon event, and Jenna's promised lunch wasn't offered until they reached the finish line. Strawberries would at least prevent her from collapsing on the sidewalk.

"I don't want anything high maintenance," she said, giving the air a tentative sniff. "And nothing that could theoretically burn through my scalp." She didn't add anything about a recent study she'd read that linked cancer with the cocamides they put in high-end hair products. If Jenna's glistening auburn locks were anything to go by, she probably bathed in the stuff.

"Oh, Gigi." Jenna laughed and grabbed Georgia by the arm, pulling her through the door with more strength than such a svelte woman should possess. "You're funny. I can tell why my brother likes you so much."

"You can?"

"Of course. You stand for everything he values." Jenna didn't lose her smile. "You're unpretentious and sweet, and you say exactly what's on your mind at all times. I bet you hate parties too. I bet you hate parties so freaking hard."

Georgia barely had time to be perplexed as a trio of well-coiffed, dressed-all-in-black stylists descended on her. Champagne was pressed in her hand, her hair was called a canvas of virgin strands, and scissors were held to her throat as she was warned not to even think about getting up out of the chair.

Okay, maybe the scissors weren't at her throat, but she wouldn't have put it past the man with the spiky blue hair to go straight for the jugular if he had to. There was a glint in his eye she didn't trust.

She fortified herself with a sip of the champagne. The bubbles ran over her tongue, feeling expensive, and she indulged in one more. Given how quickly it began warming up her empty stomach, she'd be drunk in no time. Maybe that was their plan—they wanted to drink her under the table and have their wicked way with her scalp.

"I'm taking it all," the man with the scissors announced. "And I won't hear a word of protest."

"That's fine." Georgia sat back and let them circle her like a pack of vultures, aware that the scissors weren't going to let her walk away from this unscathed. "Just make sure you set it aside so I can donate it later."

She saw Jenna shrug, and the man complied. Without any warning, he lifted her ponytail and neatly snipped it off. He dropped the discarded hair into her lap, narrowly missing her champagne, and set to work.

Georgia, aware this could theoretically take hours, drank. And like magic, her glass refilled itself again as the team set to work.

"REMEMBER THAT TIME I complimented you on your balls, Montgomery?"

Every head in the restaurant turned toward the table where he and Adam sat eating an unhealthy amount of red meat for the middle of the day. They'd been headed toward a sandwich shop near Adam's office when Monty mentioned his willingness to pay for the meal, which somehow translated itself to a steakhouse with dim lighting and several rows of scotch that were older than the pair of them combined.

"Yes, I remember, and now so does everyone else inside the restaurant, thanks."

"Ha-ha." Adam's voice didn't lower at all. "Well, I take it back. You don't have an impressive set of reproductive organs. You have a desire to be murdered in your sleep."

"She can't kill me."

"She can." Adam took an enormous bite of his rare prime rib to prove it. "And don't expect anyone to find the body. She'll cover you in cement and lay you down as part of the next house's sidewalk."

"You're alarmingly well-informed on the subject."

"Which is why you should take my advice," he said. "It's a bad idea. Not only has she expressly prohibited you from getting involved with her Homeward Bound project, but she hates surprises. See where I had to get my radius pinned?"

"Yeah, yeah." Monty tried not to let the other man's lack of enthusiasm derail him. He'd known this would be an uphill battle—his promise to scale Mount Everest coming truer sooner than he'd anticipated—but he wouldn't back down on this. He was learning he had quite a stubborn streak in him. "It was a surprise birthday party gone wrong. I heard."

Adam ran his finger along the scars on his forearm. "You heard, yet you think this plan of yours is going to end in anything but disaster?"

"Oh, it'll be a disaster. I have no doubt about that."

"This is the worst sales pitch I've ever heard."

It was probably the worst one Monty had ever given, but that didn't stop him from pressing on. "I know you guys think you're doing the right thing by not undermining Georgia's authority when it comes to her work, but you're not. You're only feeding her mistaken belief that she has to do this alone."

"I beg your pardon?"

"I'm not afraid of Georgia, and I'm not afraid of you, so you can put the steak knife down." Monty sighed and rubbed the back of his neck. This plan of his would only work if he could get Georgia's brothers to back him up—a truth he didn't like but was forced to acknowledge all the same. Arguing wouldn't work. Pleading was useless. Georgia responded to only one kind of pressure— the fraternal kind.

Goddamned pack mentality. Next time he fell in love, he was picking an only child.

"I'm right about this," he said firmly. "Georgia struggles over things for no reason other than that she thinks she has to, as if it's a source of personal triumph to have to overcome great odds. You set the bar in a weird place, you and your brothers."

"What the hell is that supposed to mean?"

"Exactly what it sounds like." Since it was clear some kind of elaboration would be required, Monty eased up and took a different approach. "Of all the men you and your brothers set Georgia up on dates with, how many would you say were willing to take her out a second or third time?"

Adam paused, his fork halfway to his mouth. "How do you know about that?"

"She told me."

"Oh." He lowered the fork. "I don't know. Most of them? Georgia never really took to any of our friends, though Lord knows we tried. She always treated them more like drinking buddies than dates. She has terrible taste in men, in case you were wondering—present company included."

Monty laughed, but only for a second. There really wasn't much about this conversation to laugh about. "To hear her tell the story, *they* were the ones who weren't interested in romance. She wasn't good enough, she wasn't feminine enough, she wasn't desirable enough."

"She's wrong."

"*I* know that, but she doesn't. It's like she has this mental block that prevents her from realizing how incredible she is." He took a deep breath. "I'm not saying it's your fault, but…it's kind of your fault. All of you."

"You're treading on thin ice here," Adam warned.

"Of course I am. Man up and join me, would you? I'm getting tired of being the only one brave enough to venture out here."

Adam leaned over the table, the yellow ring in his eyes lit into flame. "What the hell are you getting at?"

"I need your help." There. That had to be something no one had admitted to a Lennox before. "The four of you put a ridiculous amount of stock in fighting and challenging and waging a war of constant one-upmanship. I'm not saying it's necessarily bad, but I don't think Georgia ever learned that it's okay to accept her value without having to prove it first. She's afraid that if she stops fighting—if love is offered without question, or if she accepts the easy solution to her staffing problems—then she's doing things wrong. She's afraid she won't be one of you anymore."

He pulled out a closing argument worthy of a three-sixty on the Bar. "You know as well as I do that nothing is more important to that woman than the three of you. Nothing. Not even me."

Adam's mouth fell open before he clamped it shut again, uncharacteristically quiet, and Monty knew he'd broken through. It was a triumph unlike any other he'd experienced before. He'd cracked the ranks. He'd challenged the Alpha and won. He'd made Adam like him.

"I hate you, Montgomery. I hope you realize that."

Monty grinned. "The feeling is mutual. Does that mean you're in?"

"Fuck." Adam threw his knife to the table in defeat. "I'm in."

TWENTY

"WHAT DID YOU do to her?" Monty rushed to the car to help extract the strange woman who'd taken up a seat next to Jenna. It wasn't the appearance of her that frightened him so much as the fact that she was smiling—and that she was smiling through lips painted a soft shell pink.

The Georgia he'd seen walk out that door wouldn't smile through a lipstick-covered mouth. The Georgia he'd seen walk out that door would wipe the makeup off on the sleeve of her coveralls and tell Jenna from which orifice she could extract the lipstick if she wanted it back.

"Hullo, John," Georgia said, smiling even wider. "I bought shoelaces."

Oh, *no.* He cast an accusing glare at his sister. "Did you get her drunk? That's how you forced her into complicity? You shoved liquor down her throat?"

"Aren't you going to comment on how nice her hair looks?"

Monty was forced to step back and take a better look at Georgia, though he kept his hands propped under her arms to hold her aloft. He'd seen this woman drink entire pitchers full of beer, washed down with shots of whisky, without stopping for air.

"I didn't realize the champagne would go to her head so fast," Jenna said by way of apology. "I thought it might relax her."

Monty barely grunted a reply. He was too busy marveling at the changes a shorn head wrought on this woman he thought he knew so well. It would have been unfair to accuse Jenna of having taken drastic measures to alter Georgia, since the amount of makeup she wore was minor and there didn't seem to be any permanent changes to her hair color. And, if anything, this shorter hair, worn close to the head, was more Georgia's style. But he hadn't been prepared for the *curls*...

He reached up and tugged one of the short strands, watching in wonder as it bounced back into place, satiny to the touch. He wanted to dig his hands in her hair, run his fingers through those locks, kiss the long, elegant neck now bared to the sky.

"Isn't it cute?" Georgia asked, her voice loud in a mock-whisper sort of way. "Don't tell Jenna, because I don't want her to think I approve of all this needless vanity, but I love my hair. The stylist gave me this special shampoo so I don't have to do anything to it in the morning. Not even brush it. Did you know not brushing your hair was an option?"

"I like your hair no matter how it looks," he said, determined to remain neutral. But this suited her. It softened her. It gave her an almost impish quality that was highlighted by her sparkling eyes. "If it makes you happy, it makes me happy."

"They also did horrific things to the hair on other parts of my body, but I think maybe we should wait until your sister leaves to look at those ones."

"So help me, Jenna—"

His sister's eyes flew open, and she clapped a hand over her mouth. "Okay, maybe it's better if you take her inside now. It's the champagne talking, I swear. They didn't do anything against her will."

"Jenna..."

"Oh, calm your tits, Monty. The makeup washes off. Hair grows back. And you heard her—she bought shoelaces. That is literally all she purchased. I've never seen that kind of restraint in real life before."

"Georgia doesn't believe in materialism," he said with a glare, but it was pointless. Glares didn't work on Jenna. Nothing did. "It's one of the things I love about her."

"Oh, really? Do tell. What else do you *love?*"

He ignored the gleam in his sister's eyes and led Georgia inside instead. The champagne made her giggly, the makeup made her a stranger, and the hair made him want to do inappropriate things. It was better for all of them if they escaped from the public eye.

Apparently, he wasn't the only one who felt that way. No sooner had they made it through the front door than Georgia was on top of him. All the way on top of him, pushing him toward the bed and pouncing as though she were a predatory cat and he was about to be devoured alive.

He let her. It wasn't the gentlemanly thing to do when she was intoxicated, and it was probably a good idea to have a discussion about his sister's sudden interest in Georgia's grooming habits first, but Georgia's body was so warm and soft and *strong*. He might have been able to wrestle her into submission if he really put his mind to it, but his mind was otherwise occupied at the moment.

It was reeling with the confused sensations of wrong and oh-so-very-right. She tasted of champagne and lipstick—a cocktail he knew well and wasn't averse to, but which felt vaguely wrong coming from her. She also smelled of the chemical residue that came from hair salons, and her skin was more slick than usual, his hands moving over her body so quickly he had to dig his fingers in lest she get away.

"Georgia, is this—are you—did you get a *massage?*"

"I got half of a massage." She sat up, her legs straddling his waist, and lifted the T-shirt from over her head. He was relieved to find that she was still the same Georgia from the waist up, her bra a familiar and comforting tan, her stomach its customary ripple of muscle and skin. "Maybe it was closer to a quarter of a massage. I couldn't do it. I tried, but it felt so weird to have some lady rubbing me down like I was a piece of tenderloin. It was so slippery."

"It still *is* slippery," he commented, his hands running smoothly up and down her sides in a way he wasn't sure he approved of. It was too foreign, even more than the champagne kisses. His fingers hit her waistband, and he tugged at the button, too curious about the hair situation to wait any longer. "But if you couldn't handle the massage, how on earth did you make it through the— Aha. I see."

He rolled Georgia underneath him, angling her for a better look.

"I refuse to let you mock me for that," she said. "One side was all I could stand. I can take pain, Monty—you know I can—but what that woman was trying to do to me was *indecent.*"

"She and I have something in common, it would seem." He pressed a kiss on the soft curve of her belly before shucking her jeans the rest of the way off. So far, every time he'd gotten his mouth this close to her lower half, she managed to kick and scream him back up where he belonged.

"What do you think you're doing?" she asked, though

with a lazy kind of acquiescence he could only attribute to the champagne.

He grinned up at her as he continued plying her stomach with the soft press of his lips. Over belly button, along the jutting prow of her hips, lower until he reached the patch of brown curls, now halfway groomed into a neat vee. "This," he said, and pulled her legs open. "This is what I'm doing."

A warning in the back of Georgia's mind told her it was a bad idea to let Monty continue pressing those warm, wet kisses between her legs. Not only was there a high likelihood he'd end up exhausted and she'd end up disappointed, but this wasn't part of the plan. She was supposed to be encouraging him to go back home, not rolling around on the bed hoping he'd stay.

"I'm not so sure this is a good idea," she managed.

"I figure if you were willing to let a complete stranger down here, it's only fair I get a shot at it too."

She flopped her head against the pillow, too drunk to protest further. This was what rich, attractive people did—indulged in midday alcohol consumption, pampered themselves with haircuts and no-brushing shampoo and ungodly hair removal processes—and then went home to be ravaged by a persistent, golden-tipped tongue.

"I can stop if you don't like it," Monty said, that familiar anxious note in his tone.

"No, it's okay."

"Really?"

"Really." And why the hell not? Today was a day of make-believe. Her whole life had become make-believe as of late. She was going to spas and having lunch with Jenna. She was getting haircuts that literally cost the same as her truck payment. She'd been cast into the role of Lady of the Manor even though it was the last place she belonged.

If she was going to play at being a Montgomery, she might as well play at this too.

She relaxed and took the exact same steps required of her at the spa. With her eyes closed and a deep, calming breath, she gave herself permission to walk through this world of theirs, if only for a moment.

And what a world it was.

Monty gave no indication that he was anything but happy to be between her legs, and she couldn't help but remember his previous words—that he could be happy there for hours, if only she'd let him in. It had been a lie, of course, part of the education in dirty talking he'd mastered after just a few interludes, but for right now, she believed him. There were too many sensations—kissing and tongue, and oh, were those his teeth?—for her to do anything but *feel*.

"I hate to admit it, Georgia, but I think you might have been right in keeping me away from this for so long."

"What?" Georgia felt the familiar tension entering her body, tightening her muscles from the inside out, filling her with an overwhelming urge to cover up and run away. No matter how many times she lay with this man, that tension always reared its ugly head. "Am I doing something wrong?"

"No," he said, and resumed his attention to her clit. "I'm just not sure I'll ever be able to stop now."

She came. It was embarrassingly swift and wholly unexpected. One second, she was considering rolling off the bed and hiding underneath it in an attempt to get away, and the next, she was crying out and clamping her legs so hard around poor Monty's face he probably couldn't breathe.

But he didn't care, and neither did she. She was far too busy reeling in the sensation—not of pleasure, but of wonder. She'd experienced an orgasm wrought entirely by someone else's efforts. She'd experienced an orgasm she didn't have to manually elicit herself.

Yes, Virginia, there is such a thing as gratification that requires nothing in return.

"Holy hell, Monty." Her voice sounded as if from the end of a long tunnel. "You did it. You actually did it."

He pressed a soft kiss on her inner thigh before moving up the bed to hold her tight, an action so ingrained in him she wasn't sure he even knew he did it anymore. He pressed his erection against her ass, but other than a growl of contentment, he didn't make any efforts to turn the attention back on himself. "You don't have to sound so surprised. I'm not that inept."

No, but she was. Or so she'd always thought.

"By the way, I like your hair," he said, nuzzling the exposed back of her neck.

"Thank you," was inadequate, but she wasn't sure what else to say. It *was* cute, but it was just hair. "Oh, dammit. I left my ponytail at the salon."

He kept his focus on the nape of her neck, eliciting permanent liquidity. "You kept your ponytail?"

"I was growing it out so I could donate it to one of those charities that makes wigs for kids with cancer. Jenna thinks I should start a drive. She says I could talk to local salons, and she'll see if any of the women at your family's country club might be willing to drive interest. I'm kind of excited about it. It never occurred to me to try and do more than just build houses."

The kissing stopped, sending a shiver down her spine—though this one felt more ominous than sensual. "Jenna's introducing you to the country club ladies?"

"Well, um. Maybe?" Between the orgasm and the alcohol, Georgia was beginning to feel fuzzy. "Not directly. She made a lunch reservation there tomorrow, though. I'm going to learn forks."

"Forks?" Based on Monty's expression, Georgia thought maybe he wanted her to eat with only her hands from now on. "I thought you and I were having lunch tomorrow."

"Oh, dammit. I forgot. Would you mind if we rescheduled?"

"Yes, actually. I do mind." He rolled out of the bed and away from her, his sudden return to a cold, careful Monty clearing her head in an instant. "The people at that country club are snobs, and Jenna hates it there almost as much as I do. Whatever reason she has for dragging you to lunch with her isn't a good one, I promise."

Georgia's first instinct was to agree with Monty. She didn't want to go to some stuffy two-hour meal when she should be working, and she didn't want to try on any more clothes, and she definitely didn't want to waste her day hobnobbing around the Manor when she could be here with Monty.

But she didn't. Hanging out with her boyfriend wasn't part of the plan. Hobnobbing was the plan.

"Sorry," she said, knowing the apology sounded wooden. It *was* wooden. "I have to go. I already promised."

Predictably, Monty wasn't pleased with her answer. "That's great. Enjoy your meal and my sister's company. I swear, Georgia, it's like I'm not even here half the time."

"No. You're not here half the time." She sat up, struggling into her shirt. "You're here *all* the time. That's the problem."

He recoiled, all the blood draining out of his face, leaving a marbled statue forever stuck in an image of agony.

"Oh, shit. That's not what I meant." She leaped off the bed to try and touch him—desperate for one of those crazy good hugs that made everything okay—but he stepped back.

"I told you there are hundreds of hotels where I can stay instead. I'll be out of here in an hour."

"I don't want you to leave," she cried, but it was a lie. She did want him to leave. She wanted him to go back home where he belonged, where he wouldn't be wasting his talents and his passions on a woman who didn't deserve them. She reached out again, and again failed to make contact. "Don't you think it's time you made up with your family, Monty? I'm not kicking you out of here—I'm *not*—but you can't spend the rest of your life pretending this is enough for you."

Pretending I'm enough for you.

"What was Jenna's real motive in taking you out today?" he asked, his voice quiet, his face still carved of stone. "She should have gone back overseas the second I moved out."

Georgia's first impulse was to lie, but she was tired of playing by the Montgomery rules. They had stupid rules—and this was coming from a woman whose family *defined* stupidity. If only Mr. Montgomery would come out and tell Monty how much he needed him. If only Jenna would tell Monty the same thing she'd told Georgia—that they loved him, worried about him, wanted him to be happy. Everything was all so mixed up.

"She's teaching me to fit better in your world."

"You already do fit, Georgia. You fit perfectly."

"Not this world." She shook her head, marveling at how light her head felt. How not her. "The other world. The one you have to go back to, even though you're too proud to admit it."

"It's not pride keeping me away."

"I know." She felt an inexpressible sadness settle over her shoulders, heavy and somehow comforting at the same time. "It's me. I'm what's keeping you away."

He didn't argue, because he couldn't. It was true.

"Your sister can be overbearing sometimes, but she's just trying to help me fit in. I figure I'm halfway there already. I have new hair and new shoelaces and a new charity project to get underway. I'm the whole package now."

"Is that supposed to be a joke?"

If it was, she didn't feel compelled to laugh. "They're planning on unveiling me at some wedding next weekend. I think it's the same one your dad was trying to set you up on dates for. Will you come with me?"

He went from marble to brimstone in less than ten seconds.

"You did invite me in the first place," she pointed out uneasily. "So it's not too terrible for me to crash, right? Your dad will be there, and I think your brother Jake is driving in, and Jenna's been making me sit with her tailor for hours to refit one of her old dresses."

"It always comes back to that stupid wedding." He swore, a *fuck* falling from his lips with an ease she almost admired. "I can't believe they would do this. No—I can. I can believe it. That's the problem."

This was her chance. She took a step forward, but he made no move to touch her. "All they want is for you to come home, Monty. They miss you."

"They don't miss me. They miss the amount of work I took off their plates." His words were bitter, cold. "And all you're doing is feeding their delusions by playing into it. You can't go."

"I have to."

"You'll be miserable—I'm not kidding. You don't understand what those events are like. Everyone there is petty and vain and materialistic, and they'll know you're only there as a way for my dad to prove I'm not still hung up on my ex-girlfriend."

"So come with me."

He didn't move.

"You want something to keep yourself busy? You want to help me out for a change? Here's your opportunity. Be my date. Promise you'll come. Don't abandon me to those terrible people."

Not even his own words, echoed back in desperation, moved him. "It's not your kind of event, Georgia. You don't belong there."

"I know I don't." Of course she knew. She'd known her entire life. For twenty-nine years, she'd been an outsider looking in—not only at the magnificence of Montgomery Manor, but at life in general. This time with Monty might have given her a chance to walk through the walls—to where it was warm and she was cared for and she wasn't as deplorable a woman as she'd always thought—but she'd never been deluded enough to believe she could stay on a permanent basis. "I'm not stupid. I know none of this is real. I know none of this can last."

His only response was to stare. Intent and familiar, that stare said so much more than his words ever could.

Of course it couldn't last. The Bore and the Beast had always been the wrong story anyway.

MONTY MOVED OUT that night.

His entire life was packed up and returned to that single suitcase in a matter of minutes. He spent a little longer—almost half an hour—bidding farewell to Danny and her mother, thanking them for their hospitality like he was some gentleman traveler stopped in for a spell. Her own goodbye lasted seconds, if that. A peck on the cheek, one last jaw-ticking entreaty not to entangle herself with his family, and that was it.

He didn't even look back as he made his way down the steps and to his car, looking so incongruously expensive parked next to her work truck that they'd actually had neighbors call and ask if they'd either won the lottery or taken up a life of crime.

Georgia told herself it was silly to worry about him, that the amount of money in his bank account precluded starvation on the streets or any other kind of material deprivation, but material deprivation wasn't what scared her. What Monty needed more than wealth was a home—not the four walls a good construction crew could put up in a few weekends, but the feeling of love and acceptance that could be found within them.

What Monty needed was the love and acceptance that existed for him at Montgomery Manor. His family cared enough about him to make over an awkward handywoman and accept her in their ranks. If that wasn't a sign of their true regard, she didn't know what was.

She called Jenna the second Monty's taillights disappeared into the night. She told herself that she was calling out of a sense of obligation, that Jenna deserved all the facts, but she mostly needed to hear a friendly voice right now. A *Montgomery* voice. "I thought I should warn you that Monty and I had a fight. He moved out, and I don't think he has any intention of going home."

"Oh, Gigi. What did you do?"

She chomped on her lip to keep from wailing. "I'm sorry, Jenna, but I told him what we were doing. I told him about the plan to take me to the wedding next week. He practically forbade me from going—I don't think he wants me touching that part of his life."

The silence on the other end of the phone was so loud Georgia almost needed earplugs.

"Not that I blame him," she said. Looking down, she noticed blood rising from four crescents on the palm of her hand. "It was foolish to agree to all this in the first place."

"Nonsense." Jenna made a quick recovery. "We still have our lunch date tomorrow, and you need to take those new shoelaces out for a spin. I want to see how they look on."

That right there was proof of how wrong Monty was about his family. Tactful and kind and elegant, Jenna was everything Georgia could never dream of being.

"I can hear you trying to think of an excuse, but it won't work," Jenna said. "If you think my brother is determined when it comes to this sort of thing, then you're in for a nasty surprise. I've never taken no for an answer before, and I don't intend to start now."

"No," Georgia said, hoping that would be the end of it.

Jenna just laughed.

TWENTY-ONE

"THE FOURTH ONE in is the shrimp fork." Jenna brandished a tiny three-pronged instrument Georgia was pretty sure she'd seen in one of those fake alien autopsy videos.

"But we're not eating shrimp." She examined the contents of her plate more carefully, wondering if maybe there were crustaceans hiding inside her teepee of asparagus. "And don't most people just pick shrimp up with their fingers anyway?"

"Only people who are eating shrimp at an all-you-can-eat-buffet." Jenna shook her head, but the smile that had been playing on her lips all morning didn't abate in the slightest. If she really disliked country clubs as much as Monty said, it didn't show. She seemed to be lapping this up—the tables full of well-dressed men and women, the water served in wineglasses, the fact that before she'd allowed either of them to sit down, she'd forced Georgia into the bathroom to exchange outfits.

So far from loving the new shoelaces, Jenna had accused Georgia of antagonizing her on purpose, and then proceeded to wrangle her into a pair of flowing linen pants and shoes that looked like torture devices from the Middle Ages.

Georgia hadn't even fought her after the first feeble protest. Pants were pants, whether they came from Target or a boutique with a French name. And she liked the pain the shoes were inflicting, the slowly slicing band across the top that would work its way through to her bone by the time the dessert course rolled around. That pain was the only thing preventing her from breaking down as Jenna worked her way through the silverware, carefully explaining the purpose of each tine.

"There's no point in all this," Georgia said, shifting her feet so the band sliced harder. She wouldn't give in to the sensation of drowning, of feeling like her lungs were awash with suppressed tears. "I'm never going to be called upon to eat shrimp with a fork anyway. This was a silly plan when Monty and I were together, and now..."

"I don't know why it's called a shrimp fork, to be honest." Jenna ignored her with a toss of her hair. "I mostly use it for crab legs and lobster, or the occasional oyster. It's long enough so you can dig inside the claw to extract all the meat. What, Gigi? Why are you looking at me like that?"

Even though there wasn't any shellfish on her plate, Georgia picked up one of the pieces of bread from the center of the table and ripped it in half. She dug her fingers into the softest part of the roll and tugged out a handful of spongy dough.

"Ta-da. I've extracted the meat." She spoke without flourish. "It's a wonder more of you don't starve."

Jenna laughed, the sound so much like Monty's Georgia felt a pang in her chest not unlike a shrimp fork being stabbed straight through it. "Fine. You win. We'll sell you as an eccentric who can't be bothered to adhere to societal norms. We can even Diane Keaton your wardrobe if we have to."

Georgia had no idea what that meant, but she didn't have the strength to argue. *This is it, then.* The day she could no longer hoist her own toolbox. The day she gave up and started sewing shit with hooked needles.

"It certainly sounds like you girls are having fun."

To avoid having to offer a response to the large, matronly woman topped with some kind of decorative purple turban, Georgia shoved the fistful of bread in her mouth. Jenna saw her and sighed before rising smoothly to her feet. She made Georgia's new Target khakis look downright elegant. "Coco, it's so lovely to see you again."

She put such an emphasis on the repetitive, vowel-heavy nickname Georgia almost choked on her mouth of bread innards.

"I haven't heard this much laughter inside these four walls since the day Matilda's hairpiece got caught in the chandelier—and most of it was coming from me." Without waiting for an invitation, Coco fell to the chair opposite Georgia, sending wafts of floral-scented air her way. "What's the grand joke?"

"I was just telling my friend Gigi here that she could become the newest club eccentric, but that was before I realized you were still alive." Jenna executed her own seat much more gracefully. "How have you managed to hold on all these years? You were ancient when I was a kid. You must be mummified by now."

Coco cackled, the inelegant sound offset when she raised one finger and somehow managed to translate that to a waiter appearing with an enormous Bloody Mary. "I'm pickled from the inside out. I'll never die. It's Gigi, is it? Take my advice and cultivate an air of mystery instead of eccentricity. Eccentricity is all fine and good when you're old, but it's mystery that will land you the most men."

"But I don't want any men." The words were out of

Georgia's mouth before she could help it. She flushed and shoved the rest of the bread inside to prevent further mishap. She was *not* discussing the wasteland of her love life with these two women. She'd discuss it later with a fifth of whisky. Only whisky understood how lonely it was inside her apartment now that Monty was gone.

It wasn't fair. She'd been just fine on her own in there before, if sexually unsated. But what was it Monty had said? That she didn't understand how sex could be bad and still be good?

She understood now. She understood it all. Imperfect sex with a man you loved wasn't just good. It was the best thing in the world.

Jenna, never perturbed, just laughed. "I don't think I introduced her properly. Coco, this is my brother's girlfriend, Georgia Lennox. Gigi, this is Coco Carrington, who can get you all the hair you could possibly want."

"But I'm not Monty's—"

Jenna cut her off with a murderous glare. "Gigi is a philanthropist, and she wants hair."

"Don't we all." Coco patted her turban wistfully. "Am I allowed to ask what she wants the hair for?"

"Children with cancer."

"Oh, thank the stars. That's so much better than where my imagination took me. Let me think…we should probably recruit Rachel and Keiko, and you can't do anything in this town without running it by Bunny first." She offered Georgia one of her olives from the end of a toothpick. She didn't want to touch it with her fingers— this was no all-you-can-eat-buffet—so she picked up her shrimp fork and gave it a stab. Coco didn't even blink. "How much hair do you need?"

Georgia wasn't sure how to respond. She had a mouth

full of bread, an olive on a fork and a broken heart. There was no point in setting her up as some kind of Lady Bountiful, since Monty wanted nothing to do with her anymore, but it seemed like a terrible waste to let this woman walk away without hearing her out.

Throwing herself into volunteer projects had always been Georgia's way of casting her worries aside to take on the burden of someone else's, her chance to lose her sense of self, if only for a few hours.

Right now, she couldn't think of anything she'd rather do than get rid of the Georgia Lennox sobbing inside her head.

She swallowed. "As much as I can get my hands on. I was thinking we should get a few salons involved— maybe offering free cuts to people if they donate their hair, or discounted trimmings for maintenance and stuff."

Coco crunched her stalk of celery thoughtfully. "That's not a bad idea. You've got a good head for this kind of thing." She laughed out loud. "See what I did there? A good head? Mercy me, what I would give to have thick curls like yours again."

For the rest of the meal—plate after plate of food transformed into teepees and pyramids and other leaning towers—they discussed the logistics of doing a drive to raise awareness and funds. Coco was alarmingly well-informed on the subject, even after her third Bloody Mary, and Georgia felt herself relaxing more and more as the afternoon went on.

Maybe this isn't so terrible. Maybe I am capable of this kind of life. She wasn't just hobnobbing. She was successfully hobnobbing. Wouldn't Monty be surprised to see her accepting help from one of his peers?

"Well, my dear. I'll say this for you—you're an original." Coco struggled to rise, and only managed once Georgia gripped her by the elbow and hoisted her out of the chair. "Most women take years to find their feet in this set, but you seem to be planted rather firmly on yours. Though those shoes are all wrong for you. Flats are an eccentric's best friend. Flats and shawls. Remember that."

"I will," Georgia promised.

"And bring that boyfriend of yours to come see me one of these days. He should get out more. If he's not careful, he's going to end up exactly like his father."

Georgia opened her mouth to protest again, and was once again silenced by Jenna's thunderously dark blue stare.

Georgia waited until Coco was out of earshot to pounce. "Why did you let that poor, sweet old woman think I'm still with Monty? What if she tells all those other women?"

"Then she tells all those other women."

"Jenna." Georgia wanted to sound firm enough to knock some common sense into the other woman's head, but she was afraid she mostly ended up sounding frantic. "I'm going to theoretically be working with her for the next few months. This will just make things awkward."

"Only if you let it."

Georgia scanned for a sign of the shrimp fork, but the waiter had long since cleared it away.

"Besides," Jenna continued brightly. "It won't be any more awkward than when you come to the wedding with me this weekend. You're going to have to get used to nosy questions from this crowd."

Georgia couldn't have been more surprised if the tables lifted from the ground and Ouija boards started flying. "What are you talking about? Jenna—Monty and I aren't together. You know that, right? You're aware I have absolutely zero sway over him now?"

Jenna tilted her hand back and forth. "You say zero, I say a couple hundred. I like those odds."

Georgia sputtered—actually sputtered, her emotions coming out as little more than spittle and unvoiced outrage.

"You owe me one, Gigi. I gave you Coco, one of the most powerful women in Connecticut, though you wouldn't think it to look at that awful headpiece she wears." Jenna winced, as if seeing the purple turban for the first time. "You can give me a few hours on Saturday afternoon. It won't kill you."

"Actually, it might."

Jenna looked as if she wanted to drop another blasé comment or use her force to bend Georgia into complaisance, but something about the bleakness in Georgia's soul at that moment must have come through. "Oh, sweetie. I know it's asking a lot, and chances are nothing will come of it, but we need you to *try*. For Monty and for all the people who are counting on him. You're all we have right now. You're our last bargaining chip."

Georgia wavered. She genuinely liked Jenna and her family, and she knew for herself how much kids like Monty's friend Thomas needed him, but a social event like a wedding was asking a lot. It was asking everything.

"I'm no good at this sort of thing." She looked down at her feet, where bands of red, irritated skin blustered up at her. "I can't even wear the shoes right."

"You're perfect the way you are." Jenna spoke with enough certainty for the both of them. "And Coco loved you. Believe me when I say that she could have just as easily torn you to pieces and refused to ever let you set foot in here again. She doesn't extend herself like that for just anyone."

"Really?" She wasn't wavering now so much as falling, headfirst, into the void.

"Really." Jenna slipped off Georgia's tennis shoes and held them out, right there in the middle of the restaurant. "All you need to do is wear a dress and smile. What could possibly go wrong?"

TWENTY-TWO

THE THING ABOUT weddings was, no one got to see the bride until the event was damn near over.

Before the ceremony started, there was a good half hour of arrivals that put the Academy Awards to shame, limos belching up men and women in elaborately coiffed dos. There was an even longer half hour after that of chatting in the foyer, a series of uncomfortable introductions as Georgia met and was ignored by wave after wave of millionaires. And there was the longest ten minutes of her life as she and the Montgomerys found seats on the bride's side, all of them taking painstaking care to include her in their conversation.

Poor Mrs. Montgomery barely knew who she was. She kept confusing her with one of the gardeners.

Exhausted with smiling, and her head aching from all the perfume in the air, Georgia didn't remember until the processional music began that the woman for whom the entire event existed had once enjoyed ten months of Monty's love.

It was impossible to ignore that fact as a vision in white tulle appeared at the end of the nave. From where she stood behind a series of oversized hats, Georgia could only make out the long, lean lines of the bride's form and the upsweep of daintily blond hair underneath the veil. It might not have been much to an uninterested viewer, but Georgia was far from uninterested.

She was facing no less than a paragon of female perfection. In fact, from the way the woman walked, a film
vixen right down to the sway of her hips…

Wait a minute.

Georgia clutched Jenna's arm, even though she'd been
instructed eight times already to calm down and stop
grasping at her like a child missing her mother. It wasn't
totally her fault—she needed the other woman's balance
to avoid falling on her face in these stupid high heels.

"What is it now?" Jenna hissed.

"What's the bride's name?"

"Are you serious?"

"I know you told me her last name was Bridgerton,
but I don't think you told me her first name. It's not
Ashleigh, is it?"

Jenna nodded, confirming all of Georgia's worst fears
before adding new ones. "You'll meet her during the reception—I think you're going to like her. Not only do
you share the distinction of having once enslaved my
brother, but she's actually quite nice."

Georgia was already aware of that fact. Ashleigh was
nice and gorgeous and she swore like a champ and she
had a throaty laugh. She was the woman Georgia would
have handpicked for Monty to share his life with, if she
wasn't already so desperately in love with him herself.

Oh, hell. She needed a place to hide. She needed a
plague of locusts to descend on the church and start eating their way through the support beams.

As if sensing her panic, Jenna grabbed her arm and
held her in place. "I promise—she's not as scary as she
looks."

Easy for her to say. From where Georgia was standing in her spiked shoes, unable to breathe in her too-

tight dress, that woman was absolutely terrifying. Thus far, she'd been able to make it through the wedding by pretending to be some kind of distant Montgomery relation—a family friend, a visiting acquaintance, a special friend of Monty's, wink wink, nudge nudge. But Ashleigh was sure to recognize her, and would probably demand some kind of explanation for why a handywoman who wasn't actually named Holly Santos was crashing her million-dollar nuptials.

Oh, God. What had she been thinking? One successful lunch with a woman who wore a turban didn't make her one of these people. Monty was right. She didn't belong here. It had been foolish to think that participating in the Montgomery family rituals would bring anything but the extreme mortification of being put in her place.

Jenna could dress her up and give her charity projects and pretend she enjoyed her company, but Georgia would always be a duck masquerading as a swan.

A sound almost like a sob erupted from her throat, and she clapped a horrified hand over her mouth. She felt a tap on her shoulder and turned to find a kindly looking woman who might or might not have borne a striking resemblance to Queen Elizabeth extending a square of fabric her way.

"I know, love. Weddings always make me tear up too." The fabric fluttered at her, and Georgia was able to make out monogrammed letters on the lacy hem. Those letters sent her over the edge. What kind of people carried spare handkerchiefs with their initials on them? What the hell was she doing pretending this was anything but a complete and utter farce?

"Take it," the woman insisted, her face crinkling in a smile. "I have more. And don't worry—I'm sure it'll be you up there soon. You're too young and much too pretty not to have a dozen men waiting for you at home."

"WELL, BROTHER DEAR, I hate to be the bearer of bad tidings, but your non-lady fuck buddy is crying in the bathroom, and none of us can get her to come out."

"You lie." Monty lowered the remote control with a start, eliciting a series of groans from the couple at his back.

"I do, on occasion, but this isn't one of them." Jake spoke calmly, but Monty could hear the sounds of a more frantic conversation taking place somewhere on the other end of the line. "I never lie about a woman weeping— like unicorn tears, I consider them sacred."

"But Georgia doesn't cry. Not for anything."

Monty realized it was a mistake to say those words out loud when Adam and Nancy came barreling up, demanding to know what was going on. They'd been standing at the base of Old Hardwood, where a tiny helicopter was now caught in the branches, but they'd all suddenly lost interest in the aerodynamics of six inches of finely crafted plastic.

"Who made her cry?"

"What's going on?"

He lifted his hand to try and silence them, but it was difficult to keep Adam from tackling him to the ground and wrestling the phone from his grip at the same time. "Who are you talking to?" Adam demanded again.

His brother's voice cracked through. "Are you at a circus, Monty?"

"Yes," he said grimly, finding it the easiest explanation. His brother wouldn't believe him anyway if he admitted to sneaking over to Georgia's house with a grappling hook and a toy helicopter. Jake might understand the chivalrous motives of climbing a tree for a woman, but Monty doubted he'd pick up on the significance of that blue plastic circle embedded near the top. "So you'll have to speak up. What happened?"

"No one knows. Jenna and Becca are trying to talk her down, but that non-lady fuck buddy of yours refuses to open the door."

"Oh, for crying out loud. Just call her Georgia."

"I'm sorry. I thought we were still being secretive."

"So help me, Jake—if you don't stop talking nonsense, I'm going to send the circus over to come get her. Believe me when I say this is not a crew you want to take on willingly." He turned away so he could better concentrate. "Tell me what's going on."

"No one knows. One minute, we were all standing in the pew, watching your dearly beloved marry another man. The next, your non-lady—*ahem*, Georgia—is running out the door. Well, wobbling out the door. She may need to invest in flatter shoes."

"Did anyone say something to her? Is Dad pressuring her to do something she doesn't like?" He felt a warning tick flare up under his heart, and he knew in an instant he would eviscerate anyone who dared say something to hurt her. He was as bad as the Testosterone Trio. No, worse, because he'd eviscerate his own family, if that was what it took.

He hadn't actually thought Georgia would go through with it. The wedding, his family, the makeup and the dress…he'd assumed it was all a bluff, a way of smoking the fox out of his hole. It was why he'd left her apartment when he did. It was also why he'd been staying at Adam and Nancy's house instead of farther afield. He figured his family would have no reason to keep hounding Georgia about this makeover if he was out of the picture until the damnable wedding was over—and although it would have been more comfortable to hide away in a hotel room somewhere, he hadn't felt like being alone.

Adam was the closest thing to a friend he had these days.

"We don't know what the problem is, Monty." When Jake spoke again, he sounded uncharacteristically serious. "But she's upset—that much is clear. I know you and Dad are working through some kind of intense battle of wills, and I politely refuse to get in the middle of it, but I'd want to know if it was Becca in there. That's the only reason I called."

Monty swore.

"You're a regular peach these days, aren't you?"

"Keep an eye on her for me, will you? I'll be there in half an hour."

He forgot, as he hung up the phone, that he had an eager audience waiting for an opportunity to pounce. Nancy was already winding up the grappling hook, and Adam looked one pull of a pin away from exploding altogether.

"Where are we going, and who do we have to kill?" he asked.

"*We* aren't going anywhere, and none of us is going to give in to our murderous impulses." Monty looked a warning at Nancy, who bore an eerie resemblance to a mother bear about to defend her young. "And I mean *none* of us."

"I appreciate your concern, Montgomery, but—"

"I made this mess. I put her in this situation. I'll be the one to fix it." Monty took no pride in the words or in the unenviable task to come. He only felt like the biggest jerk in the world. Georgia had ventured into his social circle for the sole purpose of trying to help him patch things up with his family, and he'd abandoned her to them.

It was a cruel fate for anyone. For a woman who felt herself inadequate in almost every respect, it was unforgivable. All he'd done since the day he walked away from his family was let people down. First Thomas, now this.

"You can't seriously expect us to stay here doing nothing."

"I don't." Monty cast one last anxious glance up at the tree, running a quick mental calculation. They'd been so close to getting the helicopter to work—he either had enough time to head to the Manor to change into his tux or to get that damned Frisbee out of the tree, but not both. It was looks or love, work or play.

He knew, without question, which one he'd pick.

"How are the plans coming along for next weekend?" he asked.

"Nancy?"

She glanced bewilderedly between the two men. "Fine. Everyone has RSVPed and the deposits are made."

"Good." Monty nodded once. "Then double the deposits and have them move everything to tonight."

"There's no way we can change everything in three hours," Adam protested. "It's probably difficult for a rich bastard like you to realize, but you don't get to command the world at your leisure."

Maybe not, but he could command a Lennox. "What? You don't think you're up to the task? Not even if we made it interesting?"

Curiosity flared in Adam's eyes. "How interesting are we talking?"

"As interesting as you can stand. Anything pique your fancy?"

"Oh, hell, yes." Adam clapped his hands. "I've been waiting for an opportunity like this for years. If I manage to pull this off for you, you're taking over my cell contract. Phone number, hardware, service warranty and all."

Monty stilled. "You can't be serious."

"Oh, I'm serious. What you're asking for is nothing short of a miracle. I expect miracles in return."

"How do you know Danny won't move the ringtone later?"

Adam stuck his hand out and didn't reply until Monty reluctantly shook. "The Brother Code. He doesn't care who he's annoying as long as one of us is feeling the pain. Welcome to the family, Montgomery. It's a small fucking world after all."

TWENTY-THREE

GEORGIA SMACKED HER shoe against the sidewalk for the fifth time, hitting the heel in exactly the same place and getting no closer to removing the damn thing than she'd been ten minutes ago. That day at the Manor, Ashleigh had made it look so easy, like these things were attached by a string and a prayer.

One more thing separating me from the washed masses. Her shoe's heels had some kind of unbreakable epoxy holding them together.

"If I know my sister, those shoes cost a thousand dollars and don't exist in duplicate anywhere in the United States. Does she know you're destroying them?"

Georgia dropped the shoe with a start. She would have jumped to her feet too, but her movements were restricted by her dress and the many layers of undergarments imprisoning her inside it. "What are you doing here?"

Monty gestured to the curb next to her, and she was too bewildered to stop him from hitching his pants and taking a seat. He wasn't dressed for a wedding in his shirtsleeves and gray slacks, but he still managed to look more expensive and well-suited to the affair than she did in her borrowed dress, which she'd been informed was a delicate sea-foam green.

Sea-foam whatever. She looked like a giant mint candy.

"Here. Let me see it." He took the shoe—a shiny silver

thing—before she could protest and began gently wiggling the heel. "It's not blunt-force trauma that breaks these things. It's miles of wear and tear. You have to ease into it."

Of course he was an expert in ladies footwear on top of everything else. He *was* kind of obsessed with her orange boots.

"Can I ask why we're destroying these?" he asked after a few minutes of diligent effort. Georgia could already see the heel giving a little. "Or am I not allowed to ask?"

"They're too tall," she said. "I can't run away if they're too tall."

"Ah. I see."

He didn't say anything more, just kept working the heel with a quiet determination. He didn't appear the least bit surprised to find her sitting outside a church in full evening wear, breathing in the noxious fumes of valets parking cars, so she assumed he'd already heard the full report from his family.

There was no runaway bride at this wedding. Just a runaway guest. A weeping, emotionally fragile wreck of a runaway guest without a single bruise to cause her breakdown. All she had was a mess of a personal life, a mess of a professional life and a gaping hole where her heart used to be.

And as her shoe attested, she *still* didn't have a Girl Card to show for it.

"Got it!" Monty held the broken heel up triumphantly. "Do you want me to do the other one?"

She looked down at her still-shod foot with a frown. Killing the shoes had been more of an exercise in frustration than an actual exit strategy, but she might as well have a matching pair now. She reached to slip the shoe off, startled when Monty's hand covered her own.

"Allow me," he said, and ran his fingers along her arch. Even though his touch was hot, the press of his shoulder against hers hotter, she shivered. "I like being able to do something for you for once."

It was more than she could take. "Monty, I—"

"No, don't." He smiled, that hesitant lift of the lips that could barely be counted as a sign of joy. "I didn't come here to argue. I came to rescue you."

"You're about—" She paused and scanned the sky, where the sun was low enough on the horizon to cast everything in a nauseatingly romantic pink hue. Rich people could even command the perfect wedding sunset, it seemed. "Thirty minutes too late. I climbed out the bathroom window."

As he had yet to scoot away from her, not only his shoulder but his thigh also pressed against hers, his laugh shook them both. "Does anyone know you're out here?"

She flushed, wholeheartedly ashamed of the answer she had to give. The entire Montgomery clan was being so nice, worrying and offering support and being otherwise decent people. She was the horrible one bringing shame to them all. "No. I'm sorry. I can't seem to make myself go back inside."

"What happened?"

"Nothing. Nothing happened. A woman got married. Your ex-girlfriend got married."

"Is that what bothers you? That I once dated her? That I once loved her?"

"No," she said, and meant it. The prospect of facing Ashleigh in the flesh might have been what drove her to lock herself in the bathroom, but it wasn't what kept her there. She'd kept herself there, trapped by the over-whelming prospect of expectation.

"Does that mean you'll let me take you inside and in-troduce you?"

Panic seized her, and she bolted up despite the con-fines of chiffon and superhuman stitching. "I'm not going in there, Monty. I did it. I tried. I wore high heels and made nice with your family's friends and played the part. And it was awful."

He didn't get up, just kept wiggling her stupid shoe, acting as though nothing had happened, as if she wasn't about to break down all over again. "Of course it was awful. I told you I hate these things."

"Who cares if you hate them?" She felt a furious urge to kick the shoe out of his hand. Why wasn't he taking this seriously? She'd put herself on the line for him—offered all that she was and everything she knew. She'd put herself in his family's hands even after he'd already decided she wasn't worth sticking around for. And all he could say was *I told you so?*

"So you dislike having to be social every now and then. Big deal. You've got an entire family in there will-ing to dress me up and put me on display in hopes of getting you to come home. You've got people who care so much about your well-being they'll fly thousands of miles to attend *your* ex-girlfriend's wedding in a show of solidarity."

That got him to discard the shoe and get to his feet—but instead of defending himself, he was struck dumb, his gaze fixated on the way she was practically wearing her boobs as a necklace. Apparently, he'd missed the fact that fancy shoes meant fancy clothes, and that she was packed and squeezed into a full-length gown worthy of a high-profile wedding.

"I know I look ridiculous, so you don't have to say it." Georgia wrapped her arms around her midsection, feeling worse than when she'd been forced to meet a Kennedy in there. As in, an *actual* Kennedy. She should have listened to Coco and added a shawl. "I told Jenna it would never work. I can't pull off a strapless gown. I look like a sausage about to erupt from its casing. I feel like one too. Do you know what I have on underneath this?"

"No. Yes. No." He blinked. "Tell me."

"I'm not supposed to call it a girdle, because Jenna says that makes me sound like an eighty-year-old woman who can't let go of her debutante days. It's a bodysuit. Or, if I'm feeling stubborn, I'm allowed to say shapewear."

Monty's lips twitched. "Jenna included a stubborn clause?"

"Don't make me laugh. It's not fair! I can't compete with women like Ashleigh." She shifted on her bare feet, the pavement still warm. "And before you feel all noble and try to convince me otherwise, let me set the record straight. I don't care that I can't compete with her, because it's not like it's anything new. I'm used to that kind of pain."

"Pain?"

"Yes, Monty. It hurts." That had to be the first time she'd ever admitted it out loud. "It hurts to look at women like your ex-girlfriend, like your sister, like your step-mom, and know that nothing I do will ever compare. I don't like it, but I can take it."

"And what can't you take?"

His intently blue stare dared her to look away, full of a challenge he knew damn well she couldn't ignore. So she told him. "The pain of unwarranted hope. The pain of reaching for something I knew better than to want in the first place."

"Georgia…"

"No." She held up her hands and backed away. It was too late for that hug. She'd know it only as the gesture of a man who felt sorry for her, who'd come to get her out of a locked bathroom because she was an embarrassment to his family. "You don't have to do the responsible thing for my sake. It's not as if you asked me to get to know your sister or try to fit in at the Manor in the first place. I'm the one who pushed my way in where I wasn't wanted."

His lips fell. She was pretty sure her own did too.

"What if I were to ask you to try again?" He paused, his breathing stilled. She knew, without a moment's hesitation, that he was processing the conversation, finding a way to value it, taking his time to be kind. She wished he wouldn't. She didn't want careful, kind Monty right now. Careful, kind Monty had the potential to set her off crying again. "What if I asked you to take my arm right now and go inside to meet Ashleigh? We could dance and drink champagne and sit at my family's table. I'll even promise to be nice to my dad."

This reconciliation was exactly what she'd wanted in the first place, but the idea of facing everyone now—her eyes puffy from tears, her shoes damaged beyond repair, slinking in the back door with a guilty Monty by her side—was impossible.

"I don't belong in there," she said, afraid that to say anything more would ruin her.

He nodded, kind and careful to an inch. "I was afraid you'd say that."

That was when she noticed the Montgomery limousine

parked a few feet away. She took a moment to wave to Ryan, the family chauffeur, happy to see a friendly face with an ordinary income level for once.

"If I ask you to go somewhere for me—no questions asked—will you let Ryan take you there?"

She froze. So much for that friendly face. "What are you talking about?"

"I'm trying to strike a deal. That's what you Lennoxes do, right? Challenge, compete, trade?"

"Not always," she said, but her sullen response only seemed to amuse Monty.

"Well, see if you can muster up some of that competitive spirit for me." Before she knew what was happening, he had her hand in his and was bringing it perilously close to his mouth. She released an anticipatory moan. In addition to hugs and his warm presence in her bed at night, she missed hand kisses the most. "If you get in the car with Ryan and go where he tells you, I'll head inside and make up with my family."

She couldn't have replied even if she wanted to, because he chose that moment to drop his lips to her palm. Nothing would ever feel as good as Monty cherishing the roughest parts of her like that.

"Believe me when I say I don't like the idea any more than you do," he said, and gently dropped her hand. "But you were only trying to help by putting me back in touch with them—I know that now. I can't very well advocate you accepting assistance from others if I won't do the same."

She glanced over at the limo with even more trepidation now. Where, exactly, was Ryan planning on taking her?

"Do we have a deal? I'll tackle my biggest fear if you tackle yours?" Monty stuck his hand out in a businesslike gesture, dropping all his efforts at charm. Had he kissed her hand again or tried to pull her into his arms, she probably would have refused—those were unfair tactics, and she didn't trust her response to them. But a handshake between equals? This she could handle. This she could do.

She slipped her hand into his waiting palm, savoring what might be the last time she ever touched this man. "Why do I get the feeling I'm not going to like where Ryan takes me?"

"Because you're not." Monty's smile was crooked and sad. "I'm sorry for doing this to you, Georgia. I only hope you can forgive me someday."

"Forgive you for what?"

"You'll see." Without waiting for her to say more, he grabbed her shoe and gave it a solid *whomp* against the pavement, presenting her with a perfectly matched set of flats. She stared at the shoe, unsure how to accept this gift with anything but a howl, but then he did something even worse.

Holding one finger aloft, he dashed to the limo and reached inside. The blue Frisbee he extracted, once a brilliant royal blue, was now faded to the color of well-washed jeans.

She would have recognized it anywhere.

"Oh, Monty."

"You don't have to say anything." That small half smile again, neither happy nor sad. Just there. "I always meant to get it for you in the first place. Consider it a preemptive peace offering."

And then he walked away, leaving her with a broken shoe in one hand, a childhood trophy in the other, and a heart so full of despair she could have cried.

Again.

TWENTY-FOUR

MONTY DECIDED TO tackle Ashleigh first.

His ex-girlfriend was the last person he wanted to see after sending a flat-footed, emotionally devastated Georgia off to hate him forever, but his life was nothing if not a series of distasteful events. He ignored the pointed stares of more than one guest over his dressed-down appearance and made a beeline straight for the bride. She wasn't difficult to find. A woman all in white holding court in the center of a ballroom was a thousand times more approachable than a woman in pastel green hopelessly destroying her own shoes.

She was also a lot less desirable. Looking at Ashleigh now, her poise so ingrained she greeted him with nothing but graceful alacrity, he wondered how he ever thought they could be happy together. He didn't want a polished society wife who would make him proud at parties, someone he could admire from afar. He wanted a woman who challenged him, every day, to be worthy of her.

So far, he'd done nothing but let *that* woman down.

"Monty!" Ashleigh leaned forward to receive a kiss on her cheek and the expected benediction. "I don't believe it. You're the last man I expected to see today."

"You invited me."

"Yes, but when have those two things ever been related?" Her smile was warm and her happiness genuine—two things he could only be grateful for. "Though

I can't say I'm too surprised. Word around the ballroom is you've got some kind of girlfriend locked up in the bathroom."

Honestly—did these people have nothing better to do today than gossip about the guest list? They were at a wedding, for chrissakes. The start of two people's lives together. If that wasn't a sacred moment, what was?

This. Right now. Him standing up to his family and his past so that he and thousands of kids across the country could have a chance at a future. That was as sacred as it came.

"You'll have to forgive Georgia," he said tightly. "She gets overly emotional at weddings."

He might as well have said she grew talons. "*You* have an overly emotional girlfriend?"

"She cries at the drop of a hat. I can't take her anywhere." He forced a smile to show his willingness to move on from the subject, but he could tell Ashleigh wanted to know more. "I'm sorry she can't be here to offer her congratulations herself, but I sent her home. She really wasn't feeling all that well."

"That's too bad. I wanted to meet her."

"You already have. She's the escapee mechanic."

Ashleigh wasn't the sort to admit when she was baffled, so he had to wait a few seconds for her to figure out his meaning. He could tell when she did, surprise flashing on her face before she quickly tamped it down. "Oh. The one who fixed my shoe that day at the Manor."

He nodded. "The very same."

Then he really did change the subject. He wanted to leap on the nearest table and shout all the things that made Georgia superior to everyone in attendance—her unflagging work ethic, the determined way she cut a swathe through life, how selflessly she saw the world and how hopelessly she saw herself—but he wasn't sure he could make it all the way through without breaking down. He might have lost her. In this power play to get the most of his family, he'd forgotten which one of them would end up paying the highest price.

The most generous ones always did.

"I'm also leaving in a few minutes," he said. "I just wanted to tell you how radiant you look and to meet your Martin."

At the mention of her new husband's name, Ashleigh lit up with real joy. Monty half expected to be met with some kind of chiseled hero after that, but Martin was a nondescript man of middling years whose only conversation centered on the fluctuating value of the Nepalese rupee. He shook the man's hand and wished them well, but didn't spend too much time in the happy couple's company after that.

There was no accounting for taste.

The second task Monty prepared to tackle was the more disagreeable of the two. His family was expecting him, of course, having been watching the whole time to make sure he didn't suffer another collapse.

"I won't apologize for Georgia," he said by way of greeting. All of them were there—Jenna, his dad and stepmom, Jake and his wife, Rebecca—huddled around one another as if for warmth. It was probably the longest they'd ever appeared in public together. "And I won't ask her to either, but you can all start crafting your own apologies tonight—and they better be good. How could you, Jenna?"

"Hey, don't kill the minion. I was doing what I was told. I thought she looked fantastic."

"Of course she looked fantastic. She always looks fantastic." He knew he was speaking too loud, that this was too public a venue, but they were already the source of unending gossip. Why stop now? "But you don't start someone off at a Bridgerton wedding—you might as well have thrown her into the deep end of a shark-filled pool. *I'm* intimidated by half the people in this room, and I've known them my whole life."

Jenna just smirked. "Not my fault, brother dear. We didn't actually think you'd make her show up without you. You want to talk about throwing someone in the shark pool?"

He couldn't deny it, so he didn't even try. These weren't the people he had to explain himself to anyway.

"And you." He turned to Jake, since dealing with Jenna was impossible. "You were supposed to keep an eye on her. Why did I find her sitting on the curb in the parking lot?"

Jake was damn near smirking himself. "When someone goes through the trouble to climb out a window to escape me, I recognize the futility of pressing my suit."

"So help me…"

"We wouldn't have let anything bad happen, Monty." Rebecca took over for her husband, pressing his forearm in a soothing gesture. "I promise. I never once lost sight of her. She seemed like she wanted to be left alone more than anything else."

He nodded, accepting his sister-in-law at her word. As one who knew the pain of breaking down in the public eye, he trusted her to protect Georgia's interests.

"And you."

"I wondered when we'd get to me," his dad said, his voice laden with a thousand unreleased sighs. "I suppose it would be too much to ask to take this to another room where we can talk privately?"

Since the rest of his family showed every sign of wishing themselves elsewhere, Monty nodded and followed his dad into one of the many rooms set off from the primary reception area. There were always nooks and crannies in these kinds of places, holding ports for coats or chafing dishes, and they ended up in one full from floor to ceiling in decorative plants.

Monty was forced to stand behind a ficus. *How fitting.*

"John, I know you'll have a hard time believing me, but—"

As he was in the habit now of interrupting his father whenever he felt like it, he didn't hesitate to do so now. "I'm ready to return to work."

His dad, a man he knew to be surprised by almost nothing, could only stare.

"I don't like begging you to take me back, and I'm incredibly unhappy about a lot of things. The way you took advantage of Georgia to try and get to me is something it will take me a long time to forgive, and I'm not sure I'll ever be able to overlook the way you callously tossed my foster care project aside, but the Montgomery Foundation is too important to disappear in a petty family squabble."

"Monty, I—"

"No. It's my turn. I've been waiting twenty-five long years for my turn." He picked a leaf that was blocking his line of vision and crushed it between his fingers. The scent of it—of plant life and the open air and the woman he loved—strengthened him in ways he hadn't thought possible. "I'm going to do less hotel work this time around. None, actually. I want to be phased out. I don't care if that means you have to groom someone else to take over someday or if I have to give up my shares in the company to make it happen. I don't like working for the hotels. I never have."

"I know."

His jaw ticked. His dad was incapable of admitting anything less than omnipotence. "Of course you do."

"I'm not dense, John, nor am I particularly cruel. The idea was always that you'd split your time between the hotels and the foundation—not treat them as two full-time jobs."

"But they *are* two full-time jobs, and I'm one man. You didn't really think I could do that forever, did you?"

"Of course I didn't." His dad released one of his sighs then, that buildup of worry and air, those many details Monty knew from personal experience were difficult to shuck even for the sake of a party like this one. "But *you* did. I've been trying to get you to take less upon yourself for months now—dropping hints about your workload, urging you to start having a social life again. Every time I suggested it, you only retreated further into your office."

If Monty were a Lennox, this was where he'd challenge his dad to an arm-wrestling match or to a knife-throwing contest. They could settle things the old-fashioned way, with adrenaline and anger and an undercurrent of affection underneath it all. Instead, he had to use his words like a Montgomery. *Fucking Montgomerys.*

"Those weren't hints, Dad. They were reprimands."

He frowned. "They were meant to be hints."

"They felt like reprimands," Monty said quietly. "They've always felt like reprimands."

His dad looked suddenly ancient, the weight of decades of hard work lining his face and hunching his shoulders. Monty wished he could have said that the first emotion he felt was one of pity or affection for the man who'd given him life, but the thrum of the ocean filling his ears and his throat was one hundred percent for himself.

If I'm not careful, that could be me.

"Ten hours a day—that's my maximum," he said. "Fifty hours a week." The number sounded painfully small to Monty's ears, but he was resolved to stick to it. He'd take up hobbies. He'd take up twelve hobbies. With any luck, Georgia would agree to be at least half of them.

"I can respect that," his dad said with a nod. "But only on one condition."

Damn. He knew it had been too easy. "What condition?"

"If you ever feel like I'm reprimanding you again, you'll come talk to me, okay?" His dad's voice grew gruff. They weren't a hugging family, and they didn't start now, but this was as close as they'd probably ever get. "It was never my intention to make you feel chastised—not now, and certainly not when you were younger. I just didn't know how else to get through to you. You've always been so driven, so self-sufficient. I didn't realize how much you disliked it all until it was too late."

"Thank you," he said, and stuck his hand out, noting with alarm that it was shaking. It didn't matter much, though, because his dad's was too.

"I'm proud of you, John. I always have been. None of us would be where we are today without you." They clasped warmly, two men sealing a deal that lifted worlds off both their shoulders. "Now, about Georgia…"

Monty dropped his hand with a start.

"Don't worry. I was only going to say how well she'll do for you—for all of us. When she's not climbing up trees or out windows, she's the perfect addition to this family. Charitable, hardworking… I don't know why I never realized it before."

Monty did. Because his dad, like the rest of them, had failed to see beyond the handywoman exterior to the woman she was inside.

"I'm curious, though," his dad continued. "Where did you have Ryan take her?"

"To her execution."

"I'm not sure I understand."

"I sent her to the one place she wants to go least in the world." Monty grimaced. "Perfect addition or not, don't be surprised if we never hear from her again. Or me, for that matter. Look for my body in the sidewalk. I'm guessing that's where she'll put me."

THE DAY OF the fateful surprise birthday party that forced Adam to the hospital, Georgia had been completely unaware that plans were being hatched behind her back. In true devious form, her mom and brothers had already thrown her a small family celebration, complete with presents and cake and insults on her rapidly advancing years.

No way could she have known that a second party—this one much more elaborate in its construction—had also been underway, and she answered the call to replace a moldy roof panel at the rec center without a second thought. Naturally, when she flipped on the lights to find about fifty of her nearest and dearest screaming their joy at her arrival, she'd turned on her heel and fled. The overwhelming sensation of everyone she knew and loved coming out to celebrate *her*, and for no reason other than the shifting of her age from twenty-four to twenty-five, had been too much.

She'd been damn close to crying.

She'd made it as far as the heavy exit doors before Adam caught up with her, but he'd been quiet for once in his life, and she'd slammed the door behind her without being aware that his limb was preventing it from closing all the way.

All fifty guests had accompanied them to the hospital.

Georgia was prepared for the worst this time. When Ryan dropped her off at the Ransom Creek High School gymnasium, she lifted her skirts, clutched her Frisbee and prepared to face whatever lay in wait for her.

A surprise party wouldn't surprise her. An intervention wouldn't change her. She was immune to any and all of the persuasions of wealth Monty had at his disposal.

Unfortunately, she wasn't immune to this.

Almost every face inside the gym was one she recognized. Her brothers were there, looking their best in suits and ties, flanking their mom in the same plum-colored suit she'd worn to Adam's wedding. Most of her building crew and their families were also there, dressed in everything from their Sunday best to the flannel she saw them in every day.

Taken alone, this wouldn't be a bad thing. She knew these people, liked these people, would much rather spend the evening with them than a thousand Kennedys. But in the distance stood enough linen-covered tables to seat the whole lot of them, and a podium was set up on a stage next to a blown-up picture of a younger version of herself laughing as she straddled the empty frame of a house.

That was when she also noticed the reporters.

Among a burst of applause and a flash of cameras, a woman took the stage. Hers was another familiar face—Patty Truitt, a woman she'd know anywhere because she'd been the recipient of the first house she was contractor for. She had three older daughters and one young son, and Georgia had been tickled at the thought of how that little boy would grow up, surrounded by a protective layer of females, probably as screwed up as her in the end.

"Come on, Georgia. You're supposed to come sit with us." Adam appeared by her side.

"Fuck you, Adam."

"Ha-ha. I deserved that, but you still have to sit."

"And you, Charlie? Danny? What the hell? You guys are supposed to have my back."

"We do have your back, George. That's why we're here." Charlie led her to a table where her mom was already settling in, his hand firm on her shoulder as he thrust her to the seat.

"You look very lovely in your dress, dear, but you could at least pretend to smile." Her mom reached across the table and pushed at her cheek in an attempt to get her facial muscles to move. "This is a celebration."

A celebration of what? Her inability to meet organizational goals? The sad reality that she'd most likely be out of a job both at Montgomery Manor and Homeward Bound after this? This was the worst party of all time.

Patty murmured a few requests for everyone to be seated before she started speaking. Georgia figured it would be some kind of rah-rah, yeah-for-our-leader speech, but she was surprised when the woman began with, "One of the things no one tells you about being broke, homeless and near rock bottom is how hard it can be to ask for help."

Georgia sat up in her chair, the hair on the back of her exposed neck standing on alert. Was this going to be an intervention after all?

"I'm not going to tell you the story of how I got there, or what kinds of struggles I faced to get up again, but I will say this—at a time when I needed the most support, I found myself clinging to every scrap of pride I had left, pretending it was all I needed to make it through." Patty shot a thumbs-up in Georgia's direction, and she knew she was trapped for at least the duration of this speech. "Which is why I'll never forget what happened when I showed up one afternoon to see how the construction was going on my new home—my *family's* new home. I picked a day when I was sure no one would be around, so I wouldn't have to explain what I was doing. But someone *was* there, and I'm sure you can all guess who it was, sneaking in to do some extra work when she thought no one was looking."

There was laughter and several glances thrown her way. Georgia thought about hiding behind the Frisbee or sinking lower in her seat, but her stupid dress allowed for zero wiggle room.

"Georgia must have known who I was, but she didn't say anything to make me feel uncomfortable. Instead, she asked if I could give her a hand. Now, I'd never even picked up a hammer before, and anyone with eyes could tell she had everything under control, but I'll never forget the way she walked me through the process of framing a window. I ended up working side-by-side with her for two hours that day, and I'm pretty sure she had to redo everything as soon as I left."

Laughter again, and this time Georgia didn't feel quite as swallowed up by it. She remembered that day. She'd

gone in to build because she'd just had to fire her very
first volunteer for carrying off some of the copper wir-
ing to sell at a scrap yard. He'd thought Georgia didn't
know enough to notice.

She knew enough. She noticed.

"I don't think I picked up on the message until later—
maybe not even until I had the keys in my hands and
was able to move my kids in to their new rooms—but
that day helped shift my perspective of my situation. It
wasn't that Georgia was kind to me, or that the Homeward Bound organization changed my life. Instead, it
was how the act of being asked for help made such a
difference in the way I saw myself. It made me feel important, as if I mattered, as if I had control over my own
future again. Any of you who've been where I was—and
I know many of you have—are aware of how much that
tiny bit of control means."

Patty's speech continued for a few more minutes, this
time focused mainly on her kids and how happy they'd
been to see the community coming together as each new
house went up. Georgia wasn't stupid or blind, and she
knew the message being driven home was one Monty
planted there himself.

It's okay to ask for help sometimes, you stupid woman.
She didn't see why he had to be so dramatic about it with
a whole freaking dinner party.

But then another person took the podium right after
Patty. Hank Newell, an electrician she'd worked with on
a house they built years ago, long before she was anything more than an eighteen-year-old kid on the crew.
He talked about the day Georgia hit her thumb with her
hammer, but she didn't want to have to leave before her
shift was over, so she wrapped it in gauze and kept work-

ing. By the time night fell, her thumb was twice its size and they'd had to bore a hole through the nail to release the blood that had built up behind it.

After him there was another speaker. And another. And another. All of them told stories about Georgia—some touching, some funny, most of them enough to cause her cheeks to go up in flames.

Food was served and taken away while people talked. Reporters buzzed around asking her family and friends for quotes. At least twenty people asked where they could sign up to help her with the next big project.

And that was when it hit her.

This wasn't a celebration dinner or a way for Monty to insert a sneaky commentary on how she needed to let people help her for a change. He was fixing her staffing problem. After she told him to stay out, banned him from her site, closed the door on her heart, he'd gone ahead and fixed things anyway.

The bastard.

He'd done exactly what he said he could do—he'd given her story a face. The reporters would walk away with someone for the community to sympathize with, someone for them to root for, so they would take a more vested interest in the outcome.

She was a face. He'd made her a face, and there was nothing she could do to stop it.

"I didn't see Monty come in with you," her mom said, hugging her for what had to be the twentieth time. She'd noticed her mom tearing up during one or two of those speeches—and she cried about as much as the rest of her family. "I thought for sure he'd want to be here to see this. He's been working so hard this past week pulling everything together."

Georgia blinked. *This past week?* But that was the week he'd left her. That was the week he'd stopped caring.

She looked down at the Frisbee on the table with a growing sense of panic. Exactly when had he gone back to the house to get it?

"He's too chicken." Adam strode to join them, his hands in his pockets. "He knew Georgia would want to rip out his eyes and shove them down his throat, so he stayed away."

"Rich bastard," Danny said. "He talks big, but there's nothing there to back it up."

Charlie, as always, was the last to arrive. "I'm just surprised George is letting him get away with it. If it were *my* boyfriend sneaking around my back and sticking his nose where it wasn't wanted, I'd have something to say about it."

"I'm not twelve," Georgia muttered. "You can't goad me into going over there and confronting him."

"You sure? I'll lend you my car," Charlie offered.

"If you think you can manage it in that dress, I'll lend you my motorcycle," Danny added.

"Fuck you two." Adam never could manage to be outdone for long. "I'm the one who's all emotionally attached to the guy now. I'm driving her myself."

TWENTY-FIVE

MONTY HAD NINE hundred and forty-six emails waiting for him on his computer.

A few years ago, he'd taken a trip to Denver to oversee a hotel groundbreaking, and a snowstorm had forced him into a dead zone for a full forty-eight hours. He'd had no email, no phone, no real contact with the outside world.

He'd been so twitchy to find the thirty or so messages awaiting him on the other end, he hadn't set foot in Denver since. He didn't trust anywhere in Colorado. Boycotting an entire state was as ridiculous as not trusting calculator watches, but superstitions had a funny way of taking root and never letting go.

He allowed himself one email—to Thomas, who deserved to be the first to hear the news that everything would be back up and running again—and took a deep breath.

"Turn it off, Montgomery. It's late. You can tackle them tomorrow." Even though it took every ounce of willpower he possessed, he forced himself to shut the laptop and rise from his desk. Nothing in the office had been touched in the weeks he'd been gone, though he did notice that Sarge had managed to wrestle his way in to perform the long-neglected dusting.

He stretched and contemplated the bookshelf, wondering if two detective novels would be enough to entertain him for the night until he figured out a better way to use his downtime. What he wanted to do—sneak in to Georgia's dinner to see how she reacted to catching a glimpse of herself through other people's eyes—wasn't an option. As much as he longed to be there, he was afraid his presence would only cause her to shut down.

And she needed to hear those things. Maybe she'd never forgive him for pulling rank and swinging his full Montgomery might, but that was the risk he had to take. He didn't know how else he could break through and make her realize how important she was to the community. To everyone.

"I thought I'd find you here."

He turned at the rich, velvety voice that had grown so familiar he heard it in his dreams. "Georgia?"

"I hope you're planning on using that book as a shield, because you're going to need it."

He placed it carefully on the desk instead. "I'm not scared of you."

Sometime in the past few hours, she'd removed the dress and slipped back into her coveralls. The sight of her in them, with her shorter hair and an angry twist to her mouth, almost ended him. Ferocious, strong and stunning in every regard—there was nothing he loved more.

She pulled her hammer from out of her back pocket.

I lied. There was something he loved more.

"I mean it, Monty. I'm furious with you."

"I figured you would be."

She stepped closer. "I told you to stay out of my business."

"I know you did."

Closer still. "You had no right to make me a public figure like that. Everyone is going to know who I am and what I do."

"I'm sorry, but I thought it was high time they deserved that chance. It was selfish of me to try and keep you to myself all that time."

She released a choking sound and dropped her hammer, narrowly missing her foot in the process. "Goddammit, Monty. You're doing it again. You're not supposed to be nice and apologetic when I'm mad at you. It only makes things worse."

He grinned. "I know it does. You hate apologies almost as much as you hate surprises, but I'm not going to evoke your wrath just so you have someone to rage at. If you want to yell, you're going to have to go find your brothers."

"Don't tempt me. It was hard enough to come in here as it was."

He didn't waste another second. No way was he letting her out of this office—not until she realized how much she meant to him, not until she acknowledged her own worth. With a lunge, he had his arms wrapped around her and wrestled her to the ground.

"You barbarian!" She wriggled and flailed underneath him, her body growing increasingly warm where it pressed against his. "What do you think you're doing?"

"I'm subduing you."

"Why?"

"Because I can, Georgia. And because it's time for you to tell me a story."

She stilled but didn't stop, and he had to clasp her wrists in his hands, holding them above her head to keep her in place. Her breasts pushed against his chest, the rapid movements of her breathing only heightening his awareness of each part of her. "I don't know any stories," she said.

"Then talk to me. Let me hear about your night. Tell me how it felt to sit there in an expensive gown, surrounded by people who love you, drinking champagne and knowing you made a difference in the lives of everyone in attendance."

She stopped struggling. "I didn't notice that part. I was too busy being mad at you."

He laughed and dropped a kiss on her nose, holding himself back before he moved any lower. Once he started kissing her, he planned on kissing her forever. "You just sat through your very first night as a society lady. You know that, right? You did *exactly* what Jenna has been preparing you for."

"What?" She wrinkled her nose. "I did not."

"Nine-tenths of the functions I'm forced to attend are the same as the one I set up for you tonight. There's dinner and drinks, someone getting an award for something great they did. Long speeches. Uncomfortable clothes. You won't always be the recipient of the award, of course, but if I know you, you'll get your fair share of them."

"You're talking nonsense."

"No, I'm not. I'm talking as a man who's seen the best and the worst that philanthropy brings out in people. Some people part with money only because they have to. Others do it because they have genuinely good hearts. I promise that even though we look and act like pieces of overdressed fluff, most of us can tell the difference." He leaned down and pressed his lips against her coveralls, right where her heart was. "I know you think fitting in with my family means looking put together and knowing which fork to use, but it's not. Not really. Yes, there's an occasional wedding like Ashleigh's, which is all about name-dropping and coming up with the most impressive guest list, but most of the time, you can fill your days with whatever project makes you happiest. Houses or hair or whatever else you have planned."

"I don't…" She looked up at him, her expression full of wary regard. "I'm not sure what you mean."

He had never been more sure, especially when she paused and waited—still wary—allowing him a moment to organize his thoughts. "I'm quitting the hotels to focus solely on the foundation."

"Oh, Monty. That's fantastic."

He nodded, basking in her genuine pleasure for him, eager to offer her the same thing. "I never should have left you to deal with my family on your own, but I thought that if I could separate the two parts of my life—before and after, then and now, them and you—it would be easier for me to find a way out. But you made me realize today that I don't want out. Not all the way. If you can suck it up and tackle the occasional society wedding, then so can I."

"How many weddings are we talking?"

He couldn't help himself. "Hopefully, at least one more." Then, because the wariness in her eyes turned to outright fear, he added, "I was also hoping I could convince you to help me with that international school construction project I told you about. We could do so much together, you and I."

"Together?" Her voice faltered.

"Yes, Georgia. Together—in this and in everything." He ducked his head and said the hardest words of all. "I don't think I can do this on my own anymore. I'm scared to go back to the man I was before. He wasn't happy."

"And now?"

He allowed his lips to drop to hers. "I can't promise you much, but I can say with absolutely certainty that no man will work harder or more diligently to deserve you. You're my favorite person in the whole world, Georgia. And even though you might not see it now, I plan on doing whatever it takes to convince you."

IT ONLY TOOK about twenty minutes.

For the first five minutes, Monty made her recite the list of compliments she'd received at dinner. Her kindness and her strength, her diligence and dedication. It was a long, boring list, and she squirmed to get away, but each time she slipped in another adjective, Monty rewarded her with a kiss.

"This isn't fair," she said after she admitted to being a good swimmer on top of everything else. She was running out of positive attributes. "You act like I'm the only person in the world who can't take a compliment."

"You *are* the only person in the world who can't take a compliment."

She blinked up at him, dazed by the combination of his body pressing down against hers and the adoration she saw in his eyes, but not too dazed to lose sight of what really mattered. Him. He was what mattered—more than all the weddings and all the charity dinners and all the publicity photos she feared were headed her way.

"You're fun, Monty."

He stopped moving, startled into immobility. "What?"

"You're fun and you're funny and you're fascinating." She pressed her lips against his after each one, her rewards not nearly as heady as his, but hopefully just as powerful. "You rise to every challenge without blinking and are somehow the kindest, most generous person I've ever known despite having an obscene amount of money."

"I thought we were talking about you."

"You're *interesting*, Monty. I could spend years getting to know you and still have more to discover."

His eyes narrowed as he realized he was being paid back in full. "Oh, yeah? Well, when I look at you, I don't just see a woman I admire. I see a woman I love, and she's the most beautiful woman in the world."

She almost choked on the sob that rose to her throat. "Liar."

"No." His strong hands came down and stroked the side of her face, his touch so light and reverent she knew, in that moment, he meant every word. "You take my breath away, Georgia Lennox."

"I love you too," she whispered. It was all she could manage.

This time, she wasn't rewarded with only a kiss. She was rewarded with a full-body explosion of pleasure. She was rewarded with John Montgomery the Third— sex god, philanthropist, millionaire, man.

He was on top of her. He was inside of her. He was part of her.

And it was beautiful.

EPILOGUE

"LIFT WITH YOUR LEGS, Adam. Not your back. I swear, it's as if you're trying to injure yourself so you don't have to keep helping."

Adam dropped the bag of concrete he'd been carrying to flip Monty his middle finger. "How do you not have enough money to hire people to build your house for you? This has to be breaking all kinds of laws. You're not a family in need, for fuck's sake."

"Is he whining again?" Georgia marched by, carrying two of the bags of cement without a falter in her step. She even managed to stop and land a kiss on Monty's lips. "Adam, I bought lunch. Considering how much you eat, that's like paid labor."

"You didn't buy lunch. Your fancy cook made it. And I'm pretty sure there wasn't any gluten in it." Adam hoisted the bag again, this time using his legs. "What's the point in my eating away from home if I can't have any gluten? Nancy's killing me with this diet."

"I'll sneak you a bag of donuts next week," Charlie promised, following in his wake. "The good kind. With sprinkles."

It was Monty's turn to grab two bags of the cement and follow the siblings along the well-worn path to the orchard. There, already paced out and ready to go up, was an exact facsimile of the houses built under the Homeward Bound name. It wouldn't be the grandest establishment on the Montgomery Manor grounds, but Monty couldn't wait until it was finished. Simple and practical, its design fusing function and strength to create its own kind of appeal, it would make the perfect residence for a newlywed couple eager to move out of their parents' houses for the very first time.

He dropped the sack with a thud, breathing in dirt and cement dust and fresh air. He'd be paying for this day off by working extra tomorrow, but that was okay. Georgia had already informed him she had plenty of shit to do in the meantime. Between Homeward Bound and the dozens of other projects she was starting up, he suspected she logged more working hours than he did these days.

"Is this when I'm supposed to carry you across the threshold?" he asked, and didn't wait for a reply as he swooped her into his arms and marched across the line of dirt that currently marked the perimeter.

She kicked and flailed, but didn't release her arms from around his neck until he'd taken his time to drop a slow and lazy kiss on her mouth.

"Gross." Danny brushed past them with a sigh. "Didn't you guys do the whole threshold thing last time?"

"Yes." And the time before that. And the time before that. And pretty much every day since they'd decided this was where they wanted to build their home together. "So get used to it."

But as soon as her brothers were out of sight, he dropped his voice to a whisper, running his lips along the side of Georgia's neck as he did. "Are you sure it was a wise idea to recruit the Testosterone Trio for this? I'm half afraid they're going to forget support beams or cross wires on purpose so we die in our sleep."

"Oh, they will. This house is going to be one strong

wind away from collapsing altogether." Georgia released
a sigh of pure pleasure—a sound he was proud to state
came at regular, sex-god-elicited intervals now. "At the
first sign of natural disaster, we'll probably be trapped
inside. Whatever will we do?"

Whatever they wanted, of course. "Just remind me not
to get you a kitten for your birthday."

* * * * *

ABOUT THE AUTHOR

Tamara Morgan is a contemporary romance author of humorous, heartfelt stories with flawed heroes and heroines designed to get your hackles up and make your heart melt. Her long-lived affinity for romance novels survived a BA degree in English literature, after which time she discovered it was much more fun to create stories than analyze the life out of them.

Whether building Victorian dollhouses, consuming mass quantities of coffee and wine, or crying over cheesy 1950s musicals, Tamara commits to her flaws like every good heroine should. She lives in the Inland Northwest with her husband, daughter and variety of household pets, and only occasionally complains about the weather.

REQUEST YOUR
FREE BOOKS!

2 FREE NOVELS
FROM THE ROMANCE COLLECTION,
PLUS 2 FREE GIFTS!

YES! Please send me 2 FREE novels from the Romance Collection and my 2 FREE gifts (gifts are worth about $10). After receiving them, if I don't wish to receive any more books, I can return the shipping statement marked "cancel." If I don't cancel, I will receive 4 brand-new novels every month and be billed just $6.49 per book in the U.S. or $6.99 per book in Canada. That's a savings of at least 18% off the cover price. It's quite a bargain! Shipping and handling is just 50¢ per book in the U.S. and 75¢ per book in Canada.* I understand that accepting the 2 free books and gifts places me under no obligation to buy anything. I can always return a shipment and cancel at any time. Even if I never buy another book, the two free books and gifts are mine to keep forever.

194/394 MDN GH4D

Name	(PLEASE PRINT)	
Address		Apt. #
City	State/Prov.	Zip/Postal Code

Signature (if under 18, a parent or guardian must sign)

Mail to the **Reader Service:**
IN U.S.A.: P.O. Box 1867, Buffalo, NY 14240-1867
IN CANADA: P.O. Box 609, Fort Erie, Ontario L2A 5X3

Want to try 2 free books from another line?
Call 1-800-873-8635 or visit www.ReaderService.com.

*Terms and prices subject to change without notice. Prices do not include applicable taxes. Sales tax applicable in N.Y. Canadian residents will be charged applicable taxes. Offer not valid in Quebec. This offer is limited to one order per household. Not valid for current subscribers to the Romance Collection or the Romance/Suspense Collection. All orders subject to credit approval. Credit or debit balances in a customer's account(s) may be offset by any other outstanding balance owed by or to the customer. Please allow 4 to 6 weeks for delivery. Offer available while quantities last.

Your Privacy—The Reader Service is committed to protecting your privacy. Our Privacy Policy is available online at www.ReaderService.com or upon request from the Reader Service.

We make a portion of our mailing list available to reputable third parties that offer products we believe may interest you. If you prefer that we not exchange your name with third parties, or if you wish to clarify or modify your communication preferences, please visit us at www.ReaderService.com/consumerschoice or write to us at Reader Service Preference Service, P.O. Box 9062, Buffalo, NY 14240-9062. Include your complete name and address.

ROM15R

LARGER-PRINT BOOKS!
GET 2 FREE LARGER-PRINT NOVELS PLUS
2 FREE GIFTS!

HARLEQUIN

Romance

From the Heart, For the Heart

YES! Please send me 2 FREE LARGER-PRINT Harlequin® Romance novels and my 2 FREE gifts (gifts are worth about $10). After receiving them, if I don't wish to receive any more books, I can return the shipping statement marked "cancel." If I don't cancel, I will receive 4 brand-new novels every month and be billed just $5.09 per book in the U.S. or $5.49 per book in Canada. That's a savings of at least 15% off the cover price! It's quite a bargain! Shipping and handling is just 50¢ per book in the U.S. and 75¢ per book in Canada.* I understand that accepting the 2 free books and gifts places me under no obligation to buy anything. I can always return a shipment and cancel at any time. Even if I never buy another book, the two free books and gifts are mine to keep forever.

119/319 HDN GHWC

Name _____ (PLEASE PRINT)

Address _____ Apt. #

City _____ State/Prov. _____ Zip/Postal Code

Signature (if under 18, a parent or guardian must sign)

Mail to the **Reader Service:**
IN U.S.A.: P.O. Box 1867, Buffalo, NY 14240-1867
IN CANADA: P.O. Box 609, Fort Erie, Ontario L2A 5X3
Want to try two free books from another line?
Call 1-800-873-8635 or visit www.ReaderService.com.

* Terms and prices subject to change without notice. Prices do not include applicable taxes. Sales tax applicable in N.Y. Canadian residents will be charged applicable taxes. Offer not valid in Quebec. This offer is limited to one order per household. Not valid for current subscribers to Harlequin Romance Larger-Print books. All orders subject to credit approval. Credit or debit balances in a customer's account(s) may be offset by any other outstanding balance owed by or to the customer. Please allow 4 to 6 weeks for delivery. Offer available while quantities last.

Your Privacy—The Reader Service is committed to protecting your privacy. Our Privacy Policy is available online at www.ReaderService.com or upon request from the Reader Service.

We make a portion of our mailing list available to reputable third parties that offer products we believe may interest you. If you prefer that we not exchange your name with third parties, or if you wish to clarify or modify your communication preferences, please visit us at www.ReaderService.com/consumerschoice or write to us at Reader Service Preference Service, P.O. Box 9062, Buffalo, NY 14240-9062. Include your complete name and address.

HRLP15

REQUEST YOUR FREE BOOKS!
2 FREE NOVELS PLUS 2 FREE GIFTS!

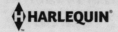

ROMANTIC suspense

Sparked by danger, fueled by passion

YES! Please send me 2 FREE Harlequin® Romantic Suspense novels and my 2 FREE gifts (gifts are worth about $10). After receiving them, if I don't wish to receive any more books, I can return the shipping statement marked "cancel." If I don't cancel, I will receive 4 brand-new novels every month and be billed just $4.74 per book in the U.S. or $5.49 per book in Canada. That's a savings of at least 12% off the cover price! It's quite a bargain! Shipping and handling is just 50¢ per book in the U.S. and 75¢ per book in Canada.* I understand that accepting the 2 free books and gifts places me under no obligation to buy anything. I can always return a shipment and cancel at any time. Even if I never buy another book, the two free books and gifts are mine to keep forever.

240/340 HDN GH3P

Name _____ (PLEASE PRINT) _____

Address _____ Apt. # _____

City _____ State/Prov. _____ Zip/Postal Code _____

Signature (if under 18, a parent or guardian must sign)

Mail to the **Reader Service:**
IN U.S.A.: P.O. Box 1867, Buffalo, NY 14240-1867
IN CANADA: P.O. Box 609, Fort Erie, Ontario L2A 5X3

Want to try two free books from another line?
Call 1-800-873-8635 or visit www.ReaderService.com.

* Terms and prices subject to change without notice. Prices do not include applicable taxes. Sales tax applicable in N.Y. Canadian residents will be charged applicable taxes. Offer not valid in Quebec. This offer is limited to one order per household. Not valid for current subscribers to Harlequin Romantic Suspense books. All orders subject to credit approval. Credit or debit balances in a customer's account(s) may be offset by any other outstanding balance owed by or to the customer. Please allow 4 to 6 weeks for delivery. Offer available while quantities last.

Your Privacy—The Reader Service is committed to protecting your privacy. Our Privacy Policy is available online at www.ReaderService.com or upon request from the Reader Service.

We make a portion of our mailing list available to reputable third parties that offer products we believe may interest you. If you prefer that we not exchange your name with third parties, or if you wish to clarify or modify your communication preferences, please visit us at www.ReaderService.com/consumerchoice or write to us at Reader Service Preference Service, P.O. Box 9062, Buffalo, NY 14240-9062. Include your complete name and address.

YES! Please send me **The Western Promises Collection** in Larger Print. This collection begins with 3 FREE books and 2 FREE gifts (gifts valued at approx. $14.00 retail) in the first shipment, along with the other first 4 books from the collection! If I do not cancel, I will receive 8 monthly shipments until I have the entire 51-book Western Promises collection. I will receive 2 or 3 FREE books in each shipment and I will pay just $4.99 US/ $5.89 CDN for each of the other four books in each shipment, plus $2.99 for shipping and handling per shipment. *If I decide to keep the entire collection, I'll have paid for only 32 books, because 19 books are FREE! I understand that accepting the 3 free books and gifts places me under no obligation to buy anything. I can always return a shipment and cancel at any time. My free books and gifts are mine to keep no matter what I decide.

272 HCN 3070 472 HCN 3070

Name	(PLEASE PRINT)	
Address		Apt. #
City	State/Prov.	Zip/Postal Code
Signature (if under 18, a parent or guardian must sign)		

Mail to the **Reader Service:**

IN U.S.A.: P.O. Box 1867, Buffalo, NY 14240-1867
IN CANADA: P.O. Box 609, Fort Erie, Ontario L2A 5X3

* Terms and prices subject to change without notice. Prices do not include applicable taxes. Sales tax applicable in N.Y. Canadian residents will be charged applicable taxes. This offer is limited to one order per household. All orders subject to approval. Credit or debit balances in a customer's account(s) may be offset by any other outstanding balance owed by or to the customer. Please allow 4 to 6 weeks for delivery. Offer available while quantities last. Offer not available to Quebec residents.

WPBPA16R

READERSERVICE.COM

Manage your account online!

- Review your order history
- Manage your payments
- Update your address

> ### We've designed the Reader Service website just for you.

Enjoy all the features!

- Discover new series available to you, and read excerpts from any series.
- Respond to mailings and special monthly offers.
- Connect with favorite authors at the blog.
- Browse the Bonus Bucks catalog and online-only exculsives.
- Share your feedback.

Visit us at:
ReaderService.com